ALL BELL BREAKS LOOSE

A Samantha Bell Mystery Thriller

JEREMY WALDRON

ALSO BY JEREMY WALDRON

Dead and Gone to Bell

Bell Hath No Fury

Bloody Bell

Bell to Pay

Burn in Bell

Mad as Bell

All Bell Breaks Loose

Never miss a new release. Sign up for Jeremy Waldron's New Releases Newsletter at JeremyWaldron.com

CHAPTER ONE

MR. T PARKED IN THE BACK OF THE LOT, REMOVED HIS KEYS from the ignition and stepped out into the darkness of the night. A mist of condensation ballooned from his lips on his exhale as he clasped his collar shut. A low-pressure front had moved in from the west, bringing with it a cold Rocky Mountain late-September snow. The first of the season.

Removing his cellphone from his coat pocket, Mr. T glanced at the screen one last time to make sure he knew the face of the person he was here to meet. Tonight, there couldn't be any mistakes. He had to get this right.

Trudging his way through swirling snow, Mr. T moved to the entrance of the university auditorium where small groups of students stood outside in tight circles smoking, playing on their cellphones, and laughing into the frozen air, each waiting to catch a glimpse of fame.

Ignoring them all, Mr. T ducked his head as he passed a line of protestors calling for tonight's show to be canceled, and entered the building—undetected—to escape the chill outside. He paused for a quick beat at the door and looked for the woman he was supposed to meet.

A heady scent of cologne and perfume mixed with pre-show cocktails filled the air. Bouncing his gaze between the blondes and brunettes, both real and fake, none matched the photo on his phone. Though he did notice a common theme among them—all the women here tonight were dressed to impress in knee high leather boots, cardigans, and scarfs, looking and acting the same.

Disappointed, Mr. T didn't see his girl among them. With a quick hand swipe over his head, he thought how this sorry pool of fans was the reward for hard work and fame. *What was the world coming to?*

He kept moving, deciding to play it safe by staying on the periphery of the crowd. It felt like cattle being corralled through the ticket handlers. He kept his eyes peeled for his date and felt the electric buzz build in anticipation of tonight's promised show.

A young woman turned and locked eyes. Mr. T smiled back, appreciating her curious sparkle that nearly slowed Mr. T's steps. He had to remind himself she wasn't who he's come here to see. The woman he was looking for was probably already upstairs waiting for him.

Walking to the bank of elevators on the south end of the building, Mr. T took a ride to the third floor and felt his nerves building as he wiped his palms on his thighs. When it came to women, he didn't have a lot of experience. Tonight, his inexperience was getting the best of him.

"It's just a blind date," he whispered to an empty elevator, tapping his toes inside his polished shoes, reminding himself to take a deep breath and relax.

Soon, the car slowed to a stop and Mr. T adjusted his tie, making sure he looked his Sunday best. Stepping out onto a quieter third floor, the rumble from below could be felt in his feet. A quick glance at his watch showed Mr. T he was early. It was a habit his mother had instilled in him as a young child, one which he couldn't break. Instead of waiting by the elevator like a fool, he slithered into the shadows and tucked his shoulders back against the far wall and began scrolling through his Instagram feed where today's hottest influencers hawked their latest adventures in travel, fashion, and women.

A quick stab of envy had him comparing his own pathetic channel against his rivals. His number of followers could be higher, and post likes greater, but he wasn't going to let it get him down. Not tonight, and certainly not as long as the woman he was here to meet, showed.

"Just you fools wait and see who I'll be photographed with tonight." Mr. T smirked when talking to his phone, "We'll see who has the last laugh, then."

Just then, Mr. T picked his head up as he heard two women arguing around the corner.

Surprised he wasn't alone like he'd thought, he turned his head and pinched his eyebrows, gazing in the direction of a conversation quickly escalating into something more. He needed to see what was happening, who was fighting. As he hurried down the hall, he couldn't make out exactly what it was they were fighting about, but he recognized at least one of the voices.

This was really happening, he thought.

His date was here—had been here all along.

Picking up his pace, Mr. T followed the voices echoing off the walls until they faded into the rumblings and murmurs from the growing crowd below. His heart hammered and he feared he might miss his chance to put a stop to whatever was happening.

He ran faster, propelling himself around the corner, balancing a single hand on the wall, when suddenly, he came to an abrupt stop. His eyes widened in disbelief. There *she* was, but she wasn't alone. Mr. T pulled out his phone and started recording the transaction.

With his date's hand pressed to her lined forehead, Mr. T could feel her anger radiating off her shoulders. A gift was exchanged, followed by the other woman turning and leaving in the opposite direction.

Standing completely unnoticed, Mr. T didn't know what to do or say.

What *could* he say?

Did he pretend he hadn't heard them fighting and risk ruining his night? Or tell it how it was and hope for the best? Again, his inexperience was causing him to doubt his own ability to solve the problem in front of him.

Looking around, he saw he was alone with his date.

He turned his head, listening for the other woman. Was it safe for him to assume she was gone?

He felt his neck pulsing with indecision. Soon, doubt crept into the forefront of his mind and he nearly turned back to the elevators when the crowd below reminded him what fame was all about.

This was his chance.

His moment to shine.

The opportunity he'd been waiting to take for so long.

And when the woman turned on a heel and walked toward the balcony overlooking the auditorium where the crowd was waiting for the biggest show of their lives, he tucked his chin, lifted his phone, and pressed record.

Mr. T had no choice but to follow because, unbeknownst to her, she was what was going to make him famous.

CHAPTER TWO

Susan was sharing the stage with Erin for Karaoke night and I stood wrapped in King's arms preparing to laugh my tail off. The girls were giggling into their microphones, carefully choosing a song they both could sing. Their choice was a throwback that brought us to our feet.

Allison and her new boyfriend, Nicholas, came onto the floor and danced next to King and me. They looked happy—we all did—shedding the stresses of life with a few drinks, good food, and great friends.

"I didn't realize Erin could sing," King said.

My body buzzed as King's lips fluttered against my ear. I slid my hands up his chest and clasped my hands around his neck as he latched a firm hold on to my hip.

I responded, "Neither did I."

Erin's voice was incredible—Susan's, too—as they turned a popular hit from the nineties into a duet. We twirled and danced, thankful Susan had brought us all together to celebrate her business's success. I was thrilled King could join us, even if my invitation was last minute.

A few weeks ago, Susan nearly lost it all by recklessly

betting everything on a single client who nearly fell through. One thing led to the next and, lucky for her, the tide turned in her favor as a miracle presented itself and saved Susan's business.

King twirled me around and my eyes locked on Susan. She pointed at me and smiled as she sang. I pointed back and we both laughed.

When the song ended, King dipped me and planted a kiss on my lips. I laughed and squeezed him tighter, hooking one leg around his thigh. We fit together like a two-piece puzzle. I still couldn't believe I was dating a homicide detective after being widowed nearly ten years prior. He was everything I could have asked for, and more. But even now, as our night wound down, I feared he'd get a call from work and be taken away from me.

"What do you say we get out of here early?"

A glimmer of desire filled King's eyes with hope. "Your place or mine?"

"Preferably yours," I said, thinking how my teenage son was home with my sister. "Unless you'd rather have ice cream as your dessert."

"What flavor?"

I slapped my hand over King's hard chest when we were interrupted by Allison. She was hanging off of Nicholas's thick arm as they strode up next to us. Nicholas had the kindest eyes of any man I'd ever seen and I liked to think Allison had a lot to do with it.

They had only recently started dating, but I liked him already. I could see the joy in my friend's eyes that sparkled like diamonds and in her smile that never left her gorgeous face. Something told me Allison wasn't going to let this one go without a fight. I liked to believe she had finally found her person.

"It's getting late," Allison said. "I think we're going to call it a night."

I said, "We were just discussing the same."

"Oh, dear." Allison was looking beyond me.

I followed Allison's eyes and we all started laughing when we found Susan back at the bar, flirting with the young barkeep. I said, "We better get her out of here before she gets herself into trouble."

"While you do that, I'm going to the restroom." King kissed me on the cheek and strode away.

We said our goodbyes to Allison and Nicholas. When I turned around, I caught Erin digging through my purse. "Excuse me?" I said as I approached the table.

Without looking up, Erin said, "It's your phone. It keeps going off."

My thoughts jumped to Mason as Erin pulled out my phone and glanced at the screen. "Sam, you're still receiving threats?" Erin looked me in the eye. "How many has it been now?"

"A lot," I said, taking my phone out of her hand and making the mistake of reading the message on Twitter. An uneasy flutter rolled down my spine.

The threats were getting personal and coming in at an increasingly high rate. It wasn't anything I couldn't handle—I'd received threats before—but, like my editor Ryan Dawson reminded me, I had a target on my back unlike anything I'd experienced since taking my fight with the chief of police public.

"If we let up now," I said, "Chief Watts won't ever resign."

Erin cocked her head to one shoulder and sighed.

Perhaps I was living in denial, or maybe I just wanted to believe no one would actually do the awful things they said they wanted to do to me. I couldn't stop simply because of a threat. I had a job to do.

"This is serious, Sam." Erin glanced to King who was walking our way. "You need to tell King." When I didn't respond, Erin asked, "What?"

"It gets worse," I said. Erin's eyes perked up and I told her, "I saw the drone again."

CHAPTER THREE

JACKIE DUMONT PUSHED HER WAY THROUGH THE KNOTS OF people standing outside the glass entrance to the university auditorium, fuming at her client Vincent Verdi for putting her on the spot.

"Get out of my way," she mumbled as she passed a couple of young women wearing entirely too much hair spray, annoyed she'd have to turn around and come back inside the same building she'd just left.

The women tossed her a look, but it didn't deter Jackie from marching forward. She needed to put a stop to this before the fire spread. Jackie paused to gauge her location when a college boy grabbed her arm.

"Do I know you?" he asked.

Jackie looked him in his eye as she snapped her elbow free and pushed onward, making a call along the way. She didn't have time to deal with unwanted attention. When the line clicked over, she asked, "Where is he?"

A voice mumbled the answer and Jackie disconnected. A minute later, she was entering the back room where Vince was sitting. She slammed the door shut and said to Vince's wingman, "Leave us."

Vince leaned back in his chair and nodded his head at Mitch to leave the room. "Get the cameras in place. The exact locations we went over before."

"On it."

"And Mitch?"

Mitch stopped and turned.

"Make sure the drone is flying high. We can't miss that shot. This needs to go perfectly."

As soon as Mitch exited the room, Jackie asked, "What the hell is that?"

Vince flicked his gaze to the cage. "It's a tiger." He smiled. "I assume by the look on your face that you got my message."

Jackie was still staring at the tiger pacing back and forth as if anticipating his next move. "Dare I ask what in the world you're planning to do with it?"

Vince leaned forward and perched his elbows on his knees. Quirking an eyebrow, he said, "Do you really want to know?" The tiger snarled and Jackie jumped back. Vince chuckled. "Look, Jackie. I'm sorry. I should have called to explain in detail what's needed of you, but this couldn't wait."

Jackie's knuckles went white as she clung to the strap of her purse. Turning her eyes on Vince, she said, "You're going to get discovered."

Vince stood and moved to the table, pouring himself another rum and Coke. "I've got it handled."

Clearly, Jackie thought with another glance to the tiger. She moved across the room and leaned against the table. Looking at Vince, she said, "I can't keep covering your ass if you keep doing dumb shit."

"Then what do I pay you for?"

"All I'm asking is that you run your ideas by me before executing them, that's all."

"You know I don't ask for permission."

"It's different now. Things have changed since your last stunt. There are people outside protesting your visit, demanding you apologize or leave now."

Vince lifted the red Dixie cup to his lips and threw Jackie a look.

"What you're doing for likes and clicks...it isn't funny anymore."

Vince took another drink before setting his cup down. "I don't know, I kind of like the direction my career is taking." The crowd noise grew louder and seeped through the walls. "And apparently they do too."

Jackie sighed while watching the tiger pace. She didn't want to ask whether Vince had a permit to have this beast inside the building. Knowing him, Vince would rather ask for forgiveness than for permission. It was one of a dozen different reasons why he needed her more than she needed him.

Jackie pointed to the tiger, and said, "So, what? Is that the big show you promised?"

"Today's shoot is big, bigger than anything I've ever done before. It's sure to make a splash." Vince winked and inched his way closer to Jackie. "But no. The tiger isn't the entire show."

"Are you going to tell me what is?"

Vince leaned down and whispered something into her ear. Jackie listened to his words and felt the blood drain from her head. Then she rolled her eyes and stared at Vince. His grin sharpened as he moved to the exit and opened the door. "Now go do your part, Jackie. After it's done, you'll receive your fair share of riches. That, I promise."

Jackie caught Vince preening as she left the room. She knew he had to make sure every detail was exact. It was important he looked his best for the cameras. After tonight, the world would certainly know who he was, if they didn't already.

CHAPTER FOUR

"APRIL?" MR. T CALLED OUT. HER BRUNETTE HAIR LIFTED off her slender shoulder as she turned around to look. "Is that really you?"

April's eyes were full of surprise as she responded with a subtle quizzical look. "I'm sorry, do I know you?"

Mr. T continued to approach, his smile widening as he dropped his gaze to her chest. Her hand was still on the balustrade. "It's me."

April tilted her head and gave him a questioning look as if deciding when and where they may have met before when, suddenly, Mr. T burst into a sprint. Charging her at full speed he shoved his arms into the center of her chest and completely lifted her body off the ground, sending her flying over the railing. A sharp shrill let loose from April's lips as she flailed her arms in the air, falling backward into the sea of people below.

Counting off the seconds—*one one thousand. Two one thousand*—then a deathly thud stilled the auditorium air.

A sharp prickle of excitement shot down Mr. T's arms as

he stopped just shy of the railing. Frozen stiff with wide and crazy eyes, Mr. T wanted so badly to lean over the balcony edge and see for himself the crowd's reaction. Vivid images of April's crumbled and broken body filled his head, and he wet his dry lips with his tongue.

He didn't flinch at the impact. It happened so fast; it didn't seem real until the people below gasped in terror. His heart-rate was through the roof, pumping out adrenaline in large doses as he reveled in the thrill of what he'd just done.

Slowly, he backpedaled away from the temptation. He had to keep cool under intense pressure as he turned around and calmly headed in the direction of the bank of elevators, leaving the chorus of cries behind.

Focusing on his breaths, Mr. T kept his eyes forward as he walked steadily. His head was in the clouds fantasizing about the fame this would bring him. His smile grew larger as he rounded the corner and marched down the hallway he'd walked only minutes before. He could still feel April's last emotion vibrating through his right hand—*absolute fear*.

A frantic roar erupted behind him like flames licking his neck, and Mr. T brought his hands together and began clapping.

This was his stage. He was the producer of his own show. And though he couldn't reveal his face, he knew the people who'd come tonight were talking about him and what he'd done to make their night the most memorable of their pathetic little existence.

"So, this is what it's like," he muttered to himself as he stepped inside an empty elevator car already waiting for him. Jabbing the lobby floor button with a curled knuckle, no one would suspect him at all. It was the actors who were remembered, never the producer.

On his way down, he straightened his brimmed hat,

smoothed out his jacket and, when the doors opened, he joined the hundreds of fans who were unknowingly helping Vince Verdi's show go viral by reporting the murder of the young woman who lay dead in the middle of the floor.

This was even better than he'd imagined.

CHAPTER FIVE

"You can't keep this secret forever," Erin said out of earshot from King, knowing it was the same drone I'd seen outside my house before. "He'll find out eventually, and when he does…"

"I know," I said, motioning for Erin to keep her voice down.

I didn't know who was behind the controls of the drone, but the thought of someone stalking me by way of a flying device wasn't comforting. As we said our goodbyes and promised to meet up in the morning, King strode up from behind and pressed his hand to the small of my back.

"So, ice cream?" I asked, a smile on my lips. I didn't want ice cream.

He said, "It's late. I'll follow you home."

King was right, even if I'd rather go to his place. I couldn't leave Mason with Heather all the time. He was my responsibility, not hers.

Threading my fingers through his, I squeezed his hand and smiled. King had a way of reading my mind. It was reassuring to know someone else in this world thought the same way I did.

We were the last of our friends to leave the restaurant and King walked me to my car before heading to his. My thoughts were on getting home to my son and cuddling up next to King on the couch, maybe sharing one more beer before we retreated to my bedroom, when my feet were pulled back to earth by a single phone call.

Settling into the driver's seat of my Subaru Outback, I answered the unknown number.

"Samantha, my name is Kovac. You don't know who I am but I have something I think you'll want to hear."

The name wasn't familiar, but I was willing to hear him out after listening to the urgency in his voice. Headlights beamed behind me, and when I glanced into my rearview mirror, I saw King waiting for me to back out of my space.

"And what makes you think I'm the least bit interested?" I asked, listening to the sounds of a crowd rattle in my ear.

Kovac raised his voice to talk over the noise. "Let's just say I have information for a story you're working."

King tapped his horn, and I waved my hand in the back window, hoping he'd see. "I'm working a lot of stories. I'll need you to be more specific." Empty promises of leads came in all the time. They were what bogged down my investigations.

Suddenly, the loud noises on Kovac's end disappeared. He asked if I knew the Starbucks on Speer and W 14th Ave. When I said I was familiar, he said, "Good. Meet me there tomorrow, 10:45AM sharp. After you see what I have to share, Chief Watts will have no choice but to resign."

CHAPTER SIX

WORKING WITH UNKNOWN SOURCES MADE ME NERVOUS. So much could go wrong, and the vetting process was way more work than I usually had time for. But I freely offered information that was hard to come by, especially, the headline I was working day and night to close.

I spent my entire drive home lost in thought about my short conversation with Kovac. By the time I curbed my car in front of my house and stepped out, King was already waiting for me. I tried to push my thoughts to the side, not wanting to mention anything about work, but King must have sensed my unease because he asked me if I was all right.

I did my best to meet his eye when I said, "Just tired. One too many drinks."

Looping my arm through the crook of his, we climbed the short flight of stairs leading up to my house. My sister Heather met us at the door. The look on her face said it all. I knew something had happened.

"Sam, I tried calling but couldn't get through."

"What is it?" I asked, thinking it was strange I hadn't seen any missed calls from the house.

King stepped forward, already assessing the inside of my house for potential danger.

"It's your phone. It kept ringing. But each time I answered, the caller would hang up."

"What was the number?"

"It was blocked."

I thought about this new mysterious source, and my paranoia that Police Chief Gordon Watts was coming after me. Could it have been either of them? If Kovac was behind this, it was unnerving that he knew both of my numbers and would only speak to me.

"I'll check it out," King said, heading into the kitchen.

"I'm sure it's nothing," I called out to him.

"I don't know how you do it." Heather uncrossed her arms and rubbed my left shoulder with her right hand. She attempted to change the subject with, "How was your night?"

I dropped my purse at the door, tossed my keys into the dish, and told her about dancing and karaoke when my yellow lab, Cooper, lifted his head and locked eyes with me. I called him over and he got up off his dog bed and trotted over to me with a wagging tail. Rubbing Cooper's head, I asked Heather about her night. Heather shrugged.

"Mason is *still* in his room playing video games," she said. "I swear, Sam, he's addicted. Do you even know who he's talking to inside the game?"

"Other gamers," I said.

Heather squinted and shook her head. "I don't get it."

Neither did I, but it was what Mason liked to do with his friends. We made our way into the kitchen and I peeked inside his room just to see him with my own eyes. Mason was in the middle of an intense battle, his thumbs working overtime across the controls. The screen exploded into a fiery inferno and Mason said something into the headset. The game looked dark and gritty and much more violent than I preferred he'd play, but I closed the door and found King filling a glass with water at the kitchen sink.

King said, "I can run a trace if you want?"

"Don't worry about it," I said, pulling a water glass from the cabinet for myself. "I'm sure it's nothing to lose sleep over."

"Samantha," Heather called from the living room, "your cellphone is ringing!"

I tossed King a look. King said, "You're going to give your sister a heart attack." I took a step toward the living room when King caught my arm. "Ignore it," he said.

"Would you ignore yours if it rang?"

His grip eased as I hurried to catch the call from my editor, Ryan Dawson.

"Samantha, you home?"

"Just winding down."

"Well, don't. I need you in Boulder."

I glanced to Heather who was already nodding her head in agreement to stay the night with Mason. I said to Dawson, "It's late."

"Get a coffee. This one is big. A celebrity committed suicide in front of hundreds of people and I need you to get the scoop."

CHAPTER SEVEN

KING STAYED BEHIND WITH MY SISTER AND SON AS I HAD no choice but to agree to report on Dawson's request. An hour later, I arrived at the University of Boulder to a chaotic scene. A light snow was falling and a dozen squad cars blocked the parking lot which forced me to curb my car two blocks away. I hurried down the sidewalk with fat flakes sticking to my lashes and prepared to get my story as quickly as possible so that I wouldn't be up all night having to write it.

I was greeted by Boulder police telling me to stand back and join the ranks of the other spectators watching with wide eyes, wondering what it was that just happened. Reaching under my collar, I pulled my press badge and held it up for the uniformed officer to see.

"Your spot is with them," he said, pointing across the lot.

I caught sight of Denver TV reporter Heidi Mitchell and her camera crew on the corner entrance of the school's auditorium reporting the late-night news. Naturally, I gravitated in her direction, stomping over handmade protest signs with homophobic slogans that had been left behind sticking to the wet ground. Packs of college students huddled around trunks of trees and eyed me from a distance.

"Did I miss the presser?" I asked a Boulder reporter.

He was a one-man show, and it was clear he wasn't sure he could trust me. I watched as he looked me up and down as if deciding whether or not I was worth wasting his breath on. I showed him my press badge, told him I was with the *Colorado Times*. His eyes lacked the flashes of recognition I expected to see.

"So?" I said. "Care to enlighten a print journalist with details of what happened here tonight?"

"Did you just arrive?"

I nodded. "Roads were a little slick coming in from Denver."

He turned his attention back to the auditorium entrance. "Word has it a celebrity committed suicide in front of hundreds of fans."

Tell me something I don't already know, I thought. "Do you know who it was?"

"Vincent Verdi was the name on the event schedule, but it could be anybody."

"Vincent Verdi?" I asked.

The male reporter turned his head and chuckled as I dated myself with my unashamed ignorance to who exactly this person was. He said, "Vince is one of the biggest, most popular YouTubers in the country. He's originally from Boulder and promised tonight would be the biggest show of his career."

"Have the police confirmed it was him who died?"

"There's been conflicting accounts whether or not he arrived at all."

I struggled to understand how a YouTuber was being treated as a celebrity. "And what's with the protest?"

"Vince is homophobic. Google him. You'll see why people either love or hate him."

Heidi finished up with her broadcast and called me over when she was done. As soon as I was within earshot, she said, "Shouldn't be surprised to see you here, but I am."

"I'm just building up my celebrity résumé for when I get fired from the *Times* and have to interview with a tabloid magazine."

Heidi laughed. Then her face got serious. She made sure no one was listening when she said, "Sam, I think I'm being followed."

"By who?"

Heidi shook her head. "I don't know. Maybe I'm just being paranoid thinking Chief Watts is worried what we might have on him."

I mentioned the threats I'd been receiving, too, then told her about the drone. Heidi inhaled a deep breath and rolled her shoulders back. "I don't like this feeling, Sam." Then she looked me in the eye. "Did we cross a line, calling for Watts's resignation?"

"He committed conspiracy to murder," I reminded her. Heidi didn't respond.

We were quiet for a beat as I realized I had no choice but to meet with Kovac now that Heidi also believed she had picked up a stalker. We needed to get to the end of this and get Watts to step aside. Then I brought us back to our current reporting when I said, "A YouTuber, huh?"

"Not exactly." Heidi met my eye. "Vincent Verdi is apparently inside, but I spoke with a witness who said it was TV actor, April Wright, who jumped from a third-floor balcony."

That name I knew, and now I was wondering more about the big show Vince promised his fans. "Suicide?"

Heidi confirmed with a single nod. "And it was caught on multiple people's livestream."

CHAPTER EIGHT

I WAS UP BEFORE THE SUN THE NEXT MORNING, UNABLE TO take my mind off of April Wright.

Boulder Police Department still hadn't officially released her name, even though word had quickly spread that she was last night's suicide victim. A flood of videos and pictures of her hit social media like a storm, all confirming her identity. It was a game of whack-a-mole as the social media channels worked to take down the offensive content. But it did little to stop people from posting what they captured.

My column was easy to write. There wasn't much to say other than April was too young to die. But what I wanted to know more than anything else was why she'd done it at all? And there, of all places?

I kept going back to Vincent Verdi.

Was he somehow at fault? Did April hurl herself over to get his attention? To bring attention to his show? If so, why? Or was it just a freak accident of being in the wrong place at the wrong time?

The more I learned about Vince, the more I disliked the man. He was Mr. Controversy himself and had a vulgar way of targeting people he disliked. Yet he had millions of followers, many of whom were attractive young women who lined up to see him.

I hated being on the outside of the investigation and wished I had a source inside the Boulder Police Department who would shoot it to me straight. I didn't have the patience to wait for another presser. Though my column was on its way to publication, the story felt incomplete.

I heard Mason come out of the bathroom and load up his school bag. He entered the kitchen mumbling a quick, "Good morning," before grabbing himself a breakfast bar from the pantry. "I'm off to school."

"Hey," I said. "I don't like how you moved your video game into your bedroom."

"I did it for you, Mom."

"You did it because you're playing a game you know I don't like."

"It's not a big deal."

"It is to me," I said, looking into his bloodshot eyes, knowing he was up later than he should have been staring into a screen instead of getting caught up on sleep. "Before you leave, I need to ask you something."

Mason's shoulders slumped, and he didn't even bother to turn around and face me. "Can't it wait?"

"What do you know about Vincent Verdi?"

Mason swiveled his head and met my eye. "Is that where you went last night?"

"You heard, eh?"

Mason nodded. "It's all over Instagram."

I told him enough about my story so he'd understand why it was I was asking.

"People are saying that Vince convinced April to jump."

I said, "People can say whatever they want, but until there

are facts proving it's true, let's leave the rumors to the trolls on social media."

"Then here is a fact for you to swallow," Mason said. "Vince is attending the Mile High Gaming Conference at the Convention Center today. How about I skip school and we can go there together? That way I can see my favorite gamers and you can ask Vince if April was his big show."

CHAPTER NINE

MR. T LAY FLAT ON HIS BACK STARING INTO THE BACK-LIT screen of his phone. He swiped his thumb over the front of his device and refreshed his Facebook newsfeed again for the thousandth time since coming home. Since returning from the college campus, he'd lost track of time. His adrenal glands were firing on all cylinders, making it impossible to sleep.

April Wright's death went viral almost immediately, and he was anxious to read every amateur report that was published before getting taken down for graphic content. It was an ugly scene, the kind of images saved for fiction. Though Mr. T was thrilled to bring the bloody show to the lives of so many boring souls, agitation caused his teeth to grind as the evening news insisted on calling April's death a suicide.

He couldn't explain why he wanted the story to be reported differently. He should be happy the police were ruling her death a suicide and not a homicide. It was what he wanted so the show could go on, but still—

Mr. T sank further into his thoughts until he was swimming in the dark pit of his mind.

Each time he closed his eyes, he replayed his night inside his head. The ride up the elevator. The stalking of his prey. The shove that started his story.

His skin buzzed with the feeling of absolute power. Nothing could compare to the taking of someone's life. Now that Mr. T was a killer—an *actual* murderer—he'd learned something special about himself that he hadn't known before. He could murder without remorse and was fine with the thought of doing it again.

"Oh, the look on sweet April's face was priceless," he howled into the dark room, laughing until he snapped his lips shut. Mr. T's thoughts got serious. The room was quiet when he whispered, "They should be talking about me. Not her. For I was the one who gave them the show of their lives."

A surge of anger boiled his skin hot. He tried to convince himself his secret was sweeter than fame, but even he didn't believe his own lies. He wanted notoriety, to be recognized now, not become an author who got famous *after* their death. Inside, he felt hollow.

Dropping his phone to his side, Mr. T rolled his neck and gazed toward the window blinds. A dim light shone around the edges. He got out of bed and opened the window, greeted by the most beautiful sunrise he'd ever seen.

He watched the bright blood orange orb of the sun rise over the eastern horizon before hiking up his boxer shorts and moving to the mirror on the wall. He stared into his dry, red eyes before squeezing eye drops into each of them. He evaluated his appearance and rated it a seven. Not bad for having not slept, but his muscular tone was definitely a ten. He flexed and combed his hair with his fingers, quickly becoming the complete package of a ten.

Mr. T loved himself more than anybody else and he worked hard to polish his physique, but there was only so much he could do to control his social status, which Mr. T thought was pitiful.

Across his social media platforms, his numbers were down. It seemed like no matter what he did, he couldn't gain the traction he desired to be recognized for his future movie star role.

"If only they knew who was behind April's murder," he said, fighting back the temptation to prematurely reveal April's last few seconds on earth. "Then I'd get what I deserve."

It was too soon, and Mr. T knew it. His time would come and he had to resist the urge to cut corners. Soon they would learn the truth, and when they did, his popularity would explode to new heights never seen before.

Settling in with his plan to slowly release the truth to the world, Mr. T flicked on the television screen and picked up the controller, rejoining the game he started last night.

Patience was a virtue he'd have to learn, but now was his time to perfect the signature move that would truly make him famous and be recognized as the star he was.

CHAPTER TEN

As soon as my son left for school, I opened up a new browser on my computer and searched Mile High Gaming Conference. It was the first I'd heard of it and I wasn't sure my son understood the incredible tip he provided, even with me telling him there was no way I was letting him skip class to attend.

Vincent Verdi was the focus of my search, but it didn't take me long to question how my son found himself navigating an online reality I knew little about. There were so many questions rolling around inside my head, especially, *my son has favorite gamers?*

The website loaded and I noticed the conference was appropriately labeled 5280—one mile above sea level—GamersCon. I skimmed the home page for details.

It worried me to think what Mason might be exposing himself to without my knowing, especially if the types of games he liked playing were any indication of what to expect from the conference.

GamersCon claimed to be the most attended conference

west of the Mississippi, featuring a variety of exhibitors, independent creators, and vendors hawking themed merchandise. It was a world unto its own and I wondered what I might be getting myself into.

I kept clicking between pages, each slowly sucking me deeper into the portal of an unknown universe.

It was a three-day festival for gamers of all genres, celebrating the culture of gaming. People across the world flew to Denver to attend and participate in the live shows, prerelease game reveals, and competitions featuring popular personalities.

It was one big party and I could see why Mason was attracted to it. But when I clicked on the next tab, it all came together for me.

Vince Verdi's face shone bright. He had a killer smile and his eyes flashed with unchecked ego. He was also to kick off Day One's competitions, which was happening today. Another handful of the world's top YouTube and Twitch influencers were also said to be in attendance.

I leaned back in my chair and stared.

These influencers had both a large audience, and the ability to persuade that audience with a single click. They were the celebrities young people admired and aspired to be. Including my son. I didn't understand it, personally. But that didn't matter. I couldn't decide, though, if Mason was right—should I attend?

Even if it was just to get a feel for who this Vincent Verdi personality was, it seemed premature of me to confront him about April. Perhaps that was the missing piece to my story? Interviewing someone who might have known April intimately. But was Vince that guy? My son made me believe he was.

I closed the lid to my laptop and headed into Mason's

room to learn more about what games he was playing. At his TV, I picked up the game cartridge next to his console. This was just one of three violent games he currently liked to play, but when I glanced at his desk, I realized the effect it was having on my son.

CHAPTER ELEVEN

WITH MASON'S HOMEWORK PAPER IN MY HAND, I RACED through the house and burst through the front door, hoping I could catch him in time. Cooper followed me to the porch, but I was too late. Mason was long gone.

Scratching Cooper's head, I turned to the house with thoughts of ending my son's screen time when I felt the hairs on my dog's back raise. Cooper let out a bark at a familiar sound, and then I felt the buzz skim the back of my neck like a bee. I ducked before getting hit by the drone buzzing my head, then I spun around and watched it stall ten feet away.

My entire body froze.

Cooper continued to bark, but I couldn't hear him.

I was hypnotized by the whirling blades as my thoughts flashed back to the terror I saw in Heidi's eyes after she confirmed she, too, thought she was being stalked.

Afraid to take my eyes off the device, I wondered if it was the same one I'd seen before. First, a few weeks ago. Then it had come to my house just yesterday.

There wasn't anything special about it. Anyone with the slightest interest could purchase the same device on the

civilian market for a small price. That was what worried me
most; it could be anybody behind the controls.

Slowly, it crept closer, and I continued to stare it down as
if it was a wild animal ready to attack. My heart thumped
louder in my chest when I saw a flash of movement dart in
the corner of my eye. I snapped my neck and was surprised to
see Erin.

"Is this you?" I asked, jabbing my finger at the drone.

Erin held the controls out for me to see and let the drone
zip up into the air. She tipped her head back and smiled up
into the clouds. I wanted to kill her.

"Why would you do that to me?" I asked.

"If you can't beat them, join them." Erin brought the
drone back to eye level and said, "I got it for you."

"I don't want it," I said after she tried to hand over the
controls. It was then I noticed Erin's red Bronco parked
across the street. Preoccupied with Mason's homework, I
didn't see it until now.

Erin landed the drone on the sidewalk and shut off the
propellers. A proud smile sprouted on her lips as if landing
was the most difficult part of flying. Then she turned to me
and said, "Isn't it awesome?"

"No. It's not. And I still don't want it."

"I picked it up last night." Erin flicked her gaze back to
the drone and grinned. "Thought it was important for us to
learn more about your stalker."

"The drone isn't what worries me. It's who's behind the
controls that keeps me awake at night."

Erin stepped up to me and tossed her arm over my shoulders. "Besides, I thought we could add it to our portfolio.
Think of how this single device could take our photojour-
nalism skills to the next level? Perhaps even use it to chase
after some bad guys?"

I stared at the idle robot and thought about it. I didn't

know how much more work I could take on without having to let something else go, but maybe Erin was right? I could see the benefits of owning a drone.

I said, "I don't know. My new smartphone has the best camera I've ever owned."

"But can it fly?"

Erin smiled as she leaned in, resting her forehead against mine.

Without getting soft, I asked, "Did you hear what happened to April Wright?"

Erin's smile disappeared from her eyes. "Sad," she said, taking a step back. "I loved her work."

"Dawson sent me to report on it."

Erin's brow knitted. "I didn't know her death was considered suspicious?"

"Mason told me this morning people are saying YouTuber Vincent Verdi convinced her to jump."

"Vincent Verdi?"

"Yeah. You know him?"

"5280 GamersCon."

"How did you know?"

Erin glanced at her watch. "Because it starts in an hour." She lifted her eyes and put them back on me. "Allison invited me to be her wingman as she drums up clients. I accepted. Thought it might be beneficial to see how we can better promote ourselves online like these influencers are doing to promote their work. You should come."

I stared at the drone, thinking it wasn't a bad idea. I said, "I saw Heidi last night. She believes she's being stalked, too."

"By a drone?"

I flicked my gaze to Erin and shook my head. "I have this feeling that something bad is about to happen."

"Nothing is going to happen, Sam. We have jack on Watts, and he knows it."

I told her about my new source Kovac and how he said he had information that would guarantee Watts's resignation.

Erin said, "This guy called you out of the blue and he actually expects you to meet with him?"

I gave her a knowing look.

"You have to be kidding me. Sam, you said it yourself. Something feels off. You can't ignore your intuition."

"I have to meet with him," I said. "We have to put an end to this."

Erin paused a beat and looked away. Then she snapped her neck, and said, "Then I'm coming with you."

CHAPTER TWELVE

MY MEETING WITH KOVAC WASN'T FOR ANOTHER TWO hours, so I headed into the newsroom while Erin left to meet up with Allison across town. I was trying to come up with a plan to keep Erin at the gaming conference while I acquainted myself with my new source. I didn't want to scare him into silence by bringing Erin along, but she wasn't going to back down easily. I'd promised to pick her up from the Convention Center before I went to Starbucks.

I exited my car and approached the entrance, still thinking about Vince as I tugged open the single glass door. Maybe I should have gone to the conference instead of coming into work.

The air was still, and the entire building felt deflated as I climbed the stairs. It lacked the buzz of breaking news. Perhaps I could use that to my benefit when trying to convince my editor to chase Vincent Verdi's relationship with April.

I weaved through the rows of desks, some empty, some occupied by colleagues working overtime to keep our struggling newspaper afloat. I found Dawson's office door closed.

Without a thought, I glanced to the time and assumed he was preoccupied with morning meetings. I peeked through the window glass and saw him shaking his head at a new face sitting across from him. Turning toward my desk, I heard his door open behind me.

"Samantha, you have a minute?"

"All the time in the world," I said with a hint of sarcasm.

"Good. You've got to hear this. It's about April."

Dawson waved me inside his office and I nodded a quick greeting to the stranger who sat and stared at me as I took the empty seat next to him. Dawson had my printed story about April Wright on his desk when he introduced me to the man sitting next to me.

"This is freelance videographer, Russ Abair," Dawson said.

Russ dipped his left shoulder and leaned closer as he extended his hand. I slid my hand into his and watched it quickly get swallowed by his vice grip. "Nice to meet you. I'm crime beat reporter, Samantha Bell."

"I know who you are," Russ said with a smile.

Dawson continued, "Russ, here, wants to sell us a video."

"Okay," I said, wondering where Dawson was going with this.

"It's a video showing April didn't jump like everyone thought, but rather, she was pushed."

"That's a serious allegation," I said, arching a skeptical eyebrow. "Can I see it?"

Dawson shifted his gaze to Russ, then flipped his computer screen around for me to see before hitting play. I tipped forward and focused on every detail I could, trying not to miss a thing as I watched the film Russ supposedly captured. Dawson let it play completely through, then he rewound the footage back and stopped on the moment in question.

"There," he said, pointing to the screen, "an arm being reeled back from April's chest."

I settled back into my seat and brought a hand to my forehead. "This is evidence," I said. "It should be handed over to the cops."

Dawson averted his eyes and turned his screen back to its normal position.

Russ said, "And miss out on a career-making opportunity? I don't think so."

I turned and faced Russ. "How many other news outlets has it already been sold to?"

Russ looked at Dawson and smirked. "Let's face it. The video will sell papers, and I'm here to help."

Dawson swept his gaze to me and stared from beneath a sunken brow. I knew that look and couldn't believe Dawson was even considering it. Then Russ asked Dawson, "You want it or not?"

CHAPTER THIRTEEN

I REMAINED SEATED AS DAWSON WALKED RUSS OUT OF HIS office. The video changed everything about April's death, and even I was surprised at what I saw.

Had the media jumped the gun and got the story wrong? It happened more times than I was willing to admit, but there was also something about Russ I didn't like that had me hesitating. Dawson didn't seem to feel the same way. He clearly wanted the video.

I heard the door latch behind me and a second later Dawson edged around his desk and dropped into his chair. With his hands on his thighs, he looked me in the eye and asked, "So, what are you thinking?"

"What am I thinking? I'm thinking I don't want to have that kind of liability on my hands."

Dawson stared and gave no indication as to what he was thinking.

"If we agree, and the *Times* purchases that video, would the police later come after us for obstructing justice?"

"I can call our lawyers."

I made a fist with my hand and rested it on the edge of Dawson's desk. "It needs to be reported to authorities."

"That's not up to us." Dawson put his hand on his computer mouse and focused his eyes on the monitor. "Was it suicide? An accident? Or murder?" Dawson asked, pondering the same questions I had been struggling to come to terms with myself.

"As of last night, it's still under investigation," I said. "Boulder PD is keeping a tight lid on this because of the names involved, but there were simply too many witnesses to deny it was anyone other than April who died."

Dawson had seen some posts on social media before they were taken down. "Before we do anything, let's check the video's authenticity," he said. "I'd hate to pass up an opportunity, especially one where we could have the exclusive."

"You think it could be fake?" I asked.

"I don't know. All I'm saying is that if Russ caught a glimpse of April being pushed, maybe someone else caught it too?"

I cast my gaze to my knees and once again found myself thinking of Vince and the big show he promised his fans on his return home tour. Now, with Russ's video, I wondered if perhaps it was Vince whose arm was caught in the frame.

I said, "I'll go to Boulder if you want—"

Dawson held up his right hand. "Don't get ahead of yourself here. We don't have the budget for another trip north, at least not until we know what story we're chasing."

And we have the budget to purchase this video? I knew what story had to be told, and over the next several minutes I told Dawson about Vincent Verdi. Dawson knew little about him, and by the look he was giving me, I knew he wasn't sold on the idea.

"Ryan, Vince is known for controversy, and he promised his fans the biggest show of his career last night. You think it's just coincidence someone of April's stature dies the night he's in town?" I tipped forward and put both hands on his desk. "Let me at least confront Vince. I can get to him today and ask him about April myself."

Dawson inhaled a deep breath before saying, "No. I need you to work the phone. First, find me something solid, then I'll grant your request if it makes sense."

I felt my jaw lock as I fought to keep my thoughts to myself. He was grounding me because of the threats I'd been receiving. The attacks against me were increasing, and this was his way of protecting his star crime reporter from whoever was stalking me. But I only saw it as an insult to keep me from doing my job.

"Forget it," I said, turning to the door and shifting my focus to my upcoming meeting with Kovac. "You're right. I have more important stories to cover than to be reporting on celebrity gossip."

CHAPTER FOURTEEN

DAWSON SIDELINING ME ONLY MADE ME WANT TO investigate Vince's possible involvement in April's death even more. As I walked to my desk, Mason's words kept ringing in my ears.

People are saying Vincent convinced April to jump.

How did this rumor get started? Was there even an ounce of truth to it? Now, having seen Russ's video, I was believing there was. I just needed to find the evidence to prove it and make a convincing case with Dawson.

Once at my desk, I booted up my computer and tapped in my password. I still had an hour before my planned meeting with Kovac and I didn't plan on wasting a single minute of my day.

First, I browsed social media to see what else I might have missed from last night. There was still plenty of chatter happening about April's fall, including more on the rumors Mason first alerted me to. But there was nothing about what I saw in Russ's video, and certainly no more images of April splayed out on the hard floor as people surrounded her like the amateur paparazzi they were.

Why did it seem Russ was the only one to have caught a mysterious arm? Could Dawson be right? Could Russ's video have been doctored?

I kept scrolling, looking for possible evidence to support either claim—suicide or murder. There were others who were making the same assumption I had with Vince, but then a single comment on Facebook stopped me in my investigative tracks.

According to this person's post, Vince and April had an affair. They didn't say when, or for how long, but posted an image of the couple together as proof to their claim. Now I knew I was onto something.

I clicked out of this page and checked Vince's online activity. There was nothing about April's death from Vince. His last post was nearly twenty-four hours ago, well before last night's event, and had nothing to do with my story.

His feed was all about himself. Vlogs. Stunts. Controversy. Everything I'd come to expect from him. Whether he had an affair with April or not, it seemed odd he hadn't given a public statement about something I was sure he knew happened at his own event.

Not wanting to assume anything, especially his reasons for staying quiet, I considered that he might be mourning. But I also thought he could be staying silent as a way to disguise his guilt.

I lifted the handset off the cradle and stood to peer over the low partition that divided our workspace just as Dawson was exiting his office. He locked eyes, and I gave him a sarcastic thumbs up which he didn't appreciate.

Over the next hour I worked the phone, first calling colleagues who might have access to someone close to April. One call led me to the next until finally I got someone close to April to not hang up on me. Her name was Justine Sisler and by way of greeting she said, "I really shouldn't be talking to you."

"I'll assume that means you don't dispute it was April who died last night?"

"Of course it was her," Justine said. "Anybody with internet knows it was April."

With pen in hand, I asked, "Did Vince invite her to his show?"

"It could have been him. Or it could have been someone from his team. I really don't know why she would have gone there. All I can say is Vince and April had a history that has me asking the same questions you are." When I asked what she meant, Justine continued, "They once did a film together, and afterward April didn't have flattering things to say about him."

"What happened?" I asked.

"Vince kept spreading rumors that they slept together." I was taking notes when Justine's next story stopped everything I was doing. "That was them. A public feud Vince seemed to thrive off of. Once Vince saw what his rumors did to bring him celebrity, he fueled it until it burned out of control. Then he'd do it all over again. Controversy was what made Vince famous. I just find it strange that April dies twelve hours after they were seen fighting, and on the night he promised his millions of followers to not miss the live show he was calling *Don't Trip. You Might Fall.*"

CHAPTER FIFTEEN

AFTER MY CALL WITH JUSTINE, I TOOK A MOMENT TO STARE at my desk and consider what she said. If Vince was seen fighting with April, someone must have known what it was about. At this point it was only hearsay—Justine didn't see it herself but heard it from a close friend who attended the event. But it gave me something to go on and that was enough to get me started.

Gathering my things, I left the newsroom and the building to meet Kovac. But what I really needed was to find Vince and question him myself. There was too much suspicion swirling around him not to hear what he had to say.

What was the fight about? In Russ's video, whose arm was it that pushed April to her death? Was April's death a result of what was said during their fight?

Don't trip. You might fall.

I picked up the pace with a sudden sense of urgency to move on this story before someone else took it away from me. The sun beat down on the crown of my head as I glanced to my phone, needing to put a call in to Erin. Yesterday's flirt with winter was now gone and replaced with an Indian summer. Temperatures were climbing to the mid-sixties, and the skies were blue. On any other day it might be paradise, but not today.

Just as I was about to press the call button I heard the same buzz in the air that stopped me in my tracks this morning. Nearly dropping my phone, my entire body stiffened, and I immediately thought of Erin as I searched for her red Bronco.

A colleague on his way into work caught my second of panic and stared at me like I was crazy. He turned his head, and I followed his gaze. The noise was coming from a landscaper nearby trimming a hedge. Grateful I wasn't being stalked, I was beginning to understand the toll it was taking on my mental health.

Heading up the sidewalk, I veered left to where I parked when suddenly I was ambushed by Russ.

"Last chance, Bell, before I take it to *9News.*"

The jerk was waiting for me. Coincidence? Or did he know my car and parking spot? I couldn't believe he'd been waiting over an hour just to sell the video, that I didn't even have the authority to buy, elsewhere.

"Have you been waiting for me this entire time?" I asked.

Russ deflected my question and said, "Forget Dawson and the *Times.* Take this video for yourself."

"What good is it to me?"

Russ grinned. "What good is it to you? Oh, I don't know. How about guaranteed massive exposure to your crime blog and a chance to finally leave this place behind?"

Russ laughed as if what I had on Vince and April couldn't compare to what he was trying to sell for a "small investment."

I stared into his flashing eyes, wondering who this guy thought he was. Why hadn't I met Russ until today? And how was it he knew so much about me? No matter what he said to try to convince me to take his video off his hands, I wasn't interested.

"No thanks," I said, sensing his desperation was a direct result of already being denied by every other news organization in town that probably shared the same suspicions I did.

"Fine." Russ showed me his palms. "I'll publish it myself and bask in the glory."

I skirted around him and made for my car. As I walked, I was struck with a thought as I discreetly enabled my cellphone's camera at my side. Was Russ part of a publicity stunt orchestrated by Vince to extend the viral wave April's story was already on? It certainly seemed possible.

Turning to face Russ, I asked, "Does Vince know you have that video?"

"There are several offers on the table but none are as good as the one I made you." He reached a hand behind his back and pulled out a business card from a back pocket. Holding it out for me to take, he said, "Take my business card and give me a call if you change your mind."

I lifted my phone and snapped his photo for my personal records.

Russ tucked his chin and asked, "What did you do that for?"

Stepping forward, I plucked his card out of his hand, and said, "Because your video has me believing you might be an accessory to the crime."

CHAPTER SIXTEEN

HOMICIDE DETECTIVE ALEX KING WAS IN THE PRECINCT at his desk reading up on the death of April Wright when his partner Detective John Alvarez appeared behind him. King said with a touch of annoyance, "Must you read over my shoulder?"

Alvarez shook his head. "It's a shame." King twisted his body around and threw his partner a look. Alvarez lifted his hands and retreated to his desk where he said, "Her best days were ahead of her."

King rolled his chair back and swiveled to face Alvarez. "You know they're saying it's a suicide?"

Alvarez frowned. "That's what *they* are saying? Or is that what Samantha is saying?"

"Everyone follows Samantha's reporting, so technically, she *is* they."

The corner of Alvarez's eyes crinkled, then he dropped into his chair and asked, "Any official report yet?"

King shook his head no. "Boulder PD has yet to give a statement." Alvarez continued to stare and King asked, "Is something on your mind you'd like to ask me?"

Alvarez looked over his shoulder to be sure no one else was around when he tipped his body forward and whispered, "IAD is in the building and was seen earlier today speaking with the Director of Public Safety."

"What's it got to do with me?" King asked, pretending not to know.

"Need I remind you?" Alvarez raised his eyebrows. When King didn't respond he leaned back in his chair and said, "Exactly. That's what I thought."

King knew the upper brass had it out for him since a Jane Doe case went completely haywire several weeks ago. They needed an escape for what quickly escalated into a public relations nightmare for not only the department but the mayor and chief of police as well. And, as if that wasn't bad enough, Samantha's reporting on the fraudulent crime statistics put out by the department and the war between Mayor Goldberg and Police Chief Watts added fuel to the fire. King knew things were ugly, but if Internal Affairs was here because of him, King suspected it was going to get a hell of a lot worse.

King closed out his computer and asked his partner, "Anywhere you need to be?"

Alvarez stood, following King's lead. "I'm sure we can find something."

King motioned for the exit but before they could leave the bullpen and the threat of IAD behind, Chief Watts appeared.

"Detective King," Watts called.

King stopped and turned, acting like he wasn't surprised. "Chief."

"A moment?"

"I'll meet you outside," Alvarez said quietly to King.

King nodded to his partner and found his way to Watts. "What can I do for you, Chief?"

Watts stared into King's eyes for a beat before saying, "I think now is the time I remind you that my job is to protect the reputation of the department, as well as the integrity of my officers."

"No dispute there, Chief."

Watts eyed King as if assessing the value behind his words. "Good." Watts said. "Then let's hope we remain on the same page in the coming week, no matter what the press might get their hands on."

King's thoughts scrambled to know what exactly Watts meant.

"It's important we unite behind the badge and not allow an external force to divide and conquer our department." Watts tipped his head back and stared deep into King's eyes. "Are we clear?"

King squinted back, looking for clues to what exactly the chief was telling him. Was he referring to IAD or something else? He wasn't sure. King didn't like what he was hearing and certainly didn't like the feeling that the worst was yet to come.

CHAPTER SEVENTEEN

I MADE IT TO STARBUCKS TEN MINUTES BEFORE KOVAC SAID he wanted to meet. A steady stream of customers funneled through the front door, and after receiving my order I made my way to a table for two and proceeded to remove the lid to my latte. A billow of scented steam puffed into the air and I took my first sip.

Darting my gaze around the shop, no one was paying any attention to me. I didn't know what Kovac looked like, didn't even have his phone number to call. But it was safe of me to assume he knew what I looked like, so I remained seated and soon found myself flipping Russ's business card between my fingers. What was his end game?

I didn't know if he was complicit in April's death, but it didn't hurt to put a little fear in his boots when telling him so. Then I remembered what I was about to do before he snuck up to surprise me on my way to my car.

Digging out my cellphone, I made the call I'd nearly forgotten about and Erin picked up almost immediately. I didn't waste any time when asking, "What's happening? Any sight of Vince?"

The excitement of GamersCon could be heard through the phone. Erin said, "I can't hear you, Sam. Hang on. I'll be outside in one minute."

"I ran out of time to get you," I told her, even though she probably couldn't hear my weak explanation. Whether she heard me, I couldn't tell.

I watched a man wearing a ski vest enter through the front door and take his place in the back of the line. I was sure it wasn't Kovac, but I kept my eyes on him just in case. When Erin got to a place she could finally hear, I told her about Russ and what it was he had in his possession.

"Holy shit." Erin gasped. "Any idea who pushed her?"

I told her about April's friend Justine and the fight April apparently had with Vince yesterday morning. "I wish I knew who saw them fighting, but once it gets around that Russ has evidence suggesting murder it won't be long before he's picked up by authorities and has his video confiscated."

"Unless Vince gets to it first."

Erin reminded me of a fear I also shared. Then I said, "But that's not why I'm calling."

"You did the right thing by not taking it."

Did I? "Erin, listen, I need you to keep an eye out for Russ. I just sent you his photo. Something tells me he might be on his way to the conference."

"You think he's affiliated with Vince?"

"That's what I'm trying to figure out."

"It would be a pretty slimy way to drum up publicity. Have someone pushed to their death at their own show just to draw attention to yourself?"

"I agree, but it's also the cheapest form of marketing and wouldn't be below what I know Vince to do."

Erin said, "My eyes are peeled, but I can't promise anything. It's a zoo here. Heck, I'll be lucky if I find my way back to Allison."

I agreed and promised I'd be there within the hour. "Once Vince arrives, don't take your eyes off of him. Something tells me he might have something else up his sleeve to distract us from what happened last night."

As soon as I was off the phone, I scanned for Kovac and sipped my coffee. A part of me thought I was wasting my time with the chief, but it was important to remind myself the reasons I was fighting on that front as well.

With a minute to kill, I checked in on Vincent's Instagram feed and wasn't surprised to see a new Vlog had been posted less than an hour ago, appropriately titled *Don't trip. You might fall.* But before I could watch his production, a tall man stopped at my table and hovered over me, making me think I'd done something wrong.

CHAPTER EIGHTEEN

THE MAN STOOD OVER SIX FEET AND DISGUISED HIS identity by hiding beneath a black nondescript baseball cap and mirrored aviator sunglasses. I stared into my own reflection. This had to be Kovac.

"Samantha?" His gravel voice was a low tremble.

"And you would be?" I asked for good measure.

He casually lifted his wrist, pulled up his sleeve, and angled his slick digital watch toward me. "It's ten forty-five. The time I told you I would show."

We stared at each other for a long pause, and I waited for him to speak first. After all, it was his meeting, and I didn't want to make any assumptions about why he'd brought me here. He stepped to the opposite side of the table and folded his frame in half as he slid into the cushioned bench across from me. It crossed my mind he might be setting me up, but I assumed I was safe by agreeing to meet with him in a public place.

Kovac kept looking around as if wondering whether or not I was alone.

"It's just me," I said.

He rolled his neck and faced me. I felt his eyes staring from behind the mirrors he was wearing. "I know," he said. "I've been watching you."

An uneasy flutter moved down my spine. I wasn't sure I could believe what he said was true, but I steeled myself to make sure not to let my fear show. How long had he been watching me? Why hadn't I felt it? Everything was happening at once, and apparently it was affecting my instinct to be one hundred percent aware of my surroundings.

An employee passed nearby, and Kovac ducked his head. I watched the young woman clean a table near ours. Kovac thumbed his smartwatch, seeming more nervous than I was.

"I need to know you're not recording me," he said quietly.

I needed to know the same, but didn't waste my breath on a useless battle. I reached for my phone, powered it down, and once it was off, I set it on the table next to my coffee. Then I stood, opened my coat, and pulled my collar down to reveal my neckline before lifting the hem of my shirt to show him my empty waistband.

"Satisfied?" I asked.

Kovac nodded and gestured for me to sit.

"Now, let's talk about why you brought me here."

"Before we get into that, there are a couple ground rules I must first discuss with you."

"Is this going to take all day?"

"You must never mention my name."

"Fine," I said, suspecting it was fake anyway. "Anything else?"

"This meeting never happened."

I brought my hands to the table and threaded my fingers.

"Once we open up this can, it can't be sealed. Are we understood?" I told him his instructions were crystal clear. "If this ever comes back to me, I promise bad things will happen to you *and* your family."

I felt my eyes squint. I didn't like how he brought my son into the mix, but it highlighted the severity of his information. Maybe he'd finally bring me what I needed to force Watts's resignation.

"You're not wrong about Gordon Watts reporting fraudulent crime statistics," Kovac said, reaching into his jacket and revealing a thumb-drive. "But what you don't know is how he is doing it."

"Okay, how is he doing it?"

Kovac pushed the thumb-drive to me. "It's all here."

"Care to give a quick preview?"

"It's a video file of a single incident where a DPD officer is in clear violation of his code of conduct. You'll understand after you watch it, but Watts is profiling a certain minority to win his PR game, and *that's* your golden ticket."

"How did you get this?" I asked, closing my hand around the thumb-drive.

"Let's just say I'm close to the source."

I lifted my gaze and suspected he was a cop, or maybe someone close to the mayor. But if what he said was true, I was concerned with what might happen to him if anyone found out he'd been speaking to a reporter.

"Now go," he said with a sense of urgency behind his voice.

I reached for my phone, slid it into my jacket pocket, and asked, "What if I have questions?"

Kovac eyed me from behind his sunglasses and said softly, "We'll be in touch."

CHAPTER NINETEEN

SWEAT DRIPPED FROM VINCENT VERDI'S BROW. HE WAS ON the floor, lying on his back with his knees bent and arms crossed, doing sit-ups. Each time he rocked forward, he grunted. Maintaining a sculpted six pack took as much dedication as sustaining his career. It was the type of sacrifice most people weren't willing to make. That motivated Vince to rise above, because he wasn't like most people. Unlike them, Vince was perfect.

The house phone rang and Vince worked harder, pushing through the pain.

Up. Down. Up. Down.

A few more reps and the phone was still ringing. Finally, it got to him. He paused his workout and yelled, "Would someone please get that?"

Footsteps scurried across the floor below. Vince closed his eyes and sucked back a deep breath as he listened to a housemate answer the call. Rocking to his feet, he leaped off the floor and hung from a pullup bar, completing his exercise.

When he was finished, he took his cellphone into his hand and moved in front of the mirror, snapping several quick post-workout selfies to share with his followers. There was nothing more enticing than a shiny, pumped up body. After posting an image across his social media pages, Vince checked his status.

Activity was up and, no surprise to him, April Wright's name was trending.

"This is good," he said. "Even in death I can ride in your wake."

Vince set his phone down on the dresser and returned to looking at himself in the mirror, obsessively checking the popularity of his recent post. Soon the story of April would take on a life of its own and, when it did, Vince would be ready to capitalize, just as he always was.

"Must I do everything for you?" a familiar voice said from the door. Vince flicked his gaze in the mirror and found Jackie Dumont extending her arm when offering him the cordless phone. "It's for you," she said.

"Take a message." Vince stripped off his boxer shorts on his way into the bathroom, not caring about Jackie seeing him nude.

Jackie averted her gaze as Vince jumped in the shower. "Vince is preoccupied at the moment. May I take a message?" Through the glass shower walls, Vince could see Jackie picking up his mess of a room. "I'll pass the message along."

Vince turned off the shower and found Jackie waiting with a bathrobe. She was eyeing the video game he'd been playing—a prerelease for today's conference.

"We're running late," Jackie said, as Vince gripped the robe and headed into his walk-in closet.

"Since when did you become my manager?" he called out.

Jackie followed Vince to the closet and leaned her shoulder against the doorframe, crossing her arms. "The moment you decided I was the one to fix your image."

Vince turned around. "My image is perfect."

Jackie's eyes drifted lazily across his bare body. "Don't fool yourself, honey."

Vince laughed and said, "I like being late. It creates a suspense that's hard to beat. Besides, people will wait if they know what's good for them."

"You'll be riding with me today."

Vince turned and glanced over his shoulder. "What about Mitch and Chas? We can't leave them behind."

"They left already."

"Left?"

Jackie nodded. "I told them we'd meet them there."

Vince huffed his disapproval. "God, you're worse than my mother."

"If your mother knew what was best for you, she wouldn't have given you so much freedom to do what you want." Jackie raised her chin and arched her look. "About last night—"

Vince pushed his arms through the sleeves of his button-down and said, "I don't want to talk about it."

"Well you should."

"It's over."

"Vince, just because she's dead doesn't mean it's over."

Vince held her eyes for a beat before turning his back with a laugh.

"That call I just took," Jackie swiped a hand over her head, "someone has a video proving April didn't jump but was pushed."

Vince didn't flinch. He continued dressing and pushed past Jackie to retrieve his cellphone off the dresser.

"Unbelievable," Jackie said, trailing behind while he obsessively checked his stats. "When are you going to learn?"

Vince rubbed his chin, giving it some thought. "Funny that no one is mentioning the tiger. I really thought that she would have been the showstopper."

"You went off script last night," Jackie barked, suddenly losing her cool.

Vince looked her in the eye and said, "I improvised."

"Are you even listening to what I'm saying? Either we address what will soon get out, or you can consider your career over for good this time."

Vince strode across the floor and stopped in front of Jackie, tucking a loose strand of hair behind her ear. Jackie stared into his chocolate colored eyes and felt her body go stiff when he said, "April was a bitch. People will realize it soon enough, and besides, soon she'll be forgotten and I'll be the only one left."

"Have you heard anything I said? This is bad—"

Vince pressed his finger to Jackie's lips and silenced her. "There's nothing you need to worry about. I have everything under control."

CHAPTER TWENTY

KOVAC STAYED AT THE TABLE AND WATCHED ME EXIT. NOT once did I look back. I had what I'd come for. Now I needed to watch it and vet it before deciding what to make of our meeting.

As soon as I turned up the sidewalk, I patted my pocket to be sure the thumb-drive hadn't miraculously fallen out—it hadn't. I continued processing everything Kovac said.

"Let's just say I'm close to the source." His words still echoed between my ears.

I couldn't wait to see what the video revealed, how it proved Watts was the corrupt cop I knew him to be. As I neared my car, I finally had the guts to look over my shoulder. Through the window I could see Kovac was gone.

Who was he, and why was he offering to help? His need for secrecy kept me unsettled.

Ever since Erin and I started our fight with Chief Watts, we had little actual evidence to make our case. We were still gathering what facts we could, and Watts knew we were digging. We were making him nervous, and I suspected he was the type of man who would be willing to do just about anything to protect his career. Including coming after me.

I turned and faced my car. Pointing the key fob at the hood, I listened as the doors unlocked. I climbed inside and set my purse on the seat next to me before backing out and turning my attention to today's next order of business.

The Convention Center was only a short drive away, and just when I was shifting my thoughts away from Kovac and back to Vincent, I received a call from Susan.

"Is it true?" Susan said as soon as I answered. "Did April Wright kill herself?"

I assumed she saw my report and how it mentioned suicide. Not wanting to get into Russ's video, I said, "I'm investigating."

"Investigating?"

Susan's voice didn't mask her admiration for April's work, and I had to be careful not to say anything to upset her.

"Does that mean it might be something else?" she asked.

"New information has come to light," I said, not needing to say anything more. Then I realized why Susan was actually calling. "It won't affect tonight. I'm still planning on attending."

Susan perked up. "Brilliant, Sam. But can I request you come alone?"

My eyebrows pulled together as visions of King flashed behind my eyes.

Susan said, "The reason being is I might have mentioned your name to a special guest."

"You do know I'm not on the market, right?" I wasn't in the mood for any more surprises today, even if Susan's intention was good.

"I know, Sam. It's not like that. But it's Public Defender Everett Atwood who's excited to meet you."

I put on my blinker and made a left-hand turn. "And what did you tell him exactly?"

"Nothing, really. He just mentioned that he is a fan of your work and would like to tell you more about his."

I took a deep breath and sighed. "I can't wait."

"And neither can he." I heard Susan's smile in her voice. "I'll see you tonight."

Ending my call, I dove the hood of my car into the pits of a parking garage and took the first empty space I came across. It was a couple blocks away from where I needed to be, but I could use the walk to clear my head.

I trotted down the sidewalk, joining the herds of attendees funneling to the entrance of the Convention Center. Banners and signs for 5280 GamersCon fluttered in the breeze, leading the way. Young people were dressed in costume, taking selfies with their expensive smartphones, unconcerned about the world happening around them.

I marveled at the narcissism and kept walking.

Not a single person looked me in the eye or cared that I was dressed in jeans and a flannel shirt. I was fine with that, as I didn't plan to stay long. I held the door open for two young women and joined them in the back of the line. Loud music thumped through the walls and mixed with the chatter inside billowing out like a trumpet. Minutes passed and the longer I stood in line, the more out of place I felt. Mason was right. I should have allowed him to skip school to come along with me. Then at least I wouldn't be standing here alone.

Several minutes later, I stepped up to the counter and said, "A ticket for one."

"What's your name, sweetheart?"

"Samantha Bell," I told the woman.

Her fingers clacked on the keyboard. "I'm not seeing your name. Did you preregister?"

"Can't I just purchase a ticket here?"

"That's not how it works." The woman frowned when suddenly a roar of screams and shouts erupted behind me.

I swiveled on my heel and glanced through the windows outside to see what was happening. A circle formed around a single man. The moment I saw him, I knew who he was.

Vincent Verdi arrived with his entourage shielding him from the onslaught of his fans. I stared without him noticing and thought how he seemed to always steal the spotlight.

Several cameras circled him like vultures, recording the girls lining up to touch him and request to have a selfie with the one and only; a picture they could share with the less fortunate.

My first impression of Vince wasn't good, but what surprised me most as I caught my first actual glimpse of the man was how he didn't act like someone who murdered only hours ago.

Was I looking at April's killer?

Within seconds Vince was ushered inside. I knew I had little choice but to follow. I turned to the woman and flashed her my press pass. It was my last card to play, but it had worked in similar situations before.

With a smile, I said, "There must be a mistake. I'm here to report on today's event."

CHAPTER TWENTY-ONE

A SHOULDER SLAMMED INTO ERIN TATE'S BACK, KNOCKING her off balance. Whipping around to scold the person who did it, she was surprised to find herself staring down the throat of a purple dragon. From behind the mask, a gruff voice apologized for accidentally bumping into her.

"What the heck? Get out of here," she said, waving him off.

Erin knew it would be next to impossible to find Russ in this crowd. There were too many faces—and costumes—to find anyone. They'd have better luck learning Russ's home address and going directly to his house than finding him here. But Erin was here for Vince too, and a quick glance at her watch told her to expect to see him soon.

Sweeping her gaze back to Allison, Erin watched her friend hand out her business card to a young hipster wearing black-framed eyeglasses and a wide-brimmed hat. "Call me," she heard Allison say. "We can discuss how I can help with marketing."

"What reality are these people living in?" Erin asked once Allison joined back up with her.

Allison's eyes glimmered as she took it all in. "One of illusion."

Erin shook her head as if deciding what planet they'd landed on when she asked in all seriousness, "And these are the people you want to work with?"

Allison met Erin's eye. "I'm simply prospecting, hoping to be a liaison between companies and influencers."

Several robotic dogs trotted in front of them, and they both marveled at the entertainment circling around them. GamersCon was Vegas for video gamers—every spectacle over the top.

"You don't regret coming, do you?" Allison asked.

"Not at all," Erin said, reminding Allison of her desire to learn more about how she could incorporate the influencer techniques into her own gig as a journalist. "I just wasn't expecting...this."

Together they walked, meandering through the crowd. "Any sight of Sam's suspect?"

"I was thinking maybe the dragon who bumped into me earlier, but then there's the man in the banana costume, that could be him, too."

"You are having fun," Allison said, reaching for her phone when she felt it buzz. Reading the message, she said, "Sam's here, but having trouble at the door. I need to go help."

Erin was standing straight, peering over the crowd. Allison followed her gaze across the room and spotted Vincent Verdi.

"You go ahead," Erin said. "There's something I need to ask Vince."

CHAPTER TWENTY-TWO

INTENT ON NOT LOSING SIGHT OF VINCE, ERIN PALMED HER cellphone and circled him from afar.

He stood over six feet tall with lean muscle mass and had that unmistakable movie star swagger. Erin was intrigued by his ego; it was what drew her closer to the man of mystery and suspense.

Vince was an attractive man with deep dimples, clean-cut and athletic. But Erin also wondered if what Samantha had discovered about him could actually be true.

Vince continued to move between vendors, acting like he owned the entire event. They reached out and he high-fived, shook hands, and hugged nearly everyone who came up to him. Even Erin could see Vince was a people person, basking in the glory of his fame.

He doesn't seem like a murderer, Erin thought as she glanced to her phone's screen one last time, reminding herself what Russ's face looked like. With Russ's image in her head, she tucked her device away into her back pants pocket and looked over her shoulder.

Allison was long gone, having disappeared into the crowd,

and now that Erin was alone, she pushed through the chaos and hurried to catch up with Vince.

Looking for a way into his inner circle, Erin wondered if she'd be able to get close enough to ask him the questions rolling around her head. It needed to happen now when the memory was fresh, when she had the opportunity to catch him off guard.

"Excuse me," she said, brushing past a couple of men, continuing to look for Russ, when she nearly collided into a stranger's back. Quick to apologize, Erin didn't know how she'd get past the wall of people now circling Vince, but she had to try.

Vince turned, and they locked eyes for a brief moment. Erin liked his pink tinted glasses, even if they were a little feminine, but Vince didn't seem to notice her admiration. He was surrounded by too many screaming fans, women who all wanted to touch him to prove he was real. Adjusting her strategy, Erin opened another button on her blouse and let her hair down.

"Will this get your attention?" she asked no one in particular.

Accentuating her slender figure, she slithered forward and watched Vince stop to take a selfie with a fan. He surprised the girl by kissing her cheek, and the entire crowd suddenly blushed with jealousy. Seeing a gap open in front of his path, Erin took it.

Wedging her shoulders between bodies, Erin was within reach when she pretended to trip. Falling forward, she reached out and gripped Vince by the arm to help catch her fall. Vince turned and helped her stand straight, his eyes drifting down her neck as his big hand gripped her waist.

"Oh my god. I'm so sorry. How embarrassing," Erin said, fluttering her lashes beneath her brow.

Vince's eyes glimmered as they circled her face. He smiled, and asked, "How about a photo to make up for it?"

"With me?" Erin fanned her face.

Vince took her phone and handed it off to a member of his team. Tucking Erin under his arm, Vince posed for a photo when Erin reached her hand to his chest and said, "I can see why April was attracted to you. Big, strong, handsome. Sad what happened to her last night." Erin looked him in the eye when saying, "It didn't have anything to do with the fight you two had the day of her death, did it?"

Suddenly a hand gripped Erin's arm and yanked her away from Vince. A red-haired woman in bright red pumps got in her face and asked, "Who are you?"

Erin shot her a look. "Who are you?"

"She's a crime podcaster," someone in the crowd shouted.

"A journalist," the redhead snarled with disgust.

"Yeah, that's Erin Tate." Another person pointed to Erin.

Looping arms, Erin's phone was shoved into her hand as the redhead dragged Erin further away from Vince. "Come with me."

Erin fought back. "Not until you tell me who the heck you are."

"Jackie Dumont, Vince's publicist, and here to offer you the deal of a lifetime."

Erin stood back and knitted her brows. "Who says I'm here to make a deal?"

"How much do you want to keep Vince's name out of the news?"

"Are you suggesting he's guilty?"

Jackie didn't immediately answer. Then she said, "Whatever you've heard, Vince ended things with April. Not the other way around."

"Then how do you explain the video that's floating around

suggesting Vince planned April's death for his big show, *Don't trip. You might fall,* to revive his career?"

"What is it you really want?" Jackie asked, seething between her teeth and keeping one eye on Vince, the other on Erin.

"A chance for Vince to clear the air."

Vince was moving, and when Jackie realized she was running out of time, she said, "Hold off on your reporting and I'll get you your exclusive interview with Vince. There is more to this story than you know. Trust me, you'll want to hear what he has to say."

CHAPTER TWENTY-THREE

I STOOD OFF TO THE SIDE AND GLARED AT THE WOMAN WHO had denied my entrance when Allison snuck up from behind and asked, "Didn't you tell them who you are?"

I spun around and wrapped my arms around my friend, so happy to see her, squeezing her tight. Allison embraced me and filled my lungs with renewed hope.

"Either my name means nothing," I said, "or my profession doesn't carry the same clout as it once did."

We locked eyes and Allison said, "I'm going to say it probably isn't your name."

"Let's hope you're right." We both laughed as I tried not to think about the time wasted. Where was Vince now? Had I missed my opportunity to speak with him? I asked Allison, "You can get me inside, right?"

"You're lucky," she said, taking me by the hand and leading me to the front of the line. "Patty woke with a migraine and had to cancel. That's why I have this extra ticket."

Patty O'Neil was Allison's chief of operations and, while I hoped she would be feeling better soon, I was happy to fill her spot. Allison motioned with her head to follow her to the counter where she flashed the extra vendor badge she'd just taken out of her purse to the ticket lady who nodded her approval. It was easy and efficient and something my press badge couldn't do. Then Allison told me to wear it around my neck. I couldn't believe how easy it was to enter the event after that.

"Where is Erin?" I asked, impressed by the madness of the crowds inside.

"Last I saw, she was making her way to Vincent Verdi." Allison swept her eyes to me and tossed me a look. Talking over the noise, she said, "She didn't say why, but something tells me you know."

I gave her a knowing look and asked her to lead the way while I broke down our investigation. Each step revealed a new detail and soon Allison was caught up to speed.

"Wow. That's heavy stuff. But I hope you're wrong," she said.

I hoped I was too, but I was afraid I wasn't. I said, "Mason said there was a rumor floating around on social media that said Vince convinced April to jump."

Allison swept her wide look over to me. We stopped in the middle of the floor. She said, "Maybe that's what they were fighting about?"

"Would you jump to your death if someone told you to do it?"

"Maybe it's not what he told her to do, but something he said to make her *want* to do it?"

I sucked back a deep breath and looked around, having thought that too. This place was hopping with activity and I was a little overstimulated by the action. The moment I spotted Erin, Allison tossed up both her hands and started waving them above her head. Erin gave us a wave back, indicating she saw us, and hurried over.

"You're not going to believe this," Erin said with bated breath.

"Is Russ here?" I asked.

Erin shrugged. "Haven't seen him."

Allison asked, "Did you speak with Vince?"

Erin's eyes flashed with excitement. "Sam, I spoke with Vince's publicist," she pointed to a redhead walking away from us, "and she's acting like they know about Russ's video."

"Did they seem worried?" Again, I wondered whose side Russ was on.

"Concerned enough to offer to pay me a healthy sum to keep Vince's name out of the news."

"How much?" Allison asked.

Erin ignored the question. It was beside the point. Erin said, "Sam, I know I said I was glad you didn't accept Russ's offer to purchase the video, but now I'm thinking you should have."

"To get it before Vince?"

"Exactly."

I thought about what Russ mentioned to me earlier, how he had multiple offers on the table. Was Vince one of those offers? It would make sense if he was.

I asked, "How can we be sure Russ hasn't already offered to sell it to Vince? Vince can afford to pay him the most. And if Russ is going after the highest bidder…"

"Unless Vince sees it as Russ trying to blackmail him," Allison said between us.

Suddenly I was concerned for Russ's safety. If he was acting on his own, he'd certainly go after the person willing to pay the most, even if it meant putting his life in danger to get the check he was after. Did he know what he was doing and who he was dealing with? How long had he been a freelancer, or was he just hoping to cash out on something he just happened to capture by sheer luck?

Erin told me she secured a meeting with Vince via his publicist for tomorrow. "We have to get the video before that meeting. It's the only way he'll talk."

My hand landed on the outside of my pants pocket. I had Russ's business card, but I couldn't guarantee we could get the film before it disappeared. "The video should be handed over to investigators."

Erin agreed. "But we can kiss our meeting goodbye if Vince gets to it first."

Which meant we'd lose our story, *and* our chance to learn why Vincent was fighting with April. I pulled out my cell and had my thumb on dial, ready to call Russ, when a stream of people stampeded past. We all turned our heads to look, and it didn't take us more than a second to realize they were all heading toward Vince.

CHAPTER TWENTY-FOUR

I WAS THE FIRST TO TAKE OFF JOGGING. WHATEVER VINCE was up to, I needed to see it with my own eyes. Allison and Erin trailed close behind as I bulldozed my way through the crowd, leading the way.

"Excuse me. Pardon me," I kept saying, threading between the hordes of people all after the same thing.

I kept my chin down and my eyes forward as I tried to figure out what was playing on the large screen ahead of me. It was some sort of video game, probably one of the new ones Mason mentioned to me, and standing on the stage in front of the pixelated wall was none other than Vincent Verdi.

The room exploded with applause. Loud cheers shook the ceiling and pulled me closer to the show. Whatever Vince was doing, the crowd loved it.

"Sam, look!" Erin said behind me.

I glanced over my shoulder and followed Erin's finger to a drone hovering above the crowd. I assumed it was filming Vince and the crowd below, but what was it dropping down?

The loud speakers shook, and my ears hurt. I flicked my gaze back to the large screen and watched the digital simulation play out. Darting my eyes around the room, it seemed as if everyone had their cellphones out recording Vince's production.

We got as close as we could before stopping. I scanned the people around Vince and looked for Russ. He didn't appear to be here. Then Vince did something I couldn't believe.

"Did you see that?" Erin screamed into my ear.

I wished I hadn't. This was a joke to him. It made me feel sick all over again.

"There is no question he knows about the video," I said.

Vince was at the controls when he paused the game. He turned to the audience, grabbed the microphone, and waved his arms to pump up the crowd.

"Don't trip. You might fall," hundreds of voices said in unison.

Vince smiled and relished his ability to manipulate a crowd. But he couldn't fool me. I was certain he was using this time to act as a distraction before the real video of April being pushed made its way to the media. This was simply his way of dulling the surprise. Then he turned back to the screen, un-paused the video game, and did it again.

My hand flew over my mouth as I gasped. Though it was only a video game, the similarities were too close to not think about the real thing. Playing the game in the first-person point of view, Vince's digital arms shoved the woman toward the banister, sending her flying over the edge.

Erin's head was tipped back as she looked on. "He's murdering the digital version of April."

Taking my eyes off the screen, I caught sight of a drone hovering above. I assumed it was filming Vince, and when it dropped a flyer, I managed to reach out and snatch it from the sky.

Allison leaned into me and asked, "What's it say?"

I read the text out loud. "When life imitates game, you become the star of your own show. Mile High GamersCon 2020."

The crowd kept chanting—*Don't trip! You might fall!*—as their thirst for pixelated blood and carnage grew manic.

Feeling a cold chill roll down my spine, I wondered how many people knew what Vince was recreating, or if they even cared. Probably not many, but maybe some. To them, it was just fun violence offered in the form of safe entertainment. But to me, it suggested what we had already assumed about Vince; that he might be the one who murdered April Wright.

"We need to get our hands on Russ's video and turn it in before this becomes a complete joke," I said, staring at the blood-filled screen.

A wave of unease lifted the hairs on my neck when I caught Vince staring from his podium. He was looking directly at me when he winked, acting like he knew who I was.

I asked Erin, "Did he just wink at you?"

"I thought he was winking at you."

Vince swapped controllers, and now he was in control of the drone that had been dropping fliers. We stood and watched it zip across the crowd before it circled above for a quick beat before plunging from the high ceiling and buzzing directly above our heads.

The three of us ducked as the crowd gasped and laughed.

With our heads bowed, Allison turned to Erin and said, "It seems you've rattled the hornet's nest."

"Then let's not get stung," I reached for Erin's hand and spun her around. "C'mon. Let's get out of here and call Russ before Vince knows we're gone."

CHAPTER TWENTY-FIVE

WE CONVENED A BLOCK FROM THE CONVENTION AND I WAS happy to be away from the noise. Erin and Allison huddled around me as I called Russ.

Anxiety swirled in my stomach. I kept looking around, expecting to see Vince strolling up the sidewalk, coming after us. In less than twenty-four hours, he'd worked his way into my dreams and turned my life into a living nightmare. Who was this guy? Why did I have a feeling he was going to get away with murder?

The phone rang and rang and Russ never answered.

"He's not picking up," I said.

"You think we're too late?" Erin asked.

I glanced to my watch and gave a wistful look. "He was awfully eager to sell it to me this morning, but it's possible he might have already found a buyer," I said, hoping Jackie wouldn't get to it first—that is, if our assumptions about her were right. I finally killed the call and asked Erin, "Did you see Jackie near Vince on stage?"

Erin took a moment to think about it. "No," she said, mentioning what Jackie looked like after Allison asked. "Shit.

She's going after the video. I know it, Sam. It's what I would do if I was her."

I swiped a hand over my head, not knowing what to do next. Erin blamed herself for giving too much away. But what I wanted to know more than anything was where Russ was now, and how we could find him. Then I asked the group, "Let's say Vince didn't know about Russ's video, then how was it he was able to recreate April's death?"

"Don't trip. You might fall. Sam, Vince is the producer of his own show. Even Jackie said it herself. *There is more to this story than you know, and trust me, you'll want to hear what he has to say.* But what no one expected was for Russ to have caught it all on film."

I hoped Erin was wrong, but something told me she wasn't. What did Vince know, and how could he explain his way out of this one? Maybe he wasn't involved, but someone near him was?

I steadied my feet by placing a hand on the brick wall and glanced up the street thinking about my conversation with Justine. I needed to know what was said, why Vince and April were fighting. If I knew that, I might know whether or not I was wasting my time chasing Vince when I should be looking at someone else.

The sound of a phone ringing had me reaching for my cell. Except it wasn't my call to take. It was Allison's. She answered her phone, smiled, and said, "It's Nicholas."

I blew out a hot breath, hating how on edge I felt. The clock was ticking inside my head. It felt like time was running out.

Allison was off to finish up work, then to meet Nicholas for dinner. We promised to call if we needed her assistance, and she wished us luck. Once Allison was gone, Erin turned to me and said, "You never told me about your meeting with Kovac."

I apologized with my eyes. "I had to go alone."

Erin nodded and looked away. I knew she was upset that I hadn't swung by to pick her up like I'd promised, but she didn't hold her grudge for long. "So, did he have the golden ticket to bring down Watts?"

I thought about the thumb-drive, still not knowing what was on it. "That's what he claims, but I have yet to check it out."

My cellphone rang. It was Russ. I answered and said, "Do you still have the video?"

Russ laughed as if expecting this conversation. "I do, but the auction is in full swing. There is another interested buyer who just came to me, so if you want it, it will cost you."

I bit my tongue, then asked, "How much?" I stopped breathing when he told me the price. It was nearly triple his original ask. "Okay," I said. "I want it. When can we meet?"

CHAPTER TWENTY-SIX

MR. T ENDED HIS CALL AND SET THE PHONE DOWN. HIS plan was working. Everyone wanted what he had. He reached up and angled the rearview mirror to his face. Removing his glasses, he swiveled his head around and combed his hair with his fingers.

"Keep dropping them crumbs and soon the clever will follow you down this trail of truth," he said, talking as if someone was in the car with him.

It delighted Mr. T to feel so important. People needed him. He liked holding the cards. It was the thrill of the chase that resurrected him from certain death. Now that he had a taste of what it felt like to be alive again, he wanted more of the same.

Turning to his laptop propped up in the passenger seat next to him, his seat squeaked as he shifted his weight around. Cracking his knuckles, Mr. T wanted to share his secret. It tore his insides up to be holding onto his words, but he also liked how much fun he was having knowing what no one else seemed to know.

He clicked out of one browser and opened up another.

There, on the display screen, were three small video feeds, each relaying back a different angle to the many cameras he had deployed out into the field.

One was inside the convention. The second, outside his house. And the third, a feed being relayed from the camera mounted to his drone. The first and second cameras were clear—no action—but it was the third lens he was keeping a close eye on.

He brought his right hand back to the drone's controls and gripped them with both hands as he peered over the steering wheel and up into the sky. Though he couldn't see the aircraft with the naked eye, he knew it was just on the other side of the building from where he was parked.

Pinching the joystick between his fingers, he focused the camera mounted to the bottom of the drone and zoomed in on the three women huddled along a quiet side street, completely oblivious to his spying. Though he couldn't hear what they were saying, he knew they were talking about him. *Weren't they always talking about him?*

It was the two journalists and a third face he didn't know. He zoomed in, snapped a couple photos, and began his search on his computer. Nothing came up. His software wasn't recognizing the face of the third, a black woman of medium height.

He turned back to the drone's camera feed. His lips curled into a smile when reading both Samantha and Erin's tense body language. Their stress was evident, and Mr. T liked to think it was because of him. He liked knowing how much he controlled their behavior. Their friend, however, was a different story.

What *was* her story? Why was she calm and collected? Mr. T then watched the black woman leave. A strange inclination fell over him to harass her, too.

Maneuvering the drone, he stalked her up the street,

wondering who she was speaking to on the phone, why she left Samantha behind, and wondered where she was off to now. A surge of excitement had his foot jumping off the floor with sudden curiosity.

"Are you someone I should know, too?" he asked the screen.

As if she could hear him, the woman tipped her head back and squinted her eyes up into the sky. She stared directly at him.

Mr. T froze and stared back. He knew the terror the drone brought to his unsuspecting victims. And she was no different. It was almost as thrilling as the fear he brought to April's eyes, seconds before she plunged to her death. Then he murmured the answer to his own question. "Something tells me you are, and I look forward to meeting you soon."

CHAPTER TWENTY-SEVEN

ALLISON STROLLED UP THE STREET AND HEADED TOWARD her car with the biggest smile stamped on her face. She murmured, "Just surprise me."

"Very well," Nicholas Bennett said. "How was the convention? Did you sign any new clients?"

"A few promising leads," she said, adding a comment about the absurdity behind Vince Verdi's actions.

"My students love Vince."

Allison pulled her eyebrows together. Unfortunately, she wasn't too surprised Vince was well-liked by teenagers. "From what I hear, he might not be that great of a role model."

"Did you know the number one career choice by high schoolers is being a social media influencer?" Nicolas added, "It's true. I polled them myself."

Allison rolled her eyes and stopped walking when a weird sense of being followed tingled her spine. Turning around, she looked at where she'd come from, but no one was there. Just a few cars and a city bus passing. Nothing out of the ordinary.

Bennett sensed Allison's moment of unease through the phone and asked, "Is everything all right?"

When Allison heard the whine, she tipped her head back and shielded her eyes from the sun. There in the sky was a drone hovering over her head about one hundred feet off the ground. Thinking little of it, she said, "It's nothing. Just a drone buzzing overhead."

"Only a drone." Bennett chuckled as if not believing the world they found themselves living in. "I'll see you soon."

Allison ended the call and tucked her phone inside her purse. She hurried away, wanting to finish up work at the office so she could get home to Bennett. Then she rounded the corner and heard someone call her name. Allison slowed her gait and turned to find a young man hurrying to catch up to her.

"Allison Doyle?"

"Yes?" Allison clenched her fingers tightly around her purse strap, giving the young man a puzzled look.

"You spoke with a friend of mine about representing him." The young man didn't give a name. "Anyway, he told me to catch you before you leave. I'm sorry to sneak up on you like this. I'm just starting out and could use some marketing tips to help get off the ground."

Allison looked around, realizing they were alone. "You're a gamer?"

"Yes." The young man smiled proudly. "And a good one, too."

"Do you have a business card? I'd love to talk over the phone and discuss how you think I'll be able to help you achieve your goals, but now's not a good time. I'm afraid I'm late for a meeting."

"Yes. Yes. Of course. I understand." The man dove his hand into his front jeans pocket and pulled out a card, handing it to Allison. "Thank you so much," he said. "I hear you're one of the best." His phone made a noise and he hurried back toward the Convention Center, seeming distracted by whatever his phone had messaged him.

Allison cast her gaze to his card and knitted her eyebrows. "Hey," she called out. "Wait! I think you gave me the wrong card."

"It's there," the young gamer responded. Picking up his pace, he said, "Check it out, and call me if you're interested. I think we might be able to work together."

"What's your name?" she asked, but it was too late. The young man was already gone. Allison flipped the card around, only to find a handwritten URL to a website she didn't recognize.

CHAPTER TWENTY-EIGHT

Twenty minutes later I arrived home, happy to find the front door locked. It was a new routine I was trying to instill in Mason—and myself. He was better about locking up when he was home than I was, but I couldn't tell him why it needed to be done.

I used my key to unlock the front door, pushed it open with my hip, and kicked my sneakers off at the door, checking my phone all at the same time. I had an hour before I had to leave for Susan's charity event, and the timing couldn't have been worse.

Sixty minutes to get everything done felt like an impossible task. Luckily, Erin offered to meet Russ, using her own money to purchase the video. Though I wasn't thrilled with the idea of her having to go alone, I now understood how she felt about my meeting with Kovac.

The house was quiet, a nice change of pace after Gamers-Con. As I stepped into the kitchen and placed my purse on the counter, I felt my muscles begin to relax. My aching bones wanted me to call it a night, curl up on the couch for an early evening of wine and movies. But I couldn't. Not with so many others counting on me to come through.

Instead, I picked up the phone and checked the voice messages. There were a couple hang ups from an unknown number and I assumed it was the same caller as before. It left me with an uneasy feeling as I wondered who could be behind the calls. Why weren't they willing to leave a message? Could it be the same person behind the drone that had been following me? It certainly crossed my mind.

This was why I had to have my house locked at all times. Mason didn't know I had a stalker, or that people on social media were wishing me bodily harm. I didn't need to scare him, and I certainly didn't want him to worry about me. He had enough on his busy plate as it was.

Moving to the sink, I filled a glass with water and stared out the kitchen window into the neighbor's backyard. I wondered if we were making the right decision by purchasing Russ's video, or just enabling him to drive the price higher.

I couldn't explain why, but I wanted him to be connected to Vince.

Once my thirst was quenched, I set my water glass down on the counter and took the thumb-drive from my pocket. Before I had a chance to put it in my laptop, Cooper was pawing at the back door, asking to come inside.

Hurrying to let him in, I passed Mason's room and stopped to peek my head inside. Mason was wearing his headset and staring at the TV. I glanced to his empty desk, then swept my gaze to his back pack lying in the middle of the floor. His homework and books were still tucked away inside, and I doubted they'd been touched since coming home.

Cooper barked again, this time louder, ending with a desperate whine of frustrated neglect. He came barreling inside the moment I opened the door and immediately jumped up and lapped his long tongue against the tip of my chin.

"Hey boy," I said, smiling. "Want to help me pull Mason away from his video games?"

Cooper wagged his tail, happy to see me, and followed me back into Mason's bedroom.

"No homework tonight?" I said to my son, reminding him of the work he forgot this morning.

"Oh. Hey Mom." Mason quickly glanced in my direction. "Didn't hear you come home."

I stared at the screen, realizing what Mason was watching. It was the same game I saw Vince use to recreate April's murder. I felt my core heat with sudden anger. "Is this your game?" I asked.

"No. I'm watching this guy, Trojan, play. It's a new game. The one I was telling you about."

I folded my arms across my chest and together we watched as Trojan streamed his game playing to the world by way of internet. To me, it was the most boring thing to watch, but Mason's eyes were bright with wonder.

Something big happened and Mason said excitedly, "His popularity is exploding. Look at all his followers." Mason pointed to the counter in the corner of the screen. "I bet this dude is making bank."

I didn't know what to say. "That's how many people are watching him play?"

Mason nodded.

"Why?"

"People might say it's because they want to check out the new game, but really," Mason turned to look me in the eye, "I think it's because he predicted April Wright's death."

My brow furrowed. "What do you mean, he *predicted* her death?"

"I mean, his avatar was on a killing spree, and one of his

kills happened to look like April. He pushed her over the rail and she fell from three stories up." Mason flicked his gaze to me and said, "Isn't that how it happened?"

"Did he do this today?" I asked, remembering what I witnessed Vince do in front of thousands of hyped up fans at GamersCon.

"No. It happened during last night's stream. I'm sure it's just coincidence because it was just a second of his game play, but everyone is replaying it as if he predicted her death."

"Does Trojan have a last name?"

Mason locked eyes when he said, "His identity is anonymous, but everyone suspects its Vince."

CHAPTER TWENTY-NINE

MY SON'S SUSPICIONS PUT A COLD CHILL DOWN MY SPINE. He showed me the second of play in question and it was exactly what I saw Vince do today. I turned to the door and told Mason to watch out for anything else that might be suspicious and to let me know as soon as anything happened.

"Mom," Mason stopped me in my tracks, "was April murdered?

I looked him in the eye and murmured, "I don't know."

In that moment my sixteen-year-old looked like a child. His eyes flashed with fear for a world he was still grasping to understand. But there was also strength and intelligence gained from the incredible experience his short life had gifted him. That gave me hope.

I said, "Just keep your eye on Trojan's stream, and report anything else you find suspicious."

"I'm not a violent person, Mom."

"I know, sweetie."

"I just like these types of games. They're fun to me."

I smiled as my heart burst with unconditional love. Then I closed his door and left my son alone, hoping I wouldn't later regret my decision to keep Mason glued in front of a violent video game stream. But he seemed thrilled to be part of my investigation and I knew he could handle the task responsibly.

Sitting at the kitchen table, I flipped the lid on my laptop and typed 'Trojan' into the search bar. I got a ton of relevant hits but didn't learn too much about him that Mason hadn't already told me. He wasn't a well-known gamer, kept his name anonymous, and had a public desire to make an astronomical amount of money. But was he Vince? There wasn't anything to suggest either way. However, after what I witnessed Vince do today at GamersCon, and what Mason said this Trojan guy did in his own game last night, I believed it was possible.

I plugged the thumb-drive into my computer port and reached for my phone. Dialing Erin's number, I left the table and walked to my bedroom, needing to lay my clothes out for tonight.

The layers to Vince's life were peeling away, and soon he'd be revealed. Whether he was guilty or not, I suspected he knew something that could lead us to April's killer.

Erin picked up after the second ring. "I just spoke with Mason. There's a new development in our saga."

After I told Erin about Trojan, she said, "This sounds like complete coincidence."

"And it could be. But the premonition happened the same night April died. What if the killer is playing out his murders before they actually occur?" I was speaking off the cuff but it was a terrifying thought. I didn't want to go down this road, but here we were, once again, chasing an evil villain terrorizing our community.

Erin asked, "When did this supposed premonition happen? Before or after Russ caught the push on camera?"

I thought about it for a second. "Not sure."

"Then we need to find out."

"Russ is expecting me," I murmured. "He's going to be surprised to see you. Do you have the money?"

"I got it. It's all here."

"Good. But I have a bad feeling about this," I said. "Just get the video and leave as soon as you can. We still don't know who actually filmed April's fall. For all I know, Russ was the one who pushed her."

Erin snapped, "Why did you have to say that?"

"To keep you alive."

We promised to message every half-hour and, after I ended our call, I did my hair and makeup, slipped into my gown and found myself sitting behind my laptop with minutes to spare.

My heart was drumming inside my chest when I opened the file Kovac had given me. Inside was a single video file which I proceeded to click. It seemed to take forever to load.

As I sat waiting for the image to appear, my thoughts rewound back to what Kovac said. I hoped he was right about this being my golden ticket to getting Watts to resign. I felt like I was being pulled in two directions and was splitting at the seams as if having to decide which path was most important. I couldn't chase April's murderer and continue down Watts's rabbit hole.

Nerves boiled up inside me and a rush of excitement had me tipping forward in my chair as the video started to play. It started out blurry and I couldn't decide what I was looking at, but as soon as it came into focus my foot stopped rocking.

Three uniformed male officers surrounded a single male suspect on the sidewalk who looked confused. There was a lot of back and forth, none of which I could hear.

Frustrated, I checked the volume on my computer and put it to the highest setting. Still nothing.

I continued watching as the biggest of the three officers

led the man to his squad car and instructed him to put his hands on the vehicle where the officer proceeded to frisk the suspect.

Up to this point, everything I saw was routine procedure. I hadn't witnessed any misconduct on any of the officers. Then the suspect turned his head and started yelling at the officer pinning him to his squad car. The officer muscled more of his weight against his thin frame and I could feel the tension between parties escalating. But what I saw happen next had me wishing I could see the officer's face.

With the suspect still pinned to the squad car, the big officer reached one hand behind his back as a second officer came into the frame and dropped something into the big officer's hand. The big officer then reached down the back of the man's shirt, acting like he was in possession of something illegal.

I rewound the video and watched the drop again. It was an inside job. The cops framed him, and their illegal activity was caught on camera. Except I couldn't see the officers' faces to know who was responsible, and I wondered if Kovac knew who they were. But then, just seconds before the video was to finish, the big officer turned toward the camera and showed his face for the first time.

The air was knocked out of me. I couldn't believe what I was seeing.

My eyes rounded, and I slammed my laptop shut, refusing to believe King had anything to do with what I just saw.

CHAPTER THIRTY

TWENTY MINUTES LATER, THE VALET HANDED ME MY ticket as I hurried inside the front entrance to the Marriott in the Denver Tech Center. Mixed feelings swirled my stomach. I didn't want to believe what I saw in Kovac's video.

What was King doing in uniform? Why would he want to frame someone? Was this Kovac helping to force Watts's resignation, or a deliberate attempt to question King's integrity and make me question everything?

It was all I could think about as I fought the I-25 evening traffic, already late to Susan's event. A part of me wanted to cancel my appearance and tell Susan I couldn't do it. Not tonight, and certainly not with everything that was on my mind. But I also knew there must be more to this video—and King's story—than a quick clip designed to raise my blood pressure.

I passed through the lobby and followed the signs while listening to my heels clack off the floor. Turning the corner, I pulled my phone from my clutch and sent Erin a message. She was quick to respond and said she was just now leaving her house.

We were safe. At least for now.

I took another deep breath and focused on letting go of work, if only for an hour or two, to be fully present in an otherwise fun environment. Relaxing my shoulders, I sprouted a smile and felt it stretch across my face. The lovely woman at the door greeted me, reciprocating my friendly expression, and checked my name off the list.

"I'm glad you could make it tonight, Mrs. Bell," she said, directing me through the double door entrance.

I stepped into the banquet hall and listened to the charming music fill the room as guests circled tables with vibrant colored flowers displayed in the center. It was a beautiful sight. As I stood there clutching my purse, smiling like an idiot who didn't know where to stand, I thought how Susan nearly lost this event to an unfortunate circumstance a few weeks ago. She'd done an amazing job putting it together, and I was proud of her.

The scent of succulent dishes and the sweet fragrance of wine drifted in front of me and I moved off to the side as I messaged my friend to let her know I had arrived.

I lifted my head and smiled as an older couple floated past. The woman hung on to his arm, and they looked content and happy. Then I turned my head and found myself watching two men in brightly colored suits leave a table and trot off together as if having the time of their lives. I kept looking for Susan, flitting my gaze across the dazzling room, guessing which of the guests came with the public defender.

"Samantha."

I turned and found Susan gliding across the floor with an average height man at her side. She added an extra flair in her stride as she smiled. I lifted my hand and waved but didn't move.

"Relax." Susan kissed my cheek. "Make yourself at home. We're all friends here."

I hated not having a better poker face. Even Susan could see this was the last place on earth I wanted to be. I said, "I'm sorry I'm late."

"I've known you for a long time." Susan turned to her friend and mentioned how many years we'd been friends. Then she turned back to me and said, "It's when you arrive early that has me concerned." We laughed, then she introduced me to her friend. "Samantha, I'd like for you to meet my friend, Garrett Todd."

"Nice to meet you," I said, shaking his hand.

"Pleasure is all mine." Garrett gripped my hand like a dead fish and winked.

"Garrett is the independent film maker I have been telling you about," Susan reminded me.

She'd mentioned her gay friend before, but we'd never met until now. Garrett was about the same height as me, had wavy blonde hair, and a mustache that filled his upper lip. His blue eyes were friendly and his optimism shimmered in everything he did.

"Ah, yes," I said. "Susan has many great things to say about you."

"As long as the stories are all great, Susan can say whatever she likes about me." Garrett cast his gaze to Susan and leaned into her.

Susan turned to me with bright eyes. "Garrett is gearing up for his film premier—"

"Coming Out," Garrett said.

Susan clarified. "The name of his movie."

"When is it set to release?" I asked.

"There are a few kinks that still need working out, but after that, I should be making the announcement soon." Garrett shifted his eyes to me and said, "You should come."

"You figure out the date and let me know," I said.

Susan set her hand on my shoulder as she spoke to

Garrett. "Samantha has many contacts in journalism. Maybe she could introduce you to a few who could help with publicity?"

We locked eyes and Garrett put his hand on his hip and quirked an eyebrow as if suddenly being handed the world.

I reminded Susan, "Allison is the marketing guru. He should really be speaking to her."

"Oh, honey," Susan laughed, "Allison is on my list of referrals too. Don't you worry."

I watched Susan's smile fade as something behind me stole her attention. I turned to see what it was she was looking at. Suddenly, Susan hooked her arm through the crook of mine and yanked me off my feet.

"I'm sorry, darling," Susan called out to Garrett. "We'll catch up with you later, but I just caught sight of the public defender who has been dying to speak with Samantha."

CHAPTER THIRTY-ONE

Everett Atwood wasn't the person I imagined. Instead of being tall with broad shoulders, Atwood was short and pudgy. His wife stood at his side and was about an inch taller than him and had crystal blue eyes that glimmered like the diamond studs in her ears. Her name was Genevieve and she was absolutely gorgeous. Together, they were an odd fit, but somehow it worked.

"Everett, I told you she would show," Susan teased him.

"It's the only reason I'm here," Atwood said, unable to take his eye off me.

"He doesn't actually mean that," Genevieve said to Susan.

Susan waved it away as no big deal. Atwood was still staring, and I was starting to feel uncomfortable. Did he find me attractive, or did he do this to everyone he met? I heard Genevieve mention something to Susan about their children, and Genevieve turned to me and asked if I had children myself.

"A teenage boy," I said.

"Then you'll understand." She gave me a single nod, brushing a tight curl of hair away from her eyes.

I smiled back, wishing I knew what it was I had missed. Then Atwood gave his wife a single look and Genevieve asked Susan to introduce her to another attendee. Susan promised she'd be back shortly and, once I was alone with Atwood, I stood awkwardly for a beat before saying, "I hear you're a fan of my blog."

"Not just your blog, also your column and your podcast with Ms. Tate."

"It's nice to know we have fans."

"Samantha," Atwood inched his way closer and dropped his voice to a whisper, "the reason I asked for tonight's introduction is to speak to you about Police Chief Gordon Watts."

We held eyes for a second, then I asked, "Are you sure I'm the right person to be speaking to?"

Atwood chuckled, holding his half-empty glass of white wine firmly in one hand. "I have nothing against your reporting. In fact, I appreciate what you're trying to do."

He was still giving me that look, the look that said I had all the answers to his many questions. I wasn't sure what exactly he was getting at, so kept my answers vague. "What can I do for you, counselor?"

"I've followed your reporting closely and I believe you might be onto something."

Atwood was referring to how I believed Watts covered up a Jane Doe murder, but we didn't have enough evidence to convict. Perhaps he knew more than I did, and I hoped that was the case. I said, "It's certainly gotten Watts's attention."

"That it did." Atwood's eyes flashed a knowing grin. "Which is why I believe now is the perfect time for my office to take a second look at some of the cases in question that got through before my arrival."

Now I was the one feeling surprised. He knew something I didn't. I listened as he continued.

"We both know the city's crime statics are fraudulent, and

innocent people are being locked away for crimes they didn't commit. The question is, what are we going to do about it?"

"We?" I said.

"It might not seem like it, but you hold as much power as I do, Samantha."

"I doubt that."

"Inside this mess you and I both know exists, is a story waiting to be told. I want to help you tell it, but I also want to make sure you get it right." Atwood's look changed. "Police reports just don't get leaked to the press without an ulterior motive. It's important we vet any information given, to be sure neither of us falls into the same fraudulent trap we're working to expose."

Staring into the depth of his eyes, I wondered if he knew about my meeting with Kovac. The look he was giving me suggested he did. Not knowing who I could fully trust, I needed him to prove he wasn't using me to root out a cop who leaked potentially valuable information for the benefit of protecting the chief of police—if Kovac was in fact a cop, like I thought he might be.

I asked, "How can I trust you?"

"I need you just as much as you need me."

Whose side was he on? How did I get roped into meeting both him and Kovac on the same day? It seemed like a coincidence to be skeptical of. My suspicions were on high alert and, though I wanted to turn my head away and look for Susan, I couldn't break eye contact for fear of turning my back. Then Atwood surprised me. "What I'm about to tell you can't be shared with Detective King."

I froze, not liking how he knew about my relationship with Alex.

Atwood continued, "Everyone is watching you two, wondering who will slip up first."

Suddenly, the room got cold. I couldn't decide if Atwood

was threatening me for his own benefit, or warning me of a distant threat looming. I hoped it was the latter, but instead of letting him continue, I swung the pendulum in my favor. "As long as it doesn't involve him, your secret is safe with me."

Atwood sipped from his glass. "Samantha, do you know who Watts is targeting to inflate his crime statistics?"

"If I did, you would have read it in my report."

Atwood's eyes brightened. "Look around, Samantha. Tell me, what do you see?"

I flitted my gaze throughout the room. Then it hit me. When I saw what he saw, I said, "The LGBTQ community?"

Atwood nodded. "And scaring the living shit out of them until a few unsuspecting victims give false confessions for crimes they didn't commit."

"If you know this to be a fact, why hasn't Mayor Goldberg stopped it?"

"Who do you think brought it to my attention?"

"So why bring me into your inner circle? It seems I have nothing new to offer."

"Because the beat reporter before you helped Watts keep a positive profile as he rose through the ranks. It's what helped him get promoted to chief. Watts isn't used to having the press turn against him, and you have him very worried."

"He should be worried," I said.

Atwood smiled, seeming to like my answer. "He's not worried about being arrested. He's concerned this story you're working is going to derail his plans to one day be mayor."

I almost rolled my eyes at the thought. *Watts. Mayor? Impossible.* He didn't have a political bone in his body. I said, "Except, I don't have anything on him."

"That will change," he said. "Together, we can correct the department and free it from the corruption both you and I know is doing more damage than good. Between you and me, the District Attorney's office is secretly building a case against Watts. I hear they have irrefutable evidence he's committed several crimes, and it's going to get ugly. While they do that, my office has discovered sufficient evidence to begin an appeals process for many who have already been wrongly convicted. But, what I need is a reporter like you I can trust, someone who can get the people of Denver to side with us instead of him."

A heavy weight draped across my shoulders as I suddenly felt lightheaded. The room spun around me as I thought about what it was Atwood was asking me to do. Was it even legal? I didn't know, but I was interested.

"It's important you keep this a secret until we're both ready for all hell to break loose."

I nodded. "You have my word."

"If word gets out of what's coming, Watts will unleash the largest disinformation campaign this city has ever seen and we'll miss our chance for real reform."

Atwood's eyes flicked to the left. I followed his gaze and saw Genevieve and Susan making their way back. He reached into his coat pocket and pulled a white rectangular card out.

"Here's my home address." Atwood slipped his business card into my hand. "Let's talk tomorrow. How's 9AM sound?"

"Perfect."

"And bring your sidekick Erin with you. There's more I need to say, but now is neither the time nor the place."

I slipped his card into my purse.

"And Samantha, remember, if anyone comes to you with information, don't automatically assume it's right."

"I never do," I said.

Atwood angled his body toward his wife and said out of the corner of his mouth, "The chief has a great instinct, and he knows his time is up."

CHAPTER THIRTY-TWO

Russ Abair ran a hand over his short-cropped hair and moved from one side of his second-floor apartment to the other, peeking behind the curtain. Only a second ago he heard a car arrive, but as he flitted his gaze across the many roofs of the vehicles parked below, he didn't see any activity.

No one was getting out. No brake lights were on. Things were quiet. Then a large diesel pickup truck blew past on the street and Russ felt the sounds of its muffler rattle the floor.

"Just a few more minutes," he said, wiping the sweat off his brow.

Releasing the curtain, the drapes fell back into place. He stepped back to the darkened living room and took a pull from his whiskey bottle. The alcohol did little to calm the anxiety swirling in his stomach, and the more he drank, the more nervous he became.

He stood up.

He sat down.

Another minute passed, but to Russ it felt like an hour.

He didn't like that she was running late. A part of him

questioned whether she'd show at all. All he wanted was to get paid and get on with his life. Was that so much to ask?

Scooting to the edge of the couch, Russ reached under the cushion and brushed his fingers against the cold metal of the pistol he was hiding. It had six bullets in the cylinder and more hidden in the entertainment stand.

Taking his hand off his weapon, he brought his fingers to his laptop keyboard. The video file proving April was murdered was still transferring onto a second disk. Cursing his slow internet speed, he wondered why he had waited until the last minute to do it. Punctuality wasn't his strong suit.

Standing, he hurried back to the window. Peeking once again behind the blinds, the view hadn't changed. Then he checked his phone. Nothing.

"She's standing me up," he said, bringing his hand to his chin and cracking his neck.

This was supposed to be his break-out moment, the single caption that would catapult his career into a larger house, faster car, and the women who loved both. All his life he'd been waiting for this moment, and now that he was close enough to smell the fame, he couldn't let this opportunity pass him by.

"Triple the price," he laughed, still not believing she actually fell for it.

Russ walked to the front door and took a look through the peephole. The hallway was empty. Not that he was expecting anything else, but where was she?

Behind him, his computer started playing a video. It was Vincent Verdi's Vlog, *Don't trip. You might fall,* and the theme music that went along with it.

A smile formed on his face. Russ had always thought Vince was a douche, someone who didn't deserve everything he had, but he admired this particular post and what it promised to do for both of their careers.

"I'm going to ruin your life, asshole," Russ said to the computer screen.

The software program chimed, and Russ dropped the blinds and hurried to take the controls. He finished copying over the video file before ejecting the external hard drive from the USB port. He left a copy on the coffee table while he locked the original inside a safe, hidden in his bedroom closet.

He wasn't stupid. He always kept a copy for himself. A memento he could someday look back on, or even use to extort the next idiot who came along for another large sum.

Russ laughed and moved to the mirror where he smoothed out his eyebrows and goatee before popping a breath mint into his mouth. Feeling like the rich man he was about to be, he couldn't deny how much he liked surprising Samantha Bell, making her feel on edge with his games.

"If only you weren't dating that detective..."

Russ looked himself over one last time when, finally, his doorbell sounded. Hurrying to the front of his apartment, he paused for a quick beat to see who was there. A redhead with shoulder length hair stood off to the side. A quizzical look crossed Russ's face as he opened the door.

"Can I help you?" he asked.

"I'm here for the video," the woman whispered.

This wasn't who he was expecting, though he was impressed by her business attire and expensive looking pumps. But the hallway was a little dark for sunglasses.

"I don't know what you're talking about," Russ said, looking her up and down.

The woman opened her purse, showed him an envelope full of cash, and smiled.

Russ stared at the stack of hundreds and thought for a beat before asking, "Did Samantha send you?"

"Who else?" the woman whispered again.

Russ paused and bit his cheek. "The video." He laughed. "Oh, yes. Right," he said, gesturing for her to come inside.

The woman entered his house, and Russ shut the door behind her. They exchanged a couple of awkward glances before she followed Russ into the living room.

Sitting on the cushion above his gun, Russ showed the woman the disk and played the video for her on his computer. The woman watched from behind her sunglasses, and when the video was finished Russ asked, "Satisfied?"

"Very." The woman's voice caught in her throat as she smiled.

Russ watched her open her purse, itching to get his fingers on the cash. Instead of reaching for the envelope of money, the woman pulled a gun on him.

"Wait? I can explain," Russ pleaded, tossing his hands into the air the same second the woman pointed the muzzle at his head and fired a single shot that tore a gaping hole through his neck.

CHAPTER THIRTY-THREE

A SEARING PAIN SHOT DOWN HIS SPINE. HIS EYES BULGED AS the instinct to survive kicked in. Russ gripped his neck with both hands and tilted forward, falling face-first to the floor.

His shoulder slammed into the corner of the coffee table, knocking it off its mark and turning him over. Lying on his back, the smell of burnt flesh filled his nostrils with the heady scent of gunpowder and hot lead.

Russ kept squeezing his neck, feeling his pulse explode against the tips of his fingers, while he stared at the couch cushion hiding his own weapon.

If only he could get to it, then maybe he had a chance to defend himself and call for help. But each time his fingers eased their grip on his artery, geysers of hot liquid shot between his knuckles.

Russ squeezed his eyes shut and clenched his teeth, fighting through the unforgiving pain. Fatigue was settling into his body despite his urge to fight and hang on. He opened his eyes when he felt the killer step over him. She was careful to avoid planting a foot into the puddles of blood pooling around his body and he watched her retrieve the disk still connected to his computer.

"Who the hell are you?" Russ coughed out the question.

The woman rummaged through his files, opened up doors and drawers. "Where is the copy, Russ?" Their eyes met. "I know you made a copy."

Russ's eyelids hooded and he could feel his heartbeat growing weaker. Looking up at her, he opened his mouth but nothing came out. He coughed and choked, beginning to drown in his own blood. There was something odd about the woman, he thought, continuing to stare. What was it? Her proportions seemed off. Then again, maybe it was only his dying brain distorting reality with whatever was waiting for him on the other side of life.

Russ blinked, and when he opened up his eyes again, she was gone.

He could hear her rummaging in the kitchen, then in the bedroom. Russ wasn't concerned about the copy locked away inside his safe; he was only worried about how he could survive if help didn't come to his door soon.

He felt his breathing grow shallow and hoped a neighbor had heard the gunshot and had called the police for him. Then a sense of calm came over his chest—a peace he'd never felt before in his life. Suddenly, all his dreams of becoming rich and famous melted into the bright light gently closing around his vision. He closed his eyes and sank deeper into the floor.

A moment later, he felt his arm being pulled. Something heavy was placed in his palm. *What was it? Was he still alive?* When his eyes opened, he felt like he was swimming on his back in a warm pool of water. Then his fingers closed around a metal object and he barely blinked when he heard a second shot fired.

CHAPTER THIRTY-FOUR

Erin couldn't believe she couldn't find Russ's apartment. Frustration was creeping up her back. She knew it had to be around here somewhere.

After feeling like she'd circled the block a dozen times, she put on her blinker and turned left onto Emerson Street. She kept glancing to her GPS mounted to the dash. It had lost connection five minutes ago and was still struggling to load her current coordinates, which she couldn't understand. Taking one hand off the steering wheel, Erin smacked the device, finally giving up on it.

Her tires crunched on the pavement as they slowly rolled south. Erin squinted through the low light while searching the addresses. Wishing it wasn't dusk, she stopped at an apartment sign, Emerson Lofts, and shook her head. This wasn't where she was supposed to be, but she had to be close, so she kept driving.

She turned onto the next street and circled back around, wondering if this was a sign from the universe to keep her away from Russ. All she could think about was Samantha's bad feeling and how she didn't sign up to meet with a potential murderer. Now she was second guessing her decision to come alone, but she couldn't turn back without getting her hands on the video proving April was murdered.

"Where is your bloody apartment?" Erin mumbled as she came to the end of the street.

She sighed, turned onto the next street, and leaned forward, gripping the GPS with her right hand to fiddle with the settings. The loud blare of a car horn had her slamming on her brakes. Erin looked up and gripped the wheel with both hands. Her entire body tensed as she braced for sudden impact. Cringing, tires squealed over the pavement and at the last second, nothing happened.

Erin peeked one eye open. Miraculously, instead of a head-on collision, the car in front of her stopped only inches away from her hood. With her heart hammering inside her chest, Erin was thankful she didn't get hit. It was entirely her fault. She'd drifted into the opposite lane when fiddling with the GPS—a foolish mistake that nearly cost her.

Squinting into the bright beams of headlights blinding her vision, Erin raised a hand to her brow and waved a quick apology with her opposite hand to a driver she could not see. The driver blared his horn in response, and Erin cursed them under her breath.

"Okay. Easy," she said, putting the car in reverse. "It was an accident."

She backed out of the vehicle's way and the rude driver sped past in a hurry. Through the flat light Erin caught a glimpse of the woman behind the wheel, who tossed her a sharp glare.

"I said I was sorry." Erin clucked her tongue.

Taking a deep breath, Erin counted her blessing and put the car in drive and continued her search for Russ's house. It was down the next block before she finally found the sign to

Vogue Apartments. It was a relief to have finally found her destination.

Parking her car on a side street, Erin stepped out and headed inside as she muttered, "Russ, after all this trouble, you better be home."

She climbed the stairs to the second-floor apartment and moved down the empty, well-lit hall until she found herself standing at Russ's door. She knocked once, and the door opened.

Erin froze. "Hello? Anybody home?"

When no one answered, Erin stepped back and looked toward the stairwell. Completely alone, she took her cell-phone into her hand and entered. After only one step into the apartment, she gasped at the sight of Russ lying dead on the floor.

Erin took her eyes off the gaping hole in his head and swept her gaze to his hand where he loosely gripped a small handgun. Without getting too close, she looked for a note. There was nothing. She then began her search for the video of April's murder and, when that too couldn't be located, she finally called for help.

CHAPTER THIRTY-FIVE

I HANDED THE VALET MY TICKET AND WATCHED AS HE trotted off to retrieve my car. I wished I had brought my coat inside with me because the temperature had fallen considerably since my arrival.

The cool autumn air invigorated me as I stood beneath the awning and kept checking my phone. Erin hadn't responded to either of my last two messages, and I was starting to worry.

A black suburban stopped a few feet away, and I watched Atwood assist his wife into the back. Our conversation was still swirling around my head. It was a lot to take in, leaving me with questions and a thirst to learn more.

As soon as he shut the door, we locked eyes. I smiled, and he nodded before circling around the back and joining his wife in the car.

Atwood was new to the city, and I liked his fresh approach to a complicated issue. I still had my doubts. Gripping my clutch, I thought about his business card and his desired phone meeting, hoping that his intentions were good. I was curious to know more about his discovery, but he was an elected official with more to lose than me. So, what was in it for him by going after the chief?

Wrapping my arms around my torso, a chill moved up my arms as I watched Atwood's vehicle drive away. Secretly, I was worried for King. Whether it was intentional or not, I didn't like how Atwood specifically told me to keep our introduction a secret.

How could I keep that from King? We told each other nearly everything, understanding nothing we shared in private would be made public without the other's explicit permission. But the truth of the matter was, going to write for Atwood would directly impact King's career no matter what position I took. I had to tell him about it whether Atwood liked it or not.

I sighed just as a slender hand pressed into my lower back. I turned to find Susan. She hooked her hand on my hip and pulled me in for a hug, saying, "Everett said you two might be working together."

I tucked my chin and gave my friend a questioning look. Susan's knowing eyes sparkled beneath the light. My body was tense. I could feel all the signs that I was on the leading edge of a big story. She didn't have to ask what it was because I suspected she already knew enough.

Atwood's red taillights disappeared around the bend, and I asked, "How well do you know him?"

"Well enough to trust his intentions are good." Susan looked me in the eye, then changed the subject. "I didn't mean to imply you should work with Garrett. I just thought maybe you could introduce him to someone who might be interested in promoting his upcoming film. If I offended you—"

"Crime is my beat," I said, getting Susan to frown. "Sorry I couldn't talk with him more. He seems like a nice guy."

Susan cast her gaze forward. "You're lucky to have met

him at all. Garrett supports good causes, but he prefers to live a quieter life." She flicked her eyes to me. "A life away from parties and the spotlight."

"Tonight was lovely," I said. "But this was hardly a red-carpet event."

Susan laughed. "Thanks."

We stood there waiting for my car and my thoughts jumped to Vince and April and the fight they supposedly had. There wasn't a single mention about my article on April all night, and I was surprised considering the remarks I knew Vincent Verdi had made regarding the gay community in the past. Maybe people didn't know who I was, or maybe they didn't want to make drama during an event designed to raise money to advance equality through research, education, and policy. Whatever the reason, it wasn't a mistake Atwood was here tonight, and that was enough to give hope where hope was needed.

I heard a familiar belt squeal and turned to find my Subaru chugging forward. The valet who'd been parking BMWs and Audis all night got out and stepped up to me with an empathetic smile. I handed him a small tip, not embarrassed at all by what I could afford to drive. But before saying goodbye to Susan, I asked, "Any chance you have any friends in the industry who have worked with Vincent Verdi before?"

Susan eyed me suspiciously. "Does this have anything to do with your investigation into April?"

I nodded once. "There's a piece to the puzzle I'm still trying to figure out."

"I'll ask around."

"Thank you," I whispered.

"But Sam, I can't get too involved in this."

"I'm not asking you to."

"I nearly lost my business once because of an investigation you were working, and I can't take that risk again."

"I know," I said, stepping to my car when I heard my cellphone ring. It was Erin. I answered, "Where have you been? I've been trying to reach you. Is everything all right?"

"Sam," Erin's voice fell flat as a rock, "Russ is dead."

CHAPTER THIRTY-SIX

EXHAUSTION WAS SETTLING IN WHEN KING CLOSED HIS eyes and scrubbed his hands over his face. The gesture did little to wake his tiring eyes. He was going to need another cup of coffee if he was to get himself through the last of his reports still needing to be written before knocking off for the night.

But something else was on his mind he couldn't shake. King reached for his phone, thinking of Samantha. It was getting late, and he wanted to see her, but he couldn't leave until his work was complete.

Alvarez sat at the desk next to him, head down, scribbling on his legal pad, doing the same as King—taking advantage of an otherwise slow day on the streets. And though King was nearly done, he couldn't resist the urge to dig deeper into April Wright's death.

April's apparent suicide was all over the news, and had since spread like wildfire across the internet, as celebrity deaths most often did. Though interested, King was happy it wasn't his case. The stakes were high and the entire nation was watching. But it was Samantha's story and, though he'd never admit it, the reason he was now digging into law enforcement databases was because of her.

Alvarez leaned back and peeked his head over the partition, surprising King when he said, "That's not our case, nor our jurisdiction."

King tossed his partner a grin.

"You have to let this go."

"You're not the least bit interested to know why she did it?" King asked.

"Of course I am." Alvarez leaned more of his weight against the divide. "But if someone finds you doing this, they'll assume it's for Samantha."

King turned his focus back to his computer. "They can think what they want, but no one will care when it gets out that April issued a restraining order against Vince just six months ago."

"Restraining order?" Alvarez's eyes pinched as he flicked his gaze to King's computer. "What for?"

"Stalking."

"If that's true, why did April attend an event hosted by Vince?"

King's fingers drummed on top of his desk. "Make him break it. Get him in trouble."

"Doesn't make sense. She'd never get away with it." Alvarez shook his head the moment his desk phone started to ring.

King quirked an eyebrow. "Maybe she didn't know it was Vince's event?"

Alvarez shrugged, took the call, and left King with his thoughts. If April wanted to get Vince in trouble, she couldn't go looking for it without someone calling her out on her own BS. Someone had to draw her in, but was that someone Vince? And if he did, why? To make amends?

"We got a possible homicide." Alvarez was on his feet,

reaching for his jacket. King asked where and Alvarez said, "North Ogden Street. Vogue Apartment building. I'll meet you at the car."

"Where are you going?" King asked.

Alvarez put his hand on his stomach and pinched his expression. "The toilet."

King memorized the street address and closed out his computer. On his way out of the precinct, two uniformed officers entered as King was exiting. Officer Matt Barber's shoulder slammed directly into King's, and King wondered if he might have done it on purpose.

King barely budged, stopped and tossed officer Barber a look. "Need to get your eyes checked, Barber?"

Barber stepped up to King without apologizing and said, "You wouldn't happen to know why IAD is interviewing us, would you?"

King angled his head and gave him a questioning look.

"No, I didn't think you did. But maybe your girlfriend would?"

"If you're looking for an excuse to use for your own bad behavior, you should start by looking in the mirror," King responded.

The officer chuckled. "Funny you'd say that King. But don't forget where your loyalties lie. I'm not the only one with a target on his back."

King's body tensed, remembering the missed calls Heather said came through Samantha's home line last night. He could feel the walls closing in. He knew it had everything to do with Samantha's reporting on Chief Watts. "What's that supposed to mean?"

Getting in King's face further, Barber said, "It means to remember who has your back when bullets are flying over your head."

CHAPTER THIRTY-SEVEN

FIFTEEN MINUTES LATER, KING AND ALVAREZ ARRIVED ON scene to four squad cars creating a blockade outside Vogue Apartments. No residents were being allowed inside, and those inside had been told they couldn't leave.

King said nothing to Alvarez about Barber's barely disguised threat, deciding it was best to focus on the work at hand. He suspected they knew something that he didn't.

King parked, and together they exited the vehicle and approached the building on foot with the red and blue emergency lights dancing off the trees surrounding them. Neighbors came out of their homes, braving the chill to see what was happening. They were huddled on front porches and stood along the sidewalk with their arms crossed. Many of them had worried expressions on their faces like, *how could this happen here?*

A single news van parked halfway up the block and visions of Samantha crossed King's mind. Soon, the cavalry would arrive and King didn't want to be here when they did.

They badged their way under the crime scene tape and

logged themselves in at the entrance with the presiding officer. King asked, "What's the word on the street?"

The rookie said, "A neighbor called 911 after hearing the
sound of gunshots. A single victim was found dead in an
apartment on the second floor. That's about all I know."

King nodded and followed Alvarez up the stairs where
they were met by another uniformed officer securing the
door. He pointed the way, mentioned the apartment number,
and at the entrance to the apartment King saw the victim
lying on the floor with a gaping hole blown out of the side of
his head.

CSI technicians were geared up taking photographs,
collecting and marking off potential evidence. Blood was
everywhere. It was like walking into a slaughter house after a
goat's throat got slit. And the smell...

King glanced around the entrance, wondering what this
guy's story was. In plain view, there was a Nikon camera bag.
King flipped up the flap and inside was a digital camera along
with several lenses and spare batteries—all expensive and
untouched. This wasn't a robbery, King thought. Something
else happened here tonight.

Several business cards were visible through a mesh pocket,
and they all shared the same name and logo that King
decided was the man lying dead on the floor only feet away.
King leaned over and read the name, Russ Abair. He said,
"Digital Media Specialist."

There was no sign of forced entrance, and besides the
bloody mess in the living room, the small apartment didn't
appear to have been ransacked like King had seen in the past
when working quick smash and grab cases.

Chief Medical Examiner Leslie Griffin was kneeling over
the victim when she waved King over. "Look here," she said
once King was near. "One gunshot wound to the neck,"

Griffin pointed with her index finger to the left side of the victim's neck, "and another here, beneath the chin."

"Okay, so he shoots himself but doesn't get it right the first time, so he shoots himself again," Alvarez said, pointing to how the victim was still loosely holding the gun inside his hand.

"That's the likely scenario," Griffin agreed, "but his hands are covered in blood, suggesting he might have fought the first wound before struggling to get the second one in place."

King stared, thoughts churning. There was so much blood. The victim must have lost it quick. It wouldn't take long to bleed out from a neck wound like the one he was looking at, so why go for the second? He wondered how far apart the shots were fired and he made a mental note to ask potential witnesses when the time came.

"Run ballistics," King said. "Make sure the bullets found match the gun in his hand."

Alvarez tossed King a sideways glance, and King flicked his gaze to the coffee table. It was knocked off kilter and a deep depression in the couch seemed to mark the victim's preferred spot when hunkered down in front of the TV.

"He was sitting there when he was shot," King said definitively, pointing to the couch.

Griffin nodded. "Blood spatter indicates that's the case."

"Anybody find a suicide note?" Alvarez was looking at the half-empty bourbon bottle.

A technician joined the circle. "Nothing yet. But I'll let you know if we do."

Alvarez bent at the waist and lifted the couch cushion. "Would you look at that?" he said.

King took one step forward, dodging the blood on the floor, and snapped his fingers at the technician. "Take a couple photos of that, will you?"

The camera shutter clicked a couple of times as King

gloved up. Alvarez stepped out of the way and King took the .357 Magnum into his hand. He opened the cylinder and said, "Not a single shot fired."

Alvarez lifted his brow. "A .357 and a Ruger SR9C—"

"9MM budget option," King said, referring to the gun the victim was still holding inside his hand. The .357 was bagged as evidence.

Was this guy a gun nut who gave up on life? Or did he feel threatened? He didn't look like someone who could muscle his way into shooting himself a second time while at the same time bleeding out at his neck. But, then again, who was this guy? And what was his story?

"Call us when the autopsy's complete," King said to Griffin. Then he gestured for Alvarez to follow him to the door. The detectives left Griffin to close out her job and headed back to the street. "We need to check who those guns were registered to."

Alvarez nodded. "And if he owned any others. I don't want any to have gone missing if this was a robbery."

Once outside, King spotted someone he hadn't noticed before in the back of a squad car and asked the rookie, "Who's that in the backseat?"

The officer shrugged. "She was inside the house when we arrived."

"Is she talking?"

The officer shook his head no. "Nothing."

King was about to ask who put her there when the woman turned her head and stopped King's heart. "Christ," he said. It was Erin Tate.

CHAPTER THIRTY-EIGHT

MR. T EXITED HIS CAR AND MOVED UP THE SIDEWALK, climbing the short flight of stairs leading to his front door when a feeling that he was being watched fell over him. He turned to look over his shoulder and scanned the neighborhood. Had he been followed? The prickles on his neck said he had been.

Squinting his eyes, he held still.

The neighborhood behind him was quiet. He could hear the gentle hum coming from the highway a mile away. Lights shone through his neighbors' windows and cast their long shadows over his paved driveway when the voice inside his head grew louder.

You're being watched, it kept saying.

A second passed and a large passenger plane flew overhead. Mr. T tipped his head back and watched the blinking lights cross the night sky. When it was gone, he stared at the sparkling stars shining brightly through the soft glow of the city lights, thinking about how it was impossible he wasn't at the center of the universe.

A pillow of condensation formed in front of his face as he

breathed, and the voice kept saying, *You're not done yet. Show the world what you've got. Make yourself king.*

Once inside, he paused to make sure he was alone before taking off his gloves. A light was on. He wasn't sure if he had forgotten to turn it off before he left, or if someone had visited while he was away. But he didn't pause to think about it. There was something more important on his mind.

Pulling his phone from his pocket, Mr. T began scrolling through his accounts. The need was driven by an addictive habit fueled by the desire to be recognized. Not enough people knew who he was or what he was capable of achieving. All his life, no one gave him the credit he deserved. Since he couldn't tell the story he was currently writing, it angered Mr. T to see his social media rivals beating him in the stats of likes, comments, views, and shares—the currency of today's online world of interaction and distraction.

They are watching you, wanting you to lose.

A crushing depression squeezed his chest tight as he climbed the stairs and locked himself away inside his bedroom. He hated the world. Hated that everyone had what he wanted. But hated even more that, despite taking the leading role in his own story, no one knew how great an actor he truly was.

Mr. T shed his pack and sat behind his computer. Though he was still putting out content for his followers, there were many who were calling him a fake, a phony, a washed-up influencer whose time had passed.

But Mr. T wasn't about to let go. He'd stood on the podium before and knew he could do it again. The new script he was working was better than anything he'd created before and, soon, people would realize just how extraordinary he really was.

Wiggling the mouse, Mr. T brought the computer to life. He typed his impossible-to-guess password and retrieved the disk from his pack and set it next to the keyboard. Before taking a look at what was on it, he needed to upload the latest drone footage to his hard drive before he forgot.

A couple clicks of the mouse and the files were transferred. He had so much fodder he wanted to share but couldn't. It was almost funny when thinking about dropping this story on the world. He was mildly delirious with far-flung fantasies, but soon his day would come. When it did, he'd make sure his speech was prepared.

Sitting on the edge of his seat, Mr. T zoomed in on Allison Doyle's face. The pixels made her seem fake. The longer Mr. T stared into her chestnut eyes, the more he couldn't tell what was real and what was only a game.

Wasn't life a game?

He tapped the mouse and clicked print. A second later, the printer spit out a perfectly clear image of Allison. He then checked to see if she'd clicked the link he'd sent her. When his data showed she hadn't, he retrieved her business card and began browsing her company website. After five minutes, he'd grown bored and spun around in his chair, catching a quick glimpse of himself in the mirror. He almost didn't recognize himself.

"You look lovely tonight, my dear." His reflection smiled.

Mr. T blew a kiss to the handsome figure staring back, then stood and took Allison's picture from the printer and pinned it on the corkboard next to the images of Samantha and Erin. His three amigos.

"Allison, honey. Don't let me down," he sighed. "I've given you an important role, and I expect you to come through. Be sure to click that link I've given you. It's a real plot twist we won't want to miss."

CHAPTER THIRTY-NINE

Even before I arrived to Russ's apartment, I knew it wouldn't be good. I uncurled the tips of my cold fingers from the steering wheel and stepped out into the night, looking for Erin.

This wasn't how tonight was supposed to go down. What had Russ done? And why did it have to involve us? I regretted my decision not to inform King about the video, but I regretted not listening to my gut even more.

I left my car beneath the large oak tree and moved up the sidewalk. Emergency bars were flashing and the medical examiner's wagon was backed up to the entrance of the five-story apartment building. I skirted around a group of three spectators and listened to the crime scene tape flutter in the autumn breeze like quaking aspen leaves ready to fall for winter.

Across the street I caught someone eyeing me, giving me a look like they knew who I was. I hoped they didn't expect me to be working because I wasn't here to report on what happened. I was only here because Erin called and sounded upset that Russ was dead.

Taking my phone into my hand, I stood off to the side and messaged her. Lifting my head, I stuffed my hands into my coat pocket and waited for her to respond. Where was she? Why wasn't she waiting for me out front like she promised?

There was nothing I could do but wait. Her car was parked across the street, but she wasn't inside. It was clear the police were treating this as a possible homicide. After a minute with no response, I couldn't wait any longer. I called Erin, but it went straight to voicemail. Something must have happened between the time she called and now.

I kept moving, skirting around the barrier and looking for familiar faces. Then I spotted King. I hurried to where I could get his attention without attracting it from others. He'd be able to tell me what was going on.

He caught sight of me but didn't look happy to see me. "Stay back, Sam. I've got nothing to say to you."

I didn't take offense; only knew he was doing his job. But when I glanced over his shoulder, I finally saw Erin.

"Did you arrest her?" I asked, pointing toward my friend, feeling my temperature spike.

"Sam, please. Let us do our job."

"At least let me speak to her."

He sighed. "You know I can't let you do that."

"I know what happened," I argued, telling him how Erin called me to the scene. "Was Russ murdered?"

King tossed me a look. His eyes pinched, and he slowly approached. "You knew him?"

"Not really. He was a freelance photojournalist who some-times stopped by the *Times*."

"Sam, things aren't looking so hot for Erin, or me. If you know why Erin was here, inside Russ's apartment, you need to do both of us a favor and tell me why."

I held his eyes and wished I could say, but couldn't.

"Were you two working a story with him?"

It was impossible to keep my secrets from him. King knew me too well to know when I was keeping information from him. "Let me talk to her," I said, "and after I do that, you can ask me all the questions you want."

King shook his head in disbelief. "I don't think so. You don't get to dictate the rules. Not tonight. If you don't want to talk, someone will be sure to get Erin to tell us at the station what you two were up to."

I flicked my gaze to the squad car. Erin's head was bowed, her shoulders slumped forward. She didn't know I was here, and I hated how vulnerable she appeared while waiting to be transported to the station. It should have been me in the back of the squad car, not her. I had to get her a lawyer just in case she found herself in any kind of legal trouble.

King was still staring as I debated whether or not I could mention the video Russ had in his possession. Then I turned my thoughts to Jackie Dumont and our race to get the video before it disappeared forever. She had to have known about it or she wouldn't have offered Erin the exclusive with Vince. Jackie knew there was something out there that implicated Vince in April's death.

It all sounded as crazy as it was. I'd known this video was trouble the moment I saw it. I couldn't believe the predicament we were in. How could we let this happen? We were smarter than this.

Finally, King looked away, and I made a break for the squad car. Slapping my palm against the window, Erin jerked her head back and was surprised to see it was me.

"I'll meet you at the station," I yelled through the closed window. "We'll get you a lawyer if you need it."

Erin nodded and was telling me something when King wrestled me away. I broke out of his arms and took a step back. We both looked at each other and I knew he wasn't happy about my actions. He had Erin in custody and refused to acknowledge how that divided us.

"Sam, don't make my life more difficult than it already is."

My feet began backpedaling away as I kept my eyes locked with his. It was nothing personal, only business, I kept reminding myself, as if needing to believe that was all this was. I was sure he could see that, but I wondered if my reporting on Chief Watts was finally catching up to him—catching up to *us*. Something told me it had.

Turning on a heel, I hurried up the block, determined to canvass the neighborhood myself. There must have been someone who saw something who could clear Erin's name.

CHAPTER FORTY

ONE DOOR TO THE NEXT, I KEPT KNOCKING, NOT WANTING to waste any time with my questions. Either the people I spoke with were witness to something, or they weren't. Up and down the block I went.

Erin was still in the back of the police car and I kept my eye on her the entire time. She was taken away a minute before Russ's body was wheeled out on a stretcher. I paused and watched him get loaded up into the back of the medical examiner's van, thinking the show everyone came out to watch was now ending.

Was his killer still here? Were they watching me now?

I didn't know and no one I spoke with had seen a thing. But they all knew something.

Some said Russ deserved it, others couldn't believe a murder could happen here. All I needed was one person to give Erin an alibi—an alibi I suspected could only come from inside the apartment I wasn't allowed to enter. Then everything changed.

The man was in his mid-fifties and shirtless. The cold weather didn't seem to bother him. He directed me to another neighbor. "Tell her I sent you and I'm sure she'll be happy to talk."

I cut across the lawn and stepped up onto her porch. The door opened shortly after I rang the doorbell. She was in her sixties with salt and pepper hair, physically fit, and with sharp blue eyes. I made my introduction, and she said, "I know who you are."

I paused for a beat, unable to decide if that was a good thing or not. "I'm just trying to figure out what happened at Vogue Apartments tonight."

"All I know is what I saw with my own eyes."

"Would you mind sharing that with me?"

"Are you going to put that in the paper?"

"Would you mind if I did?"

She shook her head and started talking. "I was walking my dog, Corky, when I passed in front of the apartment entrance. I didn't think anything of it at the time, maybe it's nothing, maybe she had nothing to do with all...this. But a woman had been standing at the door looking somewhat confused, like maybe she forgot her key or didn't know who to call, and when I circled back around maybe ten minutes later, the same woman was hurrying out of the building like she might be running from something."

So the woman got inside. "Did you see where she went?"

"Got in her car and sped off." The woman pointed her finger northwest.

"Did you hear any gunshots?"

She shook her head no. "I don't have that great of hearing as it is."

I glanced up the street. Erin's car was still parked in the exact spot I had seen it before. I asked, "What kind of vehicle was the woman driving?"

"I don't know my cars, but what I can tell is that it was a

dark, two-door sports car." The woman shrugged. "Or something."

"Did you get a good look at this woman?"

The woman's expression tightened, as if thinking hard about how she could describe an appearance. "There was something odd about the woman. Like her proportions were off."

"What do you mean, her proportions were off?"

"Like her hands were too big for her arms. Things like that."

"What color hair did she have?"

"First, I thought it was brown, but then she stepped into the light and the brown went red."

"A redhead?" I immediately thought about Jackie.

"That's right."

"Anything else you can tell me?"

The woman frowned and shook her head. "Just that something about her seemed off. Then again, I suppose if she did kill that man like I'm hearing she might have, that's all it could be."

The woman's beady eyes stared through me and I thanked her for her time before moving up the block to see if Russ's apartment complex had security cameras. But all I could think about was how the description of tonight's only other suspect besides Erin matched that of Vincent Verdi's publicist, Jackie Dumont.

CHAPTER FORTY-ONE

THE CANDLELIGHT FLICKERED ACROSS THE TABLE, CREATING a soft romantic ambience in Allison's small dining room. It was a pleasant change from the restaurant experience, and she certainly appreciated the extra effort Nicholas put into making tonight perfect.

"Can I get you another piece of cake?" Nicholas asked.

Allison laughed. "I can't believe you made me cake."

"So, is that a yes?" His eyes crinkled at the corners.

"As tempting as it is, I'm stuffed."

Nicholas stood and took Allison's empty plate from the table. After an incredible homemade meal of roasted chicken, potatoes, and greens, Allison was ready to kick up her feet and relax. Instead, she stood and offered to help clean up the kitchen.

"No. I've got this," Nicholas said, gesturing for Allison to sit down.

"But you cooked," she protested. "I clean."

"I insist." Nicholas poured the last bit of wine into her glass and handed it to her.

Allison lowered herself back into her chair and asked, "Are you trying to get me drunk?"

"I'm trying to get you to relax."

She wasn't going to argue with that. Truthfully, she was stuffed, and the wine had her melting into the back of her seat. Her ankles were swollen from having been on her feet all day, and it felt good to finally be sitting down.

Kicking her feet up on an empty chair, Allison watched her man rinse the dishes and load them into the dishwasher. She wondered how she'd gotten so lucky. He was patient, gracious, and exactly what she'd been looking for. But she also wondered if they were moving too fast. The last thing she wanted was to sabotage the good she'd found.

When Nicholas was finished cleaning up the kitchen, he swung his chair from the other side of the table and set it down near Allison's feet. Taking her right foot into his hand, he kneaded her arch with his strong hands. "What are you thinking about?"

Allison could feel it in her expression. Her scrambling thoughts were impossible to hide. "I just can't stop thinking about this person who approached me today."

"At the convention?"

Allison nodded. "His interaction with me was so odd." Nicholas asked how so, and Allison said, "It was how he chased after me to my car, almost surprising me as if wanting to catch me off guard."

Nicholas's eyes narrowed as he kept pressing the tips of his fingers deeper into her heel.

Allison continued, "I know I'm good at what I do, but *that* good?"

"Word of mouth." Nicholas swept his brown eyes up to hers. "It's the best form of advertising, isn't it?"

"Without question." Allison brought her wineglass to her lips and sipped.

"Then what's the problem?"

Allison told him about the unusual business card and how it only contained a single web address. Nicholas tried to suggest it was a mistake—and maybe it was—but Allison had called the person out on it. "He seemed intent on giving me just that one piece of information."

"Have you checked it out? Maybe it's his personal domain that hosts his résumé."

Allison shook her head. "Maybe," she said, telling Nicholas more about the story Samantha was working and what they witnessed Vince do at the convention, shocking hundreds of fans with the digital recreation of April's death.

"Cold," Bennett said.

"Samantha and Erin think April might have been murdered."

Nicholas's hands stopped moving and the house suddenly went quiet.

Allison bent her knees, put her feet down on the floor, and stood. Kissing Nicholas's forehead, she murmured, "I'm sorry to kill the mood."

"You didn't kill anything."

Allison reached for his hand and said, "I'm going to get a little work done in the study."

Nicholas brushed his lips over her knuckles. "As long as you promise not to work the entire night."

"I promise."

Once tucked in behind her computer, she heard Nicholas turn on the TV. Sports. With the mysterious business card in hand, she typed in the web address and watched the single page load. A video popped up on the screen and automatically started to play.

"What's this?" Allison tipped her body forward, intent on learning what it was she was looking at.

Two women were arguing. One of them was April Wright,

the other was the redhead she had seen with Vince at the convention—Jackie Dumont, who Erin mentioned talking to. Allison remembered Samantha telling her that rumor had it Vince and April argued the day of April's death. Maybe so, but she clearly argued with Jackie, too. Glancing to the time-stamp, the video definitely happened the same night April died.

Was this some kind of joke? Why was it given to her? Was this the person who killed April?

Allison reached for the phone and called Samantha, needing to tell her what she found.

CHAPTER FORTY-TWO

I BARRELED MY WAY THROUGH THE FRONT DOORS OF THE
police station and marched straight up to the front desk,
asking to speak with detective Alex King.

The large, pear-shaped woman sitting behind the desk
eyed me over the rim of her red framed eyeglasses. "What's
this about?" she asked.

Her tone made me believe she thought my request was
personal. Did she know who I was? How much did she
assume about my relationship with King? I didn't understand
why it seemed so many cared. How many more people were
putting our relationship under a microscope and treating it
like celebrity gossip? More than I probably wanted to know.

I said, "It's about a case he's working."

She picked up the phone and held it to her ear with her
shoulder, dialing what I assumed to be the line to King's desk.
Turning my back, I kept glancing to the clock. The walls
seemed brighter than usual and I kept blinking out the dry in
my eyes.

"Someone will be with you shortly," the woman said.

I moved to the other side of the room, read some public

service fliers pinned to the wall, and kept pacing. I couldn't keep still. My thoughts were jumping from Erin to Kovac to Vince, then circling back to Erin. There was nothing I could do but wait, and I hoped the police had figured out what I had when canvassing Russ's neighborhood.

When I heard the double doors open behind me I spun around, expecting to see King. Instead, it was John Alvarez.

Alvarez flicked his gaze to reception, nodded, and said to me, "You really shouldn't be here, Sam."

"Where is King?" My heart was racing. "I asked to speak with King."

"Sam, calm down." Alvarez swept his gaze across the room behind me and dropped his voice to a whisper. "Detective King is busy at the moment."

When he couldn't tell me where King was, I knew something wasn't right. The same bad feeling I had before was back, making me feel nauseous. Alvarez locked eyes and neither of us blinked.

I shook my head and said, "Erin didn't do this."

Alvarez scrubbed his hand over his face and pointed in the direction of the lobby. "You're free to wait, but it's going to be awhile."

"At least tell me if Erin lawyered up." Alvarez told me to relax again, tried to convince me everything would be all right, and I nearly detonated on him. "There was a security camera outside the apartments," I said. "Have you checked it out? Because you probably should. A neighbor woman I spoke with tonight mentioned seeing a suspicious woman with red hair around the time of the murder. Please tell me you know this and are looking into it."

"Sam," Alvarez reached his hand to my arm, and I backed off, "let us do our job." He paused for a beat, unsure what to do about me. "We'll call you when the department is ready to make an official statement."

"I'm not here for work," I said, getting angry.

"Until then, you can stay outside."

As bad as it hurt, and as frustrating as it was, he was right. I was crossing a line by pretending to wear a badge. But these were the same halls my husband once walked before his death over a decade ago, and somehow that still made it feel like they were mine.

I headed for the lobby with uncertainty draping over me. I didn't know if Erin was safe, or facing allegations of murder, or somewhere in between—but I assumed the worst. I called a lawyer friend and explained the situation, drank too much stale coffee, and waited for what felt like hours, hoping at some point someone would tell me something worthwhile about what they were doing to my friend.

News never came, and I passed the time searching Jackie Dumont on my phone. I couldn't stop thinking about how she fit the description of the suspect who might have killed Russ. Nothing in the photo online totally matched the witness's description that her proportions were off, but that didn't mean anything. I needed to see her in person or through a new lens. I reviewed the latest in Vince's video production from last night, hoping to catch some kind of insight there. Vincent's vlog was filled with wild antics I didn't understand, but more importantly Jackie was nowhere to be seen in any of them.

Was she covering her tracks, hoping to help Vince get away with April's murder by killing Russ, too? If so, did Vince tell her to do it? My mind was scrambling to understand when I got the call from Allison that suggested maybe my suspicions about Jackie were right.

CHAPTER FORTY-THREE

"SAY THAT AGAIN."

Allison said, "It wasn't Vince April was arguing with. It was Jackie."

"Are you sure?" April's friend, Justine, had assured me that April had an argument with Vince the morning before she died. I slowly tipped forward in my chair and stood to move out of earshot from anyone who might be listening. When Allison confirmed, I asked, "How do you know?"

Allison told me about the video she'd come across, and I was stunned into silence. When I didn't respond, Allison said, "Unless there is someone else with flaming red hair that I don't know about, it has to be Jackie."

"How did you find this?" I asked, still unclear how she obtained the video.

Allison described the person who chased her down after she said goodbye to Erin and me, and added, "I'm only now getting around to looking at the web address he gave me. If I'd have known what I was sitting on, I would have called you sooner." I sank deeper into my thoughts and, after a moment of silence, Allison asked, "Sam, are you still there?"

Moving across the room, I backed myself into a deserted corner and covered my mouth as I whispered, "Russ is dead and Erin has been taken in for questioning."

"What? Oh my god. What happened?" Allison's emotions exploded into my ear. "If it wasn't Russ who gave me this link to the video, then who did?"

My eyebrows knitted. "Did you think it was Russ who gave it to you?"

"I don't know. I guess I just assumed it might have been him. I'm not sure why."

I quickly thought about the timeline of events. Allison wasn't wrong. It could have been Russ, but I didn't tell her that. It was better she believed it wasn't.

"I don't think it was him," I said. "We would have known if he was that close to us earlier. And the video he offered me was totally different."

"I'll email you the link so you can see it with your own eyes."

I thanked her and ended our call with waves of anxiety moving up and down my spine. Uniformed officers passed by and tossed me nasty looks. They gave the impression I was being talked about behind my back, and I didn't understand why. I ignored them and waited for Allison's message to come through.

A notification chimed, and I glanced to my screen. It wasn't Allison, but a text from an unknown number. I opened it and read it with bated breath.

Don't you know better than to leave your son home alone?

Everything inside me stopped.

Who was this? How did they know Mason was home alone? Were they watching him?

My eyes rounded, and I quickly called my son. "Mason, oh thank god, you're home," I said the moment he answered.

"Are you okay, Mom?"

"Are the doors locked?"

"I think so."

"Check." I heard Mason move through the house, twisting each doorknob to confirm they were locked.

"Yes, the doors are locked. Where are you?"

I told him where I was and asked, "Where is Cooper?"

"Sleeping on his bed. Mom, what's going on?"

"Nothing." I breathed, making sure my voice was calm and confident. "Just keep the doors locked and don't answer the door if anyone knocks."

I said I would be home soon and as soon as I was off the phone, I fell against the wall and breathed out a sigh of relief. What was going on? I felt like I was losing control of my life. I couldn't trust anyone or anything. I suddenly wondered if the text came from someone who knew I was at the police, came from someone who was here with me.

CHAPTER FORTY-FOUR

NOTHING HAPPENED FOR NEARLY AN HOUR WHEN, JUST AS I felt my eyelids began to droop, Allison's email finally came through. I sat up in my chair and opened it up, reading the note she sent along with the web link.

Hope this helps. Unfortunately, I don't have a name to who gave this to me. I'm here if you need me.

I clicked the link, and the video was slow to load even with great cell reception. Once it began to play, the recording was choppy and hard to follow. It reminded me a little of the video Russ was trying to sell me. I now wondered if this was his video, too. Then it stilled and two women came into focus.

April was on the right, Jackie on the left. They were in each other's faces, but the audio wasn't clear. I had no idea what was being said, could only assume it wasn't good by the expression each of them had on their faces.

I turned up the volume and still didn't have any luck. What were they arguing about? Had Justine gotten it wrong about April and Vince fighting? If they'd argued that morning, like Justine said, why would April have come to his show just to receive more abuse? Had the fight always been between April and Jackie?

The video ended abruptly, and I stared at the screen with more questions than before. I emailed Allison back and asked if she could enhance it, make it clearer, or do whatever it took to get better audio. I was interrupted by a familiar voice.

Erin strode over to me and smiled. "Sam, you waited for me all this time? What about Mason?"

"Don't make me regret staying," I said, telling her Mason was fine. "A simple thank you would suffice."

"Thank you." Erin stepped into my arms and we hugged. "Mason is lucky to have you, and so am I."

"You're just saying that because you want a ride home," I said, thinking about the strange anonymous text from someone who knew Mason was home alone, and the feeling of being stalked that came with it.

We walked side by side through the exit and exhaled at the same time, relieved to have finally left the police station. Once we were both settled into my car, I asked if she was hungry.

"I just want to go to bed," Erin said.

Me too, I thought when asking, "So, what happened to you tonight?"

Erin told me her entire story as I drove. How she had trouble finding Russ's apartment, what she found once she arrived. "The door was left open. What was I supposed to do? Just ignore it and not see if Russ was home?"

"I would have done the same," I admitted.

"He killed himself, Sam. I saw it with my own eyes. Russ was still holding the 9MM in his hand when I found him."

I turned my head and asked, "Are you sure it was suicide?"

"I don't know what to believe anymore." Erin's head hit the headrest, and she looked as exhausted as I felt. "The police had me feeling so confused by the time their questions stopped. I couldn't tell you what was up and what was down."

Stopping at a light, I said, "After I saw you with King, I canvassed the neighborhood to see if I could find any witnesses."

"Did you?"

I nodded. "A neighbor who was out walking her dog said she saw a woman outside Russ's apartment around the time of the murder."

"Yeah? Let me guess. That woman was me?"

I raised both my eyebrows. "The description she gave me sounded more like Jackie Dumont."

"Jesus." Erin rooted her hands into the seat and pushed her spine straight. "Did I get set up?"

I caught Erin up on the latest developments, including the link Allison sent me. It was starting to look as though Jackie may have killed April for Vince, and was now attempting to cover up her first murder by committing a second.

"That's it," Erin said. "It's the killer's signature. To make each murder look like a suicide."

"Only if the deaths are related, and only if that's what happened to Russ." When a funny look crossed Erin's face, I asked, "What is it?"

"I think I might have seen Jackie leaving the scene." Erin wiped her face and sat forward. "When I was lost and looking for Russ's apartment, I almost got in a head-on collision. Geeze, Sam. That was her. I can't believe it didn't register until now, but I'm certain that was who I nearly got in an accident with."

"Did you tell King?"

"How could I? I never saw him after I left Russ's."

If King didn't question her, then where had he been? And

why didn't he come for me after I asked to speak with him? Was he even inside the building tonight?

"Don't you get it, Samantha?" Erin paused, as if still not believing it herself. "They think I murdered Russ."

"This is insane," I said, shaking my head. "You didn't do anything."

"At least someone believes me."

If Erin was set up, could it have been Vince who did it? How could I prove that? We had plans to meet with Jackie tomorrow, but now I was second guessing our decision to do so.

Then there was King. I was worried about him, too. Something was going on—something that had to do with my meeting with Kovac, or even my conversation with Atwood. Did Watts know about my conversation with the public defender? Were these events even connected? Nothing was making sense.

"There's someone else who might believe you," I said, telling Erin about my conversation with Everett Atwood.

Erin rolled her neck and said, "Sam, King needs to know your plan with Atwood. If he's blindsided, others will think he was part of it."

Without looking at her, I murmured, "I can't."

Erin tossed me a questioning look, which I caught out of the corner of my eye. "And why is that?"

Thinking about what Kovac gave to me, I said, "Because King might be the problem."

CHAPTER FORTY-FIVE

DETECTIVE ALVAREZ ROUNDED THE CORNER AND KING stood up from his desk, asking, "What the hell is going on?"

"Easy." Alvarez looked around the bullpen from beneath his brow. His shoulders were visibly tense and dark hammocks hung below each of his eyes. "Keep your voice down. There is a lot at play here."

"No one is telling me shit." King's chest heaved with frustration. He knew Samantha had come here looking for Erin, but he couldn't risk being seen with her. With both hands on his waist, he cocked his head and said, "You know this was our case, right? We should be the ones interviewing Erin."

Alvarez met King's eyes and sighed. "It's over."

"What do you mean, it's over?"

"She was released."

King held his gaze for a beat, then snapped his neck and looked away. How did this happen? One minute he was investigating a homicide, the next, Samantha's best friend was being taken in for an interview. King knew this was no accident. He was being purposely left in the dark. But why? Something told him it had to do with Samantha's reporting.

King squinted his eyes and faced his partner. "Did Erin say what she was doing inside Russ's apartment?"

"I don't know. No one is talking." Alvarez was also being kept in the dark.

King said, "Something isn't right here, partner." He turned away and let his thoughts circle back to the Director of Public Safety, trying to decide what message Officer Barber was trying to convey to him earlier.

King asked, "So, who's taking over the investigation?"

"Detective King?" a voice boomed from across the bullpen.

King glanced over his shoulder and found Lieutenant Kent Baker at the door.

"May I have a minute of your time?" Lieutenant flicked his eyes to Alvarez. "Alone?"

King shared a look with Alvarez that said, *Find out what's happening*, then he met Baker at the door and followed him into his office. "Shut the door," Baker said.

"LT, please tell me what the hell is going on?"

LT gestured for King to sit. They held eyes for a moment, then LT said, "Your personal jacket has been pulled."

King froze. The air was knocked out of him. As if things weren't already strange enough, now this? "What for?" King asked.

"A citizen complaint," LT said calmly.

King took a minute to think through his night. Then he said, "Nothing happened tonight. Today was the slowest day all month."

LT shook his head. "Didn't happen tonight. I'm still learning the details myself, but IAD is investigating."

"They're here because of me?" King couldn't believe it.

LT gave a single nod of his head.

"It must be a mistake."

With square shoulders, LT said, "The chief has accepted IAD's recommendation for suspension."

"Suspension?"

"The complaint is serious, Alex."

Caught off guard, King didn't know what to say. "Isn't a suspension a little presumptive of them?"

LT cast his gaze to his desk and said, "You'll be contacted by your union rep—"

King sprung to his feet and lunged forward. With both hands on LT's desk, King said, "LT, at least tell me the details so I know what I'm being suspended for. I have every right to fight this. It's my career you're talking about here."

Looking him straight in his eye, LT said, "I'm going to need your badge and gun."

King's eyebrows knitted. "You're not going to fight for me?"

Sweeping his eyes up from his desk, LT said in a gravel voice, "Detective, believe me when I tell you, the fight has only just begun."

CHAPTER FORTY-SIX

I WAS IN A DREAM STATE, SOMEWHERE BETWEEN FULLY awake and fully asleep, when I felt the covers lift. The warm bubble of air escaped and was replaced by a familiar presence. King cuddled up next to me and brushed his lips against my ear. "Hey."

King's protective grip was reassuring, his scent comforting. I reached for his hand and squeezed, feeling a smile tug at my lips. I relaxed in knowing both my boys were home and safe.

I'd dropped Erin at her house, promising to pick up where we left off first thing tomorrow morning. She couldn't wait to see the video of King that Kovac gave to me, and I couldn't wait to show her. I still didn't believe it could be him.

Without opening my eyes, I asked, "What time is it?"

King tightened his hold on my pelvis and nuzzled his face deeper into my neck. He told me the time, and I wasn't surprised to find it was already tomorrow.

Silence drifted over us like the warmth of a blanket and, though I knew he shouldn't be here with the drone stalking me and with me going after the chief, I didn't want him to leave either.

King's hand drifted further down my body, circled over my pelvic bone, and he pushed his fingers beneath the elastic of my underwear. My body perked, and I felt King heating up behind me. Without a single word, I twisted in his arms and stared into his glimmering eyes, thinking about what I saw him do in the video. Cops made tough decisions daily. His actions on the video didn't come from the man with me now.

He stroked my cheek with his thumb. There was a sparkle of hurt in his eye and I wanted to ask him what was on his mind, other than me. His touch was tender with a growing urgency I knew couldn't be contained. Silently forgiving him of his past sins, I hooked my hand around the nape of his neck and pulled his lips down to mine. Flashes of light lit up behind my eyes. When King rolled on top of me, I hooked my ankles behind his back and surrendered myself to the man I loved.

CHAPTER FORTY-SEVEN

THE COLD SPRAY OF THE SHOWER HIT ME LIKE PINS AND needles. It jarred my senses awake and when my chest heaved for warmth, I turned the temperature up. I stood there with my hands planted against the tiled wall, keeping my head down, remembering how gingerly King made love to me.

As the water streamed down the center of my spine, the tension in my neck lessened. My head cleared, and I was certain a part of the reason for King's surprise visit was because of what happened to Erin.

By the time I stepped out of the shower, King was at the sink brushing his teeth. He looked at me through the mirror and said, "I hate to talk shop after what we just did, but I need to know...What was Erin doing at Russ's last night?"

I toweled myself dry and responded, "She didn't tell you?" I waited to see how he would respond, but King knew my game better than anyone and waited me out. I said, "She was there to purchase a video from him for a story we're working."

"A video?"

He was still standing with his back turned but his eyes

were firmly locked with mine in the mirror. I nodded and felt my abdominal muscles involuntarily flex. "He first came to the *Times* with his offer. It's how I knew about it."

"And...what? You're competing against the paper you work for now?"

"Not exactly," I said, saying how the paper wasn't interested, which wasn't completely true. "I'm not even sure if it's real, but I saw what he supposedly caught on film—"

"And what was it?"

"That April Wright was pushed." I couldn't tell if King knew or not. He didn't act the least bit surprised by the news so I figured he did. He held my eyes inside of his and I said, "Erin said Russ might have killed himself."

King looked away and pushed his fingers through his hair.

"But I think he was murdered."

King swept his eyes back to me.

"If I'm right, that makes two deaths made to look like suicides." I could see King's mind working. There was something he wanted to tell me. I said, "I'm right, aren't I?"

King turned to face me, crossed his arms, and rested his backside against the counter. "I looked into April's background."

"And?"

"She had a restraining order put on Vincent."

"What? When?"

King shook his head. "They should have never been in the same vicinity."

My eyelids were rapidly blinking as I filed through my thoughts. "Why are you telling me this? I can't just let this go now that I know."

"It doesn't matter."

"What are you talking about? Of course it matters. Did something happen?"

King exhaled a deep breath and said, "I was suspended."

It took some convincing, but after a round of back-and-forth King told me what for.

"IAD is investigating a citizen complaint. That's all I know, but I'm sure it's political."

King didn't seem too worried. It almost seemed like he was expecting it. As for me, it knocked me off my axis and I couldn't stop asking myself if this citizen complaint had something to do with the video Kovac gave me. But before I mentioned anything to King, I said, "It's because of me, isn't it?"

King gave me a look that said, *Don't be ridiculous*.

"Do you want me to stop reporting on the chief?" I wasn't certain I could, or why I was even asking, other than I loved him.

He said, "This will blow over."

King wasn't very convincing. I said, "There is something I need you to see."

Wrapping a towel around my body, I led King back to the bed and retrieved my laptop from the kitchen table. Then I closed the door and played Kovac's video.

King watched intently and didn't react until it was finished.

"That was given to me by a man who calls himself Kovac."

King's eyes never left the screen when he said, "That's not me, Sam."

"Do you know that name? Is it someone in the department?"

"I don't know anybody by the name Kovac." King bounced his gaze between me and the computer screen. "Jesus, if this is what IAD is investigating, my career will be destroyed."

I crawled up on the bed, sat on my heels, and settled up next to King, hooking my hands on his shoulders. I said, "If it's a fake, like we think, maybe Allison can prove it."

CHAPTER FORTY-EIGHT

JACKIE SMACKED HER LIPS AND FINISHED PUTTING ON THE last of her makeup. Her eyes were bright, and she was fully awake after her early jog through the park to shake off the cobwebs of last night.

She cherished these early morning hours, providing the chance to clear her head, meditating on the silence before the chaos of her day hit. Which it inevitably would.

Every day was war when working as a publicist, and Jackie's experience hadn't been any different. She dressed in her armor, wearing a jet-black coat and suit with spiked heels to match. Her jewelry was pure gold mixed with a glitter of diamonds. It was in sharp contrast to her flaming red hair that fell in thick waves to her shoulders. Dressed for battle, she was now ready to put out the fires that were inevitably heading her way.

"Gloves up, girl," she said to herself when exiting her master bath. "It's time to fight to see another day."

Her heels clacked against the hardwood flooring as she trotted down the hallway and into her kitchen. A granite island counter with a gas stove was at the center of the room, but food wasn't on her mind. Instead, she reached for the clicker by the refrigerator and turned on the large flat screen TV in the living room. She flipped between channels while preparing her coffee. She was thrilled April's death was losing interest, but it was the homicide investigation of Russ Abair that caught Jackie's attention.

"Shit," she muttered.

Taking a deep breath, Jackie should have seen this coming. The writing was on the wall the moment word got around that April may not have committed suicide like originally thought. The details of Russ's investigation were still coming in, but Jackie knew she had to act quickly before this story eventually caught up with her, too.

She finished making her espresso and pulled her cellphone off the charger, turning it on. Her jaw was set and, though this presented a challenge unlike anything she had worked through before, Jackie knew she was worth every dollar she charged her high-profile clients. Recent developments may have been making her second guess her current fees, thinking she might have to charge Vince more for the additional efforts he was making her go through to keep his career alive.

A sharp pressure expanded her skull, and she closed her eyes until the pain subsided.

Vince was proving to be more of a headache than what he was currently worth, but she couldn't leave him now. Not after all she'd done to protect her interest. He had the most potential out of all her clients and she couldn't forget the pot of gold his platform had already made them both.

Once her cellphone came to life, it beeped with an onslaught of incoming messages and voicemails. Jackie quickly scrolled through the text messages. Only one caught her undivided attention.

911

Mitch. Vincent's boy. And the message came in less than ten minutes ago.

"Christ. What now?" Jackie murmured as she wrote back.

I'm on my way to the house now. Keep him calm until I get there.

Jackie knew what 911 meant with Vincent, and it wasn't good. He was breaking down, and she had a million possible reasons why that could be.

She put her coffee in a to-go cup, retrieved her purse off the counter, and made sure the thumb-drive was inside before leaving her apartment. She practically ran to her car, got behind the wheel and headed to the house Vincent was renting when she received a call from her assistant.

"I'll be in the office shortly," Jackie answered. "Vincent is having an emerg—"

"That's why I'm calling. I've been trying to reach you." Her assistant sounded frantic. "Where have you been?"

"Long night. I needed to clear my head." The throb behind Jackie's eyes was back. "I'll tell you about it later. What's so urgent?"

"GamersCon called and say's Vincent isn't welcomed back."

Jackie tightened her grip on the steering wheel. This had to be connected to his glorifying April's death on the big screen. He'd gone against her wishes to keep his career safe. Instead, he continued with his controversies, bringing unwanted attention upon himself when she needed him to lay cool for a while.

Jackie's assistant continued, "They say he breached his contract when he left the event early, so we can forget about the money owed."

"I'll take care of it."

"But that's not all. There's something else. It's about your schedule. You're double booked." Her assistant mentioned the scheduling conflict, reminding her about her promised meeting with Erin Tate.

"Shit." Jackie had forgotten about her meeting with Erin.

"I can cancel for you..."

"No. Just reschedule for late this afternoon." Jackie mentioned her preferred time. She needed to properly plan her response to what she assumed would be difficult questions, and though she had some facts in place, much of her story was still being worked out. "It's important everything appears to be normal."

CHAPTER FORTY-NINE

TEN MINUTES LATER, JACKIE ARRIVED AT VINCE'S HOUSE tucked in the hillside city of Boulder. Her patience was waning. She'd spent the entire drive mulling over the best way to contain Vincent, whose behavior was becoming a liability.

Somewhere between her house and his, she came up with a plan to buy some time. She parked in front and stepped out onto wet pavement, the sprinklers busy watering the green grass despite the change in season. Shaking her head at the absurdity, the yard was a complete mess with leaves needing to be raked.

Jackie followed the hedge to the front door and let herself inside without knocking. A strong odor hit her in the face and made her cringe. It was a mix between empty beer bottles and a college frat house. Disgusted, she found Mitch lying on the couch with a video game control in hand.

Jackie said by way of greeting, "You leave the lawn sprinklers on too much longer, your pipes will freeze."

Mitch paused the game, swung his feet to the floor, and twisted around to look Jackie in the eye. "Vince has locked himself inside his room. He's pissed off about something. I'm not even sure he's eaten anything since lunch yesterday. I think he's depressed, but I'm not sure about what. He hasn't been the same since...well...you know, April. I'm worried about him."

Jackie said, "Easy, Mitch. You did the right thing by calling Mama."

"Will you convince him to take his medication? We have production planned for later today, but I'm worried he won't make it."

Jackie bent and patted Mitch's cheek with her hand. "I'll get him back on his feet. I always do."

Jackie turned and left Mitch to his game as she headed for Vince. As if things couldn't get worse, Vince was unintentionally digging his grave deeper. His misbehavior was bringing them all down, and if he didn't straighten out soon, Jackie feared Vincent would bring her down with him.

She stopped at the foot of the stairs and peered into a couple enormous cardboard boxes. There were masks and suits and two paintball guns, but it was the glue and feathers that had her scratching her head. Turning to Mitch, she asked, "What is it exactly you guys have planned?"

Without looking, Mitch said, "A chicken hunt."

Jackie didn't ask. She didn't want to know.

At the top of the stairs, Jackie marched to Vincent's room. She'd seen him like this before and should have noticed the warning signs. More importantly, she knew how to correct his course, but only if he agreed to go along with her plan.

Jackie knocked on Vincent's bedroom door. "Vince, honey, it's me. Can you open up?"

Vincent responded immediately. "No. I can't."

Jackie tried the handle. The door was locked. "Vince, please, let me come in. Unlock this door."

"We have a problem," he said.

Jackie put her face close to the door. "I took care of it."

"No, I don't think you did," Vince shouted back.

Jackie paused and gave it some thought. She suspected there was something Vince wasn't telling her and now she was curious to know what that was. Did April have something else planned? Had he not told her everything that happened between them? Or did Vincent know what Jackie was up to and was about to squash her plans?

Suddenly, Vincent swung open the door and Jackie stepped back. She tried to keep her face straight and not react to the wig he was wearing.

"I'm losing my mind," Vince said, thrusting Samantha Bell's column in Jackie's chest.

Jackie took the paper into her hands and glanced to the headline. "I'm aware," she said, lowering the paper to her side. "I'll take care of them, too."

Vincent folded his arms and tossed her a disbelieving look. "How?"

Retrieving the thumb-drive from her purse, she handed it to Vince, telling him what it was.

Vince asked, "How did you get—"

"Who else knows?" Jackie looked into Vincent's eyes. "If anyone else knows about that, you need to tell me now. We can end this today, but I can't help you if you're not telling me the complete truth of what happened."

Vince cast his gaze down to his open palm and stared at the thumb-drive. His expression made it clear he was debating his options.

"We can't take any chances," Jackie said. "It's time to get ahead of this because people are coming for you whether you like it or not."

Without picking his head up, Vincent asked, "The black woman that was with Samantha Bell, do you know her?"

Jackie tilted her head, gave a questioning look.

Vince looked at her from beneath his brow and asked, "Were you seen?"

Jackie knew Vince was losing trust in her. "Vincent, honey—"

Vince pushed past Jackie and glanced downstairs. Then he turned back to Jackie and asked, "Are you being followed?"

Lifting the paper in her hand, Jackie said, "This article has you paranoid."

"But I saw her," Vince pointed at Samantha's column, "at GamersCon." He squeezed his head with both his hands, closed his eyes, and growled, "I can't take this anymore. The voices won't shut up."

Jackie cast her gaze to the column and quickly scanned the text. It said nothing other than April's death was a suicide. Meeting Vince's eye, Jackie said, "There is nothing you need to worry about, but here's what I suggest we do."

Vince leaned closer and Jackie told him her plan.

CHAPTER FIFTY

KING CAUGHT MY ARM AS I PASSED AND GRIPPED MY WAIST with his hands. His eyelids hooded, and he gave me a look of desire as he pushed his hands around my hips and toward the small of my back. My breath hitched the exact moment Erin called.

I reluctantly pulled my hands off King's shoulders and answered my phone.

"You're never going to believe this," Erin shouted into my ear, "but I just received a call from Jackie's personal assistant. She delayed our meeting. Can you believe it?"

"Until when?" I asked.

"This afternoon." A pause. "She knows I'm a witness to her being at Russ's. It was her I nearly got into an accident with. I know it was, Sam."

Erin was eager to clear her name. I couldn't blame her for wanting to do so as quickly as possible. I wasn't the least bit surprised to hear Jackie wanted nothing to do with us now that Russ was as dead as the video was missing. But what I wanted to know was how she could have planned it to set Erin up? Or was she hoping it would be me to take the fall?

Either way, it was clear Jackie was a step ahead of us all. Now I worried what she was planning to do with us next.

"Sam, what do we do?" Erin asked.

"We have to learn why Vince wanted April dead. If Jackie killed April for Vince, maybe April had something on him. Maybe she was going to leak it."

"Do you think Jackie knows about the video Allison has of her meeting with April?"

"My hope is she doesn't. And even if she does, she might not know that we know about it. That's why we need to meet with her. If we can call her out and put her on the spot, we can see how she reacts to our accusations."

"Even if she's Vincent's hired gun?"

I still wanted to know the source of Allison's video. Who sent it? How could we find them? It felt like that was the person we needed to speak to. Then again, I wasn't sure it mattered. As long as the video existed, we had leverage to use against Jackie.

"Even if," I said. "We just need to make a copy in case it gets taken down."

"Sam, you have to cancel your meeting with Atwood. The evidence he has against the chief isn't going anywhere. This other story will disappear if we don't jump on it now."

I glanced in King's direction, worried about his future and how it related to Atwood's mission to bring reform to the department. I said to Erin, "Let's not forget Atwood is a potential ally who can help your case. Why don't you come to my house and we can go from here?"

"This is kind of weird," Erin said, "but I'm already at your house."

"Outside?" Erin confirmed she was, and I said, "Then why are we having this conversation over the phone?"

"Because I know King is inside."

I moved to the front of the house, opened my front door,

and found Erin sitting on the top step with her bicycle parked in front. Cooper should have barked, but maybe he hadn't because he knew it was only Erin. Closing out my phone, I said, "He's not mad at you. Come inside."

"Have you forgotten what happened to me last night?" Erin stood but didn't move from the top step. "I like King, but I don't think I can trust him right now."

"Don't worry about him. He was suspended."

Erin's eyes lit up. "I was right," Erin said. "Was it because of the video Kovac gave to you?"

I heard King come up from behind and open the door. He placed his hand on my shoulder and said to Erin, "Tell me about Jackie Dumont."

CHAPTER FIFTY-ONE

KING SAT ON THE COUCH, HUNCHED OVER HIS KNEES AS HE
listened to what Erin had to say. Before she began, I told her
about April having a restraining order against Vince for
context. We still didn't know who brought April to Vince's
show in Boulder, but it looked like it had to be Jackie.

I listened from the table and thought it strange how only
Dawson and I had seen Russ's video—the same clip it
seemed everyone was now after. I wanted to see it again, to
learn if it was Jackie's arm caught in the frame or somebody
else's. King was trying to figure this mess out himself—
deciding if Jackie was covering her tracks after having
murdered April—despite his own career troubles. He
wanted to know everything, and I could see Erin getting
annoyed with his questioning, but I reminded her to be
patient.

After another round, I stepped in and said, "We're just
going in circles."

King leaned back and scrubbed his hands over his face.
Erin sank deeper into her thoughts and stared at the floor.
We all agreed Jackie was a prime suspect. If we planned to

meet with her later today, we had to expect the worst and not get roped into appearing to be her accomplices.

"Is it possible we could be wrong about Jackie?" Erin asked.

I tipped forward, my thoughts swirling back to what Russ's neighbor said about the redheaded woman she saw having strange body proportions. I asked, "What's giving you doubt?"

"Maybe it wasn't her I saw? Perhaps Russ was suicidal before all this happened and we're just assuming the worst in people?"

Erin was exhausted. Her head was spinning with doubt from the persistent questioning about last night. I, on the other hand, still believed Jackie should at least be questioned if not by us, then certainly the police. Then King said, "It's impossible Russ killed himself."

Erin and I both perked up. King told us about the department's initial response, what they found when investigating Russ's apartment, including the .357 hidden inside Russ's couch.

I swept my eyes to Erin, who shook her head like she didn't know. Then I asked King, "I found a witness who saw Jackie at Russ's apartment, and there were security cameras there, too. Has the department looked into either of those?"

King said, "Not to my knowledge."

"Because you already had Erin in custody?"

King shook his head. "It was only an interview, which Erin agreed to."

Erin asked, "Why? You know I don't have it in me to kill someone."

King lifted his head and locked his eyes on Erin. "I can only assume, now that I've been suspended, that it was designed to intimidate you into backing off your investigation into Chief Watts."

"And entice us further?" I couldn't believe what I was hearing. King didn't have proof, but it was a speculation that made complete sense. Suddenly, my thoughts were drifting to Atwood and the video from Kovac. This wasn't about Russ at all.

King sprung to his feet, his frustration at the whole situation coming through in his expression. "What the hell did you think would happen? That they'd just let you look into them?" He turned to me. "First, you should have notified me —or at the very least, the Boulder PD—the second you saw what Russ had." Then he faced Erin. "And you should have never entered his apartment after seeing him dead. I know you were after the video—"

"It wasn't there," Erin said.

King shook his head. "It doesn't matter. Your decisions affect real lives, and you're both treating this like you're only concerned about chasing ratings."

"Let's not forget Watts is the reason you're suspended." I raised an eyebrow. "Should we talk about what you were caught doing in *your* video?"

King squared his jaw. "We talked about this, Samantha. You know that wasn't me."

"The way I see it, you both were set up to take the fall."

Erin sensed a fight coming and stopped it before it ever got started by saying, "It was a Dodge Challenger."

King rolled his neck to Erin. "Excuse me?"

"That's what Jackie was driving."

I asked King, "Is it possible to see if it's registered to Jackie, or even Vincent Verdi?"

King gave it some thought. Then he said, "I can make some calls."

"That's all I'm asking you to do."

It would be nice to have some answers before our meeting with Jackie, but I wasn't counting on it. Instead, I glanced to the clock and thought about my meeting with Atwood. "We better get going," I said to Erin.

Erin nodded, and King asked about our plans.

Without telling him too much, I asked, "Do you trust Everett Atwood?"

King's eye squinted. "The public defender?"

I confirmed with a single nod of my head and said, "I thought maybe he could help Erin prepare a defense."

Erin eyed me. She knew I wasn't telling King the complete story, and I suspected King knew it too.

King said, "I do."

"Then you better get going. Allison is expecting you."

CHAPTER FIFTY-TWO

VINCE REACHED HIS HAND OUT AND CLOSED HIS FINGERS around Jackie's slim arm, yanking her into his room. Jackie yelped with surprise as Vince slammed her up against the wall and kicked the door shut.

"Are you out of your mind?" he said close to her face, now gripping both of her arms.

Jackie's heart drummed. "It's the only way," she said.

Vince's eyes flitted back and forth as he thought through his options. "I can't do that," he said with wide eyes. "It will ruin my image, the same image I'm paying you to protect."

"Honey," Jackie's voice calmed as she peeled his fingers free from her arm, "the media is speculating April was murdered. The way I see it, you have two options. You can either take your chances with them and have the world think you killed her, or you can do what I say and live to see another day."

"This is bad. Really bad." Vince stepped away, ripping off the wig he was still wearing and tossing it on his bed.

Jackie glanced to the wig and turned back to Vince. "What did you think would happen?"

Vince paced the room as Jackie headed into his master bath. Searching the medicine cabinet, she retrieved his antidepressants and filled a glass with water. Taking it to Vince, he swallowed the pill down without protest.

"Do what you do best," Jackie said with her hand on his arm. "Maybe, instead of this chicken hunt Mitch has planned, take my idea and work it into your production."

Vince swept his eyes up and said, "Maybe you're right."

"Own the narrative, sweetie."

"It's too close to the truth."

"I've managed far worse scandals before," Jackie reminded him as she went for his closet, sifting through his clothes and putting together the perfect ensemble. "This is a cakewalk, but only if done right."

There was a knock on the door, and Jackie turned to see Mitch poke his head inside. "Everything all right up here?"

Jackie dropped the pants she was holding and hurried to the door. "Just fine." She turned to Vince. "Isn't that right, Vince?"

"Peachy." Vince crossed his arms and scowled.

"Put those on, Vince." Jackie pointed to the clothes she'd laid out. "And call me when you're ready to film. It's better we do this now while there is still time."

CHAPTER FIFTY-THREE

THROUGH THE UPSTAIRS WINDOW, VINCENT WATCHED Jackie leave his house. Her red hair shone bright in the sunlight as she weaved between the many cars parked in his driveway. He watched her slide her index finger across the Jeep Wrangler he knew she loved before getting into her own car and driving away.

Vince knew she was up to something, but he couldn't decide what that was. The look in her eye said it all. Her ridiculous idea and the persistent need to manipulate him had him second guessing her worth.

Mitch padded up from behind and wrapped his arms around Vince's torso. Hooking his chin on Vince's shoulder, Mitch asked, "What did she ask you to do?"

Vincent's eyes were still staring out front as he told Mitch Jackie's plan.

Mitch responded, "I kind of like her idea."

Vincent's body steeled the second before he pushed Mitch off of him. Whipping around, Vince confronted his friend. "Did you call her about us? Is that why she was here?"

"She came here because she had something you needed."

"Oh, please. Wait—" Vincent paused and stared into Mitch's eyes. "I think I know what's happening here."

Mitch didn't blink. "We agreed to keep this a secret."

"Then why agree to go along with her idea?" Vincent's chest heaved. "Oh, forget about it. Screw the both of you!"

Mitch's face pinched. "What's happening to you?"

"What's happening to *me*?" Vincent's face turned red. "My most trusted advisors are derailing my career, and I'm trying to figure out why."

Mitch shook his head and headed for the door. "I know it's hard for someone like you to believe, but it's not always about you."

As soon as the door slammed shut, Vince found himself holding the thumb-drive Jackie brought him. Then an epiphany washed over him. Jackie knew too much. She would either blackmail him for an extreme amount of money, or save her butt from the disaster heading their way by ratting him out. Either way, Vincent was sure Jackie needed to go.

CHAPTER FIFTY-FOUR

WE ARRIVED TO THE PUBLIC DEFENDER'S HOUSE TEN minutes before nine. The modest two-story home on the northeast side of downtown was at the end of a cul-de-sac in what appeared to be a lovely neighborhood with manicured lawns.

As soon as I stepped out, Erin said to me over the roof of my car, "I was expecting something bigger."

"I was too," I said. Though Erin was referring to the house and not the man himself, I added, "Just wait until you meet *him*."

That's when I heard shouting coming through an upstairs window. We both turned to look and listen, and Erin asked, "You think we should come back later?"

I never intended to get caught in the middle of a marital dispute, but time was of the essence. I said, "He knows we're coming. Let's just go see what he has to show us and hope we don't get caught in their crossfire."

We followed the hedge to the front door, climbed the short flight of stone steps, and rang the doorbell. The house was quiet as I glanced around, taking inventory of the additional security Atwood had in place.

Atwood answered the door just as the garage door lifted. "Samantha, good morning."

I greeted him and watched him extend a hand to Erin. Erin didn't see it at first, too busy watching Atwood's wife, Genevieve, back down the drive in a dark maroon Audi. Genevieve never looked in our direction but I was sure she knew we were there.

"Is now still a good time?" I asked Atwood.

Atwood was still staring at Erin. Erin turned and said, "Hi. Erin Tate."

"My partner you said to bring along," I reminded him.

"Yes. Of course." Atwood blinked away his thoughts. "Forgive me for staring. It's just...you're taller and prettier than what I've seen in pictures."

Erin was used to turning heads. She took his compliment and lobbed it right back at him. "And you're shorter than your reputation suggests," Erin said.

Atwood burst out laughing, gesturing for us to come inside. His house was clean and well organized. First impression told me he had an eye for interior design and expensive taste.

"I apologize if you heard anything when you arrived," Atwood said about fighting with his wife. "Things change once you become empty nesters, and I'm afraid my wife is having a tough time with it just being me in the house."

Atwood told us about his youngest daughter in her first year at university. When he finished, Erin asked, "Where is she studying?"

"Harvard."

"Impressive," I said.

"Two on the East Coast, one on the West, and one in-state." Atwood smiled proudly, glancing to family portraits scattered throughout the house. Then he asked about Mason. "Any plans to attend university?"

Atwood's look made me flash back to last night's text about Mason being home alone. I didn't think it could have been Atwood who sent it, but my hesitation and paranoia were certainly growing the longer this went on. I was hesitant to share personal information with anyone outside my inner circle of trusted friends and colleagues.

"He's busy studying for the SATs, and I'm encouraging him to stay in-state."

"I'd have preferred them all to stay in-state." Atwood smiled, then got on with business. "I must admit, I'm surprised you showed."

We followed him to his study, and I said, "King said you were someone I could trust."

Atwood stopped and turned to look me in the eye. "You told him what we discussed?"

"No. But he's in trouble."

Atwood gave a quizzical look. "How so?"

I told him about King's suspension and added, "I need to be certain King's name isn't attached to anything you're going to reveal to me today."

"I don't recall his name being anywhere in the documents, but I can double check just to be sure."

Atwood did exactly that once settled in at his glass-topped desk. "No," he shook his head while still reading printed reports, "I don't see his name in any of these." Then he swept his gaze up to me. "But you said he was suspended?"

"Just last night." I told him about the Kovac video. "King insists it's not him, and I believe him."

Atwood's eyes darkened and got serious. "This is exactly what I warned you about," he said, reminding me how King was the first of us to slip up. "If it's not him in the video, this could be the start of Watts's disinformation campaign."

Erin's eyes kept bouncing back and forth between Atwood and me. She was doing her best to keep up, but there was still a lot she didn't know.

I told Atwood, "I have a friend helping to prove it's a fake."

"It won't be easy." Atwood sighed. "And I'm sure I'm not telling you anything you haven't already thought of yourself, but it's possible your source has already taken the same video to a competing news source."

"I'm well aware," I said, feeling the urgency grow in my stomach. But Allison was the best, and I trusted her to come through. "It's also worth mentioning that I'm being stalked by a drone."

"A drone?"

I nodded. "I've also been receiving numerous threats since we began investigating Watts."

"Not surprising." Atwood pulled a folder and opened it up. "This is the unit of officers Watts has doing his dirty work."

I caught Erin up with our discussion from last night and said, "They're targeting members of the LGBTQ community and coercing them into admitting guilt for crimes they didn't commit."

"Why?" Erin asked. "Because the cops are homophobic?"

"Possibly," Atwood's head bobbed, "but I think it's more because a certain vigilante is highlighting easy targets."

"Vigilante?" I asked.

Atwood flicked his gaze over to me. "That's right. This person, whose identity isn't exactly clear, stages underage gay hookups and then shames the individuals who respond to his posts. The department obviously doesn't publicly support the vigilante's tactics, but my office has discovered these are the exact people Watts is harassing."

I looked to Erin. "And they either plead guilty to crimes

they didn't commit, or risk being shamed by their community."

"Exactly," Atwood said. "Which then sometimes leads to unforeseen consequences."

"Like murder?"

Atwood shrugged. "And suicide." An image of April flashed behind my eyes when Atwood continued, "My fear is this vigilante character will one day wake up and want the praise and recognition the chief is taking away from him."

"Or maybe that's all this vigilante wants?" Erin suggested. "Simply for someone to get rid of the people he deems deplorable while staying in the shadows?"

Atwood handed me the reports. I opened up the files and took a look. It read like a fiction novel. The Criminal Investigation Unit worked their own active cases, but also received leads from the unknown vigilante. I asked the public defender, "Could it be the vigilante is actually one of these officers?"

"I haven't ruled it out," Atwood said.

"But if we expose those cops' names," Erin said, looking over my shoulder, "we'll have an explosion on our hands."

Atwood grinned. "Isn't that what you two wanted to begin with?"

My pulse kicked up a notch. Adrenaline and excitement, along with a healthy does of danger, stirred inside of me, reminding me what was at stake. Kovac's golden ticket was so different from what Atwood was presenting to us now that I was beginning to believe he might have been one of the officers inside the report.

Atwood stood and said, "The chief is keeping a close eye on reporters, especially the ones he knows are critical of the job he is doing, and I suspect someone knows what's about to happen." He paused as if thinking about my stalker. "It's going to get dangerous—"

"It already is," I said.

The room went silent.

Atwood picked up a hard disk and handed it to Erin. "Divide the copies between you two for safekeeping, and absolutely no spin."

"We have our personal platforms covered," I said, "but I'm going to have to get this story approved by my editor at the *Times*."

"I understand." Atwood nodded. "It's important we hit this story on all fronts. Once we open up the floodgates, we can't stop. Not even for one second. If we let up on Watts, we all lose."

Erin asked, "Who else besides your investigative team knows about this?"

"Just you two."

Erin eyed Atwood. "Then why give us the exclusive?"

"Simple. You two are the only honest reporters left in a city full of crooks."

CHAPTER FIFTY-FIVE

WHEN THE DOOR SHUT, MR. T TURNED HIS BACK AND strode toward the bedroom window. He listened and, when he heard nothing, lifted a single finger and pulled back the curtain to peek down below to the world outside.

Silently, he watched the leaves rustle in the wind. He marveled at their subtle, but obvious, changing of color. There were few clouds in the sky and everything seemed calm and organized, so much different from the chattering of voices rattling inside his head.

He was feeling frustrated with the people around him. He didn't feel listened to. His ideas were solid, if not the best. People were all talk and no action and constantly failed at keeping their word.

"What is a boy to do?" he asked himself while releasing the drape.

Mr. T turned around and took a seat at his computer. He inserted the thumb-drive into the USB jack and waited for it to load. Soon, he found himself staring at his camera bag, thinking about the story he was scripting. Taking it into his hands, he scrolled through the images, reliving each captured moment.

Something about it was off. It felt like there was something missing that he couldn't put his finger on. Though the scenes were coming together and the story itself was tightly plotted, Mr. T couldn't help but feel that his chosen villain was winning.

A chime sounded and pulled his focus back to the computer screen.

How could his villain still be winning? Why hadn't they been arrested yet? Mr. T was as calculated as the police but if they weren't going to do their job, he'd have to do it for them.

A thought came to his mind, and he scribbled it down to be sure not to forget it.

It wouldn't feel right if he wasn't somehow involved in taking down the big fish that had eluded him thus far. But how could he work the police into his story without tipping them off that it was him who was responsible for these murders?

A swelling headache settled behind his eyes and he continued clicking through old folders and news columns, looking for ideas. A solution had to be somewhere buried inside one of these folders—but where?

An hour passed, and Mr. T still had nothing. With frustration mounting, it was what wasn't being said about him in the press and on social media that really grated on his nerves. But before giving up completely, he finally navigated to the new folder and clicked the video file which immediately began to play.

The footage was grainy and not the best quality, but clear enough to know the swelling crowd and venue. The murmur of excitement brought Mr. T back to the night it all began. He recognized the chants and started to whisper them himself.

"Don't trip. You might fall."

The smile that crossed his face quickly dropped with April's fall. It was stunning. This was the first time he'd seen it from this angle and he liked what he saw. Like the director who stepped away from behind the camera to see it from the audience's perspective. It was marvelous. He paused the video, rewound it a bit, zoomed in, and couldn't believe what he saw.

"What impeccable timing," he said.

Without a doubt, it was his arm caught in the frame. He watched the clip again, this time letting it play out until the end. A stunned crowd froze before reacting to what had happened. Then they all rushed in like hyenas on a kill to photograph and video April Wright's broken body.

Mr. T chuckled softly.

No one tried to save her. Everyone was out for themselves, jockeying for the best position to capture a once-in-a-lifetime moment. It gave Mr. T a strange satisfaction, and he remembered a similar sight when exiting the elevator after having killed her.

"Animals," he said. "Wild animals."

Leaning back in his chair, he closed his eyes and replayed the start of his story inside his head. No one would suspect it was him who killed her, but who else did Russ show this to? How many others captured the same clip?

His eyes sprung open.

He was smart enough to know he didn't get to the film quick enough. He was one step short of remaining completely anonymous. Like all plot twists, this one was totally unexpected.

Twisting around, Mr. T tossed his gaze in the direction of his closet, thinking of what he was wearing the night April died. When it came to him, he asked himself if it might be beneficial to get rid of the clothes. "It couldn't hurt," he muttered.

Turning back to face his computer, he caught sight of the pinned images of Sam, Erin, and Allison. He'd expected them to be preoccupied with their fight to get Police Chief Gordon Watts to resign, yet they seemed to be getting awfully close to his own script. That was a little worrisome. Allison would be least likely to suspect his motive and sniff him out. Perhaps that was to his advantage.

"Hmmm, the possibilities."

He had reason to kill April, but murdering someone like Samantha Bell would just be business. What he couldn't decide was if Samantha was a threat to his survival or the key to his riches. He suspected the former. She and Erin were too competent to not eventually identify him. But how could he smooth out the ripples now traveling across the pond without getting caught? Tricky.

Another thought crossed his mind and Mr. T reached for a pen and scribbled a new scene into his book, crossing out old ideas, reworking the story until it was perfect. If he was to bring his villain to justice, he needed to make sure his target was exposed for being a fraud, shamed until he admitted who he was. But, most importantly, Mr. T needed him to go away for a very long time without resorting to murder. That was his intention all along. To get back at the person who constantly humiliated him and treated him like he was nothing.

Feeling heated, he needed to cool off. He moved to his TV and fired up his gaming console, hoping a few rounds of battle would settle his anxiety. Settling in, he put on his headset when a new message came in from someone who called himself White Stallion.

I know what you're up to and I want in on the action.

Mr. T paused and stared. A part of him was thrilled to be

recognized for his work, the other half of him worried he'd made it too obvious he was behind the killing spree. He took a moment to think through his response, then wrote back simply, *Who are you?*

Don't play me for a fool, Trojan. You either let me in on your game, or I go to the cops and tell them everything.

Mr. T knew exactly who White Stallion was. He'd only ever met one White Stallion in his life. Now the question became should Mr. T plan to kill him, too, since White Stallion knew what he was doing, or use him to take the fall for what Mr. T had already done?

Either way, it was time to change tactics. That included rewriting the script to include a new character in the story.

He then responded, *If you want the part, you got it.*

CHAPTER FIFTY-SIX

ALLISON WAS TIPPED FORWARD IN HER OFFICE CHAIR reading up on Russ Abair. The police had said little about his death and she hadn't heard what the outcome with Erin was last night. She studied his photo closely to be sure it wasn't him who gave her the link to Jackie Dumont and April Wright arguing.

"If it wasn't you, then who was it?" she asked herself.

When she leaned back, she thought about the drone circling above about the time she was handed the mysterious business card. It could have been anybody. With the costumes and chaos of the convention, it seemed impossible to ever know who the person was.

Allison clicked out of the open browser and went back to the video of Jackie and April. She'd been working to clear up the audio with hopes of hearing what was being said. After working on it all morning, she was getting closer.

Thinking of the drone, she asked herself if it was part of the event or something else entirely. And why bring this video to her and not the police? Did they expect her to do something with it?

A soft knock on the door lifted her gaze. Alex King stood at the door and said, "Am I interrupting?"

Allison sprouted a smile. "Yes, but Samantha said you were coming."

King entered the office and pulled up a chair. He glanced to her screen and said, "Any luck with the audio?"

"Does Samantha tell you everything?"

"I'm sure she has a few secrets she hasn't shared with me yet." King winked.

"I promise you, she does." Allison's eyes smiled knowingly. Then she said, "I'm close to nailing down the audio, but not there yet." She turned to face King. "I assume Samantha has shown you this?"

King said he'd seen it. Then he added, "Samantha and Erin are planning to meet with Jackie later today."

"Do you think Jackie killed her?"

"Not my case."

"Right. Wrong jurisdiction." Allison gave King an arched look. "So, I assume you let Erin go free?"

King frowned. "That wasn't me, but yes, the department let her go. No charges pressed."

"But it was a homicide?"

"Yes," King said, sounding annoyed. "And that's all I can say."

Allison tossed up her hands in surrender. "Then what is it I can help you with today, Detective?"

King retrieved a thumb-drive from his coat pocket and said, "Samantha didn't tell you?"

"Just that it was similar to the work I'm doing for her already." Allison cast her gaze to the memory stick and asked, "Is that the file there?"

King held it up for her to take. "Someone put my face on somebody else's body, making me look like I framed a potentially innocent person."

"Interesting," Allison said, taking the stick. "And, just so you know, I'm happy to be consulting for Denver PD no matter what my friend might be saying about your boss."

King looked into Allison's brown eyes and said solemnly, "This is a private matter. It's important we keep everything we discuss a secret."

Allison knew there was more to King's story than he was willing to share, but she didn't want to pry. "Whatever you say, Detective," she said, inserting the drive into a safe computer.

A pop-up displayed a warning on the screen and King asked, "Everything okay?"

"Did Samantha put this in her computer?"

King witnessed Allison's concern and said, "I'm guessing she shouldn't have?"

Allison removed the thumb-drive and ran it through a security scanner. "Just as I suspected," Allison said after the initial report came through.

"What is it?"

Allison pulled up the code as King scooted forward. She pointed out the line of malware and said, "Spyware. And not just your run-of-the-mill kind, either. This is professional. Disguised as part of the original file." Allison touched her brow and asked, "Where did she get this?"

"An anonymous source—"

"Who just gained access to her computer."

King stood and had his phone pressed to his ear before Allison could tell him to call Sam. As the line rang, King asked, "Can you get to the video?"

Allison nodded. "It will take some work without infecting my own device, but I should be able to do it."

King stepped out of the room and Allison could hear him warning Samantha that her computer might have been compromised. Then he was back in the office and said, "She knows what to do."

"Because I've coached her in the past." Allison's fingers worked the keyboard. "There." She spun around, tossing King a look as she did.

"What?"

"I can already tell it's a deepfake." Allison explained how she got to the source code, proving the image had been manipulated. "A deepfake is synthetic media where a person in an existing file is replaced with someone else's likeness." Then she showed him the video with the code removed. King's face disappeared, and a new face emerged. "You have any enemies?" she asked King.

"Apparently." King was staring at Officer Barber's face when his phone buzzed with an incoming message. One look and he was on his feet. "I got to run."

Allison followed King with her eyes. "Are we done here, then?"

King stopped at the door. "Work on the Jackie and April audio and please call me as soon as you get anything. I need to have a reason for Samantha to not go after Jackie herself."

CHAPTER FIFTY-SEVEN

I GOT OFF THE PHONE WITH KING AND TURNED BACK TO my car. Erin was sitting in the passenger seat poring over the documents Atwood gave us. I wasn't at all surprised by King's news. What did surprise me was that my security software didn't catch the spyware now likely infecting my computer. Kovac had to be a cop, and a dirty one at that.

I fell into the driver's seat and Erin said, "This guy, Officer Barber," she lifted her head and pointed to the open report on her lap, "he came to talk with me before I gave my statement to the detectives."

I leaned over and took a look at the report. "What did he say?"

"How ironic it was to see me inside the box being questioned on a possible homicide after accusing Watts of doing the same." Erin rolled her eyes to me. "You should have seen the condescending smirk on his face, Samantha. I just thought he was a cop who hated reporters, but now it appears to be something else entirely."

"Do you think the cops believe you were set up?"

Erin barked out a laugh. "You don't think Jackie is coordinating with the police, do you?"

"Seems like a stretch."

"Especially since there are eyewitnesses who put her at the scene of the crime."

"Unless she feels protected?"

Erin turned her attention out the window, and I followed her gaze to Atwood's front door. "We better not sit for much longer; someone might see us."

This story was escalating quickly. I didn't like the feeling of constantly being watched by the people sworn to protect me. I inserted the keys and put the car in gear. When the tires set in motion, I said, "Let's pick up your car and then head to the newsroom to speak with Dawson."

Erin sank deeper into her seat. As we traveled across town, silence filled the car. We both settled into our thoughts as if needing time to process the danger of what it was we were accusing Watts of facilitating.

Was it just his luck Erin was being questioned for a murder she didn't commit on the same night King was suspended? How deep into this was Atwood already? What other surprises were waiting for us around the corner?

I kept circling back to the evidence Atwood provided, asking myself if it was worth the emotional distress to proceed. He was making serious allegations, and now we knew it wasn't just the chief who was involved but a handful of officers doing his dirty work for supposed political gain. And, worse, it had to explain the text the other night at the station mentioning Mason being home alone. Was that officer Barber, too?

I kept glancing in the rearview mirror. Erin was tense, too. I was sure she was anxious to meet with Jackie to clear her name. We had to call her out for appearing to set Erin up for Russ's murder.

I drove back to Russ's apartment complex, and we found Erin's red bronco still parked where she'd left it. The chaos from last night evaporated with the sun, but I suspected Russ's front door would still be taped off until the investigation was complete. Besides, there was nothing there for us.

"Oh, shit," Erin said, stretching her neck.

I parked behind her car and noticed it too. Her back right window had been busted in. As soon as the wheels stopped rolling, she flung her door open and hurried to inspect the damage. I joined her a moment later. It was clear someone had rummaged through her car.

"Is anything missing?" I asked.

Erin crawled inside, opening the glovebox and looking behind the seats. "It doesn't look like it."

I looked up and down the block. Was this a random break in, or could it have been someone hoping to score a quick insight into the work we were conducting? Luckily, Erin kept all the important files at her house. Then she said, "It has to be Jackie."

"Huh?" I hurried to the door and peeked my head inside, watching her reach for something on the floor. "What? Why?"

Erin twisted around and dropped a rock in my hand. Secured to the rock by a rubber band was a square piece of paper with a phrase I recognized immediately. *When life imitates game, you become the star of your own show.*

CHAPTER FIFTY-EIGHT

I KEPT GLANCING IN THE REARVIEW. ERIN KEPT PACE behind me, glued to my tail despite the busted-out window blowing her blonde hair across her face in the cool fall air. It didn't appear she saw the tail we'd picked up, but I did.

Three cars back, a black sedan kept its distance hoping to not be seen.

I first noticed it soon after leaving Russ's street. The driver must have known we'd come for Erin's car and they'd waited. Had they been waiting all night? How soon after she was hauled to the station had her car been broken into? Was this a cop like the make and model suggested?

The next time I glanced back, I caught Erin staring in her mirror. Her expression didn't change, but I knew she saw it now, too. There was no reason to hide or try to escape. We kept our wheels straight, figuring the newsroom was as safe as anywhere else. Until then, we'd see how it played out.

But that didn't stop my heart from thumping in my chest.

I kept thinking of the quote left for Erin, the same one the drone was dropping at GamersCon while Vince recreated April's death on the big screen for everyone to see. It had me thinking about what last night's witness kept saying about Jackie, how her proportions seemed off. Could it have been Vince dressed as Jackie? I didn't know, but the thought planted its seed of doubt inside my head.

As soon as we arrived, I purposely parked out front where eyes and security cameras could keep watch over me. I was the first to step out and met Erin at her car while keeping an eye on the sedan, now parked down the block, driver staring.

"You see, we were being followed?" I asked at Erin's window.

Erin nodded. "Cops."

"If only they had the balls to show us their faces," I said, knowing they were only here to intimidate us. Then I met her eye and asked, "Is your house locked up?"

"Always. You should start yourself. It's a good habit to get into."

I told her I was working on it. "What are the chances your car was broken into by the very cops we're about to expose?"

"After the fear I saw flash in Atwood's eyes," Erin gathered her things and exited the car, "I'd say pretty good."

We left the sedan waiting and headed toward the newsroom entrance, steeling myself against whatever was sure to come our way. My thoughts bounced between Kovac and Officer Barber, wondering if they were one and the same. Once inside, I found an unhappy Dawson in editorial. He asked, "Why am I hearing about Russ's death from everybody but my crime beat reporter?"

"It's a long story," I said.

"A story that should have been on my desk when I arrived to work this morning." Dawson flicked his gaze to Erin and didn't look happy to see her.

With Atwood's files in my hand, I said, "I've got an even bigger story you're going to want to hear."

Dawson stared for a beat, then folded his arms and said, "Close the door."

As Erin closed the door, I told Dawson about Atwood and his wanting to get in on our fight against Watts. Dawson took five minutes to review the files and, when he finished, he said, "It looks legit, and I like how we caught the attention of the public defender, but are we sure we want to go down this road?"

"We're already down this road," I said. "I can't turn back now."

Dawson shook his head and sighed. "This is different. He's naming cops. We didn't have this information before. Once we take it public, it's on us to come through."

"Atwood is willing to go on record," I said, looking toward Erin. She was ready for a fight. I could see it in her eyes and the way she carried herself. Her shoulders were rolled back, her eyes narrow and unwavering. She was already planning her role. For the first time, I envied her freedom to skip Dawson's approval to begin bringing the story to our private audience.

Dawson asked, "And what does he want in return?"

"He wants to be the face," I said.

"A photo op?"

I nodded.

Dawson pushed back in his chair. "There it is. How can you be so obtuse?"

I didn't react—wouldn't give him the pleasure. I said, "I'm going to pretend you didn't say that."

"It's political, Sam." Dawson waved his hand through the air. "A career move that will only benefit him."

"You're scared. I get it. I am too, but we can't just ignore what's been given to us. This is big, bigger than anything we've worked in the past—"

"Yes. And it's also dangerous. Not only for him. But for all of us."

"It will sell a lot of papers," Erin said in a tone that sang.

Dawson tossed her a look that said, *Why are you even here?*

"Don't try to talk me out of it because you won't win. Not with the death threats I have already received." I paused to calm my racing heart. "Besides, this is nothing new for us. We've published big scandals in the past and were rewarded for our efforts."

I knew he was thinking about my safety, and Mason's too. I appreciated his concerns, but we couldn't let that stop us from finishing the job we started.

"If we stop now, they win," I said, telling him that we were followed to the newsroom after finding Erin's car broken into. Erin mentioned how she was taken in for questioning for Russ's murder, and I added, "If we don't fight these dirty cops, who will?"

Dawson's Adam's apple slid up his throat as he stared. A minute passed before he bent over and retrieved something from his desk drawer. "I'm sending you to Boulder."

"Isn't it too late for that?"

"We made a mistake when we passed up Russ's offer."

Erin shared a look with me. I asked Dawson, "What are you talking about?"

"Apparently his video may have been real." Dawson's eyebrows raised. "And if April Wright was murdered, I need you to prove it."

CHAPTER FIFTY-NINE

I LEFT DAWSON'S OFFICE FEELING ANNOYED. WE WERE four steps ahead of him on April's story. It felt like his change of heart to send me to Boulder was not only late, but also driven by an ulterior motive I hadn't yet figured out.

What did he know that I didn't? Did it have anything to do with Vincent?

Phone in hand, I texted Atwood telling him our plan was a go when Erin asked, "Why didn't you mention anything about Jackie to Dawson?"

"Because Dawson wants me to prove April was murdered *without* putting myself in danger."

"What's his deal, anyway?" Erin didn't like the way Dawson kept glaring at her.

"His deal is he's worried about losing me."

Erin huffed a quick laugh and shook her head. "We have a good thing going with our podcast and blog, but you're still working for him."

I flicked my eyes to Erin. "If it were only that simple. It's not you he's worried about. It's that we still don't know who's stalking me and sending me threats."

"He's worried you're going to get killed?"

"Aren't you?"

"Should I be?"

We weaved between cubicles and nodded our heads at my colleagues, at least the ones who bothered looking up. I thought about how Dawson's indecisiveness was killing this story softly, whether intentionally or not, and if we weren't careful, one mistake in the wrong direction and we'd lose it altogether.

Erin said, "We need to get that video from Jackie."

"If she even has it," I said, getting Erin to stop.

"You think she doesn't?"

I reminded her about the witness I spoke with last night. "She said the woman she saw outside Russ's apartment had odd bodily proportions. What if it wasn't Jackie who was there, but somebody who wanted us to believe it was her?"

"Then I want to hear Jackie's alibi myself, because I know what I saw and I'm sure it was her."

I suspected Erin didn't want our work on Watts's scandal to get in her way of confronting Jackie. I couldn't blame her. She had a lot hanging over her head. It was the same juggling act I was constantly debating with myself. No matter how much time I spent thinking about it, I still didn't have an answer. Both stories were important. Now that we were working with Atwood, neither could be put off for the other.

I asked Erin, "Doesn't it ruffle your feathers that Atwood needs this photo op? He knows his day will come if the story produces the results we all believe it will."

Erin shrugged her shoulders. "It's a small price to pay for getting a bad man out of office."

"I know. It just doesn't sit well with me," I said, thinking how it seemed no one could just do the right thing without receiving something in return.

When we stepped inside my work cubby, Erin saw the

envelope first. She handed it to me and I looked to see who it was from. "The *L.A. Times*," I said.

"Maybe your assumptions about Dawson aren't what they seem."

I opened the envelope, unfolded the letter, and silently read it. Now I understood why it seemed Dawson was giving me the freedom to write what I wanted—why he seemed afraid of losing me.

"What's it say?" Erin asked.

"They want me to come work for them." I tipped my chin, and we locked eyes. "Word must have gotten back to Dawson."

"That's a big paper. Could be a great opportunity for you."

I tossed Erin a look. "You can't be serious?"

"I'm not." Erin winked.

"Good," I said. "Because this letter was dead on arrival."

I lowered myself into my seat and tucked the letter back inside the envelope, needing to forget about it. There was no way I could accept the position, but the least I could do was call the editor back and thank them for recognizing my hard work.

"I'm not going anywhere," I said, thinking about Mason and King, and Erin, my business partner. But the more I dragged it out, the more I wondered if some part of me, deep down, really wanted to at least explore what might be waiting for me on the West Coast.

My cellphone buzzed, and I was thankful for the distraction. It was a text from Atwood.

After reading it, I said to Erin, "We're on for tomorrow morning. He'll arrange a press conference to get his picture taken and we'll release the beginning of our story simultaneously to make sure we get credit for breaking the story first."

Erin inhaled a deep breath and said, "Ready or not, here we come."

CHAPTER SIXTY

OVER THE NEXT HALF HOUR, WE WORKED THE PHONES trying to track down a copy of Russ's video. It was certainly possible he sold it before he died and we weren't willing to take any chances. Our meeting with Jackie wasn't for hours and, since I was still waiting to hear back from Allison, it felt like we had all the time in the world.

I hung up the receiver and shook my head no at Erin.

"Me neither," she muttered.

Not a single hit. I couldn't find anyone in my list of contacts who admitted buying it, though we all wished we had.

Erin tapped her pen and asked, "If Jackie killed Russ to make the video disappear, why bother meeting with us today?"

"To appear normal? Maybe gain insight into what we know about the investigation?" I didn't know. We could speculate all day about what Jackie was thinking, but the only certainty was knowing it was a race to be the first to track down both her and the video.

Was King right? Were we chasing ratings without realizing what it was we were doing?

Erin said, "It won't take other reporters long to link Jackie to Russ and connect her to the video. And, if that happens, we'll also be linked to Russ's auction."

"I don't think they're linking Vincent to either of the murders," I said, reminding Erin how Russ tried to sell me the video a second time after first being denied by Dawson. The regret burned badly, but even I didn't believe the video was real at the time.

"Tell me again," Erin leaned back in her chair, "what did you see on the video that made you think it was fake?"

I told her about the arm shoving April over the balcony rail and that it was almost too fuzzy to make out. I said, "It wasn't conclusive, and if it weren't for the fact that Jackie seemed so interested in having it for herself, I would have let it go. Her concern made her and Vince look guilty."

Erin sighed and cast her gaze to her notes. The video was all we had. An arm caught in the frame which suggested murder, with no way of identifying whether it belonged to a man or woman. I had to believe it was real. Otherwise, April's death was only suicide.

Erin asked, "Anything from Allison yet?"

I shook my head no. "She'll get it. Once she gets the audio, hopefully it will reveal why April had to go."

"All we have is speculation." Erin closed her eyes and rubbed her temples.

My phone rang, and I was quick to answer. "Heidi," I said, looking Erin in the eye. "Thanks for calling back."

"I heard about Erin. How is she doing?"

"She's fine. Sitting next to me now."

"That's great," she said, followed by a moment of silence. "Though I never heard of a reporter getting arrested like that."

"Wrong place, wrong time," I said, letting her know it wasn't an actual arrest but an interview Erin freely participated in. There was something off about Heidi's voice. She sounded tired, and I hoped that was all it was. "Did you get my message?" I asked.

She said she had. "My producer talked to Russ but, like the *Times,* also turned him down. We didn't see what he saw, and he came across as a desperate salesman. I mean, how could it be real? No one else had what he had, I checked. And with as many people who were in attendance that night, somebody else would have caught it on film." Heidi paused. "But then he died and opinions changed."

I held the phone to my ear and kept my eyes steady on Erin. Heidi didn't seem her usual self, and I wondered if it had anything to do with her concerns about being stalked.

"Sam, everyone I've spoken to about Russ thinks Erin has the video."

The crease between my eyes deepened. Heidi didn't say that everyone also thought Erin killed Russ, but her tone suggested they did.

"It's absurd, but aren't all rumors?"

Heidi tried to laugh, but it fell flat. All I could do was glance to Atwood's report fanned out across my desk and question how in the world Erin was getting framed for murder.

I asked, "Receive any new threats worth reporting?"

"Things are quiet."

"That's good," I said, catching her up on the latest details about our fight against Watts. "If you haven't already heard, there's a presser with the public defender scheduled for ten tomorrow morning."

"I'm sorry, Sam. I can't keep doing this. I wish I could. I just don't have it in me to keep fighting something I don't think we can win."

"I understand," I said, acknowledging how mentally taxing this battle was on us all. We were all suffering and the longer it dragged on, the deeper the scars got.

"Be careful, Sam," Heidi said in a soft voice. "This story... it feels different."

"I will."

When I got off the phone, Erin asked, "What did she say?"

I was at a loss for words. I couldn't tell her about the rumors floating around that she had Russ's video. Erin needed to have her head clear for our meeting with Jackie. Instead, I said, "She's out. It's just you and me against Watts."

Erin fell back in her chair with disbelief. "Let's call Jackie. Ask to bump up our meeting. We need to know if we're wasting our time so we can get ready for tomorrow."

As soon as I leaned forward, my cellphone buzzed. This time it was a call from Mason.

"Hey, sweetie. What's up?"

"You said I should tell you if I saw anything strange while playing my game?"

"Did you?"

"It's happening again, Mom. This time he's using a car to mow over pedestrians and is streaming it live."

When I asked, Mason confirmed it was Trojan behind the online acts of violence. All I could see in my mind was the rock tossed through Erin's car window.

"I don't know if this helps, or if it's what you're looking for, but it's generating tons of buzz online and thought you should know."

"Thanks," I said, thinking it might be a possible glimpse into the future. But the bigger question was, if this was another premonition, who was next?

CHAPTER SIXTY-ONE

ALLISON SAT RAMROD STRAIGHT AS HER FINGERS PECKED fiercely against the keys. She liked working under pressure—liked when the stakes were high—but hated worrying about what kind of trouble her friend might be getting herself into.

King had her believing Sam was making a grave mistake by meeting with Jackie Dumont. That wouldn't be Sam's first mistake, either. There was already Spyware on her computer. What were they trying to learn and what didn't they want Samantha to find out?

She was close to getting the audio clear on the video she was working on but, like most things lately, it was one step forward, two steps back. Her cellphone dinged. A text message from Sam.

Anything?

Allison palmed her phone and wrote back, *King's video is a fake.*

And the other?

Still working. Thinking I should give the video to Boulder PD???

Sam didn't respond right away, but when she did, she said, *Hang back until we know what the conversation is about.*

Allison sighed, set her phone down on top of her desk, and continued working.

The deepfake of King had her most intrigued. She'd read many articles on these types of videos, seen examples online, but this was the first behind-the-scenes tour she'd been on. It excited her to break down the code and learn more about the future of misinformation. But she was shocked at how close to home it struck, and at the city level, too. Perhaps that was why she was able to read it so easily. A minute later, there was a knock on her front door.

"What did he forget?" Allison muttered, thinking it was King. "It's open!" she called out.

The knocks continued, and Allison reluctantly made her way to the front and answered. A muscular man who was impeccably dressed greeted her at the door. They locked eyes, and he smiled.

Allison stood in his shadow, thinking of the mysterious man who gave her the link to the video Samantha wanted her to crack. Though it wasn't the same face as what she remembered, Allison did wonder why she'd suddenly become so popular among unsolicited introductions. Customers didn't just come to her door uninvited.

Allison asked, "Can I help you?"

"I certainly hope so." The man smiled and removed his sunglasses, revealing his ocean-glimmer gaze. "Your friend Susan Young sent me."

An awkward pause settled between them as Allison got lost in his friendly expression. She wasn't aware Susan was sending her a prospect, and she couldn't even pretend like she was expecting this. Allison leaned to one side, looking past the man and toward the street. King's car was gone. With Patty still recovering from her illness at home, Allison was the only one in the office.

"I'm sorry. I should have called. Perhaps now's not the

best time?" the man asked when seeing doubt cross Allison's face.

Allison gave him a quizzical look and asked, "I'm sorry, what did you say your name was?"

The man let out a friendly laugh. "Name's Garrett Todd." They shook hands. "Susan tried to pimp me off to Samantha, though her beat is different than the one I'm currently working."

"You don't do crime?"

"You do crime, you do the time." They both laughed as Allison told him to come inside. Garrett followed close behind and continued, "Don't get me wrong, Samantha is a lovely woman and I would certainly like to speak with her again."

"So, you two have met?"

"Yes." Garrett explained how he met Samantha at Susan's gala.

Allison suddenly remembered a conversation with Susan where she had briefly mentioned Garrett. She told this to him and apologized for not making the connection sooner.

Garrett waved it off as no big deal and said, "Nice office."

"Thank you," Allison said, adding, "I must admit, I've never worked with a film director before."

He complimented her on the décor, then asked, "What kind of clients do you generally work with?"

"Politicians, local small business owners, and I was poaching clients at GamersCon."

Garrett was staring at a piece of black African art on the wall when he twisted his neck toward Allison and said, "And hopefully now a first-time independent filmmaker?"

"Perhaps." Allison smiled. "Tell me about it."

Garrett moved from one knick-knack to another, saying, "It's a modern coming of age tale about a sensitive boy who navigates a masculine world."

"Sounds interesting." Allison watched Garrett stop to stare at her notes on King's project when, without warning, her computer screen lit up.

Garrett's eyes caught what was on the screen, and he lowered himself down in her chair to stare at the paused image. "That's her," he whispered. "April Wright." Garrett turned and gave Allison a look that made her feel embarrassed. He asked, "Who is April with?"

Feeling her chest tighten with anxiety, Allison hurried to her desk and fumbled to shut off the computer monitor when Garrett's hand stopped her. They locked eyes and a tense beat passed between them. She didn't need him to see this— couldn't afford to have him know what she was working.

"Where did you get this?" he asked.

Allison swallowed and couldn't answer.

"Are you investigating her murder?" When Allison again couldn't answer, he rolled his eyes back to the screen. "I've seen her before, but where?" His eyes squinted in thought. "That's it!" He snapped his fingers. "Vincent Verdi. She's Vincent's girl."

Allison's heart beat faster. She asked, "You know him?"

"Not personally," Garrett said. "But it wouldn't surprise me to learn he was the one who killed April."

Allison's eyebrows drew together.

"Then again, maybe not. All I know is he's homophobic and has said pretty awful things about her in the past." Garrett met Allison's gaze and asked, "What are they saying?"

"They?"

"Samantha. Her cop boyfriend…"

"That's what we're trying to find out. She," Allison pointed to Jackie, "was the last person who saw April—"

"—alive." Garrett finished Allison's thought.

Allison shared what she was trying to do, and Garrett

surprised her by saying, "I don't know if you want me to help, but I am awfully good at reading lips."

Allison stared at Garrett and debated whether she should give him a shot. Though she'd just met him, he was referred by a friend who apparently trusted him. Allison said, "Sure, why not."

Garrett leaned close to the screen as the video clip played. He watched it a couple more times, taking notes each time, making sure to comment on what April seemed to give Jackie. Allison didn't know what was exchanged, but assumed it might have been what got April killed. Then, after the fourth time through, Garrett said, "I think you're right."

"About?"

"I think whatever was exchanged got her killed." Then Garrett told Allison what Jackie said to April.

CHAPTER SIXTY-TWO

Mr. T exited the house from the side door and immediately hid behind a large ponderosa pine. He looked up and down the street to be sure nobody was looking, then peeked his head around the side of the tree to look up into the second-story window. The glare reflected like a mirror making it impossible to see inside. His gut, and the voices inside his head, told him he was being watched.

Move. Now! they screamed.

He tucked his chin and thrust his shoulders back as he hurried to the driveway pavement, pulling the hem of the dress up at his feet as he weaved past the Jeep Wrangler, heading toward his car. A second later, he opened the door to the Dodge Challenger and quickly settled in behind the steering wheel where he angled the rearview to his face. Feeling secure inside the vehicle, Mr. T took his time when fixing his hair. When he was finished touching up his appearance, he slid his shades over his eyes and revved the engine.

The vibrations of the engine tickled his insides, and Mr. T was feeling perky as he backed out of the drive. He laughed and punched the gas, getting the tires to squeal as he raced away from the house.

The wind was in his hair, and the autumn air made his blood pump hot. He was livid, knowing he'd been discovered, and relieved to be running from his problems. How could he trust that word wouldn't get out about what he'd been up to? He couldn't, and that was the worst feeling of all.

Mr. T's world was spiraling out of control. He was no longer piloting his story. He'd have to change tactics if he wanted to continue working on his script. He also had to find a way to keep an eye on this new variable that seemed to come out of the blue, like most villains did.

Dig deep into his past. Find his dirt and blackmail him into keeping his mouth shut, the voices inside his head told him.

Mr. T tilted his head and brought his hand to his kinked neck. Blackmailing White Stallion sounded much easier than having to add his name to a growing list of murders. But would it last? Or was that only a temporary solution?

Suddenly, a dog ran across the road and Mr. T's eyes widened with surprise. His thoughts flashed back to his near-collision last night near Vogue Apartments, but instead of slamming on the brakes and playing it safe, he hit the gas and accelerated toward the slobbering beast, narrowly clipping his hind legs. A roar of laughter ripped past his lips, and Mr. T tightened his grip on the steering wheel and straightened his tires before appearing to be too out of control.

"White Stallion. What a stupid name," he grumbled. "At least Trojan had meaning. Trojan, the computer malware, the one that shares the orbit of a larger one. And now the one who is constantly getting screwed."

He drove like a madman and swerved just for the hell of it. Cars he passed became a blur. Soon, reality dissipated into a series of pixels populating his vision. Before he knew it, Mr.

T was no longer on Earth but inside his game where he visualized a quick hit and run—becoming the star of his own show.

Since he predicted April's death, he was getting what he wanted. Recognition and praise. While happy his online viewership was up and he was creating a name for himself, a deep dissatisfaction remained, burrowing deep into his bones. Something was missing, the pain still present. He'd waited so long for this moment but, now that it was here, he thought he'd feel differently.

"Virtual reality lacked emotion," he said, feeling his anger grow.

He needed to vent, open his chest and let his heart beat freely. Instead, he was trapped in this fake online world, orbiting around a larger energy force, constantly telling him how to live his life. All he wanted was to be seen, to be the person he was inside and go about living his life freely.

He turned onto the next street and came to a stop at the intersection when he caught the driver next to him staring. Did he know who he was? Or just hate the person he was looking at? Wrapped in insecurity, Mr. T was locked in his gaze when the driver winked and smiled.

Mr. T turned his head away and glanced in the rearview. His cheeks were flushed. Was it the dress he liked or something else? Mr. T liked wearing women's clothes, but he hadn't experienced a hot flash like what he was feeling now in a very long time. Despite the anger boiling up inside, he felt confident when saying, "There's no reason to be ashamed, honey. You look great."

An alert on his phone chimed. It was a message from Chas. *I talked to Jackie. Word is she is meeting with reporter, Samantha Bell.* Chas told him where. *Hope this helps.*

"Indeed, it does," Mr. T said, suddenly feeling brighter about his mission ahead. The light flicked from red to green and he turned to find the stranger parked next to him, still smiling. Mr. T blew him a kiss and peeled off the line saying, "Be careful what you wish for. You might just get what you're after."

CHAPTER SIXTY-THREE

King merged into the right lane and took the Buffalo Overlook exit at the top of the hill. At the stop sign, he saw Alvarez was already waiting in the parking lot to his right. With a quick glance to his mirrors, King made sure he hadn't been followed. When the coast was clear, he eased into the lot and parked next to his partner.

His thoughts traveled to Samantha as he reached for his phone. He worried what she and Erin were getting themselves into and counted on Allison to come through with the video audio. He knew Sam wouldn't listen without a reason to back away from her meeting with a potential murderer.

He stepped out and moved in front of his car. The air was as crisp as the cobalt blue skies. He looked west into the mountain prairie—the occasional lone cloud skirting east. Bison grazed peacefully in the pasture as cars and trucks raced past on the highway.

King asked to meet at the top of the hill to keep their meeting discreet. Neither he nor Alvarez could afford to have anyone know they were still in communication, working the case together, while he rode out his internal affairs investigation. As soon as King settled into the passenger seat next to Alvarez, his partner asked, "What took you so long?"

King stared at the coating of snow blanketing the distant mountain peaks, feeling depressed and anxious to clear his name. "I got here as quick as I could." He turned to face Alvarez and asked, "What did you find out?"

"No one is talking. The investigation is sealed but there are whispers suggesting your suspension has something to do with a complaint made by a member of the LGBTQ community."

"But you don't have a name?"

Alvarez shook his head no. "Apparently, it's not the first complaint against DPD by this particular individual."

"Just a first for me."

"Bad luck, I guess." Alvarez shrugged, handing King a list of names to begin his search.

King took the paper into his hand and began reading down the list of names. "There's a video circulating showing that I framed a male suspect." King shared the details and said, "It has to be what kicked off IAD's investigation. It could be that person who issued the complaint."

Alvarez stared and sighed. "A video? Jesus. Alex..."

"It's a fake." King snapped his head up, explaining how his face was digitally manipulated onto the film. "I don't know how they did it, but I think I know who did it."

"Who?" Alvarez asked, and King mentioned Officer Barber. "I knew that guy was dirty," Alvarez said, touching his face.

"I'm sure this is why I'm suspended. If only I knew his name, I could get him to testify it wasn't me, but Barber, who set him up."

Alvarez stared ahead, retreating further into his thoughts, then asked, "What did you do to piss Barber off?"

"He knew I would be suspended." King mentioned his

confrontation with Barber last night outside the precinct. "He knows Samantha is close to uncovering his dirt. She's working with the public defender who is filing appeals to many of Barber's past arrests. Sooner or later his name is going to come up and, when it does, I'm sure it won't be pretty. They're onto him, but he got ahead of the story, so here I am."

"Shit." Alvarez's brow furrowed. This was uglier than he'd imagined. "You know they think you're feeding Samantha department fodder, right?"

King ignored what Alvarez said, knowing it was complete bullshit, and asked, "Do you know the name Kovac?"

"Is he a cop?"

"That's what I'm trying to figure out." Alvarez shook his head no and King said, "I suspect the name is an alias."

"Who is he?" King told him about Sam's source to the original deepfake video and Alvarez said, "I'll see what I can find out. By the way, ballistics came back on Russ Abair."

"And? Was I right?"

"Both slugs in the vic were shot from the same 9MM he was found holding. GSR was on his hands and the death is being preliminarily ruled as undetermined."

King turned his head. The ME's conclusion didn't sit right with him. Two shots to the head? This wasn't undetermined. Not after the video Samantha said was in Russ's possession. This was murder. "Someone killed him for that video of April falling to her death."

"That may be," Alvarez said, catching King's eye. "Nothing is finalized and, as of this moment, I'm investigating it as a homicide. The 9MM wasn't registered to Russ, but hasn't been reported stolen, either. I contacted the Federal Firearms License holder and am still waiting to hear back, but you know this works."

"Wish I didn't."

Alvarez raised one eyebrow. "Chances are, we won't know who purchased or legally owned the weapon."

"The paper trail begins," King said. "Anything else I should know before I go?"

"Actually, yes. That video everyone is after, the one you think Russ was killed for, we managed to recover the original from Russ's safe."

"Did you watch it?"

Alvarez nodded. "It's the same one the media suggested exists that no one has."

"And?"

Alvarez could understand why people were skeptical of its authenticity. He concluded, "It certainly complicates matters."

"Yet the ME's office is still ruling his cause of death undetermined?"

Alvarez shrugged and reached for the files King was still holding. Pulling out a single sheet of paper, he asked, "Is that what you're looking for?"

King stared at the DMV report. "Yeah."

"You look disappointed. Were you expecting a different result?"

"I was," King said. Samantha suspected it would be Jackie Dumont's name on the vehicle registration. "She was seen at Russ's about the same time he was murdered. Maybe she borrowed his car?"

Alvarez leaned back. "But here's the thing, Jackie Dumont hasn't been named a suspect, nor has a warrant gone out for her arrest. Russ Abair's doorbell camera proved it wasn't a woman who entered his apartment, but rather a man dressed as a woman."

CHAPTER SIXTY-FOUR

WE KICKED STONES UNTIL IT WAS TIME TO HIT THE ROAD and meet with Jackie. I didn't like her delaying the meeting or calling the shots. It made her appear guiltier in both of our eyes, but what choice did we have? Our desire to speak with her outweighed everything else. Even our own safety.

When the time finally came, we headed for the exit and strode toward my car. Since Erin's window was busted, I elected to drive. Erin tossed me a look like she wasn't happy to be riding shotgun, and I responded, "What? I don't want to mess up my hair."

Erin laughed. She knew I was joking. I was a ponytail and jeans kind of woman who put more into my work than I did my physical appearance. Besides, if what Mason saw in the video game came to be, it was better we stuck together in one car.

As soon as we were both buckled in, Erin said, "I hate to say it Sam, but we could be Trojan's next target."

Images of Vince flashed in my mind as I thought about the rock thrown through Erin's window and the note attached to it. Erin's concern had crossed my mind as well, but I didn't have the courage to admit it. At least not out loud. "I just hope I'm doing the right thing asking Mason to help," I said.

"I think he would have done it regardless."

Mason was a good kid, but like any mother, I wanted to protect him. He was surrounded by investigators and his father had been a cop. Sleuthing was in his blood. Still, I wouldn't be able to live with myself if something happened to him.

Reaching for my phone, I called my sister and asked if she could come to the house and hang out with Mason until I was done with work. Heather asked me, "When is this going to stop?" She knew something wasn't right, and I told her it was this Chief Watts story I was working. Heather said, "I can hang out with him. The boy needs an adult role model."

"Thank you," I said. The pang of guilt my sister stabbed into my side did not go unnoticed.

"But don't expect me to watch him play video games the entire time."

"Just be a healthy presence inside the house."

Once I was off the phone, I kept thinking of the intimidation tactics used to silence Erin and me. It wasn't only the online threats I was thinking about, but also Officer Barber making sure Erin knew who he was. It was also the taunting of Vincent Verdi and his arrogance in thinking he couldn't be touched that had me feeling tense. Each ounce of tension weighed heavily on me when I flicked my gaze in Erin's direction and began to think about what Heidi suggested about her—that Russ's video wasn't missing, but in Erin's possession.

Erin was on her phone, deep in thought. I hated to even question my friend. Did she have Russ's video? Erin had never kept anything from me before, so why would she start now? I asked her to go to Russ's. There was nothing surprising about any of it. Right?

Erin didn't notice me staring as I remembered the look she had when leaving the precinct last night. She barely said anything about what she saw inside Russ's apartment, but I knew the images of his murder were a constant behind her eyes.

Was that all this was about? I wanted to tell her about the rumors, but I didn't know how. Instead, I kept the wheels straight, deciding to focus on how to handle Jackie.

"She comes across as a snake," Erin said about Jackie, concerned about the danger we might be facing, and I agreed.

I asked, "Are you sure you didn't see the video anywhere in Russ's apartment?"

"She has it, Sam. I'm afraid that, because she does, it's going to disappear. Or, worse, randomly pop up out of the blue, surprising us all."

I hadn't thought of that, and I didn't like it. Erin didn't give off any signs to suggest she wasn't as worried as I was, and I was thankful to have a rock to lean on.

All signs were pointing to Jackie as being the guilty party, but if Trojan was Vince, were we the next to die like Erin's instinct suspected we could be? Could Jackie really be the one doing Vince's dirty work?

Our nerves were high and I couldn't bear to listen to music as we drove north. A part of me doubted Jackie would have the courage to show. Why would she? We had nothing to offer in return for her giving us Vince's side of the story. I shared my thoughts with Erin, and she reminded me, "Unless her story incriminates him."

"Then why tell us and not the police?"

"Trials are won outside the courtroom," Erin solemnly said.

Erin had a point. Maybe Jackie was using us to tell her

story. When I let that thought sink further into my brain, I began to believe Jackie might actually have Russ's video, and could actually give it to us, too.

We turned into the department store complex and snaked around the front before finding a place to park beneath an oak tree. Making sure I had my phone before I stepped out, I wished Allison would crack that audio soon. If only we knew what Jackie said to April, then maybe we'd know who was responsible for her murder. And know what to expect might be heading our way. Then I received a call from King that changed everything.

CHAPTER SIXTY-FIVE

"ARE YOU SURE?" I ASKED KING.

King said, "It was caught on the security camera. Alvarez wouldn't have told me if he thought it wasn't real."

"Jesus." I tossed a look to Erin. "This is good news then."

"That's one way of looking at it," King said, continuing on that motor vehicle records show Vincent owned a Dodge Challenger.

I covered the microphone with my hand and asked Erin, "Is it possible it was Vince you saw driving away from Russ's, and not Jackie?"

A wave of doubt twisted Erin's face. "It was dark. All I saw was a woman with red hair."

With my eyes, I followed a car traveling across the parking lot. That it could have been Vince who killed Russ threw me for a loop. Erin was confident in what she *thought* she saw up until a second ago. Her sudden doubt made me need to know where Vince was now.

"Did you meet with Jackie yet?" King asked.

"We just arrived. No sign of her yet," I said, thinking how I was prepared to face Jackie head on and have her answer some tough questions. But now I wasn't so sure the questions I had planned on asking were relevant.

I thought about what the eyewitness I spoke to last night said about the redhead at Russ's building, and it left my head spinning. What the heck was happening? If it wasn't Jackie who killed Russ, then who did? Vince Verdi? Was that what King was telling me?

Erin touched my shoulder and whispered in my ear, "There's Jackie. Over there."

I turned and stared at the redheaded beauty, looking for anything odd about her bodily proportions. Nothing looked off. Now I wondered if we were meeting with friend or foe.

CHAPTER SIXTY-SIX

JACKIE DIDN'T SEE US RIGHT AWAY, AND I INTENTIONALLY stayed close to the car as I relayed my conversation with King to Erin. Erin immediately started looking for the Dodge Challenger she nearly collided with last night, beginning to doubt her own story.

"I know what I saw, Sam."

"I'm just telling you what King said."

Jackie's dress was long and free flowing. She wore a leather jacket and had her hands buried deep inside the pockets. I couldn't see anything out of the ordinary that matched last night's witness, but I still thought we should be cautious until we knew exactly where she was last night—and who she was with.

Erin was particularly critical. Neither of us could believe how brazen Jackie was to be openly moving in public with suspicions of murder swirling around her.

"That still doesn't explain who put a rock through my Bronco window," Erin said in a clipped tone that put me further on edge.

"Just keep cool," I said when Jackie spotted us.

We moved to the rear of my car and let Jackie come to us. I reminded Erin of our plan to blame Jackie for the murders in hopes of getting her to confess, or admit she didn't do it, but Vince did.

"Ladies." Jackie greeted us with a smile. "I apologize for having to delay our meeting, but a girl's gotta do what a girl's gotta do."

She was so casual in her approach, I hoped she was as oblivious as she sounded. I paid close attention to her hands when I asked, "Where's Vince?"

Jackie gave some lame excuse of how Vince couldn't make it, and Erin lost it. Erin lunged forward with an accusatory growl. "When life imitates game, you become the star of your own show!"

"Ahh…" Jackie didn't budge at Erin's anger, and her smirk only made things worse. "I should have assumed you would be taking notes at GamersCon."

"It was tossed through my car window last night, and I know it was you!"

I put my arm out and stopped Erin before she brought her claws out. She was tall and surprisingly strong, yet I managed to hold her back. I didn't want to lose Jackie before this meeting even got started. That would be counterproductive to everything we'd accomplished so far. We needed to ease into our approach and use our heads to outwit our opponent, not physically wrestle them to the ground like Erin wanted.

"You don't have to worry about the video of April's murder getting out," I said to Jackie. "Russ is dead."

Jackie tucked her chin and gave a puzzled look. Was it real? Or was she acting? I couldn't decide.

Calmly, I asked, "Did you take it?"

Her lips parted, and she seemed genuinely offended. Jackie asked me, "Are you suggesting I killed him?"

I mentioned Russ's auction and how we assumed we were in a bidding competition with her. Jackie denied it all, still seeming surprised to learn Russ was no longer with us. Erin stepped into the ring, snapping like a dog. "We know you were with April the night she died."

"What was your conversation about?" I asked.

Something in Jackie changed as her gaze flitted between us. Her confidence was suddenly shadowed by looks of betrayal. "That son of a bitch," she muttered.

"What?"

Jackie turned her head away. We gave her a moment to collect her thoughts. Then, without looking, she said, "Vince set me up."

"But you were with April the night she died?"

Jackie looked me in the eye and nodded her head, admitting she was.

"Who saw you two together?" She didn't know, but assumed it was Vince. Still not knowing whether or not I could trust her story, I asked, "Did you invite April to the show?"

"I did, but now I wish I hadn't."

"Why?"

"Because she was posting about Vince being gay."

"What?" I was reminded of the mean homophobic rants I read across his social media channels. Was Jackie throwing me for a loop? Or was this man she represented actually gay?

Jackie said, "That's his secret that can't get out." Then she told us how April was quick to take her comment down, but it was too late. The damage was already done. "April breached the contract she and Vince agreed upon—"

"But so did Vince if April came to his show," I said,

surprising Jackie that I knew about April's restraining order she had on Vince.

Jackie said, "That night we agreed to put an end to their shared hostility. April just wanted Vince to stop his attacks. But he couldn't, because his hatred of her was what made him famous."

"But she knew his secret."

"Not just knew it, but had proof that Vince couldn't refute." Jackie mentioned a video without giving specifics. She swept her gaze to Erin as the world around us grew quiet. "If it gets out, everything he's built is ruined. It's the greatest irony, I know. But until April gave him what he wanted, he couldn't risk letting up."

Erin asked, "And you have this video?"

Jackie inhaled a deep breath as if deciding whether or not to say. Then, out of nowhere, we heard the air fill with screams and shouts for us to get out of the way. I turned my head and saw a dark car careening toward the three of us.

My heart raced as my eyes widened in disbelief. Did the driver not see us, or were they purposely aiming to take us out?

The engine roared, and the car moved faster. Erin reached for me, clamping her fingers around my arm, and yanked so hard my joints felt like they'd been ripped from their sockets. We both fell between the parked cars as we heard the front end of the car smash directly into Jackie's knees. I heard her body land on the windshield and listened to the glass crack as she went flying into the air. I watched it all in a state of awe, not believing what I was seeing. She landed on the pavement with a skull-cracking thud that made me jump.

My hand flew over my mouth, and I started trembling.

It was exactly as Mason warned.

Vince must have been behind the wheel, but I didn't catch the driver's face.

Against Erin's wishes, I broke free from her grip and ran to see if I could catch the plate numbers. It was too late before I even stood. The car, a Dodge Challenger, was already across the parking lot, speeding away and disappearing into traffic. When I turned and cast my gaze to Jackie, I knew she was already dead.

CHAPTER SIXTY-SEVEN

I PULLED MY HAND AWAY FROM JACKIE'S NECK AND CLOSED her eyes with my opposite hand. She didn't have a pulse. There was nothing we could do. We'd lost her.

Erin came up next to me and crouched down by my side. She placed a hand on my shoulder and a lump caught in my throat.

How did I let this happen?

Guilt swelled in my chest as I thought about Trojan's warning, that people thought he was Vincent Verdi. A Dodge Challenger killed Jackie, and everything inside me said it was the same vehicle registered to Vince. I knew who was responsible, but I didn't know how to prove it.

"Do you think she has the video?" Erin asked.

Without a moment's hesitation, I searched every pocket I could find on Jackie but came out empty-handed. There was no disk, no CD-ROM, no thumb-drive, nothing. I turned my head, locking eyes with Erin as I shook my head no.

Erin said, "I guess we should just hope Vince doesn't get his hands on it first."

I was afraid he already had.

Erin stood and said, "Here comes our reinforcement."

As I swept my gaze up, I saw a handful of bystanders rushing toward us. I knew they were here to help, but I wasn't in the mood for talking. I fell back on my bottom and rested my elbows on my knees as I sat on the pavement and continued to stare at Jackie.

"Are you all right?" a broad-shouldered man in his fifties said to both of Erin and me. "Jesus, that car came out of nowhere." He turned and gaped at Jackie. The sight made him visibly sick.

Erin asked him, "Did you get a look at the driver?" The man was still locked in on the blood pooling in front of Jackie's face, and Erin turned to the growing crowd. "Anyone?"

Another woman stepped up and said, "I took a photo of the plates. The cops are on their way now."

I joined the man in staring at Jackie. We didn't need the plate number. It was safe for us to assume we knew who the car was registered to. I met the woman's gaze and asked, "What about the driver; did you get a look at them?"

Her cheeks paled next to her round eyes, and she nodded yes. "Male. Twenties. Blonde hair. Pink shaded glasses." Her eyebrows pinched. "Are you sure you're all right?"

I blinked and felt numb inside. I couldn't look her in the eye. Finally, I turned my head away, grateful to only be shaken up while uninjured. Erin kneeled next to me, hooked my arm around her shoulder, and together we stood. We stepped back and huddled near my car, away from the prying strangers who insisted they could help.

"When the cops get here, they're going to ask us what happened," Erin said close to my ear.

"Mason warned us," I murmured. "Still, we couldn't stop it from happening." I flicked my watery eyes to Erin. "We knew this was coming and we couldn't stop it. How can we stop him if we couldn't stop this?"

Erin took me by the shoulders and looked me straight in the eye. I was grateful for her strength. "Our story needs to be consistent," she assured me. "When the police show, we can't give them any reason to block our work with Atwood. We can't let them scare us. Do you hear me, Samantha?"

I was in shock but said I understood. While we could, we rehashed what we saw, where we were in our conversation with Jackie, and what followed next. We were both convinced it was Vince behind the wheel. But there was something else worth noting.

I said to Erin, "The killer broke his pattern."

Erin broke eye contact, turned her head, and glanced at Jackie when the first squad car arrived. "Her death wasn't made to look like a suicide."

There was nothing more worrisome than a loose cannon, I thought. Vince had nothing left to lose. He was just a madman on the loose now that his secret was out. There was no telling what he would do next, or how bad it would be.

CHAPTER SIXTY-EIGHT

AFTER A QUICK MEDICAL EVALUATION, THE FIRST TWO police officers to arrive pulled Erin and me off to the side and began taking our statements. The female officer asked me standard questions that were easy to answer.

Did I know Jackie? Were we close? What had we been doing in the parking lot? I answered them to the best of my ability and kept waiting for her to recognize my name so she could begin her harassment. But that never came. Then she asked me, "Did you get a good look at the car?"

"I did," I said, telling her it was a Dodge Challenger. "This was no accident. The driver meant to hit us."

The officer gave me a funny look, and she finally asked me something that caught me by surprise. "Have you had any threats on your life recently?"

I didn't want to lie, but I saw no other choice. It was too complicated to explain and had nothing to do with what happened here. A part of me still thought that maybe a DPD officer was behind my threats, but Vince did tease us with a drone at GamersCon and a rock was thrown through Erin's car window that looked like it came from Vince. Either way, what we were planning to do with Atwood was bigger than just me. So I told the officer, "No," and kept it at that.

She scribbled the last of her notes and took my information before handing me her card. "We'll call you if anything else pops up. If you remember anything else, you can call that number there." She pointed to the center of the card with the end of her pen. "That's my direct line."

I stuffed the business card into my back pocket and leaned against the back of my car. Erin was still being interviewed by the male officer and a shiver moved down my spine. He seemed stern with his questions, but Erin kept her cool. We had nothing to hide about this incident. We wanted the same as the cops—for Vince to be taken into custody so this madness would stop.

Tucking my hands beneath my armpits, I watched a white cloth get draped over Jackie as another set of officers blocked off the surrounding area with police tape, waiting for investigators to arrive. They were treating it as a hit and run when it should have been reviewed as a potential homicide of the first degree.

When Erin was finished giving her statement, she met me by my car and said, "That went better than I expected."

As we rehashed our interviews, it was clear our stories matched other eyewitnesses' accounts. Erin was never asked about Russ or the video he had. Everything was as cut and dried as it seemed, and that made me believe the worst was behind us.

"If we let this go, will Vince stop killing?" Erin asked me.

I could hear it in her tone. Her spirit had been fractured by what we witnessed play out here today. It was nice to know she was as much human as I was. "I don't know," I said when my cellphone buzzed in my pocket. I reached for it. It was a call from Atwood. As soon as I answered, he said, "I just heard what happened. Are you all right?"

"I'm fine. But the woman we were with is dead."

"Yes. I heard. Jackie Dumont. Tragic. You're lucky though, Samantha. I think that car was meant for you."

CHAPTER SIXTY-NINE

ATWOOD SEEMED ESPECIALLY PARANOID, AND THAT MADE me nervous. What did he know that we didn't? His words kept repeating inside my head, comparing them to what actually happened. Could he be right? Had Vince meant to take aim at me and missed?

"Who was that? Was that King?" Erin asked, noticing the concern line my face.

I shook my head no. "Atwood. He heard about what happened." Erin gave me a questioning look. I said, "He thought the car that hit Jackie was meant for us."

Erin turned her head and looked at the scene, as if studying it with a fresh perspective. "Why would he think we were the target?"

"Perhaps all three of us were," I said, thinking of the Dodge Challenger and how neither of us caught a glimpse of the driver's face. Was it Vince, or another of Chief Watts's dirty cops hoping to silence our story? I didn't know, but liked to think it was Vince.

It was getting dark, and more news vans and reporters

were showing up. Erin was growing especially anxious, and I couldn't blame her with the rumor that was going around about her having Russ's video. "Let's get out of here before we have to face more questions from our own," she said.

I mentioned to one of the investigators that we'd like to leave, and they helped direct us out of the parking lot. A few miles away, we settled into our thoughts. I kept checking my mirrors, paranoid about the slightest abnormalities.

"Let's get your car and collect our thoughts at home," I said.

Erin nodded and continued to watch the city lights pass us by.

Russ's video was still missing, and I wondered if it was Vince who had it, like King thought. Jackie was surprised to learn Vince betrayed her. I was beginning to believe her initial reaction was completely genuine.

Once again, we were after Vince. I couldn't deny how great he was at hiding in plain sight for being so popular. But would he have traveled all the way from Boulder to Denver to kill one of his own? If so, why? Was he concerned about what Jackie knew? Why was owning being gay so hard? These same questions circled my head all the way to the newsroom as I tried to make sense of my day.

As soon as Erin's Bronco came within sight, she said, "I really need to do something about that window."

I pulled up next to it and saw Dawson leaving the office. He eyed my car and hurried over to me. I rolled down my window, and he greeted me with his worries.

"Christ, Samantha. Is what I'm hearing true?"

I told him everything, at least the condensed version of what happened to us tonight. "I'm okay," I said. "We both are."

Dawson said, "Maybe you should think about backing off the story with Atwood. It's not too late to do so."

There was no way in hell I was backing out now. I looked Dawson straight in the eye and said, "This story is bigger than just selling a few papers. It's about protecting the people of Denver. If we stop now Chief Watts will win, and then what? We're still on for tomorrow, are you?"

CHAPTER SEVENTY

MR. T REACHED FOR THE GARAGE DOOR HANDLE AND FELT his fingers tremble for the first time. He paused for a beat, concentrating on the throb at the tip of his finger as he stared ahead and remembered the damage done to the vehicle. How was he going to fix it without raising any red flags? The front right corner was completely crushed and there was a missing headlight, not to mention the form of a human body splintering the windshield.

A full body tremble shook his core.

The memory of what happened was coming back to him. He hadn't blacked out, but had stepped out. Stepped into his alternate reality the moment he received the message from Chas. He could still feel his foot stomp on the gas pedal, propelling him forward as he erratically weaved down the highway leading him to the impending crash.

It happened so fast and exactly how it played out before him in his game. Like the times before, in that moment of impact and death, he became the center of the universe—the star of his own show.

A door slammed somewhere across the street and Mr. T

whipped his head around, feeling his heart drum. He held his breath, waited, and listened. A wave of paranoia spiraled up his spine as he kept still.

On his way back to the house, he'd taken the side streets to keep a low profile, not needing to draw unwanted attention to himself. But it was possible he'd been followed. There were plenty of eyewitnesses at the scene of the crash, and he was certain the cops were now looking for a Dodge Challenger with a smashed up front end.

When the neighborhood dogs quieted, he pulled down the garage door in one fluid motion to keep the noise down, and turned toward the house with his belongings tucked beneath one arm. He entered through the side door, taking the stairs to the bedroom where he locked himself inside. Once the door shut, he leaned against the wall and stood still in the dim light, processing his night.

His throat closed. When his blood quaked, the dress and red wig he was holding fell to the floor and pooled by his feet. Wanting to cry, he moved to the bathroom and turned on the shower. He stepped into the cold water where he stood, fully clothed, for the next twenty minutes feeling absolutely numb.

After, he slipped into a pair of gym shorts and added a couple sprays of cologne for good measure to take the smell of exhaust and death off his mind. It worked, but only temporarily.

He messed up. Taken things too far tonight. Mr. T knew this death was different than the others, but what exactly was he feeling? Regret? A deep sense of loss? He didn't know. Truth was, Jackie was a good friend and now she was dead because of him.

"What did I do?"

His mind drew a blank when he caught sight of his camera and hurried to pick it up off the floor. He moved it to the dresser and wanted to watch the clip he filmed, to see if he was lucky enough to catch the action shot he needed to bring his story to life.

"Jackie is dead," he mumbled to himself once again, as if still not fully grasping the reality of what he'd done.

Suddenly, his loss didn't seem so bad when he reasoned with himself. "But she knew all the secrets. Her idea to go gay wasn't the vision I had when first living out my prologue."

His thumb toggled the camera's power button to on, but he couldn't find the courage to watch the film. Jackie's death was fresh on his mind. He just wished he'd been able to get the reporters, too.

"Something will have to be done about that," he said to himself when the doorbell rang.

Panic rose in his chest as his mind hurried to think who could be visiting him. He checked the time and then set the camera down on the dresser before hurrying to the window and pulling back the curtain.

Two uniformed officers were at the front door. Mr. T smirked. "I thought you'd have gotten here sooner."

CHAPTER SEVENTY-ONE

THE SILVER POLICE BADGE FLASHED AGAINST THE streetlight as the officer shifted his feet and angled his chest toward the house. Vincent's heart was pounding in his ears and his palms were damp. Swiping a hand through his hair, another officer emerged from the shadows and Vince gasped.

"What? Two officers?"

Vince looked to the street and counted only one squad car before stepping away from the window. He leapt across the room and pounced on his dresser, pulling open the top drawer before shoveling his camera, cellphone, and thumb-drives into the empty space. Slamming the drawer shut, he did a quick assessment of his room to make sure nothing was left out that he didn't want them to see—if they had a warrant to come inside.

"What else should I hide?"

The doorbell rang again, and Vince hurried to the hallway, snatching a shirt along the way. The cops weren't just going to go away; he needed to give them a reason to move on.

He pushed his arms through the sleeves and nearly

tripped on his way down. He called out to both Chas and Mitch, but neither of them answered.

"Worthless," he cursed as a pang of loneliness stitched his side. Where were they? Why did he feel like he had to do everything around here?

Suddenly, Vince missed Jackie, the one person who would do anything for him. Reminding himself why she needed to go, Vince was perfectly okay to do the heavy lifting himself, at least for tonight.

Stopping at the door, he ironed his hands down the front of his body and took a deep breath before reaching for the door handle. When his heart was calm and his story straight, he opened the door and greeted the two officers with a smile.

"Mr. Vincent Verdi?" the taller of the two officers asked.

"That's me." Vince flicked his gaze over the officer's shoulder, noticing a light left on in the garage. "Something wrong?"

"We'd like to ask you some questions about Jackie Dumont. She's your publicist, right?"

Vince stepped forward, closed the door behind him, and crossed his arms as if to keep off the evening chill. "She was."

"Was?" the second officer asked.

"That's right. Tonight, I had to let her go."

"So, you spoke to her tonight?" When Vince nodded, the officer followed up by asking, "What time was that?"

Vince gave the time.

"And was that the last time you two spoke?"

"It was."

"Was your conversation with her civil?" The air between them grew tense. "How did she take being let go?"

"Did she say something about me?" Vince's expression pinched. "Because we had an agreement."

"She was killed tonight, Mr. Verdi, in a hit-and-run accident." The officer paused for a beat, studying Vince's reaction.

Vince held the officer's strong gaze, assuming they considered him the primary suspect in both April's and Jackie's deaths. Preposterous. Did they not know whose door they'd knocked on? Thinking he should call his lawyer, the officer surprised him when he asked, "Mr. Verdi, do you own a Dodge Challenger?"

Vince's knees buckled. "I do."

"Can we see it?"

Vince ran through several options inside his head and then agreed to lead them across the driveway to his four-bay garage. With the officers hovering behind, Vince punched in the door code and nothing happened. He tried again. Still nothing. The officers glanced at each other and suspected Vince was attempting to delay the inevitable.

"How about we try the side entrance?" an officer suggested.

Vince said, "Sure. Why not?" They moved around the garage, and the moment Vince opened the door, he felt his lips part.

The cops peeked their heads inside and tossed Vince a look. "Where are we supposed to be looking, exactly?"

Vince took his eyes away from the door leading up to the guest loft and said, "I know this is going to be hard to believe," Vince said, "but I think someone stole my car."

CHAPTER SEVENTY-TWO

I PULLED IN BEHIND KING'S TRUCK, REMOVED THE KEYS from the ignition, and gathered my things before stepping out. The city lights turned the sky a deep shade of peach and it felt like a storm was blowing in. I was already missing Erin. I wished she would have come to my house instead of heading home. But I understood her desire to want to sleep in her own bed. We had a big day ahead of us tomorrow and we needed it to go perfectly.

I strode to the house and noticed the front porch light was on. Inside, I could see shadows of activity moving in the window. A smile formed on my face.

Just knowing King was here filled me with confidence. It was like having my personal security detail always keeping an eye out for me and my family, and I couldn't wait to get wrapped up in his arms.

I struggled to lift my feet as I climbed the short flight of stairs on my way inside. It had been such a long day. My shoulders were weighed down with feelings of guilt. I still hadn't processed everything that happened, but somehow it felt like I was responsible for Jackie's death.

The door opened, and I saw King glance behind me. I quickly looked over my left shoulder, paranoid I'd find someone there. There was nothing. Only the monsters living in my head. When I turned back to face King, I started to cry.

He pulled me against his muscled chest and I closed my eyes as the tears fell. I listened to his compassionate heart drum in my ear when he kissed the top of my head and murmured, "I'm sorry about Jackie, but I'm glad you're all right."

I tipped my head back and wiped my cheeks dry. "How is Mason doing?"

"He's shaken up about the whole incident."

"I should have never let him get involved."

"Heather is with him now. He's a strong kid. He'll get through it. We all will."

I regretted my decision to have Mason help us with our investigation. Now that the story of tonight's hit and run was all over the news, it was impossible to hide it from him. As King led me inside, I said, "We were wrong about Jackie. It's Vince the police are after."

"Let's get some rest," King said, not wanting to talk about it.

He was navigating in the dark, had lost his inside edge, and I could see the uncertainty swirling in his eyes because of it. I felt bad he'd been caught in the crossfire—suspended because of the story I couldn't let go. Needing to know it wasn't in vain, I asked, "Did you meet with Allison?"

King sat at the kitchen table with a cup of tea and nodded yes. I asked for specifics. All Allison told me was that King's video was a fake. King caught me up on the details.

"A deepfake?" I said, dropping my things on a chair. No wonder Atwood seemed so worried, and why King insisted from the beginning, it was a fake. "Was she able to shine a light on who the officer in the video is that framed that man?"

King made a fist with his hand on top of the table and asked, "Have you heard from Kovac again?"

"No, but now I understand why that might be." I asked, "Is that who you think set you up?"

"I don't know about Kovac, but the officer in the video is someone I know." King paused and said his name, knowing I would ask anyway. "Officer Matt Barber."

My body tensed at his name. I asked, "What are you going to do about it?"

King swiped a hand over his face. "I don't know."

He was caught between a rock and a hard place, but I thought I might have a way through. Biting the inside of my cheek, I said, "I didn't tell you the compete truth about why Erin and I were meeting with Everett Atwood."

King gave me a questioning look that said I might have just lost his trust. "If you weren't meeting him about Erin's defense, then why were you seeing the public defender?"

I'd promised Atwood to keep our plan a secret, but now that Officer Barber had crossed into both our stories, I had no choice but to bring King into the mix.

"Atwood knows how Chief Watts is inflating his crime statics and tomorrow he's making a public statement announcing his motion to file for an appeal for those victims caught in the department's scandal." I paused to give King a moment to digest. When he was ready, I continued, "He's asked me to release the names of the cops involved. The *Times* will be running the story as soon as the news breaks, but I've got the story releasing early on my blog, scheduled for tomorrow morning, minutes before Atwood's presser."

"Jesus, Sam. No wonder you've been receiving threats."

"Me? What about your suspension? The only reason you don't have your badge right now is because of my reporting."

We were getting heated. Once we both calmed down, King asked, "What are their names?"

"Without the files in front of me I can't remember them all, but one of the officers in the report is Matt Barber."

CHAPTER SEVENTY-THREE

MR. T's FINGERS WERE LACED BEHIND HIS HEAD AS HE LAY in bed thinking. The shadows creeping across the ceiling had him in a trance. They moved, but only when he wasn't looking.

Wishing he could fall asleep, his victim's faces haunted him. This was an unexpected revelation, but each time he closed his eyes visions of his victims tormented him with threats that the cops knew who he was.

He questioned for the first time if it was worth it; if he would be able to outsmart the police and get away with his crimes, or get caught and locked away forever. He wasn't sure he could do jail time. That wasn't part of his story and, therefore, wasn't something he needed to worry about.

Several anxious minutes passed, and he picked up his cellphone again, looking to see what he already knew. No one was checking in on him or wondering where he'd gone so suddenly. It hurt to see how little people thought of him. He wasn't asking for much, just for someone to notice he'd disappeared and check in on him.

You're alone and no one cares. The voices in his head taunted him, making Mr. T lose hope.

He rolled on his side, tucked an arm beneath his head, and brought his knees to his chest.

Wanting nothing more than to be held, feelings of failure seeped into his mind. The more he dwelled on himself, the darker his thoughts grew. He saw only one way out of this funk and that was to post something absurd, perhaps even controversial, to one of his many social media feeds.

He palmed his phone but couldn't find the courage to go through with his thoughts. It was a Band-Aid solution, and then what? Mr. T was still shaken up from tonight's events. He thought it best to just lie low until things cooled off.

Coward.

Flopping out of bed, Mr. T padded lightly across the floor and worked to connect his camera to the flat screen TV, finally having the nerve to watch the video of killing Jackie. He only wanted to know if he could use it in the film he was making.

Standing in front of the TV with clicker in hand, he watched the clip enough times until it was no longer real. With each replay, it became something different—a piece of art—a scene in the movie that drove his story forward. It was action, suspense, and heartbreak—the ingredients to something great. Where did he go from here?

He clicked pause a second before impact and studied Jackie's frightened face. Her eyes were alive—revealing the complete scope of the human condition. It was a small glimpse into her soul, but something he would never forget. He took a piece of her tonight that would live with him forever. But it was the two reporters who were diving out of the way that he had his eye on next.

"Do you believe in miracles?" he asked the women on screen, wondering how they managed to escape his wrath.

You're straying from the original script. Don't get lost in the story. Walk the line and remember why you're telling it in the first place.

Mr. T had lost the line. He'd forgotten why he was doing this anymore.

He sat on the couch, slumped forward, doubting his own ability to not only get the story back on track, but also be able to close it out by giving it a proper applause-worthy ending.

He wondered if he had gotten in over his head with this project. Mr. T suspected he had.

Destroy it! Start over! It's trash!

He snapped his neck and glared at the window.

When did things go so wrong?

Losing sight of his mission, he picked up his cellphone and closed down his social media accounts before he did something he would later regret. No sense in attracting attention to himself, at least not any more than he already had. Besides, he was never really good at influencing other people.

Turn the page and start a new chapter. That's what you're best at!

He tipped forward, turned on the TV, and picked up the game controller. As soon as the screen flicked on, he was quick to notice he wasn't alone. White Stallion was online. Suddenly, Mr. T remembered he at least had one admirer.

He messaged White Stallion. *I need to see you. Can we meet?*

CHAPTER SEVENTY-FOUR

A SOUND OF LAUGHER WOKE ME FROM A DEEP SLEEP. I opened one eye and reached for King, needing to know I wasn't alone. My hand padded around the mattress and I was disappointed to find him already gone. When I lifted my head, I heard the muffled sound of conversation in the kitchen—a voice that sounded like King's—and glanced to the clock.

"Shit," I said, falling back to my pillow and rubbing my eyes. I'd slept in.

It was already past seven, and the sun was up, but I refused to get out of bed. My bones were tired. The soft mattress begged me to take the day off. It was a pipedream, but Dawson's words to call this story off were still echoing inside my head.

I stretched my arms over my head and yawned.

All of last night's adrenaline robbed me of today's motivation, leaving me feeling both emotionally and physically exhausted. I wanted to quit, put myself and my family first, and do what Heidi did before the best of Vincent robbed me of everything I loved.

When my cellphone buzzed, I groaned. I hated how it had sensed I was awake.

"Do you really have to be so smart?" I asked my phone.

Rolling on my side, I retrieved it from the nightstand and instinctively found myself checking on Vince. I kept getting an error. Not a single page of his was loading. Was it my connection, or did I have the wrong URL?

Swinging my feet to the floor, I kept trying with no luck.

Did Vince go dark? Was he on the run? He had the money and resources to disappear, but could he actually pull it off? All these thoughts were circling in my head, as I couldn't believe that one of the most recognized faces on the internet seemed to have vanished overnight.

A notification popped up on my own feed that pulled my attention away from Vince. I clicked the red alert and I immediately wished I hadn't bothered to see what it was.

She's against the police.

Don't come crying to the police when you're in trouble oh, poor Samantha!

Once again, I was being attacked by a handful of online vigilantes who said I was a cop hater. It went on and on. The attacks seemed endless.

People said I should be fired, what a wasted life I lived. It was all here, publicly stated for all to see. I was gearing up to respond when I received a text from an unknown number that simply said, *How was your night with King?*

Everything inside me froze as my eyes swept across the floor and landed on the bedroom window. I paused and stared, thinking the worst. Was someone outside my window? Outside my house? Watching me sleep? How else would they have known King was here?

I tilted my head and listened for noises in the house. The conversation outside my door was still going on and the three of them—King, Mason, and Erin—were oblivious to what might be happening. Then my phone dinged again.

Does he always cook you breakfast after a sleepover?

My heart drummed against my ribs as I slipped out of bed and covered myself with a nightgown hanging on the back of the rocker. I left the safety of my bedroom, marched down the hall, gaining speed through the kitchen as I hurried past both King and Erin, and sprinted into the street looking for my stalker.

I looked up and down the block. Searched every nook and cranny over the frost-covered grass. I squinted into the morning sunlight but never once saw anything, or anyone, to suggest I was being stalked.

Where were they? *Who* were they? What did they want?

I stood barefoot, waiting for something to happen. I didn't know what to expect, or if I should expect anything at all. I shielded the sunlight with a hand over my brow and squinted into cars before looking into house windows. Then I tipped my head back and took my curiosity to the sky. It, too, was empty.

The sound of faint footsteps drew closer, and a leaf crunched behind me. But by the time I turned around, it was too late. He was already on top of me.

CHAPTER SEVENTY-FIVE

Mason slammed his shoulder into mine, and I flinched at his behavior. "Excuse me, mister."

He skirted past me with his pack slung over his shoulder, looking angry and without ever slowing down. How had I not heard him exit the house? Was I really losing my mind? What was going on with my son?

"Hey, Mason," I called after him. "What's the matter with you?"

To my surprise, he took off running, not bothering to look back or tell me where he was going. I didn't know what to do, if I should chase after him or let him go until he cooled off.

One glance down my front and I was reminded by what I was wearing. The decision was made for me. I had to let him go.

I turned back to the house, thinking how last night we only touched the surface when discussing Trojan and his premonitions that Mason alerted me to. Was that what this was about? I knew we needed to further discuss what was happening, let him know that he was doing a great service to his community by helping me with my investigation. I'd intended to get to it this morning, but now—

"Mason," I shouted one more time from the top step. He turned the corner, pretending not to hear me. I feared he may have overheard something King and I had been discussing about Vincent.

A truck rumbled down the street just as I stepped inside. I needed to shower and prepare for Atwood's press conference, no matter how much I didn't want to. As soon as I entered the kitchen, King turned away from the stove with a spatula in hand and gave me a funny look.

"Did anyone talk to Mason before he left?"

"He's upset, Sam," King said.

"About what?"

King sidestepped, reached to the counter with his free hand, and held up my job offer from the *LA Times*. "When were you going to tell us?"

I touched my face and scratched my head. Erin gave me a sideways glance, keeping her chin tucked to her chest, pretending not to be in the room. My lips parted. I couldn't believe this was what they asked me about, not my race outside in my pajamas.

"Someone is watching us," I said, showing King the message on my phone.

His eyes hardened after he read the text, and he hurried outside, still holding the spatula.

Erin asked what the message said, and I told her. She responded, "Someone knows we're working with Atwood."

I didn't ask when she arrived, or if our own reporting was set to go as planned. Instead, I said, "It has to be the cops we're investigating, but how do we prove it?"

"You haven't told him," Erin said, referring to King, "about what we're doing, have you?" I gave her a look that said I had. "Sam! Atwood specifically told you not to get King involved."

"I had no choice," I said.

"And why is that?"

"Because the officer, Matt Barber, in Atwood's report, is the same cop who King believes framed him in that video Kovac gave to me."

Erin inhaled a deep breath. "If that's true, this is bad, Sam."

I glanced at my watch and checked the time. We needed to go if we wanted to arrive early. Lifting my gaze to Erin, I asked, "Are you sure you still want to go down this road with me?"

"Even if we backed out now, it would be impossible to erase everything we know."

"Good. Then let's get ready to go."

King came back inside and I asked him if he saw anything. "Nothing," he said. "But someone was definitely watching us if they knew I was here cooking you breakfast." He leaned over the kitchen sink and peered out the window.

"I don't know what to do," I said.

King turned and responded, "I should come with you today, just to have a second set of eyes on your back."

I shook my head no. "You can't."

King's brows knitted. "What do you mean, I can't?"

"It's best you stay low until IAD's investigation is complete. And, also, this might not be the best place for you to hide."

"What are you saying, Sam? You want me to leave? And, just for the record, I'm not hiding." King flicked his narrow gaze to Erin, then asked me, "Are you considering flying out to Cali?"

He couldn't let this job interview go, but I couldn't decide why. Was he disappointed I hadn't mentioned it to him, or did he think we could both use a change of scenery?

"We'll talk about it later," I said, not wanting to get into it now. "After today's presser, you won't want to be associated with us any more than you already are."

CHAPTER SEVENTY-SIX

LESS THAN AN HOUR LATER, WE WERE STANDING ON THE steps of the capital building watching a drone hover above our heads while we waited for the public defender's press conference to begin.

"I'm beginning to really hate those things," I said to Erin.

Erin shielded her eyes from the sun with her hand. "That one looks friendly."

I eyed the drone, wondering if it was here to watch us or just an extension of another news team nearby. I didn't want to think about being stalked or threatened. Instead, I brought my eyes to Erin's and quirked an eyebrow. "You know it's illegal for drones to be flying over public buildings, right?"

Erin went back to staring at the machine. "Maybe they have a permit?"

I swept my gaze across the gold dome of the state capital and thought how the only reason I was okay with this particular drone was that it was illegal and I didn't suspect it would be flying for long—eventually the pilot would be forced to land.

Our backs were to Civic Center Park as I kept checking

my phone, expecting to hear from Atwood any minute. I wondered where the governor was and if Mayor Goldberg would be tuning into today's press conference when I spotted two uniformed patrol officers on foot. They reminded me of Chief Watts and why we were here at all.

"Hey," Erin said, "There's the pilot."

I followed Erin's gaze and was surprised to see I knew who he was. It was Garrett Todd, the documentary filmmaker from Susan's charity event, and Susan was with him. We made our way to them and, when Susan spotted us coming, we waved.

"What are you doing here?" I asked Susan as we hugged.

"Everett mentioned what he was doing today and asked for us to join."

"I hope he didn't reveal the big surprise," I said, turning my attention to Garrett, quick to notice his camera bag full of gadgets slung over his shoulder. I said to Garrett, "And I thought you didn't stray too far from home?"

Without taking his eyes off the sky, Garrett landed his drone with skilled precision. "Something tells me that I'm going to want to hear what Atwood has to say."

Garrett gave me a knowing look, and I smiled. I didn't know exactly what they knew, but they obviously knew something.

Susan lowered her voice and said she heard about what happened to Jackie. "I'm sorry, Sam. Were you two close? I saw your face on the news last night. What happened?"

"It's a long story," I said, overhearing Erin mention to Garrett how flying a drone over public buildings was illegal.

There was movement at the podium but still no sign of Atwood. Where was he? And why hadn't he messaged yet?

Susan asked, "It didn't have anything to do with why Atwood called us all here today, did it?"

I thought about one of the last things Jackie said before

she died, and then it was all I could think about. The irony was how Atwood was fighting for the LGBTQ community while a suspected murderer was apparently part of that same community but didn't want anyone to know. "I'm still trying to figure that piece out," I told Susan when two officers confronted Garrett about his drone.

With surprise in his voice, Garrett turned to us and said, "Document this. If things escalate, I want it all caught on camera."

The officers were speaking to him about the illegal flying of his drone. Garrett's concern to have the interaction filmed made me think there might be something else going on, too.

Erin pulled out her phone, and so did Susan. They both started recording, though the interaction never escalated past a stern lecture. I kept looking for Atwood, but instead spotted Heidi Mitchell. I hurried over to where she was setting up to report with her team, and she was quick to apologize for yesterday. "Don't worry about it," I said.

"No, Sam. I will worry about it, because it wasn't right for me to expect you and Erin to fight the DPD on your own. We started this together, we end it together."

I mentioned a little about Jackie, the insight she provided, and Heidi said she saw her station's news clips of what happened. She reached for my hand and squeezed. "That's why I made sure it was me here today."

More news vans arrived and soon the steps were buzzing with activity, but still no sign of Atwood. Then a woman with short-cropped hair who was expensively dressed took the microphone. She abruptly canceled the presser with no explanation.

CHAPTER SEVENTY-SEVEN

HEIDI TURNED HER HEAD, AND WE SHARED A LOOK OF confusion. Neither of us knew what was going on. Something wasn't right, and I didn't have a good feeling about this. Excusing myself, I stepped off to the side and tried calling the public defender.

With my phone pressed to my ear, I could barely make out that Garrett was still talking to the police. I wondered if they were going to give him a ticket or would decide to let him off with only a warning. The line clicked over and went straight to voicemail.

I dialed again but still couldn't reach Atwood on his cell. Then I called his office, but again got only his voicemail. Where was he? What happened for him to cancel at the last minute? He should have at least sent me a text to let me know what was going on.

Fisting my phone in my hand, I rooted my knuckles into my side, wondering what had happened. The bad feeling in my stomach hardened and, when Susan caught my eye, I waved her over.

"I guess this wasn't part of the plan?"

"Do you have Genevieve's number?"

Susan nodded, dug out her phone from her purse, and made the call when Erin trotted over to me, meeting me back at the bottom of the capital steps. Erin said, "I just spoke to the woman who canceled the event."

"What did she say?"

"Someone from Atwood's office gave her the call. Told her to cancel. Didn't give a reason."

It made no sense. Had it not been for Atwood approaching *me* with this plan to out the DPD, I would think I was being played. I looked over my left shoulder. Heidi and her team were packing up their news van, on their way to the next story. Had they been told what happened? The small crowd that gathered was beginning to leave, too.

"I think we should continue as planned," Erin said, reading my mind.

I kept darting my gaze from one street to the next, thinking about how to respond. Our scheduled post was about to go live, but we still had time to cancel it.

"We have to hit pause," I said, thinking about how someone was watching my house earlier. "At least until we figure out why Atwood canceled."

Erin nodded. "Okay. I'll go do that now. In the meantime, find out what the hell is happening."

As soon as Erin was gone, I made my way to Susan, who was just getting off the phone. She turned to me with a grave expression and said, "That was Genevieve. Everett was found dead early this morning."

CHAPTER SEVENTY-EIGHT

ATWOOD'S DEATH MADE TWO DEAD IN LESS THAN TWENTY-four hours. I secretly feared I could be next. We didn't know the cause of Atwood's death—whether it was natural or otherwise. Everything was coming at us fast and I was reacting on pure instinct.

I tossed Susan a look. She said, "Go! I'll meet you there."

I took off sprinting toward the car, quick to catch up with Erin. She was inside my car, connecting her cellphone's Wi-Fi to her laptop computer to cancel our blog post. I climbed into the driver's seat and said, "He's dead. His wife found him early this morning."

Erin snapped her neck and gaped. "Was he murdered?"

I cranked the engine, slammed the car in gear, and punched the gas. "I don't know."

Erin worked as I drove. With one hand on the wheel and the other on my phone, I called Dawson. "He's dead. Atwood is dead," I screamed into the phone.

"What? How?" I told Dawson what I knew, which wasn't much. He said, "Samantha, please come back to the news-room. We need to put some kind of protection on you."

"Sorry, Dawson, but I need to know what happened. I'm heading to his house now. I'll keep you posted."

Then I hung up, knowing Dawson was thinking the Angel of Death was shadowing my every move. A part of me thought he could be right. Though I didn't want to think about my own mortality, I knew Dawson might be right about one thing: the timing of Atwood's death screamed foul play.

With a white-knuckle grip, I weaved between the congested traffic, slowly reliving the last conversation I shared with Atwood. He seemed especially nervous. I originally thought it was because of how close the hit and run came to taking both Erin and me out. But now I suspected that nervous tone was caused by something different. Was Jackie collateral damage? Or was she the intended target like I originally thought?

Erin closed her laptop and said, "We have his reports. Is it possible he knew this might happen? Is that why he specifically stated for us to keep the papers safe in case something happened?"

I didn't want to make any assumptions, but I suspected Erin might be right. "Where is your copy?" I asked.

"In my safe at home. And yours?"

I reached into the backseat and dove my hand into my bag, retrieving the files. "Here," I said, tossing them on Erin's lap.

Erin opened it up and went to work to see what we might have missed. As she did that I thought about my son, where he went, what he was doing now. Did we miss another of Trojan's forewarnings? Was it possible these stories were overlapping? Or was it just their timing that made me think they could be connected? Then it hit me.

I asked Erin, "What are the chances this is connected to Vincent?"

"I don't know." Erin cast her gaze back to the report, pointing to the center of the page. "But I do want to know more about this mysterious vigilante the police seemed to be working with."

Soon we were meandering through Atwood's neighborhood and weren't surprised at all to find the street had been blocked off. We parked and got a visual on his house. The place was crawling with cops. It seemed more like a raid than an investigation.

Erin closed the report and stuffed it under her seat. "I really hope he died of natural causes. It wouldn't be difficult to connect us to his cause."

I didn't want to think about it. I opened my door and stepped out. There was a stiff breeze blowing and I unlocked my cellphone and snapped a few pictures, wanting to document as much as I could.

The police had set up a tent in the front lawn and blocked a great deal of our visual. It was a deliberate effort to keep whatever happened a secret. To make matters worse, not a single reporter besides us was here to cover the news of Atwood's death.

We watched from a safe distance without anyone noticing, witnessing boxes being taken from the house and loaded up into a crime scene unit van. I wondered what they contained, what the police hoped to find inside. From the looks of it, the warrant was allowing a full-scale criminal investigation.

"What do you think they're doing?" Erin asked.

"I don't know," I muttered, worried this might be Chief Watts's way of making Atwood's investigation disappear.

Just when I was going to make my way toward the house, Lieutenant Kent Baker stepped out of the tent, followed by Chief Gordon Watts. What was he doing here? Now I knew this went beyond a simple conspiracy to manipulate crime statistics and moved into murder. But how could I prove it and present it to the police when they were the ones taking out their opponents?

"Oh, shit," Erin said. "You've got to be kidding me."

Their presence here wasn't a coincidence. It couldn't have been. My cellphone rang, and I was quick to answer. It was Dawson. He said, "Samantha, the TV networks are breaking news."

"I'm here. No one is speaking. They aren't letting us in," I said.

"Samantha, this isn't about Atwood. The local stations are saying a DPD officer has been suspended for misconduct. There's a video. King's face is all over the news. Do you know anything about this?"

My heart stopped. This couldn't be happening.

"Unfortunately, I do," I said, feeling the heat of the fire spreading.

CHAPTER SEVENTY-NINE

KING SAT ON SAMANTHA'S COUCH WITH COOPER AT HIS side, flicking between news channels, waiting for the press conference to begin. He kept reading Samantha's invitation to fly out to Los Angeles and meet with the editorial team at the *LA Times*. He wondered if she'd accept it.

"You think she's going to take it?" he asked the yellow lab next to him.

Cooper lifted his ears and looked King in the eye with a doubtful look.

"I don't think so either."

King exhaled a deep breath and went back to watching the news. He didn't want Samantha to leave—couldn't see living without her—but he understood opportunities like this came only once in a lifetime. The real question for him was: if she went, would he follow?

He sat forward and stretched his back. There was nothing worse than having nothing to do. The suspension stripped him of his purpose. He missed his partner, too. But the stress at work was building, seeming to get worse year after year. Maybe Sam's job offer wasn't such an issue. If he went with her, he could retire and try something new. It might even bring peace to his relationship with Samantha, allowing them to spend more time together.

King surfed the channels, growing bored. The news wasn't going anywhere fast, and he finally turned off the television, giving up on caring about something he already knew. Flicking his wrist, he checked the time. He needed to get out of the house and get on with fighting for his job.

Before leaving, King made sure Cooper had enough food and water before locking up the house behind him. He pretended not to notice the undercover parked up the street. Were they stalking Samantha, or was he the one they were after?

King's thoughts flipped to Matt Barber and what Allison said about Sam's computer being infected with Spyware as he strode without hurry to his car parked at the curb. He slipped into the driver's seat and checked his mirrors. The undercover's face was blocked by a dark shadow. He cursed the glare cutting across the glass and reached for his cellphone inside his jacket pocket. He put a call in to Alvarez and began to drive.

"Whatever it is you're calling me about, you better make this quick," Alvarez answered, swearing King would eventually get them both fired if he couldn't stay away.

King made a turn up the block and kept his eye on the rearview. Seconds later, the undercover followed his exact move. Now he was certain he had a tail.

"Listen, there's someone keeping a close eye on Samantha's house. It's an undercover." King told him that he just left Sam's. "Now they're following me."

"You're losing it, partner," Alvarez said, mentioning he heard what happened to Sam.

"I don't think I am," King said. "But what else are you

hearing? Should I be worried yesterday's accident was intended for Sam?"

"Victim, Jackie Dumont, was DOA. Still searching for the vehicle involved. It's a hit-and-run case. Nothing more."

"Sam thinks Vincent Verdi is responsible."

"I'm not surprised you said that," Alvarez concurred. "Vincent reported his Dodge Challenger stolen last night when a couple uniformed officers visited his house to question him about his whereabouts."

King pulled onto a side street and parked. He knew Sam was right about this story. She was on to something. But why weren't the police? King said, "Listen, Samantha isn't wrong about this. She has a source—can't say who it is—but she has a list of names inside the department who apparently are doing Watts's dirty laundry."

"I want to help, I do, but this is—"

King told Alvarez about the deepfake video and Alvarez went quiet.

"Christ. You saw this yourself?"

"It's him," King said. "Barber is out to get me. But, get this, he's also in the same Criminal Investigation Unit I saw listed in Everett Atwood's own investigation into the department's misconduct."

King watched the undercover pass, seeming to have missed King's turn. Alvarez was suspiciously quiet. King wondered why his partner didn't ask questions about what he knew the public defender was up to.

"This suspension has nothing to do with me and everything to do with Sam," King said, waiting for Alvarez to mock him with a witty, *I could've told you that*. "I have the original video that will prove my innocence, but I don't know who I can trust." Alvarez was still quiet. "After all that, you've got nothing to say?"

Alvarez sighed and spoke in a whisper. "The public

defender was found dead early this morning. It's a disaster over here."

King's round eyes stared with disbelief. "Everett Atwood was found dead?"

"Yes, and let's just say it's one police report that can't get leaked to the press."

King didn't take offense.

Alvarez concluded, "Sorry, partner. That's all I can say."

King killed the call and swiped a hand over his head. He couldn't believe it. Sam's source into Chief Watts's misconduct was dead. He glanced in the rearview, wondering if it was Barber who had been following him or someone else who wanted to make sure their secret didn't get out. Either way, King's hand was being forced. He had no choice but to fight back.

CHAPTER EIGHTY

VINCE WOKE SUDDENLY WHEN HE HEARD A LOUD NOISE downstairs. His heart was pounding in his chest as he reached for the remote clicker, quickly turning off the television. Sitting upright in bed, he stared at his closed bedroom door and waited for something to happen.

The noise he thought he heard didn't come back right away. For a moment, he wondered if it was in his dream. Then he heard the sound of rummaging coming from the floor below.

What the hell is going on? His eyes widened a fraction. Someone was inside his house.

He reached for his phone and swung his feet to the floor, pulling on a pair of boxer shorts on his way to the door. Armed with only his phone and wits, Vincent swung the door open with thoughts of his night filling his mind. Ghosts of April and Jackie haunted him in his sleep.

He moved on the tips of his toes to be sure he wasn't heard and stopped at the top of the staircase. There, he tried to get a visual on what was creating the heavy footsteps moving from one side of the house to the other. It sounded like maybe two, maybe even three, men. Were the police back with a warrant? Did they find his car?

Slowly, he moved down each step, keeping a sturdy hand on the rail and debating whether he should announce himself or just surprise whoever was there. He kept moving. This was his house, and he was prepared to defend it, whatever the cost.

At the bottom of the steps, Vince stepped over the cardboard boxes stuffed full of costumes. It reminded him of the failed chicken hunt skit that Mitch created but never came to fruition. Worse, it also reminded him of Jackie and her silly plan for Vince to go gay.

Get ahead of the news before the world learns my secret, Vince mocked Jackie silently, suddenly feeling lightheaded.

He reached for the wall and balanced himself against it, feeling his throat close up. Vince filled his lungs with oxygen, warding off the impending panic attack he could feel building in his chest.

It still hadn't fully hit him that Jackie was gone. A piece of him was missing, and it killed him to know he'd never be able to get her back. Flitting his gaze throughout his empty and disorderly house, Vince just wanted things to go back to how they were when he caught a shadowy figure move swiftly between rooms on the far side of the house.

Snapping his neck, he held still and stared. When the figure came back, Vince was quick to hide behind a wall. He watched with bewilderment before deciding to attack.

His pulse rose with each step closer to the person. There appeared to be only one, and Vince was grateful for it. Was it Chas? Mitch? Vince couldn't tell. But he was certain that whoever it was, he was going through his things.

Vincent shouted, "Put your hands up, asshole?"

The man startled and turned around. Mitch.

"What the hell are you doing?" Vince asked. "You nearly gave me a heart attack."

Mitch was wearing a headdress of colorful feathers and a black-as-night, skin-tight leather suit. "Maybe if you hadn't slept in, you would know," Mitch argued, seeming pissed off.

Anger swelled Vince's lungs. "Where's my car?" he asked. When Mitch didn't respond, Vince said, "You should know I reported it stolen."

Mitch said, "Jackie is dead."

Vince clenched his fist and charged Mitch. Running at full speed, his eyes went wild a second before impact. Wrapping his arms around Mitch, he tackled him to the floor. Mitch clung tightly to Vince, hooking his legs around his waist. They tussled and rolled a couple of times. Before they knew what they were even fighting about, their lips were locked in a passionate kiss.

CHAPTER EIGHTY-ONE

VINCE FISTED MITCH BY THE COLLAR, LOCKED HIS ELBOW, and pulled away. Lying on his back, Mitch hooked his hand around Vince's skull and pulled his mouth down to his own. They shared another quick kiss before Vince dug his knuckles into Mitch's sternum and sprung to his feet.

Breathing heavily, Mitch propped himself up on one elbow as Vince squeezed his head with both his hands. Vince's muscles were visibly tense, tightly wound balls glistening beneath the light. Vince couldn't believe this was happening.

"It's okay," Mitch said. "It's time we come out and be who we are."

Vince scowled and snapped, "Get over yourself. This can never come out. *Never*. Do you understand?" This was exactly what Jackie had wanted.

"You're better than this," Mitch said from the floor. "We can't keep hiding who we are."

"Oh, no, mister." Vince burst out laughing. "We can. And we will."

"No one cares."

"My fans care."

"You'll get new ones."

"Like it's that easy." Vince shook his head, laughing cynically. He made sure to look Mitch in the eye when he said, "I know this is tough to hear, but I never loved you. You should just get your crazy ideas out of your head now and forget everything that happened here today."

"You lie!" Mitch shouted, yanking off his headdress and tossing it at Vince, hitting him in the legs. Vince turned his back and walked away. "Where are you going?" Mitch called after him.

"There are some loose ends that need clearing up."

"You can't just leave me here all alone."

Vince stopped and faced Mitch. "When I come back, I need you to be gone."

"Gone?"

"The party's over, Mitch."

"What about Chas?"

"Forget him, too."

Vince knew Mitch would have a hard time accepting the end of their relationship. Mitch said, "I didn't believe Jackie, but now I think she might have been right. You did it, didn't you? You killed April."

Vince didn't answer. He just ducked his head and headed for the door with tears in his eyes.

CHAPTER EIGHTY-TWO

ALLISON WAS SITTING AT HER DESK, STARING SLACK-JAWED at the TV. She couldn't believe what the news was saying about King, nor, more importantly, why he didn't alert her to how this might happen to him. He must have known this was coming, right? Why else would he have come to her asking for help?

She turned her head to the hallway feeling like she needed to hide this from her employees. They knew Allison was friends with Samantha and that Samantha was dating King. It could quickly become a distraction if she let it. Turning the volume down, she continued watching.

How had these TV reporters gotten the same video she knew was a fake? Who gave it to them? How many other copies were out there? Did King know? Did Samantha?

Thinking about her visit with King yesterday, word would soon spread that she was associated with him. Reporters would be knocking on her door asking her about his moral compass along with other questions she didn't want to have to answer. And, though it might be bad for business, she needed to focus on what she could do to help King get through this.

Allison cast her eyes to her USB port and wondered where the drive had gone. In a panic, she began her search while listening to King's name continually get smeared by reporters across networks. It seemed to only get worse the longer it went on and, when she couldn't find her copy, a moment of alarm rang in her ears.

"Oh, shit," she said, realizing she hadn't seen the video file since before Garrett Todd's surprise visit yesterday. He'd arrived right after King left. Did Garrett follow King here? Was he waiting for him to leave? Did he take the video with him?

Beginning to tear her desk apart, she worried Garrett may have taken the file by mistake. Allison picked up a stack of papers and watched the thumb-drive fall to the floor, exhaling a breath of relief. She bent and picked it up, saying, "You're losing your mind, girl."

King was going to need this for his defense. Allison would have it ready for him when he came looking. Allison looked up to find her colleague Patty knocking at the door. She quickly turned off the news and called her inside the office. "You look better. How are you feeling?"

"I'm feeling so much better," Patty said, smiling and taking a seat across from Allison. "I wanted to ask you about this project with Garrett Todd."

Allison's forehead creased as she sat forward, bringing her hands to her desk. "It's in the very early stages," Allison said. "It should be a fun project to work on if we're given the chance."

Patty cast her gaze to her lap and bit her bottom lip.

"What is it?" Allison asked. "You don't have a problem with the content, do you?"

Patty shook her head. "No. It's fine."

"Then what is it?"

Patty looked up and said, "It's just strange how we're all connected."

"What do you mean?"

"Well, I was doing my research and discovered Garrett worked on a film with Vincent Verdi and April Wright several years ago."

Now Allison was the one doing the thinking. "Did they?"

Patty nodded. "Can you imagine being gay and working on the same set as someone like Vince? It must have been so hard for Garrett."

"Yes. It must have been," Allison murmured, lost in her thoughts.

"I saw the aftermath of April Wright's death, and it's disappointing Vincent hasn't made a public statement given the size of his platform."

"Then it's a good thing we're working with Garrett and not Vincent," Allison said, putting some pieces together.

She reached across her desk and took her phone into her hand, calling Samantha. As the line rang, she shooed Patty out of the office and told her to close the door behind her.

Once Samantha answered, Allison said, "I figured out what Jackie and April were discussing the night April died."

"What? How?"

"Well, it wasn't actually me, but Garrett Todd, Susan's friend—"

"Yes, I know who he is," Samantha said.

"He can read lips and he was certain Jackie said she'd kill April if April didn't give her something."

"What did April have that Jackie wanted?"

"I don't know, and what Garrett saw her say in the video doesn't answer that. I'm still working on clearing up the audio, but I think he might be right." Allison told Samantha about Patty's information—that Garrett had worked with April and Vince.

Samantha said, sounding surprised, "Wait, back up. Garrett Todd came to your office and you showed him the video of April and Jackie?"

"Did you not hear anything I said?"

"This is news to me," Samantha said. "Who else knows you have the video?"

"Only Garrett. What's going on, Sam? Is Patty right? Could Jackie have known April was going to die? Why are all these people you're interested in connected?" When Samantha didn't respond, Allison asked, "Samantha, is everything all right?"

"The public defender is dead," Samantha murmured. "And I think it might have been a couple bad cops who killed him."

CHAPTER EIGHTY-THREE

KING'S CELL KEPT GOING TO VOICEMAIL, BUT I KEPT trying until he finally answered. I said, "Did you hear the news?"

"I heard, and I was meaning to call you. Do you know how it happened?"

"How what happened?" It didn't occur to me until after I asked that King didn't know about his face circulating morning news. "Alex, listen to me. The fake video of you planting evidence made the local news."

King cursed. "Jesus. They're one step ahead of me."

"One step ahead of us both," I said, filling him in on what happened to Atwood. "Listen to me, where is your copy now?"

"I left it with Allison."

"You need get it back, preferably the one that shows Barber's face instead of yours."

"Yeah. Yeah," King said. "I'm on it, but Sam, there was an undercover at your house this morning. It must have been the person texting you."

"Do you know who it was?"

"Unfortunately, I don't," he said. He was never able to get a clear visual on the driver. "Also, I heard about Atwood. I spoke with Alvarez a moment ago. Get this, Vince reported his Dodge Challenger stolen last night."

"No surprise there."

"Watch your tail, Sam. It's clear someone is worried what you know and how you'll use it against them."

I glanced over my shoulder, looking back at Atwood's house. What was really going on inside? How could I do the job Atwood was prepared for without getting knocked off myself? The story still needed to be told, but was the risk of putting my friends and family in danger worth it?

I asked King, "How can we prove it's Barber who is threatening me?"

King didn't answer. Instead, he cursed. When I asked what was happening, he said, "I'm being followed again."

"Is it Barber?"

"I don't know. But it's a different car than before."

"You be careful, too," I told King. "It's possible Barber might try and provoke you to do something he could later give to IAD. Or, even worse, a desperate news desk."

We were both under attack—being flanked on all sides. I didn't see this ending well for either one of us but we couldn't quit when we were this close to discovering the truth.

"If anyone is going to stir the pot," King said seconds before ending his call, "it's going to be me."

CHAPTER EIGHTY-FOUR

"C'MON. LET'S GO," I CALLED OUT TO ERIN. WE LOADED into the car and I was starting to turn the wheels when my cell buzzed with another call. Thinking it was King, I was quick to answer.

"Samantha, it's Heidi. Hey, I just got back to the newsroom and saw what's happening to King. I'm so sorry."

"It's fake. I promise you that."

Heidi didn't doubt it. "Listen," she said, "can you swing by? There's something here you should see in person."

She promised it would be worth my time, so I didn't argue; I could hear the urgency in her voice. When I relayed the message to Erin, she said, "You think it's a good idea to show your face at a network that is currently bashing your boyfriend's reputation?"

"If it was true, maybe. But we have nothing to hide, and neither does Alex."

I raced across town, thinking more about how a handful of dirty cops were intentionally ruining King's career. This was my fault, my fight. Unfortunately, King was caught in the crossfire—taken as collateral damage in a desperate attempt to silence me.

"What do you think Heidi has?" Erin asked.

I suspected it had something to do with Chief Watts, and told Erin as much. "This isn't about King," I said. But the fact that Heidi didn't feel comfortable discussing it over the phone had my head spinning.

Once we arrived, we found a spot near the front and headed inside. We checked in at the front desk, were handed our visitor passes, and took a ride up the elevator to where Heidi was waiting.

As soon as the doors opened, a thick wave of optimism crashed against me. The energy here was young and full of hope—so much different from print journalism and the sorry place I worked. As I watched Heidi hurry toward us, it was impossible not to wonder what it might be like working for a paper as big as the *LA Times*. Would it be like this, or feel aged and out of date like the *Colorado Times*?

"Thanks for coming on such short notice," Heidi said by way of greeting.

"What's this about?" Erin asked.

Heidi's eyes met with mine and I asked, "Did you hear what happened to Atwood?"

"That's why I called you here." She waved for us to follow and led us to the other side of the floor where we entered a small windowless conference room with a Smartboard and table. Heidi shut the door and said, "We need to keep what I'm about to show you private."

Erin and I both gave each other a look and agreed to play by Heidi's rules.

Heidi said, "Only my producer and I know about this but that's about to change."

My mind raced, anxious to know what she could have learned that we hadn't already discovered ourselves. If this was about Atwood like she suggested, then why were we the only ones at his house? Did Heidi know he was dead?

Heidi lay a folder flat on the table and opened it to reveal several still photographs of Atwood's lifeless body. His eyes were closed and his jaw hung open like he was in a deep sleep. It wasn't a gruesome image and, though I didn't see a time-stamp on any of the pictures, I knew they had to have been taken sometime early this morning, probably by a crime scene tech.

"Where did you get these?" I asked, fingering through the pictures of a dead public defender.

"A protected source working the investigation."

I knew by the look on her face she wasn't going to reveal her source's identity. I asked, "Why leak it to the press?"

"Still trying to figure that part out. But it's clear someone wants everyone to know not only that Atwood is dead, but what he was doing before he died."

I stepped up to the table and watched as Heidi spread several more pictures across the table. "These were sent via email and I assume taken by cellphone. Regardless, I'm assured the source is trustworthy and they look authentic to me."

"Who's the man next to Atwood?" Erin asked, pointing to the John Doe on the bed next to the public defender.

"Geoff Little," Heidi read from a printout pinched between her fingers. "A male escort they suspect was there to entertain the public defender."

"Atwood was gay?" Erin said, sounding surprised.

Receiving leaked material from an active investigation was incredibly unusual, especially given the high-profile stature of the victim. Naturally, I was skeptical that this was leaked for anything but to cast Atwood in a bad light. As Heidi read more from the unofficial report, I wondered who this source was and what else was found inside Atwood's house. There were a lot of holes in this story. My main priority was protecting Atwood's investigation.

I flicked my gaze to Geoff Little's face and wondered if this was what we overheard Atwood fighting with his wife about. Was this man at Susan's event? I didn't recognize him, but that didn't mean he wasn't there.

"Cocaine and alcohol were found on the nightstand next to both victims," Heidi read.

It was too soon for an autopsy to be complete, but would the medical examiner expedite the order because of who Atwood was? I hoped so, but I wasn't going to hold my breath until an official report was made public. That could take weeks.

Heidi finished by saying, "It appeared their little party of two got out of hand, causing them both to overdose."

"Is that what you're guessing, or is that what your source says?" I asked, reaching for the report she was reading from.

"It's what my source assumes happened."

She handed me the report. I hated how unofficial it was— a simple text email with quick one or two sentence bullet points. None of it added up, and certainly didn't reflect the man I knew. I'd just spoken with him last night. Was this another setup? A smear campaign designed by the Chief in an attempt to hide his own crimes? It certainly appeared to be that way.

As if reading my mind, Heidi asked, "Samantha, when was the last time you spoke with Atwood?"

"Last night." Knowing where Heidi was going, I stared at the report and added, "I sensed he was paranoid, but he didn't seem afraid for his life. I just assumed it was nerves talking ahead of today's press conference." Then I swept my eyes to Heidi's and said, "You're not going to air this, are you?"

"Not if it was up to me, but I'm afraid our producer wants

to run with it. They don't want to make the same mistake twice."

"You have to stop this," I said. Passing up Russ's video was something they couldn't fix by airing this unofficial report. "It could derail Atwood's entire intention of bringing account-ability to the police department."

Heidi tossed a look to Erin, then swept her eyes back to me. "Unless you can give me something to convince them otherwise, I'm afraid this story is going to air sooner rather than later, no matter what I think is true."

CHAPTER EIGHTY-FIVE

WE WERE ON AN IMPOSSIBLE MISSION WITH THE MINUTES passing fast.

I stepped off the elevator and headed toward the exit with Erin one step behind me. Geoff Little was on both our minds as we left the newsroom, squinting into the sunshine.

"We're not going to be able to do it in time," Erin said quietly into my ear.

My eyes were busy scanning the parking lot in front of me. I couldn't admit that Erin was right. "Then let's hope King's story is enough to calm today's news desk until we figure it out," I said.

Erin reached for my arm and spun me around. I immediately regretted wishing King's story to continue on, especially considering we didn't know what else they had on him or if they'd try to hit King again with something bigger. I hoped this was it, but suspected there might be more coming.

Raising my chin, I said, "King's story is already out there and we have a solution for it."

"And Atwood? What are we going to do about him?"

"No one is going to fight for him but us."

"Do you think it's true? Did he really overdose the night before he was going to officially announce his fight for criminal justice reform?"

I let my thoughts unravel for a beat before I said, "I don't know, but we need to figure out who this Geoff Little is and how he ended up in Atwood's bed."

We knew so little about Atwood, there was no way to know if what Heidi had was real or not. Was he in the closet? A drug user? Neither of those things really mattered, but the chief of police was making us all look like fools while we chased our tails. I was sure he was having himself a good laugh at our expense.

At the car, Erin suggested I call King and have him bring the original video of Officer Barber to Heidi. It could be just enough to delay Atwood's report long enough for us to learn if his death was an accidental overdose or murder of the first degree.

I was on edge as I drove—hyperaware of our every move being closely watched. I kept glancing to my mirrors, wondering who was watching us now. I never saw anyone, but that didn't mean they weren't there. As I settled into our drive, paranoia gave way to feelings of betrayal. Atwood was married to Genevieve. He never revealed anything about his sexuality other than being straight, and I wondered if that hidden part of himself was part of his reason for needing to be the face of this movement.

Erin said to me, "According to Jackie, Vince hid his sexuality. What if Atwood was gay, too?"

We were attempting to connect possibly unrelated events, dividing the facts into camps of truths and unknowns. The more secrets we uncovered, the more likely it seemed our two stories would eventually cross, if they hadn't already.

"Geoff Little looked like a little boy," I said.

"Some men have baby faces," Erin tried to reason.

"And some men like their partners underage," I countered, thinking about the vigilante the cops were using to target their own victims.

When I shared my thoughts with Erin, she turned to me and said, "Did Atwood get set up?"

I hoped he was smarter than to fall for something he was aware of happening, but I didn't know. This was all so weird. If he had been tricked, it scared me to think about who exactly we were dealing with, what they had planned next, and if we could be so easily deceived, too.

Erin was thinking out loud, figuring out how we could find out who this vigilante was when my thoughts traveled to Kovac and the many gadgets I saw him with. Garett also had a lot of gadgets, but I didn't think he was Kovac. Why hadn't Garrett mentioned his visit with Allison yesterday when we saw him this morning? I had suggested he meet her when I met him at Susan's event. Wouldn't he have told me he'd followed up on that?

I turned on the on-ramp and slammed my foot on the gas, watching the RPMs climb as I thought about Vincent and how I believed he was responsible for the death of Jackie. It seemed like the only story I could control the outcome of, and I didn't want to lose him before answering my questions. I worried he was going to hurt someone else before we could stop him. And, if he was after me, I wanted to make sure he knew I wasn't afraid of the truth.

Erin asked, "Where are we going?"

Traveling north at a fast clip, I said, "To ask our boy Vince why he killed Jackie."

CHAPTER EIGHTY-SIX

FORTY MINUTES LATER WE ARRIVED AT VINCENT'S HOUSE tucked in the hills of Boulder. Like most houses in rich neighborhoods, I suspected we were under constant surveillance from security cameras, doorbell ringers, or even snooping neighbors peeking from behind the curtains. Someone knew we were here.

"Looks quiet," I said.

"Aren't all neighborhoods like this?"

I gave Erin a knowing look and continued assessing the situation. There were a half-dozen expensive cars parked in the drive, but not one of them was the Dodge Challenger that hit and killed Jackie. Had it really been stolen, or was Vince just trying to cover his tracks by hiding it? Either way, Vince had a lot of explaining to do.

Soon, my thoughts drifted to April and then to Russ and Jackie. I thought about Atwood and knew I had to add Geoff Little's name to the list as well. We needed to get Vince to talk and admit to his sexuality if we expected to progress our own investigation. I wasn't sure how it was going to happen, but maybe I could lure him in with the work Atwood was set out to do with hopes of Vince wanting to help. It was a stretch, but it was the only angle I had besides Jackie.

"Look, someone is coming out," Erin said, pointing.

My gaze went to the front door, but nothing happened. Then I caught movement out of the corner of my eye, surprised to see a person stepping out from the side door of the garage.

"You recognize him?" I asked Erin, staring at the young man carrying big boxes in his arms.

Erin nodded. "I saw him at GamersCon but couldn't tell you his name."

My heart was beating fast in my chest. It felt like we were close to unraveling the mystery. Who was this man and how could we use him to get to Vince?

"Is he moving out?" Erin asked.

That's what it looked like. "Let's ask him," I said, opening my door. Our car doors shut, and the man startled. "Hi," I said with a smile.

He quickly turned to the trunk of his car and shut it. Then he faced us and said, "This is private property. You can't be here."

"Where are you going?" Erin asked. "Moving out?"

He gave her a confused look. I let the silence settle between us but he didn't answer. "We're here to speak to Vince; is he home?"

The young man flicked his gaze to an empty parking spot in front of the four-car garage where the concrete was lighter in color. I swept my gaze up from the fresh oil stain and into the windows of the loft above. By the size of it, I assumed it was a separate living area, perhaps this man's home.

"He's not here, is he?" Erin said.

The man cleared his throat and said, "You just missed him."

"When can we expect him back?" I asked.

"Better yet," Erin added, "do you know where he went?"

The man stayed silent, and I watched his eyes blur into a distant stare that seemed to cut right through us. I asked, "Do you rent the loft above the garage?"

"Look," he snapped, "Vince isn't home and I don't know when he's expected to come back. Now, if you'll excuse me, I have to finish up what I was doing."

Erin turned to me and said, "Maybe he's off to see his boyfriend?"

The man abruptly turned around, slack-jawed. A tinge of embarrassment colored his cheeks—or was it jealousy? "I'm sorry, I didn't catch your names." He paused as I watched his eyes flash with recognition. "Wait a minute, I know who you are. You're the reporters from GamersCon. I thought Jackie handled you?"

"Vince handled her for us," I said, hoping to shock him into talking.

"You're wrong."

"Am I? Where is he?" The man glared through red, swollen eyes. It looked like he'd been crying or was about to begin. "Why are you protecting him?"

"Please," his voice cracked as if our questions were too much for him to handle. "Just go and leave me alone."

CHAPTER EIGHTY-SEVEN

KING KEPT HIS EYE ON THE COROLLA IN THE REARVIEW AS he turned onto a side street where he pulled to the curb and parked. His tail did the same. Flinging the door open, King hurried to the car behind him to confront the driver and ask him why he insisted on following him.

"You wanted to speak with me; well, here I am," King yelled through the window as he banged his hand on the glass. The window tint was too dark to see inside, but King stuck his nose to the windshield and called for the driver to step out.

The driver's body was still, but King could see he was fiddling with something beneath the steering column. What was it? A gun? King hoped not. He wasn't armed himself, but could grapple with the best of them if he needed to.

"Don't make me break the glass," King growled.

The door opened, and the driver called out, "Easy. Relax."

King reached for the door frame, yanked it open, and asked, "Who are you and what do you want?"

With one foot planted on the pavement, the driver raised

both hands and said, "That's far enough, Detective. You can back off now."

King glanced to the man's cellphone and suspected he was being recorded. "And so can you," King shot back. "Or I can have you arrested for harassing a police officer."

"If only you had the authority." The man chuckled as if knowing King had been suspended. "Besides, you think the public would actually believe your story over mine? I don't think so."

"Are you willing to chance it?" King clenched his jaw. "Because I am," King said.

"Look here, all I want to ask you is how many more innocent people will be locked up because of your actions?"

King's eyes narrowed. "You're a reporter?"

A knowing glimmer flashed in the man's eyes. "Do you have something against gays, Detective King? The video the local news stations are circulating sure makes me believe you do."

King angled his head and wondered how many other small-time reporters were out looking for him now. If this guy could find him, so could others. More importantly, though, King wanted to know how this fake video was leaked to the press about the same time of Atwood's death. Was that coincidence? King thought not.

The young reporter continued, "Rumors say DPD are targeting members of the LGBTQ community to inflate the Chief's crime statistics. Care to comment?"

"Who told you that? You have proof? That's a big statement to make for a rookie."

"I have my sources," the reporter said. "I'd be happy to quote anything you have to say on the matter. Who knows? It might help your case."

King knew better than to respond. He'd seen plenty of stories get misrepresented by the press and knew how quickly they could spin out of control by a simple misinterpretation. But as King stood there staring into the eyes of this hungry new reporter, he thought maybe he could make him an offer where they'd both come out on top.

"Turn off your camera," King demanded. "And let's make a deal."

CHAPTER EIGHTY-EIGHT

I WATCHED OUR NEW FRIEND GO BACK INSIDE THE HOUSE, stepping through the same side door to the garage he'd come from. I wondered what happened to him to make him so emotional. It couldn't have been his conversation with us. He was like that before we arrived.

As soon as the side door shut, I hurried to the front door and rang the doorbell. Erin followed and once she was behind me, she whispered, "You think he was lying about Vince?"

"No," I said, listening for movement inside. "I just want to see who else might be home."

We waited a minute before hitting the button again. I heard the chime followed by the same sounds of silence. I wanted to get inside, get a feel for if Jackie was right about Vince, learn what else he might be hiding. Was Vince the person she said he was? Would he be willing to admit it if I asked? How would he react if I did?

I turned back to the street and headed for the car. I hoped we hadn't let Vince get away. Erin said, "Should we wait and follow this guy? Maybe he'll lead us to Vince."

It was a tough decision. Ideally, I wanted to wait here and

go searching for Vince. But since I couldn't be in two places at once, I said, "Let's leave Vince to the police."

"Are you serious?"

Looking Erin in the eye, I said, "I want to know who we were just talking to before we decide if he was lying to us."

It was clear we struck a nerve with the man. Because of that, I thought we might be onto something. But what was it? Was it that we hinted at Vince killing Jackie? Or that we let him know we knew about Vince's secret?

We circled the block and parked up the street, staked out the house, and waited. The sun was beating down on us, keeping the car warm. Erin scrolled her phone, and it didn't take her long to learn the man's name.

"Mitch Unger," she said. "He's been with Vince from the very beginning, before he was a successful YouTuber."

"Boyfriend?"

Erin shook her head. Nothing indicated they were lovers. However, when it came to Vince, we couldn't judge a book by its cover. Erin added, "There's a third amigo, Chas Douglass. Apparently another friend Vince grew up with."

Interesting. Where was he? With Vince?

Time passed slowly, and I wondered if we were wasting it waiting for something to happen here instead of figuring out who might have killed Atwood. My thoughts turned to my son, and I called home, hoping he'd be there.

"Hey," I said when Mason picked up. "I just wanted to talk about earlier."

"Mom, are we moving?"

"What? No. Of course not."

"Then what was that job offer about?"

"I've been recruited for a job at the *LA Times.* I was meaning to tell you about it. I just didn't get the chance."

"But you brought it home, so you're at least thinking about taking it."

"Do you want me to?"

Mason didn't answer right away. "I don't know."

"We'll talk about it more later," I said. "It's a decision we can make together."

When I was off the phone, Erin said, "You're actually thinking about taking it, aren't you?"

I held her eyes for a quick pause before requesting to see Atwood's report. Erin reached under her seat and handed me the files. "No harm in at least discussing your options with them."

Erin was right. I'd be lying if I said I wasn't the slightest bit curious to know more about what the editors at the *LA Times* expected from me. It was worth having that conversation, I thought, as I pored over Atwood's documents, this time making sure not to skip over any lines.

Flipping through the pages, I dug deeper into the names of each of the victims Atwood was planning to file an appeal for. His report went as far back as sixteen months, and there was a clear pattern of how each of the victims found themselves being convicted of a crime they didn't commit. It was exactly as Atwood told us before, but now I was seeing it through a new set of eyes, making it much clearer than before.

I lifted my gaze and stared through the windshield. "They were victimized twice," I said, getting Erin's attention. "First, by falling for the vigilante's trap, and second by the police who coerced them into making false confessions to crimes they didn't commit for fear of being shamed for who they were."

"These men hadn't come out," Erin whispered her revelation.

"No. And I suspect no one knew they were gay. Otherwise, why admit to something you didn't do?"

We couldn't forget these men were suspected child predators, too. But two wrongs didn't make a right, I said to myself, imagining Genevieve finding her husband with another man and the surprise and shock she must have felt. How would she explain that to her kids? Was this part of Atwood's claim to how relationships change when you become empty nesters?

I wondered where Genevieve was last night, and why she hadn't been home. Was that part of their fight we witnessed? Did she ever come back home after our visit? Or had she been home through it all, knowing Atwood was upstairs with another man?

I shot off a quick message to Susan asking if she could find those answers for me. I wasn't counting on Genevieve to open up so soon after learning of her husband's death, but I was willing to take a chance if it meant bringing us some much-needed answers.

"This asshole can't even show his face, but can shame these unsuspecting victims because they fell for his stupid trap?" I said, rattling off my frustration with this vigilante whose name we didn't know. It made me sick to my stomach. But then a name stood out from all the others. "Shit," I gasped. "Look here. How did we miss this?"

Erin leaned over and read the name I was pointing to. "He meant nothing to us before."

"No." But now he did.

I couldn't believe it. I was looking at Geoff Little's name in Atwood's report. Now I knew that finding him dead alongside Atwood couldn't be a coincidence. "How is it that Geoff is found with Atwood when he should be behind bars?"

"Maybe he was released for good behavior?"

"Or maybe it was just as I suspected and someone was destroying Atwood's credibility before he had a chance to ruin theirs?" But what I really wanted to know was how Chief

Watts and his men learned what Atwood was up to. Did we give him away?

A cold chill moved up my spine and spread at the nape of my neck.

If our report went out like we planned, Geoff Little's name would have been mentioned first, discrediting the entire bombshell we now held in our hands. But someone got to him first. Someone knew what we were up to, just like Atwood suspected. That was the most frustrating part of this investigation—how did they know?

Then I remembered the suspected Spyware infecting my computer, and an ill feeling settled in my stomach. Had I unintentionally given them Geoff Little's name? Were they rubbing it in my face by leaking Atwood's police report to the press? It seemed like they were, showing me who was boss.

"Sam. Look," Erin said, pointing to Vince's house. "Mitch is leaving."

He exited from the house instead of the garage. "How did he get into the house?"

"There must a door inside that connects the two buildings."

We watched him hurry to a dark blue Toyota Prius and climb inside. We jotted down the plate number and then he was off, driving away fast.

Erin asked, "What do you want to do? Follow him?"

I shook my head no. "I want to get inside Vince's house."

CHAPTER EIGHTY-NINE

Erin didn't like the idea, but I knew this was our only shot at getting a glimpse into Vince's private life to learn exactly who we were dealing with. We gave it some time to be sure Mitch wasn't coming back before going in, and my anxiety nearly killed me.

My knee bounced, and Erin's fingers drummed on her thigh. We were both uneasy about what we were about to do, but we'd been in similar positions before and the risk was usually worth the reward. I hoped that would be the case this time, too.

Ten minutes passed with no sign of Mitch when I asked Erin, "Ready?"

I nodded, and Erin turned to me. Her eyes were steady and full of focus. I inhaled a deep breath and reached behind me into the back seat for two pairs of leather driving mitts I kept in my car during winter. I handed Erin a pair and said, "Here. Put these on."

We stepped out and walked the sidewalk following Vince's driveway to the garage where we edged the house and made our way to the back. Along the way we peeked inside windows and looked for any sign of life. Inside was dark and quiet, and I was certain no one was home.

Erin tried the back door and neither of us was surprised to find it locked. Needing to get inside, we debated our options while taking in the expansive backyard bordered with a tall privacy fence. Breaking a window might set off a house alarm, which was something we couldn't chance, though neither of us was waiting around doing nothing. With few options left on the table, we were nearly about to call our mission a failure when Erin said, "Is that door cracked open?"

I turned and followed her gaze to the door we'd seen Mitch using. It didn't appear to be fully latched, and I wondered if he'd left it open on purpose.

We hurried over and pushed the door open with my finger. Inside smelled like oil and gasoline. Each bay was clean and housed a different motor vehicle. There were a couple motorcycles and a boat—toys of young money—but most interesting were the nude calendars of women hanging on the wall above the tool bench.

Did Vince really like this stuff, or was he living two separate lives in an attempt to hide his secret? I thought it must be exhausting to be him—wondering how he kept up the façade all these years without anyone knowing the truth.

To our right was a staircase which climbed into the loft. We followed it to the top of the stairs and stopped to look around. We found a guest house complete with a full bath and kitchen, just as I'd suspected. The bed sheets weren't made, and dirty dishes filled the sink. It was sparsely furnished and had little to offer in the form of entertainment, but when we checked the closet, it was full of men's clothes and expensive shoes.

"There's nothing here that leads to the house," Erin said, opening and shutting random doors.

"It must connect from the garage," I said, thinking of the layout of the house as seen from the street.

We moved back to the garage and peeked around for a minute before Erin opened a door and turned to look at me. "Hallway," she said. "This must be it."

I moved across the concrete floor and peeked into the black abyss. "Only one way to find out," I said, sharing a quick look with Erin. Taking the lead, I moved swiftly, keeping one hand on the wall to balance my steps. We traveled thirty feet before coming to another closed door. I whispered, "Go ahead. Try it."

Erin twisted the knob. As soon as the door opened, she screamed in terror as a large Bengal tiger lunged at us.

CHAPTER NINETY

WE STUMBLED BACKWARD A COUPLE STEPS BEFORE crashing to the floor. The tiger growled as we scrambled on all fours over the cold tile floor with our hearts lodged in our throats. It wasn't until ten yards back that we realized the tiger was caged. It had happened so fast. Neither of us expected to come face-to-face with a big cat.

"What the hell does Vince have a tiger for?" Erin asked.

The tiger stared at us and we stared back. He bared his long, sharp fangs and clawed at the bars caging him inside his little box. He was hungry for a big meal or pissed to be trapped, and I wondered if he'd been set intentionally by Mitch, or maybe even by Vince.

"More importantly," I said, "what other surprises are waiting for us around the next corner?"

Erin rolled her eyes over to me, and I lifted a brow.

We knew we couldn't turn back now, but we were hesitant to proceed. Together we stood, gathered our courage, and sucked in our guts as we passed the beast, hurrying into the next room and making sure to close the door on our way out.

I had a thick dose of adrenaline propelling me forward as

we went to work, clearing rooms, combing through Vince's things. We searched two rooms, both revealing little, before striking gold in the third.

"What's all this stuff for?" Erin asked.

"Props for his videos, I guess," I said, picking up a costume. There were feathers and rubber chickens and a suspiciously familiar red wig. I picked it up and asked Erin if she recognized it.

"It could have been the one I saw," she said. "Honestly, though, I can't say for sure."

I held the wig out in front of my face thinking about Russ's murder and the man dressed as a woman who visited him the night he died. But if this was the wig I suspected Vince wore the night we believed he killed Russ, why didn't he disguise himself when plowing over Jackie? It seemed like he was giving up, losing strength. That was a good sign, considering how close it felt we were to capturing him.

I snapped a quick photo with my phone and continued looking around, my head swiveling on my shoulders with reminders of Jackie everywhere. Her presence could be felt, and I thought what a tough job she had containing someone as erratic as I knew Vince to be.

A poster across the room caught my attention and I had to get a closer look. I couldn't believe his arrogance. I had never seen somebody so into themselves. He was a unique individual, a bit immature as well, but as I stared into his eyes gleaming from the poster of himself all I could hear was, *When life imitates game, you become the star of your own show.*

There were framed cutouts of past articles about him next to awards and memorabilia reminding him of his greatness, no matter where he was in his house. Nothing suggested he was gay, and that had me curious to know why he would hide that about himself even in the privacy of his own home.

I took the steps down and moved to the living room,

finding the same gaming console as Mason had next to the large flat screen TV. Next to it lay the same game I found the other day in Mason's room. I picked up the controls and turned on the TV. The game loaded, and I was immediately taken into Trojan's account.

My heart started beating faster.

The rumors about Trojan being Vince were true after all.

I cast my gaze to the controls and wondered if it was here that he thought up how he would kill each of his victims when I heard Erin call from the other side of the house.

"Samantha, come quick. You're going to want to see this."

I quickly turned everything off and followed Erin's voice to a back bedroom. When I entered, she held up a drone for me to see. She asked, "Look familiar?"

It was similar to the machine that had been stalking me. But was it the same one? I had to assume so because all this time I thought it was the cops who were harassing me when now it appeared it may have actually been Vince.

"Look at all his cameras and video editing equipment. There must be at least fifty grand worth of stuff here," Erin said with a hint of admiration coming through.

I could tell she wanted to sit in the driver's seat and begin poking around, but we'd already been in the house long enough. I worried if we didn't leave soon, someone would discover what we had done.

I pulled my cellphone from my back pocket and began documenting everything I saw when I noticed Russ's video sitting next to the computer keyboard. Taking a photo of it, I called Erin over, happy to learn Erin hadn't taken it like the rumors suggested. "That's Russ's video, the same one he tried to sell to me."

"If Vince killed him for it, why leave it out in the open like this?"

I didn't know, but I didn't have to watch it to know what

was on it. Vince had either forgotten what he was doing with it, or he was getting sloppy with his work. Either way, he certainly didn't expect us to break into his house and be the ones to discover it. I snapped a quick picture when Erin crouched to the floor and found something that surprised us both.

Bending my knees, I crouched next to Erin and together we read the name written on a piece of masking tape. Erin tilted her head and asked, "Why would Vince have Garrett Todd's name in his house?"

I thought about the film Vince, Garrett, and April supposedly all worked together on. Then I thought about Garrett's documentary, *Coming Out*. Something told me Garrett might have known Vince was gay, but perhaps was too afraid to say anything. But one thing was for certain; Garrett was hiding something from us and I intended to find out why, and what, that was.

CHAPTER NINETY-ONE

WHITE STALLION TOOK HIS EYES OFF THE TELEVISION AND checked the time. He was waiting for Mr. T to arrive and was annoyed because he was running late. Killing time, he ordered and relaxed with a beer, always keeping one eye on the television above the bar.

He was glued to the breaking news of Denver's Homicide Detective Alex King and kept shaking his head, knowing an innocent man was being taken out.

The media was tearing the detective apart—discrediting his character, questioning his entire career—over one video clip White Stallion knew was partially fake. It was a shame to watch because White Stallion knew Alex King was one of the few good cops working alongside so many bad.

"They should have asked me the names of the bad cops," he muttered into his glass as he sipped his draft beer.

His vigilantism had taken a backseat in recent weeks. Now, White Stallion had more pressing issues to attend to and wanted to see how this all shook out for Vincent Verdi. Then he could go back to his usual ways of luring in sick child predators to shame or hand over to the bad cops willing to do the dirty work for him. Like Mr. T, White Stallion was on a mission of his own. The difference between them was clear: he was winning while Mr. T was not.

The news replayed the video of the officer planting evidence again, and White Stallion kept looking for signs of digital manipulation on the officer's face. He never saw any, at least not from where he sat, and was impressed by their work.

"If I could do the same, my job would be so much easier." He smirked.

Growing impatient, he turned his head to the entrance to check again for any sign of Mr. T's arrival. Nothing. While Stallion wondered who the officers would decide to frame next if he wasn't feeding them a constant supply of names to go after.

He liked what he did; considered it a necessary evil in a world full of injustice and corruption. It was important people knew who the predators were, living in their community, but really what White Stallion liked most of all was the control he had in deciding who lived and who died.

A shadow caught in the corner of his eye and White Stallion barely paid Mr. T any attention when he took a seat across from him. Together they sat silently watching the news until it switched over to a commercial.

White Stallion hunched over his beer and faced Mr. T, assessing his clothes, always judging a man by what he chose to wear. "God," he said with grave disapproval, "you're even starting to dress like him."

Mr. T raised a single eyebrow and asked, "What gave me away?"

"You mean how did I know it was you killing all these people?"

Mr. T snapped, lunging forward. "Keep your voice down. Someone might hear you."

White Stallion smirked, a knowing glimmer catching his

eye. "Where should I begin? How about the *Don't trip. You might fall.* event? Or your history with April?" Mr. T stared expressionless, so White Stallion kept going. "No, no, no. It was your arrogance to predict the deaths before they happened."

"Okay, that's enough."

"Are you sure? I can keep going if you'd like?" White Stallion amused himself. Liked the games he played. He enjoyed establishing his dominance over someone who clearly thought he was the brilliant one. His eyes crinkled at the corners when he said, "When life imitates game, you become the star of your own show. You came up with that, didn't you?"

Mr. T flicked his gaze to the TV, clearly annoyed by White Stallion's assessment. He said, "I was only trying to protect our secret."

"*Our* secret?"

Mr. T locked eyes with White Stallion's. "You know what I mean."

"And what has it gotten you?" White Stallion laughed as if he knew all along this was how it would be. "Look, I know that this wasn't what you wanted. I get it. I do. Things sometimes have a way of spiraling out of control, but I'm here to help. That's why you asked to meet, isn't it? Because you need my help?"

Mr. T gave him a skeptical look. He tried to maintain his façade, act like what he was hearing didn't bother him. White Stallion could see the cracks forming. Mr. T was losing it.

"I won't make you admit you need my help, but did you at least bring what I asked for?"

Tears welled in Mr. T's eyes as he reached his hand inside his pocket and pulled out a CD-ROM, handing it over to White Stallion. White Stallion took the disc into his hand and chuckled.

"You won't regret this," White Stallion said, standing. "By the time this is all over, the two of us will be at the top of our game."

CHAPTER NINETY-TWO

Susan was standing outside Allison's office pounding her fist on the glass door and calling for her to open up. Feeling irritated, she yanked on the door, rattling it on its hinges hoping someone would respond to the noise. Finally giving up, she pulled out her phone and called. The line rang to Allison's cellphone, but she never answered.

"Why call me here if you're not willing to let me inside?" Susan said frustratedly.

She turned her back and looked to the road, wondering if Allison stepped out, having forgotten Susan was on her way. Another minute passed before she heard the lock unlatch behind her. Susan turned to find Patty opening the door.

"Sorry it took so long," Patty apologized. "Allison has the place locked down after we learned what happened to the public defender." Susan stepped inside and Patty asked, "You knew him, right?"

Still upset and coming to terms herself, Susan said, "We were acquaintances. Is Allison here?"

"In the office," Patty said, motioning with her hand.

Susan hurried to the back of the office with Patty on her

heel, acting like she was waiting for Susan to reveal more. At Allison's door, Susan knocked.

"Hey, darling. C'mon in," Allison said, tossing Patty a stern look with her eyes, telling her to leave.

Susan closed the door behind her. "Can you believe Samantha wants me to ask Genevieve about last night? Where she was? If she was home? If she knew what Everett was doing? It's ridiculous. Completely insensitive. Tell me I'm not wrong."

Allison gave her a funny look, like she didn't know the details of what happened.

Susan caught her up. "Apparently Everett was found naked in bed with another man." She touched her head, feeling her spine slump forward as she cast her gaze downward. "He was going to change the world."

"Samantha must have good reason to ask you to do something like that." Allison paused before asking, "How did he die?"

"Genevieve thought it might be an overdose." Susan blew out a heavy sigh and asked why Allison called her here.

"A friend of yours, Garrett Todd, came to see me." Allison watched flashes of recognition cross Susan's gaze. "Did you send him to me?"

"I might have mentioned your name to him. He's working an interesting project and is going to need help marketing it when he's finished."

"Yes. His documentary. Have you seen it?"

"No. Why do you ask?"

"Patty discovered Garrett had a past connection to Vincent Verdi and April Wright. It might be nothing, but..."

Pushing herself up in her chair, Susan said, "Are you suggesting he had something to do with April's death?"

"I'm not suggesting anything," Allison said calmly. "But Garrett may have lied to me." Allison told Susan about the audio of the video showing Jackie speaking to April minutes before April was killed. "Garrett guessed at what it was they were saying—and he was close—but his guess wasn't completely right."

"What are you saying, he lied to you on purpose?"

"Do you think he did?"

Susan shook her head. "It could be an honest mistake. Can I see the video?"

Allison pulled it up on her screen and Susan moved around the desk to get a good look when the office door opened. They both picked their heads up and were surprised to see King entering the room.

"Hey, sorry to interrupt," King said, "but I'm going to need a copy of my video."

"I thought you might be back," Allison said, opening a drawer and retrieving the file for King. "I'm sorry to see what's happening to you."

King looked away, turning his attention to the computer screen. "Is that what it looks like?"

Allison nodded. "We were just about to watch it."

Allison hit play, and King asked, "You cracked the audio?"

Allison smiled as the three of them huddled around her desk and watched as Jackie and April exchanged a tense conversation. They listened as Jackie said, "If you don't hand over the files, Vince will kill you sooner rather than later. Now just give me what he's after and we can all go home."

"Shit," King said, standing straight. "This isn't good. Does Sam know about this?"

Allison said, "Yes, well, no—"

"Which is it? Forget it." King cursed, getting Sam on the phone before she made the grave mistake by going after Vince blind.

CHAPTER NINETY-THREE

ERIN'S HANDS WERE ON MY SHOULDERS AS WE PEEKED OUR heads outside. The sun angled from the west as a buildup of clouds moved in from the east. There was no sign of Mitch, no new cars parked in the driveway, and the neighborhood was absolutely quiet.

I whispered, "I think it's safe to go now."

Erin's fingers refused to let go of me as we exited the garage, leaving the door slightly ajar—exactly the way we found it on our way in. We edged the house and ducked between the trees, not wanting to be seen. It was a couple tense minutes but once back in the car, I asked Erin, "Do you think anyone saw us?"

Erin was sunk deep into her seat, peering over the windowsill and breathing heavily. "No. I think we're good."

With the keys in the ignition, I hesitated to leave. I knew what had to be done, but I couldn't bring myself to do it. Erin turned to me and gave me a funny look.

"Why does Vincent have Garrett's name on a piece of tape?" I turned to look her in the eye. "Is he in danger? Should we be worried about him?"

The crease between Erin's eyebrows deepened. Nothing we found inside proved Vince killed anyone, but the evidence we did find suggested he could have. Again, there were too many coincidences, and the evidence was suggestive, but there were enough unknowns to give me reason to doubt he was the one responsible.

Erin said, "Do we have reason to believe he's not guilty?"

I sat gripping the steering wheel, piecing together the events that led us here. Were Vincent and Garrett working together? If so, why? Did this have something to do with the film Garrett, Vince, and April worked on together? Or was it about the documentary Garrett was putting the finishing touches on? Something happened on that film set years ago, and we needed to find out what that was. But how?

I told Erin about Trojan, and said, "It's him. Vince is Trojan."

Erin asked when I discovered it, and I told her. Then she perked up and got excited. "Sonofabitch! We have him, Sam."

My gut told me we did, too. Our problem was how to get the police to see what we saw without having to jump through legal hoops. It wasn't like we could just reveal what we found without incriminating ourselves in the process, but at least we knew we'd been right all along.

Then my phone buzzed with a call that left us both feeling startled.

CHAPTER NINETY-FOUR

King was talking in my ear, but I couldn't hear what he was saying. Susan was in the background fighting me on calling Genevieve, and Allison was telling her to keep quiet and let King talk. Finally, King snapped and told them both to be quiet.

"Garrett had it wrong," he said, finally clear enough for me to hear him. "Allison figured it out. She broke the audio on the video."

I turned and met Erin's curious eyes. "What were they discussing?"

"Jackie said Vince would kill April if she didn't give him what he wanted, not that Jackie would kill April."

"But didn't April give him what he wanted?"

None of us knew for sure. We just knew something was exchanged but didn't know what. Did it have to do with April knowing he was gay? It had to have. But what I really wanted to know was if Garrett lied to Allison on purpose. Was he helping cover something up for Vince? I hoped it was just an honest mistake. No one knew where he was or what his intentions were.

"Alex, listen to me. Ask Susan if she knows where I can find Garrett."

A rustle of static filled my ear, and Susan got on the phone. "Samantha, I'm not sure where he is. I can call to find out, but he likes to get his work done at a café on the east side." She told me the name of the place and said, "Or you can try his house?"

"Where's his house?" I asked.

She told me the address, and I committed it to memory.

Susan said, "I don't think he intentionally lied. Garrett's a good man and whatever this is about, I'm sure he would like to help you out."

I hoped she was right, but I didn't have it in me to tell her that I was worried about his safety. "Please don't let him know I'm looking for him," I said. "I'd like to surprise him if I can."

"Whatever you say, but Sam, I can't ask Genevieve about her husband. You know it's not my style to stick my nose in someone else's private life."

I wanted to tell her about the escort Atwood was found with, how it strangely related to his own investigation, but King was back on the phone before I had a chance. I asked King, "Does Allison have the news on?"

"No."

"Turn it on for me, will you?" I heard King playing with the remote.

He asked, "What am I looking for?"

"I need to know if Atwood's police report has been made public yet."

"It leaked?"

King sounded as surprised as I'd been when Heidi showed it to me. "Heidi has it," I said, starting the car.

"No. I don't see anything. Unfortunately, they're still mostly interested in me." King sighed, mentioning how

Alvarez warned him that this would be a damaging report if leaked. Then he asked, "Why do I get the feeling you know more about what happened to Atwood than I do?"

"Because I probably do," I said, telling him about what Heidi received and how we linked the male escort, Geoff Little, to also being one of Watts's victims of police corruption.

"I don't recall seeing that name in the report," King said.

"But did you recall any of the victims' names, or were you only concentrating on Matt Barber?" I didn't want to fight with King, but that was what it sounded like we were doing. "Look, we have ourselves a copy of Atwood's report. But if Geoff Little should have been in jail, how did he get in Atwood's bed?"

King grumbled, and I could hear his frustration seeping through the line. I knew he was wishing he could do more to assist, but without his badge his hands were tied. Then he asked me where I was. I knew I couldn't tell him without him worrying for my personal safety.

"There's something else I should tell you. I found the video Russ Abair was trying to sell the paper."

"Where?"

"It's here, in Boulder."

"Sam, what did you do?"

"Nothing you need to know about."

"You need to stop now and let the police do their job." When I didn't respond, King added, "Did you hear me, Samantha? This is serious. If what you say is true, you need to bring it to Boulder PD's attention."

Staring at Vince's house, I said, "You do your job, and I'll do mine."

CHAPTER NINETY-FIVE

VINCE'S EYES WERE BLURRY, AND HE STRUGGLED TO KEEP the tires on the road. He kept wiping the tears away with the back of his hand, driving aimlessly up the canyon, then back down, before circling around the city of Boulder.

Vince didn't know what to do with himself. He hated where he was at, what his life had become. He wished he could be the man he was without being weighed down by shame. But he couldn't. He'd tried before, but he always reverted back to pretending to be the man people wanted him to be.

He stopped at a red light and reached for his cellphone. Scrolling through his gallery, he landed on a picture of him and Mitch. His eyes welled with more tears and his throat closed up. Soon, he was a blubbery mess of unstoppable pain.

"I'm sorry," he cried. "I'm so sorry."

Flitting his gaze around, he looked to see if anyone was watching. Though his windows were tinted, it was easy to forget he was hidden inside. The light turned green and Vince dropped the phone into his lap, thinking about his last kiss with Mitch.

He wished he could take back what he said. He didn't want to hurt him, but knew he had. Mitch had been there since the beginning, never straying from their friendship. He would do anything for Vince and didn't deserve to be treated that way.

"You'll never forgive me." Vince shook his head. "I don't deserve to be forgiven."

After a while, he began his way home when the tears were replaced by feelings of regret. He needed Mitch more than he was willing to admit. They were good together, but Vince wasn't ready to let his secret out just yet. There was too much on the line. He'd worked too hard for all he'd achieved. It was his life—*their* life—the one he created for both of them, and if he stopped being the great influencer, Vincent Verdi, he'd lose it all.

With a thumb over his cellphone's screen, Vince wanted to text Mitch but knew he had to say his piece in person.

"Please still be at home," Vince said, hoping Mitch hadn't left the house yet.

He punched the gas and watched his speed climb. An hour after he left, Vince could see his home again. In front of his house, a car he didn't recognize was parked.

Vince eased on the brakes and pulled off to the side. Was it paparazzi? Cops? He tried to read the plate number, but he was too far away. After a minute of staring, he finally decided it was an older model Subaru Outback. He could be wrong, but what did it matter?

Peering through the trees, he could see the Prius was gone. He presumed Mitch was gone too, and in that fleeting moment he felt his heart sink. He was lost in his heartbreak when the side garage door suddenly opened.

Mitch?

His heart fluttered with excitement and time paused as he waited to confirm that he still had a chance. Then his eyes popped with disbelief, not believing the two faces coming out of his house acting like they knew they were doing something illegal.

Lowering his brow, Vince glared as he watched Samantha and Erin scurry between the trees and vehicles before getting into the parked Outback without ever noticing he was watching them.

Did she just break in? Mitch wouldn't have let them inside, would he?

Vince didn't know who to trust or what to believe.

He sank deeper into his seat and waited for them to leave, listening to his heart pound with anger. It seemed to take them forever. He wondered what they were doing, who they might be calling. Vince thought back to the police visiting him last night and knew right then and there that he needed to get these two reporters off his back. They'd been after him since his show, convincing no one that he was responsible for April's death. It was getting old.

His thoughts jumped to Jackie and her ridiculous plan. Why was she so concerned with making his secret public? She should have trusted he could figure this out himself. But now, with her gone and these reporters snooping around, his secret was coming out whether he was ready to face the truth or not. What the world couldn't understand was why he had to keep April silent in the first place.

"The world can be such a cruel and unforgiving place," he said, biting down on his knuckles.

April knew it better than anybody but Vince. He couldn't let these two reporters control the narrative to his own story. A crime beat reporter was looking to report on crime. He worried what he might have left out for them to find inside. They had to be stopped, Vince thought as he watched Samantha's taillights flash a moment before they left.

It was Mitch's fault they were inside his house. Vince was sure of it. Mitch was getting back at him for saying their relationship was a mistake by leading them here. Though it might be too late to get ahead of the story, Vince could certainly decide how it would end.

CHAPTER NINETY-SIX

WE ROLLED THE DICE AND DECIDED TO TRY GARRETT'S favorite coffee shop east of downtown first, because it was closer. Susan's tip paid off.

"Funny how much he gets out for supposedly being a recluse," I said when we spotted Garrett leaving the café.

"Everyone is a recluse compared to Susan," Erin responded.

Garrett looked completely innocent in the same neutral colors from this morning, blending in with his surroundings. I watched him casually stroll up the street, phone in hand, oblivious to the potential dangers heading his way. It was like watching the walking dead. I just couldn't imagine him wanting to work with Vince. So why was his name found on a piece of tape at Vince's?

"We better make our move before he catches an Uber," Erin said.

I was missing our forewarnings into the future. Without the premonitions coming from Trojan, we were left with only our wits. My increasing feelings of anxiety kept me off balance. There were too many unknowns. Until an arrest was made, I knew my fears wouldn't stop.

We exited the car and quickly caught up with him, pretending like this meeting was completely coincidental. I said, "Garrett, what a surprise to see you here."

He picked his head up and gave us a double take, genuinely surprised to see us. He didn't miss a beat when he said, "Sorry I couldn't stay for the press conference, but the police were determined to make sure I didn't want to stick around for it."

My gaze drifted to his bag slung over his shoulder, and I assumed his drone and other film equipment were inside. What else was tucked away? Did his desire to film Atwood's presser have anything to do with the documentary he was making? I was sure they were connected. Though there was no crime in any of that, I still wanted to know what work had to get done before he could release it.

Garrett asked, "Did Atwood eventually show, or was he too chicken shit to fight?"

Though I was taken aback by his comment, I didn't let it show. "Why would you say that?"

"I've seen it before." He flashed Erin a wide smile. "Probably got cold feet. People like him are all talk until they start receiving pushback for taking a stand. It takes a brave man to be the face of the queer community, and frankly, I didn't think that short man had it in him."

Garrett seemed bitter about something. I couldn't tell if it was because Atwood failed to follow through on his commitment, or something else completely. Either way, it was a sharp contrast from the optimistic man I had come to know.

"He's dead," I told him.

Garrett was stunned into silence. After a long beat, he asked, "When? How?"

"The cops are still trying to figure it out," Erin said, giving him enough information to leave him satisfied.

I asked, "Do you know Vincent Verdi?"

Garrett flicked his eyes over to me and asked, "Did he have something to do with it?"

I stared without saying anything.

"Yes, I know him," Garrett said, shifting his feet. "He's only the most popular homophobic in the West. When Vince is talking, it's safe to assume he's attacking someone. And let's be honest, this shouldn't come as a surprise. I'm like anyone else when deciding to keep my friends close, but my enemies closer."

"So he's an enemy?" I asked, wiping the smirk off his face.

"We have a history."

Erin asked, "When is the last time you two spoke?"

Garrett knitted his eyebrows. "Am I in some kind of trouble or something?"

"We believe Vince is targeting people from his past, people who might know a secret he doesn't want to get out."

"From his past. But I—"

"What happened on that film set you, Vince, and April worked on together?"

Garrett looked over his shoulder and rubbed the nape of his neck when asking, "Is that why April was killed?"

"We're beginning to think so. But I just spoke with my friend, Allison Doyle. She mentioned you stopped by her place yesterday."

"Yes." Garrett's eyebrows pinched. "You and Susan referred me to her."

"Why didn't you mention you visited Allison when I saw you this morning?"

"And waste your time with me discussing search engine optimization and CPC advertising? I'd be happy to discuss it with you, but I don't think that's why you tracked me down."

"You were wrong," Erin said. "Allison cracked what was really said on the video."

"Wrong? How was I wrong?"

"Jackie told April that Vince would kill her if she didn't hand over the video, not Jackie."

"I was only reading lips. You can't possibly think I was hiding that from you, or anybody else, for that matter."

"Any idea what Vince wanted from April? Something that might also have to do with you?"

Garrett kept shifting his weight around, shoving his fingers through his hair. He was growing increasingly paranoid when he finally came out and said, "Who else knows you came to speak with me? And how did you find me?"

We didn't answer. Instead, we kept hitting him with the questions we needed answered. "What happened on the film set the three of you worked years ago that makes Vince so worried?"

Garrett leaned forward and got in my face. Pointing to his chest, he snarled, "Are you trying to get me killed? Because the way I see it, wherever you are, death follows."

"You have the power to stop this, but we need to know what happened, Garrett." Erin reached for his arm and he slapped her hand away.

"Just stop it." Garrett began backpedaling. "If I tell you what happened on that set, Vince would certainly kill me."

CHAPTER NINETY-SEVEN

HEIDI STEPPED OFF SET AND WAS HEADING BACK TO HER office, needing a moment alone to collect her thoughts, when she caught her boss staring from across the room. There was a brief pause as she looked into his gaze, knowing the glimmer was a look that said ratings were up.

Though she was sick and tired of covering Alex King's story, Samantha got exactly what she'd wished for. She heard her name being called from near the bank of elevators and she turned to see who was calling. A young man with a visitor pass slung around his neck hurried across the floor with one arm extended out, offering her his phone.

With a quizzical look on her face, she glanced to his hand and asked, "What's this?"

"It's for you."

Heidi looked the stranger in his eyes. "Who are you?"

"The messenger boy." He grinned.

Finally, she took the phone and pressed it to her ear. "Hello?"

"Are you in a safe place where you can talk? I need to make this quick," King said.

Heidi recognized his voice and responded, "No. But give me a minute."

"Make sure to bring the boy with you."

Heidi motioned for the young man to follow and asked King in a low whisper, "Alex, what is going on?"

"It's hard to explain exactly, but I'll make this quick. Your station is airing a fake. It may appear to be me in the video, but I wasn't the one planting evidence."

"Then who did?"

"My messenger has the original video proving it's not me."

"Alex, I—"

"Take it, Heidi. Watch it. After you see for yourself, you'll notice my face will be replaced by another officer's face. His name is Matt Barber, a member of the Criminal Investigations Unit. That's your story right there. Not me."

Heidi stepped into her office with the young man trailing behind and closed the door once they were both inside. "Did Sam put you up to this?"

King ignored her question and said, "Geoff Little, the man the public defender was found with this morning, was a victim of Officer Barber. I can't give you the exact details at this moment because I don't have access to police files, but I'm guessing after you dig into this story, you'll find that Barber coerced Little into pleading guilty to a crime he didn't commit."

"Then how did he end up in Atwood's bed? Because I was given the police report and it's not looking good for Atwood."

"That's the million-dollar question," Kind said. "And I'd be hesitant to publicly share anything in that report until the ME's autopsy is complete."

"Are you suggesting Barber put Geoff Little in Atwood's bed?"

"Look into it. It shouldn't be hard to figure out now that you know where to look."

"I will, but Alex, how can you prove this new video showing Barber isn't also a fake? Because that's what people will assume now that the other video is already out there."

"Air it. Let the people decide, and I'll do the rest."

Heidi wasn't sure what else King had planned. She didn't want to know, either. She was more curious to see what King was sharing and couldn't wait to play the new video herself. "I'll take a look," she said, "and I promise to fight for it to air, but that's about all I can do." Before she ended the call, she whispered how sorry she was for what was happening to him.

CHAPTER NINETY-EIGHT

Vince was slow to exit his car. With one foot planted on the ground, it felt like the entire world was watching him. For the first time in his life, it wasn't a good feeling.

He looked around, peering into his neighbors' windows. The air was so still, and the neighbors quiet, it had him nervous.

Closing his car door gently, he was afraid of attracting unwanted attention. He didn't know what to expect or what was waiting for him inside as he made his way to the house. Oddly enough, he found himself wishing he'd made an effort to meet his neighbors, the same people he was certain who knew about his relationship with April Wright. While his work life was in the spotlight, Vince had kept a low profile at home, and that was what he planned on doing now that he felt the need to hide.

The closer he got to his house, the faster his feet moved. He immediately went to the garage door and cursed when he found that Samantha had left it open. Peeking his head inside, he wondered what she had been looking for. And what she might have taken with her. Then he closed the door and entered the house through the front door like any other day.

In the foyer, he stood for a moment, quietly listening, hoping someone was home. Again, it was as quiet as the street when he called out, "Honey, I'm home!"

His smile faded when his call wasn't echoed with a response. A small piece of his heart broke, and Vince was beginning to realize that he was losing everyone he ever loved.

Moving through his house, his home was as empty as his heart. He caused this. Caused his family to split. There was no one to blame but himself, and that really tore him up inside. Vince didn't make bad decisions or have regrets. He was loved by everyone. Wasn't he?

"You reap what you sow," he muttered to himself as he climbed the stairs on his way to Mitch's loft.

The tiger growled as he passed, but Vince paid him little attention. Without Mitch, he was going to need to get rid of that thing sooner rather than later. When he knocked on Mitch's door no one answered. Without hesitating, he opened the door, only to find the entire loft desolate.

Missing his friend, Vince edged the bed and touched his sheets before his eyes landed on his own pink shaded sunglasses. He picked them up off the dresser and felt his lips pull into a smile.

"You were thinking about me?" Vince assumed Mitch was. Why else would his glasses be in Mitch's room? Vince hadn't left them there.

He set his glasses down, hopeful Mitch would be back so he could apologize for what he said earlier. Then he opened and closed drawers, happy to see Mitch's things still inside. It didn't appear he'd taken anything with him. Vince considered that a good sign. There was still hope, he thought, when opening another drawer. "I'm sorry, Mitch. Please come hom—"

Vince burst out laughing when he found a red wig that reminded him of Jackie. But it was the memory of Mitch wearing it while dancing in his underwear that kept Vince laughing. Those were the moments he cherished most—the memories that he wanted to create more of.

Sitting on the edge of Mitch's bed with wig in hand, Vince was thinking that maybe Mitch was right. Again, tears welled in his eyes as he nodded his head, thinking how he could do this—be the person he was born to be without being afraid of what the world thought of him. But it made him angry to think Samantha broke into his house and violated his privacy, as if deciding his future for him.

Standing, he tossed the wig to the dresser and thought how everything in his house suggested he was gay. The clothes, the shoes, the décor. Living with two men. Everything.

He stormed back to the main house feeling completely violated.

Did she take photos to print? He had to assume she did.

Beginning to freak out, he reached for his phone and reactivated his social media accounts, surprised to see a number of his fans turning on him. They questioned if he was the one responsible for the spree killings, if he really killed April like the rumors suggested. This was what he feared—the reason he couldn't come out and tell them the truth of who he was. They'd turn on him just as they were doing now. Vince knew he needed to release new content to get ahead of this, but he didn't know what to post.

With his eyes flitting across the walls, Vince realized his mistake.

He took off running across the house and passed through the living room, his fingers raking the back of the couch. He could almost see Mitch lying back, relaxing with his video game controller in hand. He kept running. When he reached the editing room, he boomeranged himself inside feeling his heart beat even faster.

It was gone.

He looked to his left, his right, but it wasn't there.

Hyperventilating, Vince tore the office apart as he cried, "No. God. No. How could you be so stupid?"

Then he dropped to his knees and clenched his fists. The video Jackie got from April was gone. He had to know who had it—Samantha Bell, or Mitch?

CHAPTER NINETY-NINE

No one was sorrier about what was happening to King than himself.

He ended his call with Heidi and pushed his cellphone back into his pants pocket, then reached across the seat for the binoculars. Turning his attention to Barber's house, he knew that his career and reputation should speak for themselves. If only he could get access to his own file, then he could show the public he was one of the good cops. But that was also what made IAD's investigation so odd. They should have his file. What was missing? Why couldn't they see that his suspension was politically motivated?

"Politics." King grumbled his disapproval.

He had everything riding on Heidi and Samantha's ability to learn how Geoff Little found his way into Atwood's bed, and he trusted they'd be able to come through for him. But he wasn't certain they'd be able to do it before time ran out.

King glassed the house and watched Barber's wife feed their two children. The scene was calm inside. King wondered if Barber's wife knew she married a prick.

"How does it feel to be surveilled, asshole?"

He swept his gaze to the same undercover vehicle that was following him earlier. It was parked in front of Barber's garage. King couldn't believe how stupid he was for leaving it out in plain sight, as if wanting King to put the pieces together. Rookie mistake.

The front door of the house slammed and King swept his gaze to an angry Barber heading straight for King. Running up to King's window, King buzzed it down as Barber greeted him. "What the fuck do you think you're doing, King?"

"Easy, partner." King casually rested his arm on the sill. "I'm just here watching your back. It's what us cops do for each other, isn't that right?"

"That's bullshit."

"You're right." King winked. "I'm here to let you know two can play your game." He reached for the tinfoil wrap in the passenger seat and handed it to Barber.

"Whatever it is, I don't want it."

"It's breakfast. The one you watched me cook. I thought you might want to try it, seeing how interested you were to mention it to Samantha."

"Take a vacation, King. You're only digging your grave deeper. Though I'm not sure that's even possible now that your face is all over the news."

"I know about Geoff Little," King said, changing his tone. "Where he came from. Why you used him. You pricks thought you'd actually get away with it, didn't you?" King laughed.

"Geoff who?"

Looking Barber in the eye, King could see that Barber knew who Geoff Little was. He continued, "But here's what I can't understand: why target the LGBTQ community? Is it because you're an insecure homophobic? Or is it because someone gave you easy targets to pursue? I'm going to guess it's a bit of both, but mostly I'm going to assume you chose them because someone did the work for you."

"My face isn't the one plastered across news desks."

"What happens when this vigilante you're working with wants to be recognized? You think he'll seek media attention himself? Or ask for help?"

Barber's jaw clenched. Worry crossed the younger officer's face, but King didn't let up. He continued his attack by saying, "Putting him on the stand would be a nightmare. He'd ask for leniency and you'd have to give it to him. What? Did you actually think Atwood didn't speak to this person before making the decision to go public?"

"Go ahead, King. Make use of your girlfriend. Then we'll see how much leniency IAD gives you in your own investigation. We all know there is a leak in the department and I'm not the only one looking forward to the day you're gone."

"You can dream of me moving on all you want, but know this: your name, as well as that of the other officers Watt's has recruited to do his dirty work, will be named. And when that happens, we'll see who likes early retirement better." King pointed to Barber's house. "I'm sure your family would like seeing more of you."

"Are you threatening my family?"

King started his car and put it in gear. "Your moment of reckoning is coming, and I'm looking forward to watching the show."

CHAPTER ONE HUNDRED

MR. T WAS TUCKED SAFELY INSIDE HIS CAR, IN A QUAINT neighborhood, sitting calmly behind the wheel with his fingers drumming on his thigh. He smiled at the mature trees and manicured lawns, appreciating the sidewalks without any cracks. It was a beautiful day with the autumn colors flickering in the light—a nice surprise when he'd expected to find something completely different.

"This place is clearly on the up and up," he said into his phone, filming himself. "Investment and home prices are on the rise, and I can think of no better place I'd want to bring my story to an end."

Mr. T knew he wouldn't broadcast his show to the world today; he'd learned that no one cared. That didn't bother him because he could easily see for himself how beautiful the ending would be.

"Art is in the eye of the beholder."

Closing his eyes, he tipped his head back and smiled as he imagined seeing his work being played across the country on large projector screens. People would appreciate his work, marvel at the art and amount of work involved to make it the masterpiece it was. There would be awards and recognition; fans would gather and demand he create more.

"That, my friends," Mr. T opened his eyes and continued talking into the camera, "is how it will happen. You heard it first from me."

He laughed and rolled his gaze back toward Samantha Bell's house. However, nothing could happen until his characters arrived on set. Speaking of, where was his star? She wouldn't make him wait all day, would she?

"Doesn't she know to never make the director wait?" Mr. T said amusingly.

He toyed with the idea of luring her in with a prank call, perhaps just a text. But he had nowhere to go, nothing better to do, so he decided to wait it out. Besides, surprising her would add drama to the scene and that was *always* a good thing.

He passed the time filming scene-setting shots—a few dog walkers and bicyclists making use of the sunshine before winter settled in for good. He didn't bother hiding who he was, for no one paid him any attention. He was a ghost and had come to recognize his newest superpower was his ability to hide in plain sight.

"You like this new me, better?" he asked the camera, thinking of the three amigos. "Because I'm starting to think it's a good fit."

Mr. T stared into Samantha's front windows, wondering if Allison was still working through the audio on the video clip he had given her. He figured it wouldn't be too long if she hadn't figured it out already. What really tickled Mr. T was knowing Samantha's son witnessed Trojan predict, and execute, each of his killings. Priceless.

"The greatest joy in my life right now is knowing I'm toying with the son of the journalist who is set on solving a case the police seem disinterested in solving themselves." Mr.

T smiled at the camera. "It's almost like they don't care that I've killed three people."

Mr. T had a plan for that, too, because he would never fully believe the police didn't care.

Reaching into his pocket, Mr. T pulled out the second CD-ROM he had kept for himself. Flipping it between his fingers, he remembered White Stallion suggesting he might be stupid enough to believe the police would never solve the murders. What White Stallion didn't predict was how he would be outsmarted by Trojan.

"And he thought I'd actually let him in on our little secret." Mr. T tsked.

Mr. T was on to him from the moment White Stallion first reached out to Trojan. And when he requested to meet with White Stallion, Trojan came prepared with two discs, one in each pocket, deciding which one to give White Stallion at the last minute. It depended entirely on how White Stallion fit into Trojan's equation. White Stallion gave him the answer he needed to help him decide, and now Trojan was asking himself, "But what to do with this second disc?"

The way Mr. T saw it, he had two options. The first was to give Samantha the disc and be done with it. The second was what he was leaning toward, and what a surprise it would be for both of them if Trojan decided to uncover White Stallion's mask and reveal his true identity.

Mr. T burst out laughing. He could hardly contain himself. He was excited with the possibility, tickled with power.

Both options had their benefits. One would keep Mr. T in control, and wasn't that what this had been about from the very beginning? But revealing White Stallion's identity would be almost comical.

"What a fool he is," Mr. T said, looking directly into the camera's lens. "He had no idea how great an actor I am. The tears I forced myself to squeeze from my eyes. He believed I would actually turn on the man I love. White Stallion, you have no clue what is coming, but you'll surely find out, my friend."

Mr. T cackled. Then his lips snapped shut and everything went quiet when he caught movement on the street in front of him.

"This can't be," he said, dropping the camera to his lap. His lips parted, and he kept his gaze on the man walking to Samantha's front door. His presence was going to change everything. Mr. T didn't like what he was seeing.

CHAPTER ONE HUNDRED ONE

I COULD FEEL ERIN GLARING AT ME OUT OF THE CORNER OF her eye. This was partially my fault for not having the patience to ease Garrett into talking about what happened on that film set so many years ago, but I couldn't blame him for wanting nothing to do with us.

"He's right, you know?" I said.

"About what?" Erin responded.

I turned and met her eye. "Death follows us wherever we go."

"Only because we're on Vince's heel." Erin gathered her hair into her hands and tied it into a ponytail, beginning to make her way back to the car. I watched as she pulled her phone from her pocket and begin typing a text. When I asked who she was messaging, Erin called over her shoulder, "Susan. Maybe she can get Garrett to talk?"

Thinking she was right, I hurried to catch up to her and asked, "How old would Garrett have been when that film came out? Thirteen, fourteen? And Vince would have been, what? Eighteen, nineteen?"

Erin kept walking. "What are you getting at?"

"Barber's vigilante targets sexual predators. It's clear he believes he's doing the community a great service by luring these people out from the shadows."

Erin stopped and turned to me with a creased brow. "And you think what, that this vigilante is Garrett?"

I arched a single eyebrow. "All we know about Garrett's film, *Coming Out,* is it's about a sensitive boy learning to live in a masculine world."

Erin stopped and asked, "Did he say that?"

"Something like that."

"It's a bit of a stretch, even for us. Don't you think?"

"Do you have any better theories?"

"My head hurts, Sam. I need to get some caffeine in me before I start trying to fit square pegs in a round hole."

Erin continued to the car, and my thoughts kept churning. Again, I was missing Trojan's premonitions. At least his fore-warnings gave us a heads-up to what might be coming. Now we had nothing, and not knowing was worse. Maybe naming Garrett as the vigilante was a stretch, but I couldn't shake the possibility that Vince could have acted on his own suppressed sexual desires with Garrett Todd. But if I was right, was Garrett the vigilante? Was April witness to it? Was that the reason she was killed?

My phone buzzed with a text from King. As soon as I was finished reading his warning, I scanned the horizon and said, "Christ. We need to go."

Erin heard the urgency in my voice and asked, "What is it?"

"That was King." I looked over my shoulder. "He said to be on the lookout for Barber. He just put him on notice."

"What does that even mean?"

I wasn't totally sure, but had some ideas about what King was up to. I didn't like it. Erin and I both concluded Barber could be coming after us and as soon we settled back into my car, I received another text from King.

Erin asked, "Is it him again? What's going on now?"

"He gave Heidi the original video and now she just needs to convince her producers to run it."

"I hope this works, Sam, but King's right. Once Barber sees his face on the news, he's going to assume it was us who gave Heidi that video."

"Because Barber is probably the idiot who first gave it to me," I said, thinking about Kovac. I still didn't have proof Kovac was Barber, but I liked to think he was. It made it easier to hate Barber for trying to pin this all on us, while also trying to ruin King's career at the same time.

We headed back to my house, needing to safely file away my copy of Atwood's report, when my son called me with a frantic sounding voice.

"Mason, can you hear me?" I said over Cooper's barking.

"Mom, there's someone here pounding on the door and windows calling for you."

"Calling for me? Do you know who it is?"

"I wouldn't dare open that door with what he's saying."

I didn't dare ask what Mason had heard. Instead, I asked, "Does he know you're home?"

"I don't think so. I'm hiding in my room, but I'm afraid he's going to break in."

"Keep Cooper barking and call the cops," I said, hearing loud knocks echo in my ear. Who was this lunatic at my house looking for me? And why did I think this person might be after my son? Was it Barber? It had to be. But if it was, would the police do anything when they came?

"Hang tight. Okay, Mason?" I said, slamming my foot down on the gas pedal, knowing I was only a minute away from rescuing my son. "I'm almost home."

CHAPTER ONE HUNDRED TWO

I HELD THE STEERING WHEEL IN A TWO-HANDED WHITE-knuckled grip as I took the car faster than I'd ever taken it before. We were so close to the house, yet it seemed like we wouldn't make it in time. A minute felt like an eternity and I kept glancing at the clock, worrying about Mason.

I said, "I hope that sonofabitch is still there so I can see who has the nerve to come to my house to scare my son."

We didn't know what to expect to find waiting for us when we arrived, but King's warning about Barber mixed with the soft quiver in my son's voice had me racing to stop whatever might be about to happen.

Every muscle fiber in my body flexed as I jerked the wheel and skidded around the bend. Erin hung onto the door and leaned into the turn as we sped toward my house. Once my front porch was in sight, I stomped my foot on the gas pedal before slamming on the brakes, skidding to a stop.

A man in a hooded black sweatshirt came around from the back of my house and, instead of running away, he came straight for us. That's when I recognized through his angry, shadowed face who it was.

"Christ," Erin gasped. "Does he know we broke into his house?"

"How could he?" I was more surprised he knew where I lived, but if Vince was my drone stalker, this wasn't his first visit to my house.

Erin bent over and dug in her purse, searching for her can of mace.

I unbuckled my seatbelt, keeping an eye on Vince.

A part of me was relieved it was him approaching and not Barber. Barber scared me more, but I worried what Vince might be hiding inside his pockets. Locking eyes, I hoped Erin was right about Vince's reasons for being here. I didn't want this to be about my son and the premonitions he'd witnessed. I needed it to be about us. Then maybe we could talk some sense into him before he decided to kill us, too.

"We have to confront him," I said, listening to the drumming inside my chest.

"Just so long as we don't incriminate ourselves."

Flashes of what happened to Jackie blinked behind my eyes. I didn't like the position we were in but we asked for it the moment we decided to enter his house without an invitation.

Vince lengthened his stride, sprinting for our car. We flung our doors open at the same time and braced ourselves for impact. I could hear Cooper barking like mad through the front window and watched Erin aim the can of mace at Vince's head.

"Stop!" Erin screamed. "Or I'll shoot this in your eyes."

Vince dug his heels in and came to an abrupt stop. Breathing heavily, he asked, "Where is the video you took from me?"

I shared a quick questioning look with Erin before responding, "What video are you talking about?"

"Stop with the games," Vince snapped. "I know you broke

into my house and took what was mine," he yelled, stomping his foot hard on the concrete. "I saw you leaving my house, dammit!"

I knew we could have been seen, but I didn't expect Vince to be the witness. Thinking through my answer, I stared into Vince's dark eyes, suddenly feeling bad for him. I couldn't imagine having to live my life pretending to be someone other than who I was. It must have been a nightmare having to live the lie, causing unnecessary misery along the way. As he stood there heaving through breaths with his shoulders hunched forward, he looked like a man-child needing to be held by his mother. Oddly enough, I wanted to be that mother I knew he needed.

In a compassionate tone, I said, "You mean the video Jackie took from April? Or the video you stole from Russ?"

His eyes went wild. My bet at guessing what he was refer-ring to paid off. But where it went from here was anybody's guess. I was acting on instinct and faith that he'd do the right thing when faced with the truth.

Erin kept the can of mace steady when I asked, "Where did you stash your Dodge Challenger?"

"You nearly killed us," Erin barked.

Vince's hands hung to his sides, and I watched him clench his fists into tight balls as he tucked his chin and flared his nostrils like a raging bull about to charge.

"April gave you what you wanted." I continued applying the pressure, knowing we were close to breaking him. "Yet you still killed her. Why?"

Erin said, "Must have been something big."

I took another stab at guessing what was actually happening inside his head. "It didn't have anything to do with Garrett Todd's documentary, *Coming Out*, did it?"

Vince's eyes rounded into large white disks. "What did you say?"

"Garrett Todd is making a film, *Coming Out*. He hasn't told you?" When Vince didn't respond, I continued, "I thought since you two had worked together he would have shared his project with you. Unless you hadn't told him you were gay but he figured it out himself?"

Vince's look changed. Suddenly, his spine curled, and he looked a foot shorter, as if his body had shrunk. I didn't know what he was planning next, but I felt he was about to lunge forward and attack in a last-ditch effort to silence the two people who clearly knew his secret and had the ability to tell the world. When he made his move, I flinched, taking a step back before blinking the surprise out of my eyes.

"What the...?" Erin said, equally bewildered by his actions.

Instead of attacking, Vince turned and sprinted in the opposite direction. Then we watched him climb into a parked car and speed away without another word said.

CHAPTER ONE HUNDRED THREE

"No. No. No." Mr. T kept swiping his hand over his head. He couldn't believe his eyes. "What are you doing here? You're going to ruin everything."

Slapping his palm against the steering wheel, his core began shaking. Mr. T thought about the odds, thought about opening the car door to warn him he had it all figured out and that he didn't need to be here now.

"You have it all wrong," Mr. T said. "I'm here because of you."

Mr. T watched Vince rap his fist against the front door, calling out for Samantha. When nothing happened, Vince jumped off the porch steps and moved around the side of the house. Mr. T assumed he was looking for a way inside, struggling to decide if he should risk showing his face or not.

Then it hit him. "You went home, didn't you?"

Vince must have found out the video April gave to Jackie was gone.

I have it, Mr. T wanted to tell him, but was afraid Vince would then blame him for the video's disappearance.

Tires squealed behind him and Mr. T whipped his head

around, jumping back in his seat as a Subaru Outback roared past. He watched it stop in front of Samantha's house, and Mr. T lifted his phone to record whatever happened next.

Sitting in the director's chair, he watched Vince sprint to the car. Samantha and Erin swung their car doors open and Erin pointed something at Vince, getting him to stop in his tracks.

"This is gold," he said, and kept filming. "Everyone is doing great."

He wished he was closer to hear what they were saying. He cracked his window with his free hand, but he was still too far away, so he made up his own script to go along with the scene.

SAMANTHA: Standing tall, unafraid. "*I know you murdered April.*"

VINCE: Angry, with fists clenched. "*I murdered no one!*"

SAMANTHA: "*We have proof.*"

But Mr. T couldn't have predicted what came next. Suddenly, Vince turned completely around and sprinted to his car where he sped off like a bat out of hell.

Feeling his heart race, Mr. T didn't know what to do. Was Vince coming after him? Going home? Then he remembered what he had done, suddenly regretting his decision.

You can't do that!

Do it. End it with a bang.

You'll get caught. You've already taken it too far.

His conscience battled it out. Pressure built inside his head. Mr. T squeezed his eyes shut and clamped his head between his hands, listening to the many opinions shouting to be heard.

Do it, you fool. Show the world what you're made of. They'll forgive you when they learn why you did it.

When Mr. T thought about what White Stallion had, he made his decision. This was how it would end. Turning the camera on himself, he said, "By the time this is over, *I'll* be at the top of my game."

Then he clicked out of the cellphone camera and made the call.

"Nine one one, what's your emergency?" the dispatcher answered.

Mr. T inhaled a deep breath and said, "I just killed my lover and have two hostages. Come quick. I'm not sure, but I think I might kill them too."

CHAPTER ONE HUNDRED FOUR

WHITE STALLION WAS IN A GREAT MOOD WHEN HE ARRIVED back to his house. His meeting with Trojan went swimmingly. He couldn't have planned it better himself, and still couldn't believe Trojan gave him exactly what he wanted while asking for nothing in return.

"What a fool!" White Stallion howled into the ceiling as he unlocked the door and stepped inside.

After dropping his keys into the bowl at the door, he headed straight to his office, unable to contain his excitement to finally see the video he'd been waiting to get his hands on for years. He'd meticulously prepared for this day. Now that it was here, White Stallion was ready to relive the moment that changed everything.

"I'm the vigilante hero here to destroy you," he sang, and skipped down the hall, light on his feet. "I'm here to do the work others don't have the courage to do themselves." He whistled a jovial tune as he spun the disc around his finger.

Entering his office, he flipped on the light and closed the curtain. "This is my coming out party and I want you to be a part of it. Come one, come all, everyone is invited!"

White Stallion dropped into the chair and rolled himself to his desk. He had saved Trojan from making the biggest mistake of his life.

"You protected the wrong man, Mr. T, and will thank me later for what I'm about to do."

White Stallion's fingers jumped over the keys as he typed in his computer password, anxious to expose Vincent Verdi's lie.

"You are as gay today as the day you came onto me," he said with a sharp grin, thinking revenge was sweeter than honey.

White Stallion couldn't wait to see Vince's fans turn on him. He opened the CD-ROM case and three flimsy head-shots fell out. Two landed on his lap, the third on the floor. He bent and picked up the one from the floor and placed each of the photographs in a straight row on his desk like a police lineup.

"Was this some kind of joke?" he muttered, trying to figure out what Trojan had given him. "Or a message?"

He knew the three women; had met them all this week, actually. There was Samantha on the left, Erin in the middle, and Allison to the right. A pin size hole was at the top of each of them. But what did this have to do with the video?

"We shall find out," he said, inserting the disc into his computer.

His video player popped up on screen and White Stallion pressed play. His heart was hammering, and a cold sweat spread over the back of his shoulders. He drew his eyebrows together. It didn't take him long to see this wasn't the video he was expecting. It wasn't the one he had asked Mr. T to give him. Instead of a video showing Vince prey upon him as a teenage boy, it was clips from Mr. T's killing spree.

White Stallion watched each one with great fascination. The shots were filmed from a first-person perspective and added a unique narrative to the story. Though he expected what was coming, he couldn't stop watching. It was like looking through the eyes of the killer.

First, April plunged to her death as two arms extended out from the screen and pushed her over the edge. Then it was a personal behind-the-camera account of witnessing Russ being shot twice in the head. Finally, he saw two hands on the steering wheel as the car veered for an unsuspecting Jackie Dumont.

White Stallion cringed and felt his stomach twist with each murder, but for some reason he couldn't look away. The perspective was fascinating and unique, almost like it was him who had committed the murders himself. But this was useless to his own documentary. Did Trojan give him the wrong disc?

"No, you're making a film of your own," White Stallion concluded.

Suddenly, the screen cut out and an electronic voice spoke through the speakers. The voice sounded oddly like his own, but he knew who it was. Trojan said, "When life imitates game, you become the star of your own show. Lucky for you, I saved the best for last. Death is knocking on your door. Sweet dreams, my friend."

CHAPTER ONE HUNDRED FIVE

WE HAD NO CHOICE BUT TO FOLLOW VINCE. GRIPPING THE car door, I dropped back into my seat and slammed the door shut. Erin knew what I was going to do before I made the decision myself. She managed to snap her buckle first. Once I'd done the same, we were off chasing Vince.

"Hurry, Sam, he's getting away!"

I was going as fast as my car allowed, but it wasn't fast enough. I hated leaving Mason home alone without first checking in on him, but the threat he'd alerted me to was getting away. And fast.

Erin kept pounding the dash, pointing her finger through the windshield, telling me to hurry up. I kept focused on the road and dialed home with my free hand. Mason answered. I said, "It's me. He's gone."

"How? Where are you?" Mason sounded confused.

"It's a long story, but when the police come, tell them it was Vincent Verdi who was trying to break inside."

"Vincent Verdi? Mom, does he know I was helping you solve these murders?"

I wouldn't be surprised if Vince knew my son was helping

us figure out his next move. I said, "Write this down." Then I gave the description of Vincent's car and the plate numbers— at least the ones I could remember. "We're following him now. I'll text you when we know where he's going."

Mason was relieved and promised to call the police. He told me to not do anything stupid.

Erin was still navigating, keeping sight of Vince, but we were one red light away from losing him. He led us through the city on what could have been a wild goose chase. We assumed he knew we were following him, and that made me nervous to think what he might have planned for us.

"You don't think he's leading us into a trap, do you?" Erin asked.

"Anything is possible with him."

I hated how unpredictable he was, but also wanted to understand what sparked him in the first place. I assumed it had something to do with the video he was after. But which video was that?

Vince turned on a side street somewhere west of downtown and slowed as he wound his way deeper into the quiet suburban neighborhood. My body was tense, the air stale. Neither of us spoke as we blindly followed him deeper into his plans, struggling to get our bearings with each second that passed. My thoughts kept jumping between Vince and my son. By the time he finally curbed his car and parked, I realized where he had led us.

"Where are we?" Erin asked, looking around.

I only knew because Susan had given me this address earlier today. I said, "This is Garrett Todd's neighborhood."

Erin furrowed her brow. "Sam, this is exactly what Garrett warned us would happen."

"Did Garrett come home after we spoke to him?" I assumed he had, and so did Erin.

When we locked eyes, I regretted pressuring Vince into

talking in front of my house. We revealed too much and received nothing in return.

I said, "Vince thinks we know what happened on that movie set."

"Garrett's not going to be happy we led him here," Erin responded, growing increasingly nervous about the situation.

I texted Mason the address to relay to the police. Despite Erin losing confidence, I hoped my gamble with Vince earlier would pay off. I couldn't afford to get it wrong. Another mistake could be the end of me. Never mind the possibility that we might have given away the information that could get Garrett murdered.

The tips of my fingers were cold as I glanced to what had to be Garrett's house. "We need to tell Garrett that Vince is outside," I said, realizing I didn't have his phone number. When Erin agreed, I called Susan.

Susan picked up after the second ring and I asked, "Have you heard from Garrett?"

"No. Why? Did something happen?"

"Can you tell me his address again?"

"Did you check the café first? You were right there the last time we spoke."

"Garrett was at the café. We spoke to him earlier."

"Then why are you asking for his house address?"

"We followed Vince to what we believe is Garrett's house."

"Vince is there now?"

"He knows we know about them being on set with April," I said, mentioning how Garrett was certain Vince would kill him to keep whatever happened on that set a secret.

"I'll try calling him. But, Sam, you need to call the police. This doesn't sound good." When I didn't respond, Susan threatened, "If you won't, I will."

We waited for Susan to call back. It felt like she was

taking forever. Vince hadn't moved since we arrived and Erin asked, "What do you think he's doing?"

"Nothing good, I assume."

My phone finally rang. It was Susan. "He's not answering or responding to my texts. Sam, you have me worried about him."

The sounds of sirens got closer, and I asked Susan, "Did you call the police?"

"I'm about to."

The sirens stopped as the first cop roared up to the house with emergency lights flashing. Now we really didn't know what the heck was happening, but I was hoping maybe Garrett caught sight of Vince and called the police himself before something bad *could* happen.

"Forget it," I said. "They're already here."

CHAPTER ONE HUNDRED SIX

KING CIRCLED THE BLOCK, PRETENDING TO LEAVE BARBER'S neighborhood before taking up his new position half a block away. He had everything riding on his plan, but there was no telling whether it would work or not. That was entirely up to what Barber decided to do next.

"What are you going to do?" King kept saying. "Take my bait and lead me to your source?" King hoped so.

It was a bold, risky move, but after he'd confronted Barber, King knew Barber would have to respond. Where, and how, was anybody's guess. King was ready to follow whenever Barber was ready.

King knew Barber was nervous. He saw it in his eyes. The way they flashed with worry, thinking King might actually bring his source to Samantha and reveal the Chief's scam. But who *was* Barber's source? Would Barber need to warn him to keep his mouth shut before that could happen? King hoped he would. It was the best-case scenario. King already knew Barber was complicit in Watts's scheme. Now all he needed was proof that a vigilante existed—evidence he could use to exonerate his own name.

King kept checking the time. With each minute that passed, he worried Barber would call his bluff. Then, at the fifteen-minute mark, Barber exited his house.

"Show me the money," King said, starting his car.

Barber was in a hurry. King wondered if Heidi broke the news. There was no way of telling, but it didn't matter now. Soon, the tide would change. When it did, King would be ready to ride the wave.

Barber backed out of his driveway and sped off. King followed, maintaining a safe distance as he followed him north. For a quick beat, King thought he was heading to Samantha's. It had crossed King's mind Barber might want to take his frustration out on her, and King welcomed the chance to bust his skull at thinking he could continue to stalk Samantha without repercussion. To King's relief, Barber swung west and increased his speed.

King matched his exact move and speed, wondering where this wild goose chase would end. Barber sped faster, then slowed to a near crawl. He continued driving in the erratic pattern of ups and downs, having King ask, "What is he up to? Have I been made?"

They approached an intersection slowly, and when the light turned yellow Barber took off, racing through. King swore he'd been spotted but hit the gas regardless. He blew through the red light with his horn blaring to stop the other cars from crashing into him. Barber shot back by tossing on his sirens. King was starting to lose hope.

Struggling to keep up, King's engine roared, and he managed to stay on Barber's tail. He soon led King into a neighborhood he wasn't familiar with, and to a house where a second officer was already waiting.

CHAPTER ONE HUNDRED SEVEN

MY HEART POUNDED. WE COULDN'T UNDERSTAND WHY THE officer seemed to be focused on Garrett's front door instead of on Vince. I flicked my eyes back and forth. Vince still hadn't moved. He remained as still as a shadow, and I was confused who called and what emergency the police were responding to.

"Do you think Garrett called the police?" Erin asked me.

It had crossed my mind. But why hadn't the police knocked on his door? The officer took position behind his cruiser, busy talking into the radio clipped to his shoulder as he stared at Garrett's house.

"Why aren't they going after Vince?" I asked.

A second unmarked car arrived, parking adjacent to the first black-and-white. The door swung open and Erin cursed. "Holy shit, it's Officer Barber."

We couldn't believe it. This couldn't be coincidence. Now I thought my assumptions about Garrett being Barber's vigilante were right. But if he was, that didn't explain why they seemed focused on Garrett's house when they should have been looking for Vince.

Erin suggested in a low whisper, "What if we just point Vince out?"

The situation was growing more intense. It wasn't like we were the department's two favorite people. What could we do besides wait?

Just as things seemed to be getting more desperate, additional uniformed officers arrived, followed by a SWAT tactical van. They were putting on vests, pulling out the big guns. I had a bad feeling about this but didn't know what to do. Something huge was about to go down and we couldn't figure out what.

"We stay put, keep our eyes on Vince."

"We can't just sit here, Sam. We have to do something."

"And risk getting shot?" I argued, knowing that if we moved now, it could easily make things worse.

Erin turned her head and said, "They're surrounding the house."

My mind was churning. Was Garrett not the person we thought he was? I kept flicking my gaze between Vince and Garrett's front door. Or did Vince set this up? I thought about Russ and Atwood and the dozens of innocent citizens having been coerced into admitting to crimes they didn't commit. Was Garrett next? It certainly seemed so.

When I shared my thoughts with Erin, she said, "If Vince did call the cops on Garrett, why would he still be here?"

I turned my head, and we locked eyes. "To watch it go down."

Erin gave me a knowing look, then turned her focus back to the house. She leaned forward and said, "It looks like they're going to bust down the door."

My entire body froze as I watched, anticipating the worst. Holding my breath, I waited when suddenly the front door opened and Garrett came out with a baffled look on his face.

Dozens of boots marched in and another dozen guns were

raised, all pointing their muzzles at his chest. Barber was shouting for Garrett to raise his hands in the air. Garrett looking stunned, wanting to know what this was about.

"No. This can't be. They have it wrong," Erin whispered.

I wondered if they did. Time seemed to have stopped, and I was so nervous. I didn't want to watch but couldn't look away. My mind knew what was about to happen, but I refused to believe that it was possible. Then Garrett told Barber something as he slowly raised both hands.

Barber continued yelling, pointing his gun at Garrett's chest as he moved in closer. Then Garrett made a fatal mistake. He took one step back, tripped on something behind him, and dropped one hand below his waist to steady himself. Barber fired a single shot into Garrett's chest.

CHAPTER ONE HUNDRED EIGHT

Erin screamed. I felt like the wind got knocked out of me. Erin covered her mouth with her hand and my eyes were round disks as my entire body froze, not believing what we just witnessed. On my first breath, I flicked my gaze to Vince, then back to Garrett. Neither of them was moving, but my heart was pounding.

What was Vince doing here? Did he know this would happen?

My mind replayed what I just saw. Again, I watched Garrett drop like a stone as soon as he was hit by Barber's bullet. He crumbled to the ground, folding onto his side. The shot was too close and too powerful for it not to have been fatal.

I turned back to Barber. He was crouched in a defensive stance as he cautiously approached Garrett with his gun still pointing at the center of Garrett's back.

"Someone needs to help him," I said, not liking how slow the response was from the other cops. "He needs medical attention."

Erin reached for my hand as if knowing I was going to

kick my door open. She was too late to stop me. I sprinted toward Garrett, needing to see if he had been armed. Was this police shooting justified or a terrible mistake?

I kept running toward his house, thinking how Garrett didn't strike me as a violent person. I didn't know what to believe anymore. I yelled his name as I ran, needed him to know that a friend was here—that he wasn't alone.

"Stay back," an officer shouted at me, blocking my pursuit.

He clamped his fingers around my arm and spun me around. I kept screaming, reaching for Garrett's attention. "Garrett! It's me, Samantha. You're not alone! Don't give up. You're strong. You can do this!"

Garrett tilted his head and fought to look in my direction as his body squirmed on the ground. He looked to be in agony.

Barber hovered over him, gun drawn, finger on the trigger, acting as if Garrett still posed a threat.

"Hang in there. I saw it all," I screamed, fighting free from the officer's vice grip. "They're not going to get away with this."

Barber caught sight of me, must have heard what I said, and swung his firearm on me as he pivoted his stance. I stopped and tossed my hands in the air, staring into the darkest eyes of any man I'd ever seen, wondering if I'd be shot next. Then I was scooped up from behind and wrestled to the ground where my hands were zip-tied behind my back. The officers stood over me and I turned my neck back to the house. I was relieved to see two officers treating Garrett's wounds.

"Hang in there," I whispered as I watched Garrett gasp for air like a fish out of water. There was too much blood and his color was fading fast. I kept yelling for him to fight, to hang on, but I wasn't convinced he was going to make it.

Then an officer hoisted me to my feet and, when I lifted my head, I locked eyes with Vince.

Vince stared with wide eyes from behind the glare of his windshield. He put his car in gear and left the scene before anyone but us knew he was there.

CHAPTER ONE HUNDRED NINE

AN HOUR PASSED BEFORE I WAS FINALLY SET FREE. NO ONE bothered asking what I was doing there, though I was sure they had plenty of assumptions. Erin remained behind the lines, keeping one eye on me while making sure to not get caught up in custody the way I did. It was a smart move as it allowed her to keep track of what was happening, who was coming and going, documenting things I couldn't see myself.

Time passed slowly as I waited to be released. Not long after I watched Garrett get shot, an ambulance arrived on scene and whisked him away to an area hospital. I prayed he'd make it, but knew it would be a miracle if he did. I couldn't figure out how Vince seemed to have pulled off the impossible.

"You let Vincent Verdi get away," I said to the officer guarding over me. "He was parked right there," I jutted my chin to the now empty spot across the street, "the entire time, playing you like a fiddle."

"Have a nice evening, Ms. Bell," the officer said, turning his back to me.

It didn't matter what I said. Nothing could convince them

Vincent had fooled them into killing an innocent man. I felt helpless. I kept asking myself if I was only making things worse by wanting to get to the bottom of why April had to die.

Garrett had warned me that death followed me wherever I went. Then he proved it by getting shot here tonight. I took my phone from my back pocket and checked on Mason. When I knew he was fine, I called Dawson.

"They shot him, Ryan. The cops shot Garrett Todd," I cried, telling my editor what I witnessed and why Garrett Todd mattered.

When Dawson asked if this had something to do with Atwood's report, I said it did. "The two stories are loosely linked." But mostly I was afraid because Vince managed to manipulate the police into silencing the last person on earth who knew what happened on that set that he didn't want anyone to know about. "It's why April is dead. It's why they all had to die," I said.

Dawson said, "Don't be so hard on yourself."

I was my biggest critic but I could also hear the regret in his voice. It was the tone that said he wished he hadn't ever sent me to Boulder to cover April's death.

"You don't understand," I said, doubting every thought that crossed my mind, wondering why it seemed Vince was untouchable. I'd never met anyone like him. It bothered me to know he'd get away with this. "Vince did it while sitting only feet away. He watched it all happen."

"I know this is tough, Sam, but there is a silver lining in all this."

"I'd love to know what it is, because I could really use some good news about now," I said, catching sight of Erin leaning against the hood of my car with her arms folded over her chest.

"The story has changed on King's video. It's come out

that the one with King in it is a fake. Now the focus is on Officer Matt Barber."

I stared at Erin and wondered how the new video clip would be received.

"It's confusing as hell, Samantha. I'm not sure anyone will buy it as the truth, but it's a good first step." Then Dawson told me to go home, get some rest, and together we could review everything that happened tonight when my head was clear.

As soon as I was off the phone with Dawson, I spotted King's car parked half a block down the street. It took me a moment to realize it was him, but when I saw he was sitting inside, presumably wanting to stay out of sight, my entire body lifted as I made my way to my man.

Once I climbed inside, he reached for my hand and pulled me to his lips.

I said, "Erin shouldn't have called you here."

"She didn't."

My eyes bounced back and forth with his. "Then how did you know where to find me?"

"I followed Barber."

I pulled back and gave him a questioning look. He told me that after he confronted Barber, he was led here. King saw everything that happened and had a totally different reaction than I did. "I don't know it for sure yet, but I think Barber might have just found a way to silence Atwood's key witness."

The cops were busy working the scene, combing for evidence inside.

I asked, "What happens to Barber now?"

King said, "The department will review the shooting and he'll be put on paid administrative leave, maybe assigned desk duty for a while."

I tucked a loose strand of hair behind my ear. "Heidi aired the original video."

King nodded his head like he knew she would. Then I followed his gaze and watched Erin hurry to our car. She banged on the glass and I opened the door. Erin said, "They opened Garrett's garage. You'll never believe what they found inside."

CHAPTER ONE HUNDRED TEN

VINCE PULLED INTO HIS DRIVEWAY AND PARKED BEHIND the Prius. His arms fell to his sides as he sat with the engine off for a minute, taking in several deep breaths as he attempted to collect his thoughts.

He'd never witnessed a man get shot before. It was a lot to handle. Nothing was making sense. He was now scared for his own life. He knew too much, had seen too many people from his life get killed. He had theories as to why people were getting killed, but didn't want to admit that he might be the reason why. Things were getting out of control and he didn't know what to do.

Checking his phone, Vince scanned the initial reports about an officer-involved shooting. No names were mentioned, but they would be by morning. He just hoped that Samantha would leave his name out of it—hoped she was the only one who saw him there.

The loft light above the garage came on but Vince wasn't ready to face Mitch, or anybody for that matter. He just wanted to be left alone so he could spiritually connect with Jackie and have her tell him what to do.

"Please, Jackie. You always know what's best for me. Please come back to me."

Vince heard a noise and looked behind him. When there was nothing, he swept his gaze between the dark shadows with paranoid thoughts telling him he was being watched.

They're coming for you next.

On the edge of a mental breakdown, Vince counted to three before jumping out of his car and hurrying to the front door. He fumbled with his keys in the dark but managed to get the door open and closed before anything could happen to him.

He reached for a light switch when a door somewhere in the house slammed shut. He jumped and reeled his hand back to his side before sliding his back down the wall, hugging his knees to his chest. Whimpering in the dark, he felt his insides begin to tremble. It was impossible to erase the image of Garrett getting shot. He could still hear the sound of the gunshot echoing in his ears. He was soon on the floor crying with his face buried inside his hands.

"I didn't know. I'm so sorry," Vince sobbed when thinking about what happened on that studio set so long ago. "I didn't mean to hurt you, Garrett."

April knew it then, as he knew it now. What Vince did to Garrett was wrong, but Vince didn't see it that way at the time. He was only acting on his infatuation, responding to a young flirtatious boy and learning who he was, what he was feeling. Yet his actions had haunted him the rest of his life, and he did anything to keep it a secret.

But he was also concerned about what Samantha might say. Vince knew she had followed him to Garrett's and suspected she knew about their past as well. It was why she was digging. Now it was anybody's game to bring out their history and right the wrongs of his past.

The harder Vince cried, the more difficult it was to stifle

his sobs. His pain was too deep. Finally, he released everything he'd been holding inside for so long—mourning all that he had lost.

When Vince settled down and wiped away his tears, he was surprised to find Mitch standing and staring at the bottom of the staircase. Mitch's brow was furrowed with pain, and Vince felt ashamed for having Mitch watch him cry. He felt so vulnerable. It only made Vince angrier for appearing so weak.

"Go away," Vince snapped, turning his head away while wiping at his tears.

Mitch ignored Vince and slowly approached. "You're hurting," he said, lowering himself next to Vince on the floor and rubbing his back.

Vince continued crying. "They shot Garrett. The cops shot him."

Mitch wrapped his arms around Vince and held him tight. "It's over."

"I never wanted him to die."

"You don't have to worry anymore."

Vince lifted his head and stared into Mitch's eyes. Mitch took Vince's face into his hands and they touched foreheads. "You're free, Vince. You're finally free."

Vince swallowed and nodded as Mitch peppered his lips with kisses. "You're free."

CHAPTER ONE HUNDRED ELEVEN

"C'MON, SAM. WE HAVE TO GO BEFORE THEY CLOSE THE garage door."

I turned to King. "You need to leave." King's expression tightened, but he knew I was right. He couldn't stay. He wasn't welcome by the department that had suspended him. "Go to my house. Be with Mason, please?"

King nodded and started his car. I gave him a quick kiss goodbye before joining Erin as we ran back toward Garrett's house.

Word about his death had spread like wildfire and we were no longer the only journalists on scene ready to report the police shooting. News vans were beginning to line up and a helicopter even circled overhead, making it impossible to hear the sounds of my heart beating wildly in my chest. But I could certainly feel it.

"There," Erin said, pointing as we got near. "You see it?"

"I do," I said, not believing it. But there it was, a dark-colored Dodge Challenger with a smashed in front end and cracked windshield.

"That's it, Sam. It has to be."

There wasn't any doubt in my mind. It was the exact vehicle we saw hit and kill Jackie Dumont. But how did it get here? Was Garrett really the person behind the murders?

"How do you explain that?" Erin asked.

I couldn't, but it was clear the police knew what they had found. Why they decided to keep the garage door open for everyone to see was beyond me. Perhaps they were diverting the attention away from Barber. Or maybe Garrett really was the mastermind behind the murdering spree. Either way, teams of investigators were going in and out of Garrett's house like they had found their guy.

We stayed off to the sidelines and watched the police work. Soon, I caught sight of Barber transferring vehicles and noticed the smartwatch he was wearing. I pointed it out to Erin and said, "It was the same one I saw on Kovac's wrist."

"I'm sure it was him," Erin said. "And I hope he gets what he deserves."

"Ms. Bell? Ms. Tate?"

We turned and found Detective Alvarez calling our names. He had a stern look on his face and I didn't like his tone. Forcing myself to stand taller, I said, "Rarely do we get officers requesting to be interviewed."

"And rarely is it I find the exact two people I'm looking to speak with so easily."

"This isn't about how your colleagues treated my friend earlier, is it? Because I recorded everything," Erin said.

"What can we do for you, John?"

"I have to make this quick, but since I knew you were here, I thought you'd like to know we found each of your photos inside Garrett's house. It appears he may have had you listed as possible targets."

"What else did you find?" I asked.

John scratched his chin and had a look of regret on his face, wishing he never came to speak with us. He was doing it as a favor to King, and I appreciated his willingness to divulge what he knew.

"We saw what was parked in the garage," Erin added. "Is Garrett responsible for the murdering spree the police have been investigating?"

Alvarez gave a knowing look and let us know more details would be given at the press conference. Then added, "Let's just say, I think you're lucky to be alive."

CHAPTER ONE HUNDRED TWELVE

WE WATCHED ALVAREZ WALK BACK TO THE SCENE WHEN Erin asked, "Why did he tell us that?"

I was as confused by the news as Erin. But John was a good man, and I appreciated his willingness to at least let us know we may have dodged a bullet when dealing with Garrett. It still wasn't fully registering though.

It wasn't only the fact that Garret had our photos, but he also somehow had Vince's vehicle in his garage. If he did steal it, why? And why had we missed the signs suggesting Garrett might be a person of interest? Were there any signs to begin with? This was Susan's friend we were thinking about.

We stood there asking ourselves what we could have done differently, grasping to understand our own shortcomings, when a crowd began to form around the podium. Not wanting to lose our spot, we took our position near the front, waiting for the press conference to begin.

Police Chief Gordon Watts made his way to the podium and Erin voiced the irony of him being the one to address the media. "I'm sure he's only here to protect Barber from our investigation into them both."

"Let's hope we get more than a cold stare," I said.

Watts adjusted the mic to sounds of shutters clicking. Tentacles of microphones hung over his head and a dozen cameras focused on him. I stared with hopes of him looking me in the eye but he never did. The chief was fixated on delivering a quick synopsis of what happened and I couldn't wait to hear what he had to say.

"At approximately 4:43 PM we received an anonymous call alerting us to a homicide and potential hostage situation. All units in the area responded and, upon arrival, joined our tactical team in securing the house. Before our officers could enter, the homeowner opened the door and disobeyed our officer's direct orders to show him his hands. At that time the suspect lowered his right hand to his belt and reached for what the officer believed was a weapon. One of our officers responded with a single shot and secured the perceived threat."

I couldn't believe the spin I was hearing. I turned to Erin. "*Weapon?* Garrett tripped."

The chief continued, "Upon initial search of the premises, our officers found no evidence to suggest a homicide had occurred at this property. Neither did we find any hostages like the call suggested. At this time in our investigation, it is our preliminary belief our suspect was home alone, and this may have been a suicide by cop situation."

Suicide? Was Garrett dead? I could feel my chest squeezing the air out of my lungs. Was it possible Garrett swatted himself? It didn't make sense. When I thought back to everything that happened, I once again returned to Vince. Both April's and Russ's deaths were made to look like suicides as well.

When a reporter asked about the Dodge Challenger in the garage, the chief responded by saying, "A dark navy-blue Dodge Challenger was found in the suspect's garage during the initial search, and it does match the description of yesterday's hit-and-run incident that resulted in the death of Jackie Dumont."

I realized the chief was purposely avoiding Garrett's name, so I made it a point when asking, "Are you saying Garrett Todd murdered Jackie Dumont?"

The chief turned, and we finally locked eyes. He paused for a beat as if surprised to see me. "We're not making any definitive conclusions at this time, but it's our belief the suspect may have been responsible for Ms. Dumont's death as well as that of two other unsolved murders both Denver and Boulder PDs are investigating."

A sudden uproar of questions followed as everyone assumed he was referring to April Wright and Russ Abair. I leaned close to Erin's ear and said, "You're not buying this, are you?"

"I wish I wasn't, but it makes sense, Sam."

The chief said, "We are still learning the details and, unfortunately, I just received news the suspect passed away on the way to the hospital. I'd like to remind you that our investigation is still ongoing, but we'll keep you updated on the latest developments as they come. Thank you."

Slowly, everyone but me moved away from the podium. Something about this didn't add up. It felt raw, a bit spoiled, and I couldn't move. Erin put her arm around my waist and held me for a long time before I finally asked, "Why does it feel like we lost?"

She looked me in the eye and said, "Because, in a way, we did."

CHAPTER ONE HUNDRED THIRTEEN

THE FEELING OF LOSING WAS AWFUL. INSIDE, I WAS grieving all that had been lost. Too many had died for me to feel like justice had eluded us all. But what bothered me most was seeing Garrett get shot by a cop I knew was dirty.

I didn't want to believe this was over. Vince was still out there. But Erin was right. The press conference made our investigation feel final, and so did seeing Vince's Dodge Challenger parked in Garrett's garage. That was the real shocker, and we spent a long time sitting in my car after the presser, reviewing our notes on Garrett to see what we might have missed.

Finally, I asked Erin, "Was this his coming out party?"

"I don't know if we'll ever know."

It wasn't just about what happened to Garrett that kept me feeling like more had to be done. It was also that it felt like Watts and Barber had won, too. The pain was almost as bad as feeling like we could have stopped this from happening in the first place. We missed something, but where? What was it?

It was well after dark by the time I dropped Erin at her

car. She opened the door to step out and had one foot on the pavement when I said, "I could have sworn it was Vince we saw steering the car into Jackie."

Erin said sympathetically, "Get some rest, Sam. We missed the mark. It happens."

I didn't know if she truly believed that or was just trying to make me feel better about how this investigation ended. When I arrived home, Mason was sitting on the couch with King and it was a beautiful sight to see. As soon as Mason saw me, he jumped forward and said, "Mom, you've got to see this."

I set my things down at the door and stood in front of the TV, curious to know what had Mason riled up. The last thing I wanted to be doing was watching the news, reliving what I already knew, but this time it was good news. I turned, glanced to King, and asked, "How did they get that?"

"Someone with access to his personal jacket is sticking up for him," Mason said. "Isn't that exciting, Mom?"

"It certainly is." I sat on the couch next to King and he put his arm around me and kissed my forehead. "This certainly changes things," I murmured.

"He might actually get his badge back," Mason said eagerly.

"I'm not out of the woods yet," King said, reminding both of us to be patient.

After explaining how it could have only been Lieutenant Baker to gain access to his personnel file, King changed the topic and made sure I knew about Heidi releasing the original video. Dawson had already seen it and let me know what was being reported. I was happy for him. This was what we needed. After we discussed the irony of how Barber's video was released at approximately the same time he was shooting Garrett, I asked, "Did you watch the presser?"

King nodded and asked how I felt about it.

"Confused."

Not a second passed before we were interrupted by my cellphone ringing. None of us were surprised. It was going to be a long night. I knew Dawson would be expecting my column on his desk come morning. But this wasn't him. This was a call I couldn't ignore.

"Genevieve," I said, answering my phone.

"I'm sorry to be calling so late, but I saw the news of what happened and thought of you."

"How are you doing?" I asked.

"I heard my husband's police report was leaked to the press."

I paused before responding. "I'm trying to use my influence to stop them from airing it, but I'm not sure if they'll listen."

Genevieve thanked me, then said, "But you should know it's true."

I paused and stared, asking myself if I had heard her right. "You know what was said in the report?"

"Enough." Genevieve sighed heavily. "I know what it looks like, and what you think happened, but Everett fell for Geoff while he was awaiting sentencing."

I opened my mouth, but no words came out. Could this be right? I had to believe Genevieve knew her husband best, but it explained why Geoff hadn't been behind bars. It wasn't worth asking if Genevieve knew Geoff responded to an ad promising to meet with an underage boy, as reported by Atwood, or if she knew the cops investigating her husband's death were blackmailing the same men Everett had been fighting to free. I just assumed she did and thought maybe it wasn't as black and white as I'd hoped it to be.

"Everett was a good man," Genevieve said. "A good husband, and a great father to our kids. He's going to be greatly missed."

"I enjoyed getting to know him," I said, sympathetically. "If anything, I hope he's at peace now."

"I do too." Genevieve paused a breath. "But that's up to you, Samantha."

CHAPTER ONE HUNDRED FOURTEEN

It was late, and precipitation was building on my windows as snow flurries floated from the sky. Genevieve's parting words left me feeling like there was something more I could do. Not only did I want to ensure Atwood would rest easy, I was also hoping to find my own peace in all this.

I heard the television turn off, and King came into the kitchen. Two strong hands fell to my shoulders, and I pulled back from my work to let King rub the tension from my neck.

"This can wait," he said.

"It really can't," I responded.

Atwood's report was spread across the table, and I was reviewing everything I'd acquired since that first night covering April's death. The stories felt connected because of Barber. He made this personal the moment I received my first threat, but a part of me needed to redeem myself for missing the signs I should have seen on Garrett.

I touched King's hand and twisted around to meet his eye. "Did Mason mention Vince came to the house earlier?"

King nodded. "I wish you would have told me sooner."

"He was after a video."

"Did you take it?"

I arched a single eyebrow. "No."

"Then why come chasing you for it?"

I was still trying to decide that myself, but I shared my theory about Garrett being the vigilante in Atwood's report. King had the same thought when Barber led him to Garrett's house, but then the Dodge Challenger changed the story.

King said, "After I confronted him, I was hoping he'd take me to his source—Atwood's vigilante. But now I wonder if he was only responding to the emergency call."

Something about Garrett being behind the murders didn't make sense to me. It was too convenient, and I told King. "Garrett personally told me Vince was the enemy."

"You still think Vince is responsible for all these deaths?"

"I do," I said. "He's an escape artist and has a secret to hide."

We debated how Vince's car got into Garrett's garage and why he even went to Garrett's after I confronted him at my house. We discussed how my photograph ended up in Garrett's house, and though I didn't have an answer for any of it, I did think I had a reason for Vince to want to silence Garrett.

"It's possible Vince sexually assaulted Garrett on that film set and April was witness to it."

King asked, "Then why kill April and not Vince? Because that's what the Chief alluded to tonight. That Garrett was responsible for the murders."

"And you believe Watts?"

King gave a look and sighed.

I reminded King how I had seen Russ's video in Vince's house. Then I sprang to my feet with a sudden revelation. Sifting through papers, I thought about the drone stalking me, the red wig I picked up when going through Vince's things, and how Trojan predicted each death.

"What, Sam? What are you thinking?" King asked, watching me work.

I touched my brow and recalled the way Mitch closed his trunk the moment we surprised him at Vince's house and that it seemed he wanted us to go inside once he left the house.

King asked, "What is it?"

I stared at the table, still lost in my own head with thoughts churning faster than I could keep up with. "Maybe it wasn't Vincent," I whispered.

"What are you talking about, Sam? You think it was someone else?"

I squinted and felt the pressure build inside my head. Was Mitch protecting Vince? Or was he setting Vince up? Why? Were they a couple?

I typed a few quick keystrokes on my laptop and shot an email off to Allison. Then I picked up the phone and called, hoping she was still awake.

CHAPTER ONE HUNDRED FIFTEEN

VINCE WOKE IN A COLD SWEAT FROM ANOTHER NIGHTMARE. This time it was Garrett getting shot. Fisting the sheets with both hands, his heart hammered against his chest. It felt like a nine-inch nail was being driven through his heart and he was afraid to move. It took a moment to remember where he was, who he was with. Finally, his memory came back to him.

Looking around his bedroom walls, the overwhelming feeling was back. He gulped for air, but his lungs refused it. Uncertainty crept into his thoughts and, when he rolled his head to the side, he saw that Mitch was sound asleep next to him.

Did I scream in my sleep? Vince wondered.

The look on Mitch's face said he hadn't.

Mitch looked at peace. Vince knew he was going to be the only person to help himself get through these trying times. But how long would it take for Vince to feel normal again? What was normal? He didn't know. Mitch believed he was free, even if Vince wasn't convinced himself. However, Vince knew it would take some time for him to believe his secret was finally buried in the past forever.

388 JEREMY WALDRON

Slipping out of bed, Vince made his way downstairs to the kitchen where he made himself an ice water. He chugged the first glass and was making himself a second when he caught sight of Mitch's cellphone charging on the counter. Next to it, the disk he had thought he'd lost lay in plain sight.

Vince wondered if Mitch had been the one to take it, or had it only been misplaced? Though skeptical of its placement, Vince was thrilled to know it hadn't made its way into the hands of Samantha Bell.

He set his glass down next to the sink and scooped up the disk as he hurried into the editing room, where he plugged it into the computer. The video loaded, and he started to choke up all over again.

"This would have destroyed me," he whispered. "Thank you, Jackie. Thank you for getting this from April."

His eyes were blurry from the tears. A blanket of relief draped over him, trapping in the shame he was feeling inside. Vince feared this wasn't the only copy, but had to trust that it was. When the door creaked open behind him, Vince's insides jumped as he spun around.

Mitch stood at the door. "I left it out for you so we can destroy it together."

"You knew about this?"

"Garrett did, too."

Vince tilted his head. "That's what you were looking for earlier today. You were after this video? That's why I couldn't find it?"

"He was going to expose you, Vince. Like he did to so many others."

"What are you talking about? How do you know this?"

"The cops were using Garrett to bait and expose sexual predators—men like you—to use for their own hidden agenda."

"No. That's not me. It's not who I am," Vince pleaded.

"You were on his list. And don't lie to yourself, the evidence is right there." Mitch snapped his elbow and pointed at the computer screen. "You're lucky Garrett reached out to me—"

Vince's lips parted. "He contacted you?"

Mitch gave a knowing look. "Wanted to expose you for what you did to him."

Vince's chest heaved with anxiety as he worked to connect the dots. "That's what his film was about? Me?"

Mitch stepped forward and grinned. "Samantha, she's a gem, isn't she? I didn't expect her to lead you to Garrett, but it was fitting as you got to see my work in person."

"Mitch, no. You didn't. You couldn't have." Memories of seeing the cop shoot Garrett flashed behind Vince's eyes.

Mitch inched his way closer and flicked his gaze back to the video of a much younger Vince and Garrett. Vince's body stiffened as he kept a careful eye on Mitch. It was his tone, the sharp glimmer of uncertainty in his eyes, that had Vince on edge. It was like he was speaking to a stranger instead of the friend he thought he knew. If Mitch killed Garrett, did he also...Vince noticed something in his hand, but he couldn't tell what it was.

Mitch continued tiptoeing closer, saying, "If not for Samantha, I might not have picked up on Garrett's intention. Turns out her investigation into Chief Watts was a blessing for both of us."

Vince gripped the armrests on his chair and rolled himself away from Mitch, remembering the red wig and how he found Mitch dressed as a woman. "What did you do? Did you show Samantha this video?"

"No, you fool. Garrett wanted it for himself. Not Samantha. I was going to take it to him."

"You were what?!"

"Vince, baby, Garrett knew April gave it to Jackie, and he

also knew if he could present it to the world they might actually listen and for once see that you're not who you say you are."

"I didn't kill April," Vince choked on his words.

"No, you didn't. I did."

Vince's breath hitched when he remembered how Mitch had accused him of murdering April. That was why people loved what he did at GamersCon. It had all been Mitch's idea to get people to react. His eyes welled with tears. "Mitch," he said, "please tell me you're lying. I had this under control. April didn't have to die. She gave up the video. It was over."

"You're wrong. April still knew what happened. She was the only witness. I was protecting you. Protecting us." Mitch pointed at his chest. "That's what this was about. What it's always been about. *Us.*"

"No," Vince said. "I had nothing to do with this."

"You had everything to do with this," Mitch argued. "If not for you assaulting Garrett on that movie set, none of this would have happened."

"That's not true."

"I'm sorry," Mitch said. "But it is. And you know it, too."

"People think I did this. You understand that? They think I murdered these people."

"I always knew you were safe. As soon as people knew what happened, the evidence would have exonerated you. Besides, you always managed to escape when backed into a corner. There was no reason for me to think this time would be any different."

"How could you do this to me? You ruined my life!"

"I know you suspected it was me, you just didn't want to admit I was cleaning up your mess."

"Don't turn this around on me!"

"You couldn't admit it for fear of losing me. I'm the only person you have left. I did this for you. To protect you. To protect our secret, and you nearly blew it when you told me you never loved me. Don't you understand: I set you free!"

Vince cried, "No! You ruined everything!"

Mitch reached behind his back and pulled a gun. Pointing it at Vince, he said, "I thought you might say that."

Vince showed Mitch his palms and pleaded, "Mitch—"

Feathering the trigger with his finger, Mitch said, "I'd think real hard and fast about what you say next. It could decide whether you live or die."

CHAPTER ONE HUNDRED SIXTEEN

I SWITCHED HANDS AND WIPED THE SWEAT FROM MY PALM. The phone was still pressed to my ear, pleading for Allison to pick up. King kept his eyes on mine, an ear tilted toward my phone, waiting for Allison to answer as well. I hated how it took Garrett to die to put it all together, but I knew I finally had this right.

The line clicked over. Allison answered, "Samantha, I'm so sorry about what happened to Garrett."

I heard bed sheets rustle, and I assumed she was with Nicholas.

"I should have called," Allison continued. "Is what they're saying about him true?"

I said, "Check your email."

"Okay," Allison dragged the word out. "Now, as I make my way to my computer, care to tell me what this is about?"

I kept calm but my brain was wide awake, ready to run. "The link to the video you received of Jackie and April. I've attached a picture of someone I'm hoping you'll recognize." I heard Allison lift the lid on her laptop, followed by keys clacking. "Tell me, was that who gave you his business card?"

A beat of silence hung on the line. "Who is he?"

"Is it him or not?" I snapped impatiently.

"Yes, Samantha. It was him. Now tell me, who is he?"

I lifted my gaze and met King's eyes. He stared like he knew what I was going to do without me having to tell him. I could see it in his eyes that he didn't like my idea, but I couldn't let it wait. This was my last shot at getting ahead of this story and determining who was responsible for all these murders before they slipped away and disappeared forever.

I said to Allison, "Mitch Unger. Vincent's right-hand man, and the last person who saw April alive."

CHAPTER ONE HUNDRED SEVENTEEN

I PRACTICALLY HUNG UP ON ALLISON. AS SOON AS I WAS off the phone, I stepped forward and slammed the lid on my laptop closed. King took one step forward and clamped his fingers tightly around my arm. "Sam—"

His fingers subtly twitched and I could feel his worry move down my arm. I looked him in the eye and said, "I have to go."

"That's fine. But not alone."

King's tone made me believe I didn't have a choice, but I argued with him anyway. "I need you to stay with Mason."

King clenched his jaw and gave me a look. "Then this can wait 'til morning."

"It can't. You know it can't."

King turned his head to the kitchen window, then snapped his gaze back to me. "Look outside. Are you out of your mind?"

"I understand you're worried, but Mitch gave Allison the link to the video and we need to ask him why."

"Must you go tonight? You know why Mitch contacted Allison."

I stared with thoughts shifting back to the victims. I could still hear Genevieve's plea for me to continue her husband's work. It was all I needed to remind myself that this was what had to be done.

I said, "Look, Mitch clearly wanted us to think Jackie killed April. Why? If he's responsible, then Vince is either in danger or they're both planning their escape."

"And if they're in on it together?" King's mouth pinched. "What will visiting them tonight accomplish besides pissing them off and putting yourself in danger?"

Making either of them mad was the last thing I wanted to do, but I had to keep them off balance just long enough to make the police see the truth. I said, "The police are going to close this case quicker than tomorrow's news cycle without having all the facts. You really want that to happen? Because I don't."

"And what? You think Mitch will just hand you the evidence you need to prove he's guilty?"

"I can do this. I *have* to do this. The treasure is right under the department's nose, and they don't even know it. They don't *want* it."

King swiped a hand over his face, and I cocked an eyebrow before telling King my plan. He stared for a long minute before rolling his neck with a disapproving look falling over his face.

"It will work," I said.

"I don't like this plan at all. You can get in serious trouble." He sighed and finally let me go.

"I don't plan to commit a crime. Only get to the bottom of what's going on." Knowing King was still hesitating to let me go, I fisted his shirt and pulled him in for a kiss. Muttering against his lips, I said, "I have to do this. It's the only way. If we don't do this now, we may never know the truth."

CHAPTER ONE HUNDRED EIGHTEEN

KING WALKED ME TO THE DOOR. ON MY DRIVE NORTH, I got Erin on speaker phone. "It was Mitch—Mitch gave Allison the link to the video of Jackie and April arguing," I said, telling her how all the pieces fit together. "He was the last person to see her alive."

"You think he killed her?" Erin asked.

"Makes sense, right?"

There was a long enough pause for me to think Erin wasn't buying it. I explained my reasoning, reminding her of Mitch's odd behavior in Vince's driveway. Then I said, "What if Vince didn't leave Russ's video out like we thought, but it was Mitch?"

It was so quiet I could almost hear Erin thinking. I assumed she was recalling how we caught Mitch by surprise, how he seemed on edge about something. This was why I was driving to Boulder in the middle of the night.

"But he left the door open for us," Erin argued.

"Did he?" I wasn't so sure anymore.

What was he doing earlier? Why did he seem to be in a hurry? Were we delaying his plans to kill Garrett? Or was he covering his tracks from the previous murders? If he was, he did it poorly.

"I hear what you're saying, Sam, but why set up Vince? Vince gave him everything. There's too much to lose."

Her guess was as good as mine. Everything I came up with was only speculation.

"Perhaps he was jealous of Vince's success, or angry that Vince couldn't admit to being gay. We thought he was protecting Vince by not letting us talk to him, but maybe we never had to talk to Vince in the first place," I said. "But it doesn't matter. If it's not Mitch, it's Vince, and they live together. I'm going to catch them by surprise."

"And what if whoever is guilty decides you should join the others six feet down? What then?"

King had already instilled those thoughts in me. Erin putting it out there added to my second thoughts. I eased into Vincent's neighborhood, parking across the street from his house.

"In ten minutes," I told Erin, "call Boulder PD. Report a break-in. Hopefully by then, I'll have all the answers we need."

CHAPTER ONE HUNDRED NINETEEN

Vincent tossed up his hands and fell back into his chair. He couldn't believe Mitch would actually point a gun at him. "What are you going to do, shoot me?"

Mitch cocked his head and grinned, giving Vince a look that suggested he was at least considering it.

"Where did you get that thing?"

Mitch reached behind his back and pulled his cellphone from his waistband. He brought the device to life, pointed it at Vince's face, and pressed the record button.

"Are you filming this? You can't be serious?"

"It's my story," Mitch said, extending his arm further across the room. "No. No. Let me rephrase that. It's *our* story, and I'm letting you decide if it will be a happily ever after, or ends in tragedy."

Vince's toes dug into the floor as his eyes skirted the room, looking for anything he could use to defend himself. He had few options and was afraid Mitch would shoot him no matter what he did. With both hands still raised, Vince turned back to Mitch, realizing he no longer knew who he was.

"You hurt me, Vince," Mitch's voice quivered. "You don't know how close I came to giving Garrett this video." He swung the gun's muzzle toward the computer screen. "And I demand you apologize."

Vince was still looking for his way out without making it seem too obvious. It seemed like an impossible situation. Mitch had him trapped in the small room, and Mitch knew it.

Looking Mitch in his eyes, Vince said, "I'm sorry."

"Now mean it," Mitch growled as he waved the revolver in the air.

"I mean it," Vince pleaded. "I never wanted to hurt you. You have to believe me."

"Then why did you do it?" Mitch asked angrily.

"I don't know. Jackie's plan had me all stressed out— I couldn't come out. I was afraid that what happened to April might happen to me. Maybe I was feeling guilty for what I did to Garrett years ago and how I was trying to hide it. What I did was wrong, I know. But like you said, you were protecting us and so was I. I love you, Mitch. I truly do. Now please put down the gun."

Mitch held still for a moment to let Vince's words sink in. Then he raised both his eyebrows when he asked, "Do you love me enough to tell the world?"

Vince held Mitch's stare. His moment of hesitation was enough of an answer for Mitch to know Vince could never come out to the world. Feeling his throat close up, Mitch turned his head away, snapped his wrist, and pointed the gun at Vince. Then he fired.

CHAPTER ONE HUNDRED TWENTY

THE SILENCE AFTER HANGING UP WITH ERIN WAS haunting. I checked my mirrors before glancing above to the streetlights. I took a moment to relax the worries voiced by both Erin and King. I watched the fat snowflakes lazily fall from the sky while thinking about the drone. I had to listen to my intuition because, inside, my heart was telling me I was right.

I checked the time and exited the car. Neighboring houses were as dark and motionless as the surrounding air. The neighborhood seemed to be tucked in for the night, but Vince's front porch light was on.

I moved with ease over the wet pavement that would soon freeze over as the temperature dropped. Ten minutes was all I had to get in and out alive before the police arrived. If it all went according to plan, that would be all the time I needed. I also had to factor in the weather and the possibility the response might be delayed because of it. It was a tall order to handle, but I believed I could do it.

A pillow of condensation formed at my lips as I intently listened to each footstep hit the pavement. Thick wet snowflakes stuck to my jacket as I headed straight for the garage, thinking about the layout of the house I remembered from our escapade earlier.

At the door, the knob was cold to the touch but turned easily. I slipped inside undetected and paused for a moment to allow my eyes to adjust. It took longer than I hoped. Inside was as dark as space, but as soon as I could make out the stairs, I began climbing up into Mitch's loft.

At the top, I pressed my ear gently against the door. Again, it was quiet. Not a single hum or click to be heard. With a deep breath of courage, I opened the door and, because of the streetlights shining through the window, I could see the bed was empty. Then a gunshot cracked the air.

I flinched, and my heartrate spiked through the roof. The shot came from the other side of the house and I took off running toward it. Sprinting through the hallways, I kicked open the door and hurried past the tiger, swiping its paw at me as I ran.

There were grunting noises and the sounds of large bodies slamming against the floor. I followed the noises, leaping down the stairs two at a time while balancing one hand on the railing to keep from falling. At the bottom, I heard Vince's voice. He sounded scared.

Knowing at least one of the men was armed, I approached cautiously. Who was he with? Mitch? Passing the living room and creeping down the hall, I moved to where Erin had found Russ's video earlier. I didn't know what to expect, but my mind already saw the gun in Mitch's hand.

With my heart pounding hard and fast, I pressed my shoulders against the wall and slowly peeked into the office, surprised to see I was wrong. It wasn't Mitch who had the gun, but Vince, and he was pointing the gun at Mitch's head.

CHAPTER ONE HUNDRED TWENTY-ONE

THE MOMENT MITCH SAW ME, HIS EYES ROUNDED AS HE pleaded for me to save him.

"Help!" Mitch screamed. "He's going to kill me, too."

Vince jumped and swung his head to look in my direction. His face was pale, his eyes wild with disbelief. I'd surprised them both and wasn't exactly sure what to do. What happened before I arrived?

"Shut up," Vince growled, jamming the sharp muzzle of the gun deeper into the back of Mitch's skull. Mitch winced and Vince turned to me. "Samantha, don't believe him. He did this. He's the dangerous one. Not me."

"Look who's holding the gun," Mitch said. "He just fired a shot but missed. He's trying to frame me for the murders of April and Jackie knowing he won't get away with them if he doesn't."

"He's lying," Vince interrupted, his face reddening with anger.

"Samantha, I know you know it, too." Mitch's chin was to his chest as he crouched forward with both hands in the air, but his eyes were glued on mine. "It wasn't Garrett like the police are suggesting. Vince framed him. Why, you ask yourself? Because Vince sexually abused Garrett when they both worked on a film years ago with April. That's why Vince killed April. She saw it all and had evidence to prove it. Look, there." Mitch pointed to the computer. "It's on Vince's computer if you don't believe me."

I swept my focus to the black computer screen. A thumbdrive was in the terminal. My mind raced to decide who to trust. Not wanting to take sides, I kept a close eye on the gun when suddenly Vince swung his arm back over his head and released the butt of the gun handle against Mitch's skull like a hammer.

I squealed and covered my mouth. Blood squirted from the back of Mitch's skull as he toppled over. It was impossible to look away. Mitch kept getting back up, fending off the blows as best he could, but Vince was like a wild animal, completely out of control as he kept hitting Mitch. When he was finished beating Mitch, Vince turned to me and said out of breath, "He's lying. He's the one. He killed April. Not me."

"Why would I do that?" Mitch said from under his arms. "It's your secret you were hiding." Then his pleading eyes swept back to me. "He's been watching you, Samantha. Afraid that Chief Watts would eventually blackmail him into admitting guilt to a crime the department couldn't solve. See the drone?" Mitch pointed to the machine across the room. "I know you recognize it. It was him. Vince is the dangerous one, not me!"

Vince hit him again. This time harder. Mitch toppled forward, placed his hand to the back of his head, and was finally quieted. I didn't know what or who to believe, but the fact that Vince hadn't turned the gun on me spoke volumes.

"Vince," I said, "put the gun down."

"He's wrong, Samantha," Vince said, still pointing the gun at Mitch. "Garrett knew what Mitch was up to, and Mitch killed him for it. It's part of the story he's creating, and he's given us all a role in the script he's writing."

"I believe you, Vince. Now, please put down the gun."

"I can't." Vince tightened his grip and applied more pressure to the trigger. "If I do, he'll surely kill us both."

"Look at me." Mitch rolled to one side and said from the floor, "Do I look like a killer?"

As soon as I swept my eyes to Mitch, I saw Vince flick his gaze to me. Then Mitch kicked Vince's legs out from under him and he fell hard like a tree, dropping the gun in the process. Mitch sprung to action, pinning Vince to the floor with his knee, and hurried to reclaim the gun for himself. It happened so quickly, I didn't have time to react. As soon as it was in his hand, Mitch took aim at me. "Now get on your knees and lace your fingers behind your head before I decide to kill you, too."

CHAPTER ONE HUNDRED TWENTY-TWO

I THOUGHT ABOUT RUNNING BUT SAW MYSELF GETTING shot in the back. Calculating the minutes since I'd left my car, I suspected the police had to be here soon. I was counting on Erin. I hoped she wouldn't fail me now.

"Okay, easy," I said, looking Vince in his red eyes.

Was it possible they were playing me? They were both great actors if they were. Mitch was still pinning Vince to the floor with his knee and he struggled to breathe. I didn't think Vince was faking as I watched him plead with Mitch to get off.

Slowly, I kneeled where I was standing and laced my fingers behind my head.

"No. Over here." Mitch directed me with his gun to where he wanted me.

"Only if you get off him first," I said, adding critical seconds to come up with a plan on how to end this.

Mitch stood and stepped back. Keeping the gun on me, he said, "Now move."

My knee popped as I stood but I ignored the pain as I moved forward and dropped my knees down to the floor next to Vince. Vince was clinging to his neck when he turned to me and whispered, "I'm sorry."

Turning his camera on me, Mitch pointed at me and said, "Please state your name for the camera."

Now I knew what Vince was referring to earlier. This was Mitch's story—the one he'd been recording. I kept my mouth shut, trying to keep track of the time inside my head. Where were the police? How long did I have? Was it still snowing, or had it stopped?

"No?" Mitch angled his head to the side and said, "Fine. I'll do the honors." He introduced me from behind the camera. "The relentless investigative reporter, Samantha Bell, everyone."

I stared into his eyes as I watched him clap a round of applause. Mitch was having a grand old time, cackling into the air, thinking he was so clever. Finally, he sat on the edge of the desk and propped his camera next to him using a tripod. Vince and I watched as Mitch popped open the cylinder of his pistol and lined up the five remaining bullets from the chamber into a straight row.

With his thumbs brushing the brass, Mitch muttered, "Vince ruined everything when he went looking for this video at your house. I had it under control. Everything was falling where I wanted it. Though now that it's here, care to see it for yourself?"

Mitch lifted his head and, when our eyes locked, I felt my body go stiff. "Not really," I said.

A glimmer caught his eye. He seemed surprised by my answer. "You're not the least bit curious as to why he came looking for it?"

"I know why."

"Yes. I should have known you'd say that." Mitch clucked his tongue and laughed. "Of course you know why." Carefully choosing a single bullet, Mitch continued, "Vince doesn't appreciate me. He's only into himself. I'm sure you know that now after having gotten a glimpse into his private life. It's why I had to create my pseudonym —Trojan."

Our eyes met, and a cold wave moved down my spine. I thought about all that my son had seen, what Trojan did to give us a prediction into what would come next. Did he show the world a quick preview of what he was going to do to us now?

"Your son told you it was Vince, didn't he?" Mitch's eyes shifted to Vince.

Vince was staring at the gun, trying to anticipate what Mitch was going to do next.

Mitch said, "It was so fun pretending to be Vince, but then White Stallion—I mean, Garrett—saw through my plan and ruined everything."

White Stallion? Garrett? I put another piece of the puzzle in place. "So, you found a way to place Vince's car in his garage."

"Yes, but not to frame Vince."

"Then why did you do it?" I asked.

"Garrett wanted to help, but I knew his secret. He was the vigilante baiting people like Vince to give up to the cops. He had to go, so we'd be safe." Mitch leaned forward and rested his elbows on his knees as he stared at Vince. "You see, I was protecting you, but you still don't believe me."

I rolled my gaze to Vince. He was still and quiet, no longer with us in the room.

Mitch turned his gaze back to me and continued telling me why he had to do it all. "You were so close to seeing me meet with Garrett. He was still inside the café, I'm sure of it, and you and your blonde sidekick had no idea." Mitch smirked. "Though, I have to admit, I wasn't sure how I was going to get past that one, but you never found out I was there."

"Why did you two meet?" I asked, wondering where inside his head Vince had taken off to.

"Garrett thought I was giving him this video," Mitch tossed up his thumb and pointed it at the computer, "but I had a change of heart and gave him your picture instead."

I could hear Alvarez's words ringing in my ear, how he thought we dodged a bullet with Garrett. Mitch must have seen the glimmer of recognition flash across my eye because he needed to tell me it wasn't Garrett who killed these people, but him.

"But it wasn't only your and your friend's photos I gave Garrett. I also gave him the films of my murders. After the cops realize what they have, they'll think it was him who killed April and Russ and Jackie."

"You framed an innocent man."

Mitch shrugged and bobbed his head. "That may be, but the true irony is how that cop Barber shot his own informant." A big smile sprouted on Mitch's face. He thought he was the smartest man living. "I saw it on the news," he said, "and assume he and the chief will get away with it."

"Then it was over," I said. "Garrett will go down for your murders."

"Just as I planned."

"So why keep us here? We didn't do anything."

Mitch flicked his eyes to Vince. "It could have been finished, and still can be, but it's not up to me. Isn't that right, Vince?"

Vince blinked and lifted his head, suddenly back in the room with us. "I won't say anything. You know I can keep a secret."

"Me too," I added in agreement, thinking it would be a miracle if Mitch let us go on our word alone.

Mitch kept shaking his head. He couldn't take his eyes off

Vince. There was something more going on between them, but I couldn't figure out what.

"All I ever asked of him was to come out. Be the person he is." Mitch swung his eyes to me and smiled. "He's a beautiful person, Samantha. Such a beautiful person. The world will see it, too, if he ever gets the courage to show them."

"I'm sure he is," I said.

Mitch repeated my words as if seeing through my lie. He reached for a bullet and said, "But now, he and I will play a game of you love me, you love me not."

I saw where this was going as I watched him load a single bullet into the chamber and snap it shut. Spinning the cylinder, Mitch pointed the muzzle at Vince.

"No, Mitch. You don't have to do this," I pleaded. "Let me help you tell your story."

"Sorry, Samantha, but you're wrong. If you know anything about Vince, it's that he needs to be prodded into action." Mitch paused and held Vince's stare as he said, "You love me—"

He pulled the trigger, and I flinched. The hammer clicked but nothing happened.

I kept pleading with him to stop. "You don't need another murder on your hands. It's Vince you're pointing that thing at. You love him, don't you?"

Mitch jumped off the desk and marched directly for me. He reached for my wrist and yanked my hand forward, placing the gun in my palm. I snapped my fingers wide open, not wanting anything to do with it.

"Take the gun, Samantha. You're right. I couldn't live with myself knowing I killed him, but if you did..."

Mitch kept fighting my hand, attempting to force me to take his gun. No matter what I said, he wasn't backing down. It was useless. I knew too much. Mitch was never going to let us walk out of here before someone died.

"Take it, Samantha," Mitch kept yelling. "We have to finish this game."

I kept reeling my arm back to my side, and he kept yanking it back. The gun was still pressed into my palm. I was afraid it would accidently discharge, but Mitch couldn't get me to hang on. My fingers were so tightly curled into themselves I thought my bones were going to snap. Then, suddenly, a beam of light flickered across the wall. When I turned my head, I could see flashes of red and blue in the window. The police.

Mitch saw it, too, and cursed as he planted the sole of his boot into the center of my chest, knocking me backward. He pointed the gun at Vince's head and said, "You love me not."

Time stalled as I watched him squeeze the trigger for a second time. The hammer clicked, and again, nothing happened. Then he lifted the gun to his temple and, with sweat dripping from his brow, he said, "You love me—"

This time the gun went off.

CHAPTER ONE HUNDRED TWENTY-THREE

THE AIR WAS KNOCKED OUT OF ME. I BLINKED, NOT wanting to believe what I'd just witnessed. Then Vince let out the most terrifying shrill I'd ever heard, and it was impossible to erase the memory from my head.

Vince lunged forward and crawled his way up Mitch's lifeless body before taking Mitch's face in his hands. "Mitch. Mitch." Vince kept shaking Mitch's head, pleading for him to come back. But I knew that was it for Mitch. The hole in his head was too big—there was too much blood.

I started breathing hard and felt my body tremble. This was so much worse than seeing Garrett shot. Everywhere I looked, I saw spatters of blood and fragments of bone glittering the walls and floor. The back wall was painted in a thick red and all I could hear was Vince crying and pleading for him to change his mind.

"You asshole," Vince kept saying. "I loved you. Now I'm left with nothing."

Vince's cries grew louder as I heard the police banging on the front door. When I finally realized what was happening, I wondered how long the police had been there—if they heard the gunshot, too.

Crawling across the floor, I dodged the blood and went for the thumb-drive. I handed it to Vince. "Take it," I said.

Vince fell back on his heels and gave me a confused look.

"Take it, dammit!"

"But—" Vince stammered, shifting his eyes between Mitch and me.

"I don't want to know what's on it. That's between you and God," I said. When Vince still looked confused, I added, "You suffered enough already, now take it before the police find it."

When Vince finally took the thumb-drive into his hand, I ran to the front of the house and announced to the police, "I'm coming out and I'm unarmed." I slowly followed through on each of my actions so there wouldn't be any misunder-standings. The last thing I wanted was to get shot myself. With my hand on the knob, I said, "Opening the door now."

As soon as the door opened, the responding officer asked, "Miss, are you all right?"

I cast my gaze to the officer's hand firmly placed on his weapon. I imagined I felt a lot worse than I looked. I said, "I'm fine."

"We had a report of a burglary. Is this your house?"

"No. It's mine." Vince came up behind me. "Domestic dispute with my roommate," he said.

I flicked my gaze to him, surprised, as he told the police about Mitch. The front of his shirt was soaked in blood and his fingers were red. I hoped the best for Vince but my job here was finished. We didn't need a plan, as there was already an agreement between us that his secret was his to share.

As Vince led one officer to his home office, a second officer escorted me to his patrol car where I gave a statement. I told them I was here to request an interview when Mitch lured me inside where he proceeded to commit suicide in front of us after admitting to killing April, Russ—disguised as Jackie—and Jackie—disguised as Vince. By the time I was finished, I found Erin and King waiting near my car.

"What the hell happened?" Erin asked as King pulled me into his arms.

I wasn't at all surprised they had come for me. My plan was risky. Much more so than I'd expected.

"Mitch killed himself," I said, digging out my car keys, demanding King drive me home.

Erin swiped a hand over her head. "Jesus, Sam. Why?"

"It was him. He was our guy."

CHAPTER ONE HUNDRED TWENTY-FOUR

Two weeks later...

I was rummaging through my closet, wishing I hadn't procrastinated in packing for my trip to Los Angeles. Turning my head, I yelled toward the hallway, "Mason, have you seen my carry-on?"

I couldn't find the suitcase anywhere. When Mason didn't answer, I stopped rifling through my clothes at a blood red blouse. I pulled it from the hanger and brushed my thumb over the weave as I thought about Mitch and Garrett.

I hadn't been sleeping well since the day it all ended. I pretended like it didn't bother me even though it did. Instead of talking through my emotions, I dove headfirst into work to keep me distracted. I worked relentlessly to fact-check everything Mitch said that night before taking his own life. I needed to know that was the end of the murder spree. I even went as far as checking the security camera at the café where he said he had met with Garrett. It was all true. Garrett was there with Mitch minutes before Erin and I arrived.

"What is that boy doing?" I muttered to myself as I hung

the blouse back in my closet and headed for Mason's room, afraid if I didn't get packed soon I'd miss my flight.

I knocked on Mason's door and, when he didn't answer, I cracked it open to see what was going on. He was sitting in front of his video game with his headset on his ears.

He'd since taken up a new game—a decision he made himself—one I fully supported. Mason simply said he grew tired of the old game, but I suspected it was because of Trojan. I never told him about what happened that night at Vince's, just that we caught the bad guy, but I'd definitely spent many nights lying awake thinking about the audience Mitch captivated when pretending to be Vince.

"Hey," I said, tapping Mason on his shoulder.

Mason paused his game, and I asked about the suitcase. "It's in my closet," he said.

"Heather will be here soon," I reminded him. "She's bringing dinner."

"Good. I'm starved." Mason made an exaggerated groan as he gripped his belly with both hands.

I laughed and reminded him to behave and treat my sister with the same respect he would me while I was gone.

Mason said, "Mom, I know you said you're just going out there to hear what they have to say, but I'm fine with whatever you decide."

"It's just an interview to get to know each other. I won't make any big decisions without you," I assured him just as I heard Erin arrive at the front of the house.

I left Mason to his game and met Erin in the living room, greeting her with a smile. She peeled off her coat, kicked off her shoes, and said she had news for me. Great, I thought. Just what I needed. More news. "If it's something I need to know now—"

Erin lifted her head and looked me in the eye. "You have no idea."

"Then follow me to my bedroom. I need to pack. I'm running late as it is."

Erin followed me to the back of the house, and couldn't believe I wasn't already packed for my trip. She said, "An attorney's office has taken up the class action appeals Atwood started."

I stopped and turned. "Who?"

Erin told me the name of the firm and smiled. "His legacy continues."

It was great news, but still premature of us to pop the champagne.

We'd since published a lengthy piece in the *Colorado Times* about Atwood's findings into Chief Watts's scheme to throw the LGBTQ community under the bus to make his own crime statistics appear better than they were. We finally had an overwhelming amount of evidence that was impossible to ignore, thanks to Atwood, and our story was the talk of the town. Even Dawson was blown away by the response. The community had our backs. It felt like we were finally on top. Which only made my trip to LA feel like I was giving up on everything we'd worked so hard to achieve.

"Now, if only Watts would fold under the mounting pressure, then maybe we could complete our victory lap," I said, packing my bag.

Erin was looking through what clothes I was taking with me when she said, "Wear this if you don't want the job, and wear that if you do."

"That's the advice you're giving me?"

Erin quirked a brow. "It doesn't come cheap."

Soon, I was wheeling my bag to the front of the house when Allison arrived with a new laptop computer for me. "I can't accept this," I said.

"New job. New hardware."

"She's not actually going to take the job," Erin argued

from behind. "It's all part of the strategy to increase our Podcast sponsors. Isn't that right, Sam?"

I gave Allison a look that said I didn't know what I was going to do, then slid my old laptop out of my suitcase and replaced it with the new one. I zipped up the carry-on and set it near the front door, checking the time. I was expecting my Uber ride to show any minute, and I was growing more anxious by the second.

Allison said, "I've beefed up your security system since I won't be there to fix it for you if something happens."

"Nothing's going to happen," I said. "And I'm only going to be gone a couple of nights."

"If you wear that ugly dress, you'll be back for good," Erin said from across the room.

"Thank you," I said to Allison.

We'd been on edge since we broke our story, just waiting for someone to threaten us. But since Garrett's murder, the threats never came. The online chatter and mysterious text messages stopped, too.

The best part, though, came when IAD investigated the deepfake pinning Watts's scheme on King, and finally linked it back to Officer Barber. We decided to press charges, but I was just happy to hear the DA was throwing the book at him, hoping it would get him to talk and reveal the details to Watts's scheme.

The front door opened, and Heather and Susan stepped inside, chattering like birds in spring. Heather reached out and handed me a large bag of Chinese food. "You didn't say everyone would be here for dinner. I don't think I bought enough."

"Because I didn't know," I said, taking the heavy bag of food to the table.

The girls were making themselves at home. I suspected they had planned this to remind me what I would lose if I accepted the job. As we laughed to the sounds of corks coming off and plates being handed out, I had to admit it was a brilliant plan. Just thinking about living a life without them had me choking up.

"Samantha, have you heard? Vince just put out a public statement," Susan said, pulling me aside. "He's come out, now admitting he had an inappropriate relationship with Garrett Todd on that movie set forever ago."

"He said this?"

Susan's eyes smiled. "Across his social media channels. He blames himself for what happened and is seeking treatment with hopes of moving past it."

I often wondered if I did the right thing by giving Vince the only known evidence of his assault on Garrett, but now I knew I had. "That's great," I said, thinking how Garrett could finally rest in peace.

Mason ran to the front of the house. "Turn on the TV. Everyone has to see this."

Erin was closest to the remote, and Mason told her to go to channel nine. The house went silent as we huddled around the television and watched Heidi report from City Hall.

"Denver Police Chief Gordon Watts was just arrested after publicly announcing his resignation."

They showed the clip of Watts's arrest and there was a collectively held breath.

"King did it," Mason said excitedly as he pointed to the TV. "He made the arrest!"

The house erupted into cheers and hugs.

"We did it!" Erin said, falling into me.

We laughed, hugged, and cried. A weight had been lifted off our shoulders. I couldn't believe we'd actually taken down the chief. Then my cellphone buzzed with an alert.

"Oh my god, I have to go," I said, giving my son a hug goodbye.

Mason wished me luck, and I promised to call when my flight landed. When I turned around, Heather handed me a to-go container full of food. "Your favorite."

"Thank you."

Heather turned to Allison and said, "Just think: I moved here to be closer to my sister and now she's thinking about leaving."

"What's that say about you?" Allison said to Heather before giving me a funny look. She asked me, "Is this it, then? Are you going to take the job?"

I smiled and winked. A part of me was hoping to leave trouble behind. "I'll let you know."

Allison stepped forward and gave me a hug before pushing me out the door. Then I was off to sunny California for the biggest interview of my life.

Tap here and begin reading the next Samantha Bell adventure, TO BELL AND BACK. You're not going to believe the surprise Samantha has waiting for her in California.

A WORD FROM JEREMY

Thank you for reading ALL BELL BREAKS LOOSE. **If you like the stories I'm writing, don't forget to rate, review, and follow. It really helps my books get in front of new readers.**

AFTERWORD

A special thanks to my editor and brilliant proofreaders for cleaning up the errors I missed. I couldn't do it without you.

One of the things I love best about writing these mystery thrillers is the opportunity to connect with my readers. It means the world to me that you read my book, but hearing from you is second to none. Your words inspire me to keep creating memorable stories you can't wait to tell your friends about. No matter how you choose to reach out - whether through email, on Facebook, or through a review - I thank you for taking the time to help spread the word about my books. I couldn't do this without YOU. So, please, keep sending me notes of encouragement and words of wisdom and, in return, I'll continue giving you the best stories I can tell. Thank you for giving me an opportunity of a lifetime.

Never miss a new release. Sign up for Jeremy Waldron's New Releases Newsletter at JeremyWaldron.com

ABOUT THE AUTHOR

Waldron lives in Vermont with his wife and two children.

Receive updates, exclusive content, and new book release announcements by signing up to his newsletter at: www.JeremyWaldron.com

Follow him @jeremywaldronauthor

 facebook.com/jeremywaldronauthor

 bookbub.com/profile/83284054

CPSIA information can be obtained
at www.ICGtesting.com
Printed in the USA
LVHW031518060521
686701LV00003B/652

9 781953 570062